Alma's Journey

Alma's Journey

❦

Taylor Samuel Lyen

iUniverse, Inc.
Bloomington

Alma's Journey

iUniverse books may be ordered through booksellers or by contacting:

iUniverse
1663 Liberty Drive
Bloomington, IN 47403
www.iuniverse.com
1-800-Authors (1-800-288-4677)

ISBN: 978-1-4697-0036-6 (sc)
ISBN: 978-1-4697-0037-3 (e)

Printed in the United States of America

iUniverse rev. date: 02/10/2012

Old Map Of Abbeville[*]

❧

ALMA AND EDGAR'S CABIN
ABBEVILLE ESTATES
JEFF JR. MEMORIAL PARK
ABBEVILLE LIBRARY
ABBEVILLE TOWN HALL
JOHN JR. MEMORIAL PARK
ABBEVILLE LIBRARY PARK
ABBEVILLE TOWN HALL PARK
ABBEVILLE CEMETERY
ABBEVILLE ELEMENTARY SCHOOL
ABBEVILLE SAVINGS AND LOAN
BELCHER BROTHERS MORTUARY
DAMASCUS CHURCH
CREMATORIUM
ABBE FAMILY MAUSOLEUM
SPRING CREEK PARK AND CAMPGROUNDS
ABBEVILLE TOWN MORGUE
PRESTON MEDICAL CLINIC
FABRICS PLUS
ABBEVILLE CEMETERY CHAPEL
KNEAD 2 FEED BAKERY

---

* *This map, yellowed by age, was clutched in the hand of a blind gold miner found in an abandoned mine off Prospector's Trail; the remains are reported to be those of Elder Jacob. Note: The darkened areas are empty lots.*

SANDERS ATTORNEY AT LAW
BLUE GOOSE TAVERN
ABBINGTON FARMER'S MARKET
SALMON CREEK WINERY
TREE TRIMMERS BARBER SHOP
HAIR FALLS SALON
LAS ABUELITA'S COCINA MEXICAN RESTAURANT
ABBEVILLE GENERAL STORE
MEADOWS AUTO SERVICE
EMMA JANE'S WOG FARM
SALMON CREEK STABLES
CALIFORNIA STATE PARK AT YUBA RIVER

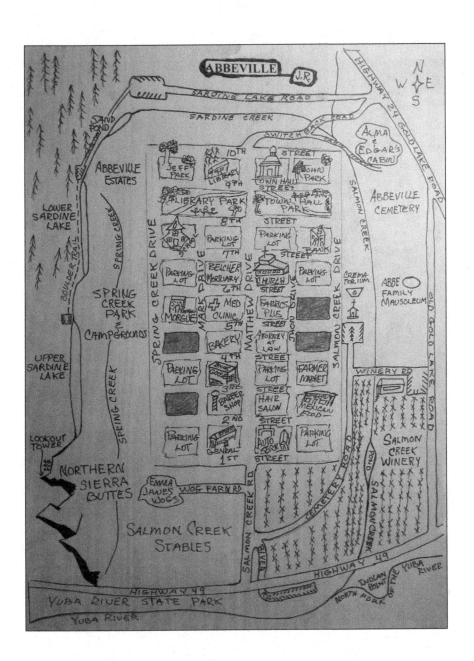

Marie
Whose heart has gone away and exists
In some curved dimension yet undiscovered

Judy Guerino and Marie Lyen, Celestial Sisters who walk among
The stars on streets of gold as pure as transparent crystal.

Preface

❦

Regard this world as a star at dawn
A bubble in a stream
A flash of lightening in a summer cloud
A flickering lamp
A phantom and a dream.

Vairacchedika

If we are stars at dawn, do not our mythologies and sciences clearly explain why? My sense is no, at least not yet. Most of us take comfort in believing that what we experience is reality. As a practical matter, we believe a chair is a solid piece of furniture that we may sit on without fear and believe a horse is a horse, of course. Then, where do the bubbles bursting in a stream and lightening flashes through summer clouds go? The answers to these questions fall within the realms of science, religion, philosophy and/or the machinations of our subjective introspections.

Abbeville was a small town located in the Northern California Sierra Mountains, where people had lived and worked for two hundred years. Then, within the flickering of a lamp, Abbeville and its two hundred year history virtually disappeared. Alma's Journey is the story about mysterious forces that obliterated the people and town of Abbeville and the equally mysterious forces that created the people and town of Newtown.

Those that enjoy having mysteries end with all of the loose ends tied up for them in a neat bow may find Alma's Journey unsettling. Those needing to have a book open with fireworks to keep their interests may not have the staying power to understand character development in the sleepy town of Abbeville. For the patient and diligent sleuthhound, however, when all is said and done, when all the information has been fairly weighed, only one reasonable solution will be found that accurately describes the events that took place in Abbeville and that are taking place in Newtown.

s/Taylor Samuel Lyen
August 2, 2011

Table of Contents

Book One

❧

Alma and the Sisterhood

Chapter 1

❧

Monday, October 4, 8:18 a.m.: Upper Sardine was a pristine mountain lake before Fish and Game poisoned it to kill the squawfish. Everything died including the bugs. Except for a few expert fly fishermen like Edgar Whitman, this pure glacier bowl rarely gives up its bounty. Edgar limits out early on Rainbow and Brook trout. He stands at water's edge, as he's done for fifty-five years, ever awed by the sight of sheer granite plunging into the ice-cold lake with rock beaches and teetering boulders. Water so clear and still, everything at the bottom of the lake is plainly visible.

"It's like fishing in an aquarium," he says to Fenway.

Her blond eyelashes glistening in the morning sun, she lovingly looks at him with sanguine brown eyes. Like a kid Edgar chuckles to himself at the thought he and Fenway can play hooky and go fishing. Thanks to a long Indian summer in the Sierras this year, Edgar gets to extend the luxury of fly-fishing through the end of November. Otherwise he would be cutting a hole in the ice to fish, which is doable, but would play major havoc with his arthritic knees and shoulders.

A leisurely walk back along the trail to the truck is always an adventure. Fenway's curiosity sends her sniffing at and around every rock, snag, and bush that attracts her attention. She episodically marks her territory and worse. Ever so often she scares out a sagebrush lizard or a garter snake that escapes into the lake, only to become a meal for some large trout. Once in a while a reclusive meadow mouse or pocket gopher or rabbit runs from cover, risking certain death in the talons of flying predators. This morning Fenway noses over small rocks, uncovering beetles to Edgar's delight. What sights, sounds, and smells beyond human detection does Fenway sense, only Fenway knows. At the edge of the parking lot, Edgar throws the doggie poop bag into the campground's receptacle. He opens the cab door to his old PRO-4X. Fenway barks and circles before jumping in the truck, positioning herself head out the passenger side window ready for the ten-minute ride down Switch Back Road to the outskirts of Abbeville.

Since birth Edgar and Alma have lived in the grand log cabin built by their father in the early 1930's. They are the last of the founder's lineage that created Abbeville. The town now boasting seven hundred fifty inhabitants is located about nine miles below Sno-Park at Yuba Pass. Except for Abbeville Estates, which is plainly visible from Highway 24, Abbeville is nestled in a high mountain meadow off highway 49 at the end of Salmon Creek Road with hundreds of homes cloaked within the dense mountainside forest below Volcano and Sardine Lakes.

Fishing pre-dawn to sun rise on a Monday beats having to open the Abbeville General Store and Lodge at five in the morning. Edgar is finally beginning to take his foot from the proverbial gas pedal, breaking down two months ago to hire Bridget Silver to manage Abbeville General in his absence. A month ago he stopped cooking and pumping gas, hiring Ted Michaels to do that for him, as well as keep the books, be the stock boy and be Bridget's guy Friday. Edgar also decided to keep Daisy May on as the waitress at the cafe. Daisy is twelve years Edgar's senior and worked at the store before Edgar could smile. Funny how he's easing out of the business while Daisy is going full throttle. Yep and still it's good to be alive and fish with his best friend, Fenway, the best dog in the world.

The road off Switch Back to Whitman's cabin disappears into forest, where it crosses a narrow bridge over Salmon Creek and runs to a large turnabout in front of the one-level, twenty-seven hundred square foot cabin. Out of the truck, Edgar gathers his fish. He and Fenway climb the broad steps up the steep incline to the cabin. Atop the deck the eastern sun captures the grandeur of the Great Northern Buttes in full view. Fenway bolts across the deck to the front door jittering all about and wagging her tail. She anxiously waits for Edgar to catch his breath. Edgar's pace slows almost to a standstill as he turns to admire and pay homage to the mountain that dominates the Sierra forests and all creatures below.

From Fenway's ever-ready gung-ho perspective, the door is opening all too slowly. She quickly wedges herself between the opening door and cabin muscling through so hard she springs the door open pulling the doorknob from Edgar's hand. Fenway charges around the rooms sniffing the carpets and furniture. At last she lands on the large throw rug in the kitchen rolling on her back. She expects loves and scratches from Edgar. He roughs her up with all the affectionate scratches Fenway needs for the moment.

"Good girl; yes you're a good girl, Fenway. But, I have to leave you and get to work!"

The thought of Alma soon returning home compels Edgar to quickly clean the morning's catch. He cannot linger in the throes of jubilation, knowing Alma will soon come through the door eager to prepare breakfast for him. Sure enough, fifteen minutes later the door swings open.

"What's for breakfast Edgar? Shouts Alma."

Edgar begins to stammer, "Fresh rain . . . rain . . . rain . . ."

But before Edgar can answer his sister, she answers her own question, "fresh rainbow trout again!"

Finally able to untie his tongue, Edgar spits it out, "Sorry Sis, yes it's rainbow trout again and I want it breaded, fried in garlic butter with lemon and a pinch of salt. I'd love some of your coffee and country fried potatoes too."

"B-o-r-i-n-g . . . b-o-r-i-n-g . . ." his sister sings out in a dull, monotonous tone.

They laugh wildly at the absurdity of ever being blasé about such a delicacy.

Fenway hates fish. She slowly walks to the deck to find her bowl of exquisite dog food Edgar hand makes from fresh nutritious ingredients. There will be no commercial dog food made with diseased, disabled road kill and euthanized zoo animals, dogs and cats ground with their flea collars, pet tags, preservatives and plastic death bags for Fenway. After her sumptuous breakfast, Fenway jumps on the hot tub cover next to Edgar's chair, curls into a ball, and snoozes.

Edgar forks the first flakes of garlic butter fried trout and places it in his mouth. His expression tells the tale—Alma's cooking tastes superb as usual. He takes a sip of coffee and jabs another bite of the succulent fish, closes his eyes, and sighs happily.

"Alma, this is magnificent."

Alma smiles knowingly.

With hunger satisfied, Edgar and Alma move to the back deck of the cabin and sink into their chairs. The view is one of natural rugged beauty contrasting with the intrusions of humans. Below the craggy cliffs of the Northern Sierra Buttes sits the small town of Abbeville immersed in fields of wildflowers, a splendid scene of natural beauty, breathtaking in every dimension, which never ceases to astound the senses. Out of step with nature, the grey stone-studded hillside of Abbeville Cemetery and Abbeville Estates cut into the side of the Buttes present man's accomplishments, which pale against the forces of nature. Edgar lights his favorite cigar and settles down further in his chair. Smoke from his cigar drifts southward, as the eastern sun plays with the forest shadows surrounding the cabin. With eyes closed Fenway gives a big sigh.

"What do you have planned for today, Sis?"

"I think I'll go to town and visit Jane at Fabrics Plus."

"Jane's is having a baby?" Edgar inquires.

"No, Jane is a little too old to have a baby, Edgar, besides Jimmy Brown is enough for any parent to handle."

"Then, why are you going to visit Jane?"

When Edgar was young, Alma used to think her brother was brain damaged or dumb as a post. Edgar was a jokester; he was always joking. She never came to fully appreciate his constant pushy flippancy. But, in time, Alma came to accept the truth that's the way her brother was; and, he probably will never change. So, she developed the strategy of laughing when Henry is genuinely funny, not encouraging him when he is irritating and responding rationally to his cornball comments and questions.

To get fabric, buttons and sewing thread to make a dress."

"A dress? For what?"

"The Bicentennial Festival?"

"Alma, the festival isn't till summer—a full ten months from now!"

"I don't want to put things off to the last minute, Edgar."

"With the festival ten months away you got a powerful lot of time to sew a dress; don't you, Sis?"

"Ed (Alma always calls Edgar Ed when she's had enough of his pushiness) the festival is closer than you think. You'll need all the help I can give you setting up the general store for the winter storms. I'm already meeting with my bicentennial planning committee. We probably won't finish until January, early February. Then, things will be busy pushing you and the town council to put everything together. Who knows what the future holds? Yes, getting my dress made will only take a couple of weeks, and I'd rather take the window of time I have now to start and finish the project. I'm afraid once things get rolling on the festival we will both be busy beavers until summer."

"Good point Alma."

"What's your day going to look like Edgar?" Alma says diverting him.

"Hum, I think Fenway and I will go down to Meadows Garage and check on the chainsaw repair. Then, we'll go down to Salmon Creek Stables and see if Washington has finished cleaning the store's wood burning stove and heater for the winter. On the way back I'll drop by the library to see what new books Bob Winston's has set out for Abbeville to read."

"That's a pretty ambitious day you've set out for yourself."

"Yeah I've been putting off my reading for too long and want to get back to reading a few good mystery books this winter."

"It's about time. You haven't picked out a book to read in years."

"Yep, plus while Fenway and I are strolling through town visiting everybody, we'll be plugging the Bicentennial Festival like you want."

"Ed, how long do you expect to be strolling around glad-handing everyone and doing everything you want to do?"

"A few hours maybe more. You know how those things go Alma. It's like asking how long is a piece of string? There's no way of exactly knowing how long I'll be gone."

"I know you're pretty busy these days. But, try not to stay too long with Bob at the Blue Goose."

"I didn't say anything about the Blue Goose did I? Or, did I?"

"No, say "Hi" to Bob for me anyway."

Edgar nods his head and smiles contently.

Alma sits by her brother's side as he melds into the fragrances of cedars, junipers, pines and redwood trees, the jabber of Salmon Creek below them. Watching Edgar enkindles Alma's maternal instincts. Alma has cared for Edgar since the beginning. Their mother Jane Francis died giving birth to Edgar. Their father's death followed a few years later. Alma never had time to have children. Sacrificing her childhood, she became the Abbe family matriarch early in life. As a child of ten through womanhood, she and Daisy May ran the Abbeville General Store, made soups, salads, sandwiches, and specialty dishes, waited tables, pumped gas, served as postmaster, managed and cleaned the twelve-room Abbeville Lodge atop the store.

During the last months of his life Alma remembers her father enjoying simple pleasures. He was a gentle soul.

"Pumpkin," her father would say smiling, "Could you fix me a bowl of soup?"

Alma would always say, "Sure Dad, soup's on its way."

He loved Alma's soups, which always surprised him. Tomato and basil soup, chicken soup with thick noodles and marjoram and tortilla pepper soup with cilantro were his favorites. She provided care for her father until his passing. Edgar has no recollection of his father on his own. Telling stories about the way she saw her father, Alma created the memories Edgar has cherished over the years. Alma was mother, father and sister to Edgar. He knows no other family.

Alma's zeal, work ethic and high moral character earn her admiration and prominence in the eyes of the then tiny community. She is a dynamo raising Edgar and working the store is the only life Alma knew. Then when Edgar turned twenty-five, Alma finally has a chance to venture into the world; and she jumped at the chance. Thailand is her first venture outside the Sierra's. Taking her love of cooking to the next level, Alma is fortunate to have her cooking experiences staged in several of the finest kitchens throughout Thailand and China's Sichuan, Hunan, Shandong and Beijing provinces. Greatly influenced by eastern religions, Alma studied Taoism, as it was practiced throughout Asia. But she struggled constantly, resisting her heart's desires to return to Edgar. But, somehow, she found the strength to stay on her journey for the better part of a year.

When Alma arrives back in the United States, she doesn't call Edgar. Travel whets her yearnings to know more about cultures and religions. She enrolls in San Francisco State University and picks class offerings designed to fit her interests. On top of her general education requirements in English, mathematics and history, Alma loads up on anthropology, sociology, philosophy, comparative religion classes and courses in women's studies and archeology. During the three semesters and a summer session she attends SF State, her appetite for learning is voracious. Alma's high grade point average and contacts at school help open the door for her to further develop her skills in the culinary arts. She is invited to enroll in the California Culinary Academy and quits the university after summer session.

Alma's travels gave her an incredible, but spotty, culinary education in regional Asian cooking. Studying at one of the most prestigious cooking schools in the world, Alma more than rounds out her cookery. But again, the call of home is strong; and, she leaves the Academy before finishing their program. Nonetheless, Alma established a solid foundation to build upon for a lifetime. After her two-year odyssey, she returns home to her beloved Edgar and Abbeville.

In Alma's absence, Edgar operated the family business. On her return, Alma's stature in the community continues, as if she had never left. She encourages Edgar to continue running the business. Alma is content to influence Edgar and Abbeville without assuming the mantle of formal leadership. She has learned to lead through humble submission to greater powers than worldly command. She loves preparing Edgar's breakfasts. Today, fresh salmon, a toasted bagel, organic sliced tomatoes, thinly sliced red onion, cucumber, capers and cream cheese. Tomorrow, he may have to fend for himself. She enjoys preparing resplendent dinners for Edgar's return from work. On occasion she eats dinner with him. A loving sister and brother, Alma and Edgar engage close, deep conversations, at times unspoken. They find enjoyment in simple pleasures. They play checkers, scrabble and a variety of card games. They are devoted companions. They will never part.

From outward appearances Alma, Edgar and Fenway live a serene life in an idyllic setting. Alma, however, lives multiple lives at multiple levels. There is the practical, influential shaper of public opinion that is Alma. There is Alma, the artist in the kitchen. There is the Alma, whose life is busy with committee, charity, and community work, clothes making and a variety of other projects. There is Alma, who spends most of her time walking wilderness trails. She communes with nature at the highest levels; wild animals walk with her like pets. There is the Alma of the Sisterhood, a society of women that have gathered in the wilderness since before the founding of Abbeville.

The women of Abbeville are aware of the forces revealed in the wilderness and the Sisterhood that gathers to commune with these ancient forces or "shadows" as they are often called. As to the nature and purpose of the forest shadows, however, the women are divided.

Situated in the Knead-2-Feed Bakery, Fredrika Cameron Handley weaves her fabrications before willing eyes and attentive ears.

"I heard Alma was dancing nude again in the high meadows." she says in a hushed voice.

Looking around the bakery to see who's listening, Bunny Grimmer responds, "She's a mystic or, maybe, a witch or worse!"

Edna Pinkney contributes, "I've heard others say they have seen Alma whirling and twirling in the luminescence of the midnight moon dressed in magical garments."

Interrupting Holly Spears says, "Yes, Alma sets aflame the forest paths upon which she twists and sways, her hands, face and body glow from within, a radiant energy, her freely flowing gown hurling sparks, electrifying the grasses, wild flowers and trees she passes."

"How long is our town going to fawn over this woman, this demonic spirit posing as an angel?" Joyce Lawrence says with hackles rising.

With her feathers all ruffled Jenny Hobbs spouts, "Someone needs to take her down to earth."

"I suppose you're going to confront Alma? I think not. The only one here that can take on Alma is Fredrika," Bunny declares.

"Thank you ladies for your vote of confidence," Fredrika says absorbing the praise, "Revenge must be served on a cold plate and we are too riled to do anything quite yet, but the time will come."

Fredrika and her group have spread false rumors about Alma for decades. Those new to Abbeville like and appreciate Alma. They see her as a nice old woman, who quietly lives on the hill with her brother and his dog. The newbie's disregard the rumors. Alma is, after all, in her mid-seventies and is not likely to be prancing and dancing in the forest at midnight. The younger generation view Fredrika and her girlfriends' preoccupation with spreading rumors as a pathetic attempt to be the center of their small worlds. They seem to spin yarns to occupy and brighten their uninteresting lives. But the gossip mill keeps spinning lies, as many people live to hear the evil whispers in this small town.

Clever twists of truth are always woven into the poisonous fabric of Fredrika's falsehoods. Alma, on the other hand, is untied from the anchor of gossip. She is a free spirit, free to find her own path, her essence of childhood. Alma does enjoy walking in the woods. As the world sleeps in the arms of darkness, who knows whether Alma is dancing to the divine music of the universe?

Monday, October 4, 12:34 p.m.: By the time Edgar and Fenway begin their jaunt through town, Alma is home from the fabric shop, pinning the dress pattern on the fabric she will make into her summer dress for the Bicentennial Festival. By one o'clock, Edgar and Fen reach the memorial fountain that is dedicated to Jeff Abbe Junior, who died in the Second World War. They spot Bob Winston, taking his lunch break.

"Bob, Bob," Edgar calls waving Bob over to him.

Rolling on his feet, begging for attention, Fenway intercepts Bob. After scratching Fenway's tummy, Bob extricates himself from her charms and walks over to Edgar, who's sitting on one of the park benches encircling the fountain.

Bob sits down and says, "Edgar how's the fishing these days?"

"Excellent, you know the fishing around here as well as I do Bob. It couldn't be better. Bob I want you to do a favor for me. I know you're on your break and have to get back to work, so I'll be brief. How about saving me a trip to the library and pick out a good murder mystery for me? You can bring it down to the Blue Goose after the library closes, and I'll buy you a beer."

"I don't know Edgar, sounds like you're bribing a public official to me."

"OK Bob, make that two beers."

"Done and I don't want to hear you complain about the book I select for you either."

"Done."

Bob is and has been Edgar's friend for years. He knows what Edgar likes to read better than Edgar does himself. With that Edgar stands to leave and remembers.

"Say Bob, I need another favor if you don't mind."

"It's going to cost you."

"I'm willing to pay the price Bob. I need for you to place a poster or two in the library advertising the upcoming Bicentennial Festival in Abbeville."

"Glad to be of service to you and the community Edgar."

Edgar and Fenway cut through Library Park and across Ninth Street to the schoolyard fence.

The schoolyard bell signals the end of the 1:30 recess. Kids freeze in their spots, except for Jimmy Brown and Curtis Dean, who couldn't stay still if their lives depended on it. Mrs. Torrance sounds her police whistle and the children walk to class, except for Jimmy and Curtis who run past everyone to be the first through the door. Fenway runs over to the schoolyard fence and begins to bark.

"Hello I want to play too," Fen seems to say to the kids.

The children laugh and giggle into the classroom. Fenway watches the last child enter the schoolhouse before she darts along Eighth Street, across Matthew Drive, across John Drive, and into the Abbeville Savings and Loan building. Edgar goes to the door waves at everybody. He calls to Fenway, who's already on her back having her chest and stomach scratched by the customers. Taking time to talk with the savings and loan manager, Martin Lawrence, Edgar puts the bite on him to put an Abbeville Bicentennial poster in the bank.

"Sure thing, no problem there Edgar. You can count on me."

Edgar leaves and waits for Fen in front of the Damascus Church across the street from Belcher Brothers' Mortuary. After fruitlessly waiting for Fen, Edgar walks down the drive. Fenway roars out of the bank across the drives and barks in front of Preston Medical Clinic. Stepping out of the clinic, Florence scratches Fen's stomach and gives her a doggie bone, allowing her next patient to slip quickly into the clinic without being lovingly accosted by Fen.

"Fenway girl," calls Edgar.

Fen races toward Edgar and catches him in front of Fabrics Plus. Edgar waves through the window at Jane, who smiles and waves back enthusiastically. Although Edgar has no intention of going in the fabric store, a land strange to most men, Fenway has other plans. She flashes through the open door into the shop with Edgar taking long strides in pursuit.

"Hi Edgar. Alma was in here buying material for her new dress for this year's Festival."

"I know. What did she buy?"

"Oh I don't know if Alma would want me to tell you the details. I can tell you she bought an Eco friendly, rich, plain weaved cotton stemmed, sweetbrier dress fabric, teal blue and black elastic thread and several new bobbins."

"Thanks Jane. I know less now than when I came into your store."

"Aw poor Edgar. Would it help to tell you the dress has side pockets?"

"At least I understand what side pockets are Jane. Thanks. Fenway! Fen! Let's go. Good-bye Jane."

"Take care, Edgar."

"I almost forgot, Jane. Could you do something to let people know about the Bicentennial Festival? Alma wants to give everyone plenty of advance notice."

"Sure thing Edgar. I'll work something up to highlight the event."

"Thanks Jane."

Charges out from the fabric store, Fenway crosses Matthew Drive and runs to Stella May who owns the Knead-2-Feed Bakery. Stella hugs Fenway, giving Fen all the love she needs.

"Fenway girl, I can't give you any cookies, they'll make you sick sweetheart."

Fenway looks at Stella and wags her tail excitedly. Edgar follows Fenway into the Bakery.

"Stella May, good-day. I'm not on restriction like Fenway. Do you have any German chocolate cake left?

"Lucky you Edgar, you've got the last German chocolate cake of the day."

Edgar couldn't be happier as German Chocolate Cake is Alma's favorite and when Alma is happy, Edgar is happy.

"And I'll take a dozen of your glazed old-fashioned donuts too, Stella."

Stella puts a baker's dozen glazed old-fashioned donuts in a box for Edgar and wishes him well.

"Stella," Edgar speaks almost apologetically, "you're so kind to Fenway, she's turning into a spoiled baby."

Behind the cookies, cakes and pie counter Stella May has already slipped two butterscotch biscotti to Fenway who stands waiting for more.

"Born to be spoiled. Fenway's such a love, how can anyone refuse her allure?"

"So true Stella, so true. Fenway is a beauty and a rare one at that!"

"Yes you are so lucky to have Fenway. I know she is dearer than life to you."

"No doubt about that Stella May. Which reminds me I'd also like a Boston cream pie to take home. Got any?"

"Sure do. That comes to $22.50, Edgar and I'll throw in the tax!"

"Sweet. Next time you're in my store I'll repay the favor."

"No problem Edgar. That's all right, although I do have a soft spot for that peppermint ice-cream you have at the store."

"You can take that one to the bank Stella May. Where's that dog gone?"

The thought of cakes and cookies wipes Edgar's rational mind as clean as a *tabula rasa*. He's forgotten to tell Stella about advertising the festival.

No sooner did Edgar say good-bye to Stella than Fenway runs out of the store and down Matthew Drive. She automatically turns into the Blue Goose Tavern. Edgar, standing in front of Sanders Attorney at Law Offices, calls Fenway.

But Fen is hunkered down behind the bar with Nick Simmons' two Chihuahuas, Taco and Bell. They engage in mutual sniffing behaviors, as do all the most curious and friendly of dogs. Fenway is having so much fun that she doesn't hear Edgar calling.

Nick, the tavern's owner lures Fen to the street with a Slim Jim, which he tosses to Edgar. Fenway bounds across Matthew Drive and begs Edgar for the spicy meat stick. Slyly Edgar puts the Slim Jim in his pocket and sharply looks down the street as if he sees something. Fenway looks down the street too. The Slim-Jim-slide-of-hand maneuver works.

Scratching Fen behind the ears, Edgar lovingly tells Fenway, "Those things are not good for you girl. Who knows exactly what's in the stick Fen?"

Fenway smells the lingering scent of the Slim Jim from Edgar's fingers, but losing interest in his lecture, she trots down the street and ducks into the Farmer's Market, checking out all the empty food stalls. The market is closed on Mondays and is free of any food scraps. Fenway's curiosity is captured just the same. What wonderful aromas Fen smells from what was. Edgar waiting in front of the closed market doesn't see Fen slip under the back flap onto Salmon Creek Drive.

Knowing Fenway eventually comes back to him like a boomerang, Edgar makes a cameo appearance at the open door to Tree Trimmer's Barber Shop. Ranger Patrick O'Reilly, a town council member, Bill Silva, the president of the town council and "Bronco" Brown, a former rodeo

Brahma bull riding champion, town council member, church elder and owner of the Bar-B Cattle Ranch, occupy the three barber chairs. Larry Sherman, manager of the Lookout Tower Conference Center is on the bubble waits for the next chair. Augustus "Auggie" Castro steadily cuts each head of hair, while Edgar and the boys carry on in conversations.

"Where's your faithful doggie companion Edgar? Did she run away with another fur ball?" Bronco laughingly delivers what he thinks is the funniest line of the day.

"Funny Bronco, how are the mad cows at the Bar-B Ranch doing today?"

"Now, you're hitting below the belt, partner. I was only trying to be friendly like."

All the guys laugh at the banter between Bronco and Edgar. All of them are on the town council and know each other well.

Ranger Pat changes the subject. "Did you hear about the old mines caving in above Sand Pond? Trapped four tourists inside for more than eight hours."

"News to me," Edgar responds, "What happened?"

Ranger Pat continues, "Dr. Preston attended to the injured until they were medically evacuated to UC Davis Hospital. All are doing well."

"Good to hear that," Edgar replies.

Whatever the boys at the barbershop want to talk about, no town council business is discussed in any manner. If Abbeville's gossip mill got wind of council business being conducted at the barbershop, all hell would break loose. The double hex lies in the fact that McWhinney Thurston's boyfriend is Auggie, the barber, who is sure to blab to McWhinney. Accordingly, conversations flow about sports, fishing and hunting, national politics, the weather, what's new on the Las Abuelitas Cocina Mexicana Restaurant menu and other scintillating topics.

Leaving his friends and fellow councilmen, Edgar feels ethically obligated to cross the street and say hello to the ladies at the Hair Falls Salon. Still Fenway is nowhere in sight.

"How are you young ladies doing today? You look gorgeous." Edgar greets the three women, trying not to stare at the most unsettling sight of women with little aluminum pieces stuck in their hair and different colored hair sticking in all directions.

"You can cut the crap Edgar. You're not funny," fires back Emma Jane Walters who owns the wog farm.

Emma Jane's comment brings the salon group to the height of laughter, reminiscent of the time when the three gray witch sisters, who shared one eye and one tooth among them, lost their one eye. Edgar stares and smiles weakly at the three salon beauties enjoying themselves at Edgar's crest-fallen expense. But he muddles on.

"I'm glad I've brought a smile to your faces today ladies," Edgar continues, "Emma Jane Alma needs two dozen of your finest eggs tomorrow to make her famous wog egg potato salad for the Abbeville Bicentennial planning committee's next meeting?"

Laughter comes to a screeching halt, as the mention of Alma's name brings a sense of decorum back to the group, as if Edgar had waved a magic wand. Seeing the gray witches return to normalcy amuses Edgar.

"Of course Edgar I'll have them ready for Alma by noontime tomorrow," responds Emma Jane.

Edgar thinks, "My sister is one powerful woman in this town. I can handle the men with a baseball bat, but Alma calms the waters by the mere mention of her name."

He thanks Emma Jane and the other ladies and bids them a fond farewell. Thoroughly lost in schmoozing with his friends at the barbershop and bantering with the women in the salon, Edgar completely forgets about the Bicentennial Festival.

"Edgar, I think I saw Fenway go into the Mexican restaurant down the street," a green-faced Simone Fletcher announces, through her Missha Green Grape Yogurt Sheet Face Mask.

"Thank you Simone," says Edgar, without so much as a look or comment about the mask, as he's leaving the salon in search for his dog.

Actually Fenway stays clear of Mexican restaurants, ever since she accidentally stuck her nose into a bowl of abuelita's habañero diablo chili at last year's Summer Festival, for which she spent a day in the pet hospital in Sierra City, not a pleasant experience.

Edgar loves Abuelita's cooking. Several years ago, he leased the building and property to the Santiago family and hasn't regretted it.

"Buenos dias, Abuelita, como éstas?"

"Good, good Señor Edgar. How may I serve you today?"

"I'd like two of your Road Kill Tacos, Concha."

Abuelita's Cocina Mexicana Restaurant is famous for its "road kill" specialties, which present the finest in Mexican foods, made with a variety of forest critters and forest-grown vegetables, a Mexican-Sierra fusion cuisine. The restaurant of course receives the highest ratings from the Sierra County Health Department. Abuelita's Cocina serves two menus for breakfast, lunch and dinner: its Road Kill Menu and its Comida Mexicana Traditional Menu. Edgar likes the Road Kill Tacos because if he guesses what kind of meat is in the taco he gets a free drink.

"Tastes like pocket gopher to me Concha?" Edgar ventures a guess.

"No Señor Edgar, no es pocket gopher, es carne de ardilla."

"Squirrel meat again! That's the third time in a week you've had squirrel meat tacos Concha. That's not fair!"

"Bueno Señor Edgar, I'll give you a free drink anyway. Que gustaria?"

"Half orange Fanta and half Coca-Cola please."

"Señor Edgar alli va Fenway atras Meadows Garage."

"Thanks Concha I see her, Adios."

"Buenas suerte con la carne ardilla."

Although Edgar only saw a flash of Fen's tail he is sure she has gone into Meadows Garage to find owner Mo Jackson's black Labrador retriever puppy Rambo. In sort of a walking-skip-running stride, so as not to spill his orange-coke beverage, Edgar arrives at the Garage a little winded.

Edgar can hardly wheeze out, "How's the chainsaw coming along Mo?"

"I still have my fingers Edgar and the chainsaw is fixed, oiled and ready to go. That will be $17.85 to get it back. You look pretty out of shape my friend."

"That I am; and the cost for repairing my chainsaw is a bargain at twice the price Mo. Thanks. I'll be going and will I be seeing y'all at the Blue

Goose later?" Edgar asks, slinging the chainsaw over his shoulder, while carrying the bag of bakery goodies in the same hand and holding his free drink in the other hand.

"Sorry, I can't make it tonight. I've got the blacksmith's tractor and backhoe to fix. I'll be out of commission a few days. But I'll return."

"I'll be waiting with bated breath for your return Mo," Edgar hollers back on his way down Salmon Creek Road toward Highway 49.

Mo shouts back, "I didn't know you fly-fishermen believed in bait-fishing Edgar?"

"We don't any Mo. Get it?" Edgar laughs at his cornball joke until tears come to his eyes.

Mo yells, "I don't get it Edgar."

Fen and Rambo are still chasing each other and almost trip Mo, who's looking down the road shouting at the top of his lungs.

"See you later!" Edgar bellows, continuing down the road to Salmon Creek Stables.

"Not if I see you first!"

Fen sprints Wog Hill Road to sniff Emma's wogs. Weighed down by the bakery goodies, the chainsaw and his free drink, Edgar chases Fen the best he can. At the top of the Road he's greeted by Emma Jane Walters, freshly back from her day at the Hair Falls Salon.

"I'll be darned Edgar, if that Fenway of yours don't love to sniff wogs. You know I'd be upset if Fenway starts scaring my precious wogglings!"

Out of breath Edgar gasps, "Yes, Emma Jane I know. Fenway wouldn't hurt a fly let alone spook one of your prize chickens. Your hair turned out well Em."

Shaking her head Emma says, "You take good care of the Fen, Edgar. They don't make them like that anymore. She is so gentle. My chickens love seeing her. All the same, Fenway looks like a big freight train under full steam. The younger chickens do get nervous seeing her for the first time. Oh and thanks for the compliment."

"You're welcome Jane. Take care too and get your prize wogs ready for the Bicentennial. They're a crowd pleaser. And you're welcome."

"No doubt about that Edgar; I'll be there."

As fierce as Emma Jane sounds she has a heart of gold especially for animals, particularly for her incomparable wogs. Em was born and raised in the Deep South, a white slave. She was treated like an animal. Beaten day-in-and-day-out and indecently assaulted. She lived with the wogs, and they became her family. Her heart would break every time one of the masters came out to her quarters and wrung the neck of one of her dear wogs. Her only escape from such inhumanity came when she was left for dead. Somehow Emma Jane was raised from the dead and found her way to Abbeville. She would never kill a wog under any circumstance. Em only sells chicken eggs to people whom she knows for sure love animals and will handle her precious wog eggs with loving care. Alma spends lots of time with Em at Wog Hill Farm.

Washington, the blacksmith works and lives about five hundred feet from Wog Hills Road, a quarter of a mile out of town, down at the junction of Salmon Creek Road and Highway 49. When Edgar and Fen reach Salmon Creek Stables, Washington has Edgar's wood burning stove and heater loaded in the back of one of his trucks ready to go.

"Good to see you and Fenway."

Fenway loves Washington and throws her body on his feet. Washington Reyes is incredibly built. Fenway feels like she hit a cement truck. Although she takes all the heavy-handed loving and scratching the big blacksmith gives her.

"That was one bear of a job Edgar. Cleaning that antique stove of yours was hard work. If you want them in tip-top shape you need to bring that baby in every year for servicing."

"You're right, you're right, I get busy fishing and lose track of time Washington. Sorry."

"True Edgar. It's only been about a decade since I last worked on your stove and heater."

"Time flies Wash, time flies.

Then, Edgar finally remembers the Bicentennial.

"Say big guy, this year's big festival is coming soon; and it's going to be a doozy!"

"I hope so Edgar. The last few years the festival seems to have fizzled."

"I know. This year is the bicentennial year and Alma's been planning with her committee for something special. Will you show for the Town Hall meeting in February to help?

"You bet Edgar, you know you can count on me to come through."

"Maybe you could put a couple of large signs on the outside of the stables so people driving by on 49 can see them?"

"You bet Edgar."

"Good. How much do I owe you Washington?"

"Let's wait till I deliver the goods to the Store tomorrow. We can settle then."

"Sounds like a plan Washington. See you tomorrow."

With the morning's fishing trip, walking around Abbeville and chasing Fenway, Edgar is pooped. He only waves, as he goes past the Abbeville General. He limits his time at the tavern to two beers he owes Bob.

Monday, October 4, 6:34 p.m.: When Edgar gets home he remembers that he left the library book, *Mystery of Blood Hollow,* at the Blue Goose.

Thank goodness Alma is taking a nature walk or Edgar would have to lose at playing twenty questions with her, again. He puts the German chocolate cake and Boston cream pie in the refrigerator. The glazed old-fashioned donuts didn't make the trip back home. He puts the chainsaw in the shed and retires to bed with Fenway. Tomorrow is another day. Edgar will rescue the book from the Blue Goose on his way home from the General Store, unless, after having a few beers with Bob and the gang, he forgets.

Chapter 2

⊙❧⊙

Sunday, November 28, 1:07 p.m.: Life is as laid-back as one can imagine in Abbeville. Bell chimes at Damascus Church echo through the valley marking the end of Reverend Henry's last service. Pealing bells also mark the beginning of Henry's after church race to Edgar and Alma's cabin for a lunch of trout leftovers and the weekly game of chess. Forty-five minutes later, a knock at the Whitman cabin door signals let the games begin.

Hearing Alma shout, "It's okay to come in Henry," Reverend Johnston opens the door and seats himself at the kitchen table.

Alma finishes clearing the kitchen table as Edgar sets out pieces on the chessboard. Driven by her dislike of fish and her uneasiness around Reverend Henry, Fenway meanders to the deck and settles on her pillow.

Picking out two pawns, Henry says, "Which hand Edgar?"

"Your right hand Reverend."

"My goodness, you have white again!"

Alma softly interrupts to ask her boys if they need anything before she goes. Edgar is absorbed in his game.

"Reverend do you want some of my sautéed asparagus spears and Spanish rice with your rainbow trout?"

"Absolutely, my dear Alma, thank you."

"And my dear," the Reverend continues, "I'd like a napkin and glass of lemonade too?"

"I like? I like? I like? People in hell like ice water too Henry," Alma delivers the line with a laugh.

"Whoa," Henry says caught a little off guard."

He recovers with a laugh, "Funny Alma, very funny. May I trouble you for a glass of lemonade, Alma, pretty please?"

"Of course Reverend, a glass of lemonade is just the ticket for washing that dry sermon taste from your mouth."

Reverend Johnston winces and says, "That hurts Alma. So you think my sermons are dry. How would you know? You've never been to church in your entire life! How do you know my sermons are dry?"

Alma without missing a beat replies, "I don't have to cross the Sahara desert to know hot, dry winds blow across it, Henry"

"Pawn to king's three Henry," interjects Edgar, "You two can duke it out later. Let's play chess!"

Alma's spirituality is grounded in nature; Henry is spiritually grounded in Christ. Because she knows there is no conflict between Jesus' teachings and nature, her beliefs easily embrace Henry and his beliefs. He, however, is stuck within the boundaries of his theology. Henry believes his way of connecting the theological dots is the only true way to connect the dots. He loves Alma with "Christian Love" and is careful not to be drawn into her "Naturalism," which he knows is a snare set by the devil to trap him. When Alma pokes fun at him and he genuinely laughs, she knows Henry realizes every word he speaks does not necessarily come directly from the mouth of God. He faces his arrogant self and laughs at the irony.

Edgar and Henry's relationship is more labyrinthine. When they first met, they almost came to blows, but not really. Their verbal exchanges, however, sent mixed messages to the ears of those listening to them exchange barbed views about every subject one can imagine. That was when they were younger, thought in absolutes, and could get more fired up about issues. Over the years, Henry and Edgar have mellowed and manage a convivial relationship, keeping their adrenalin in check.

Today, people who know Reverend Henry and Edgar would never expect warlike posturing beneath either of their calm, happy-go-lucky exteriors. The community only experiences the light, considerate, compassionate, trustworthy, and friendly sides of the two.

"Pawn to queen's bishop four," replies the Reverend, and the war sublimates to the game of chess.

Edgar takes the full allotment of time before moving.

Although Henry doesn't exactly believe in God in the same way as Edgar believes, their theological differences will never kill their cherished relationship. To ensure their relationship matures and deepens, they keep their association restricted to the small window of time on Sunday afternoons, when they play chess. Henry and Edgar never do postmortems on their games. Between the warlike chess moves, peaceful gambits are at play. In between the attacks of white's pawns and the charge of black's knight, Edgar and Henry discuss how to alleviate the hardships their townspeople face. Well aware of the substantial influence they exert in Abbeville, they put aside selfish interests, sublimating their differences. Like flipping a coin, if their wins and losses were totaled, the score would be a virtual tie.

"Knight to king's bishop three," Edgar refocuses his attention to the chessboard.

"Pawn to queen three," replies Henry.

"Pawn to queen four," counters Edgar.

As expected the game ends stalemated.

Reverend Henry thanks Edgar for the game and looks for Alma. They forgot she mentioned she was going somewhere. Alma has slipped away in the forest, while their heads were filled with chess strategies that insulated them from hearing doors opening and closing and Alma's fading footsteps.

"Edgar, please, let Alma know how much I love her and her cooking," Henry says warmly.

Edgar gives Henry a big brotherly hug, "I'll be sure to convey your love to the cook and your best wishes."

"Love in Christ my brother."

As the sun sets beyond the Northern Buttes, turning the gathering dark clouds golden, Henry leaves. Edgar closes the door on the upcoming storm. He listens to the weather forecast that confirms light snow overnight in the Sierras, continuing through Monday. Satisfied that he will not have to cut holes in lake ice to fish, Edgar relaxes on the sofa with a cigar and Fenway's head in his lap. He waits another hour or so, hoping Alma will return, but knows otherwise. He misses her companionship.

"Nothing against you girl. I hoped to see Alma before we went to sleep, that's all."

Fenway looks at him as if to say, "Sorry, I can't tuck you in bed Edgar, I don't have opposable thumbs."

Sunday, November 28, 9:25 p.m.: Alma is out for the evening and won't return until Tuesday morning, in time to cook breakfast. Edgar goes to bed with Fenway by his side. They will fly fish Culbertson and Bullpen Lakes early in the morning. The lakes are two miles from Forest Route 17 into the higher elevations of the mountains, a short romp for Fenway, but something a bit more for Edgar. However, Edgar figures it's the last of the Indian summer fishing and worth the effort.

"A little snow doesn't really mean the end of summer Fenway. That only happens when the ground is frozen solid, right girl?" Edgar says patting Fen.

Alma rides her Vespa to the outskirts of Foresthill. Season's first snow won't stop the sisters from meeting. By anyone's standards Alma's walk up Mosquito Ridge is several miles over very difficult terrain. As night falls, a bold moon rides high above a smattering of dark golden, but soon ominous looking clouds begin moving inland. The moon stays bright enough to light the forest floor, allowing Alma to easily find Black Rock clearing, one of the meeting places of the Sisterhood. Protecting the natural resources and ensuring public safety, Fish and Game closes Mosquito Ridge Road to public transportation. Chances of running into another human being on the ridge at night are nil. As Alma closes in on Black Rock, freshly fallen snow crunches beneath her feet, telegraphing her approach to Florence and to Chinook, the alpha male of a wolf pack hunting deep in the forest.

Alma enters the clearing and embraces Florence, who is petting wolf pups not old enough to keep pace with a hunting pack. Sensing Alma's arrival, Chinook breaks off the hunt and trots the pack back to Black Rock clearing. Perceiving a world beyond human comprehension, the pack welcomes them, nuzzling and licking the two human females. Scratching the wolves behind their ears and stroking their backs, Alma greets the wolves in a calm voice.

"I know, I know. Your lives are hard, your hearts are strong; nature has called you to fill this space and time in the wilderness. You do well what nature requires of you. Yes, you do."

Alma and Florence hug Chinook and pour their love, their warmth on him. Chinook remains upright, dominant and ever vigilant. By contrast, Fenway would have melted into gaga-land and unashamedly rolled on her back with paws limp and curled, submissive and vulnerable with no thought of vigilance. As foreign are the worlds of the wild from the civilized, Alma and Florence know Chinook and Fenway are the same in spirit and heart. Few humans understand this truth, as they tend to see and judge only by outward appearances.

Faced with constant starvation, the wolf pack soon returns to the hunt. With heads lowered, noses close to the ground for scent and communication, Chinook leads the pack from the clearing, leaving their pups in the care and protection of Alma and Florence. The wolf pups—some huddling, others sprawling in the snow—sleep soundly, confidently under the wings of the Sisterhood. Conventional wisdom says the relationship between these two women and the wolf pack is uncanny, unbelievable. The truth is for centuries, some few women of the Sisterhood and the wolves have always shared great trust. Alma and Florence are one with the pack and the wolf pack is one with these sisters. They continually test their faith in the wilderness and faithfully follow the ways of nature. Scripture ensures that some day the lion will lay down with the lamb. For the wolves and the Sisterhood, this is a promise that has been kept for centuries.

Natural depressions in the granite provide places for Alma and Florence to set ablaze a small fire. Their faces feel ribbons of heat penetrating the night's cold air that heightens their awareness of the grandeur of nature. Looking inward through each other's eyes they see the unfathomable depths of their personal worlds. Communing in silence, their worlds reveal tenderness, peace, and mystery. Through the tree-filtered moonlight and light falling snow within the great expanse reaching toward Hell Hole Reservoir, they watch the Sierra Nevada's knuckle-topped mountains punch the night's darkness. Alma and Florence connect beyond ten thousand things. In the darkness, they experience calm, power and mystery of the universe wherein their worlds revolve. Half Alma's age Florence possesses spiritual gifts surpassing Alma's. In time, Alma will relinquish her flame, as it has been done in the Sisterhood for many centuries, before the founding of Abbeville.

The frenzy of the hunt is close. Sounds of the wolf pack pursuing prey next to camp bring the sisters and the pups to their feet. A large terrified mule deer crashes through the brush into the clearing, wolves' teeth deeply sunk into its throat and haunches. Insatiable wolves mercilessly pin the doomed deer to the ground. Tearing raw flesh, spilling the deer's entrails on the ground, wolves rip through the dying animal's tough hide and soft belly with their two-inch long teeth. Molars powerful enough to crush the thighbones of moose are heard crushing knee and leg bones. The struggle is soon over. The kicking stops and deer's cries become last gasps for air. The dense forest quells the hoofed beast's final squalls.

In a show of supreme confidence, standing, ears and tail held high, Chinook walks to the kill. With disinterest, he looks at his would-be challengers and subordinates. They avert their eyes. Chinook gives deference to the sisters, allowing Alma to walk to the lifeless mule deer and cut pieces of meat for Florence and her. A slight motion is detected in the pack. Chinook glances and gives a low growl. As eyes cast to the ground, all movement in the pack ceases. Chinook feeds. Afterwards, the pack is allowed to eat the remains of the kill.

Alma sits at Florence's side. They give thanks. The aroma of meat roasting over the fire rides the breezes pushed by the impending snowstorm. The mule deer carcass lies behind them, being devoured by the wolf pack. The pack gives way, as Chinook returns to the deer and chews chunks of meat from its rump. Satisfied, he walks from the carcass, permitting the pack continue feeding. Wolf pups that can chew pick at the carcass and eat scraps from the snow. The younger pups suckle.

Florence observes the skies. Dark pendulous clouds partially obstruct the moon. Alma and Florence watch snowflakes appear from the darkness into the fire's light, only to vanish before reaching the ground. Lighted by flames from the flickering fire, the trunks of the great pines and the undersides of their branches glow. Stomachs full, the wolf pack sprawls out in the clearing and falls asleep.

"Florence, like these snowflakes, I will soon pass from sight."

"I know."

"Are you ready?"

"I am. I am upheld by the hand that created all."

Nature's chapel of the pines is peaceful.

But, nothing attracts the attention of predators better than the lingering scent of a fresh kill. First, at a distance, then, louder and louder, the sounds of large tree limbs breaking wake the pack. Instinctively, the wolves face the impending danger, ready to attack in defense of the wolf pups and the humans. Side by side they wait for the mystery to unfold. Within seconds, three hundred pounds of crazed animal storms the clearing and rises to full height on its hind legs—firelight dancing wildly on its chest and jowls. Pawing the air, the bear lets out a deafening, blood-curdling roar.

Florence whispers to Alma, "This bear doesn't appear to be interested in a diet of grass, flowers, and sarsaparilla berries."

Before the wolves launch a ferocious defensive strike, Florence moves forward and strokes Chinook's back assuring everything is well. She lovingly picks up and holds one of the pack's links to immortality to her breast and caresses the pup. She looks into the eyes and soul of the bear. Time and space freeze in what feels like an eternity. The bewildered bear stands down. The wolf pack shows no signs of aggression. The befuddled bear quietly turns and disappears to the forest darkness from which he came.

"You are ready," Alma declares.

Florence with eyes closed bows her head in assent. Like the mythical Uroboros, Alma and Florence create themselves anew with each venture of the Sisterhood. Never can they, nor ever would they, even if they could, return to what they were. Forest experiences constantly alter their kaleidoscopic understandings of reality. Chinook howls into the night, as if giving tribute to a greater power. The wolf family sleeps safely in the clearing, huddled in the snow for warmth until the pre-dawn hours, when the pack will hunt again.

Book Two

✦

Winter's Deadly Touch

Chapter 1

⇖⇗

Friday, December 31, 6:30 p.m.: Highways 49 and 24 to Abbeville are choked by one severe storm after another, as blizzard conditions pound the sierras. Twenty feet of snow blanket the town, burying all of Abbeville's drives, streets, and roads. Abbeville is cut off from the world and isolated. However, two hundred years of winters have taught the town's inhabitants to adapt well to harsh conditions. New Year's Eve day, Ellen Jackson's Hair Falls Salon thrives, as a steady stream of women's hair is washed, colored, cut, premed, and eloquently quaffed for the evening's celebrations.

Ellen, who is usually home by six o'clock on most holidays, is not home by the appointed hour. Mo Jackson calls the salon at six-thirty to see what his wife is doing. No answer. High winds and heavy snows continue. He walks out on the front porch and peers into a solid wall of whiteness for signs of Ellen. Nothing. He can't see the salon or the Mexican restaurant down the street or Abbeville's General Store across Matthew Drive. Mo immediately calls the sheriff department to

report his wife missing.

"Happy New Year. Sergeant Dirk Jacobson Sierra County Sheriff Department speaking, how may I assist you?" Comes a cheery greeting from the desk sergeant.

"My wife Ellen has not come home from work today. She owns the Hair Falls Salon here in Abbeville. It's not more than a stone's throw from our home. I really don't know what else there is to say, except I'm worried, really worried."

"Sir, what is your full name?"

Sighing hard into the phone Mo says, "Oh, I'm sorry. My name is Moses Timothy Jackson."

"Thank you Mr. Jackson. With the blizzard hitting hard in the Sierra's where you are it's impossible to do anything immediately. The road's closed and all surveillance and rescue helicopters and planes grounded.

"I understand Sergeant. I can't see any of the buildings across Second Street or Matthew Drive."

"When was the last time you saw your wife, Mr. Jackson?"

"When she went to work at about eight o'clock morning."

"With the roads closed, how did you get to work?"

"I own Meadows Garage. Ellen has been able to go back and forth the short distance between our house and the beauty salon using our mini-cab tractor two-stage snow blower."

"Have you gone over to the solon to check out what's happening?"

"The snow's too deep to make it by foot; Ellen has the snow blower."

"Mr. Jackson how do people get to your wife's salon in this blizzard?"

"Years ago Edgar Whitman and I thought of the idea to connect our business establishments across Matthew Drive. Three large portable wooden road covers across Matthew Drive—one at the front of town between my service station and the general store, one in the middle of town between the Medical Clinic and Fabrics Plus and one at the end of town between the library and town hall. Each street from Second to Ninth Street has a small portable cover connecting each business that faces Matthew Drive. Anyone making it to town can walk straight through most of the town."

"I've never heard of that. If the snow is deep enough to bury the town, how do the inhabitants of Abbeville get to town?"

"Everyone digs a snow tunnel from their home to the snow tunnels along the streets in their neighborhoods. Almost every home is connected to the town through our system of snow tunnels."

"How long are the tunnels and cover ways used?"

"Depending on the year, four to six months."

"The whole of Abbeville is honey combed with passage ways?"

"Yea, almost the entire town is interconnected, snug as bugs in a rug."

"So why don't you travel through the tunnels and portable road covers to your wife's beauty solon?"

"I can't get through. The blizzard and snow fall collapsed the tunnel from my house to the street cover across Second Street."

"Mr. Jackson maybe your wife is holed up in someone's home or is stuck in one of the structures covering the streets or one of the honey-combed passage ways?"

"Maybe so, but I'm worried and fear the worst has happened to her."

"Why do you fear the worst, Mr. Jackson?"

"I don't know. I feel something terrible has happened to Ellen."

"Okay, Mr. Jackson. I've recorded your report. As soon as we can get to your town, a search and rescue operation will begin. But, most likely, she will show up alive and well tomorrow. In the meantime let's hope for the best and please keep us informed."

"Thank you sergeant, I appreciate all you can do."

"No problem. I'm sorry I had to ask so many questions. I'm new to the area. I see from our records, missing persons reports from Abbeville are common during the winter months. Most of the reported incidences turn out well with people safely appearing in a day or so."

"That's reassuring Sergeant Jacobson I'm hopeful too, but scared at the same time. Nothing like this has ever happened to Ellen."

Friday, December 31, 7:00 pm: Mo can't stay still and wait for the snow plows to make their way from Sierra City to open the roads. He grabs a shovel and begins to dig out from the front of his house. The snow towers over him; soon the relentless winds, sleet and snow overwhelm his efforts, driving him backwards. Nevertheless, he presses on because Ellen may be just a few yards from him. He returns home to find an empty house and exhausted he falls asleep.

Saturday, January 1, 7:15 a.m.: Early the next morning Mo Jackson is up and at it again.

"Maybe Ellen drove the snow plow toward Matthew Drive for some reason," he thinks.

The thought doesn't make sense, but he has no choice. He shovels through his parking lot to the wooden cover across Matthew Drive. But, shoveling up to Second Street is impossible. The walls of snow are twelve feet high. He has no place to shovel the snow, except behind him. His efforts are unrewarded this New Year's Day. He finds no trace of his beloved wife.

Later, news that Ellen's missing quickly spreads as people rub elbows in the maze of Abbeville tunnels. Saturday's Damascus Church New Year Day services are fertile grounds for speculations and lengthy discussions about what happened to Ellen. Others find their way to the Blue Goose Tavern to converse. Come Saturday afternoon, the Knead-2-Feed Bakery and Abbeville's General Store are chat and gossip centers for the latest news on Ellen's whereabouts.

Sunday, January 2, 12:30 a.m.: Distant clattering of snowplows, working to open highway 49 over Yuba Pass down through Downieville, doesn't disturb the sleeping citizenry. Only when the clanking tractors begin to clear Gold Lake Road above Abbeville, clamor up Salmon Creek Road, and down Switch Back Road is the town awakened. Mo grabs his shovel and heads out the door, welcoming the noise.

Monday, January 3, 8:10 a.m.: Bruce Dean, a land developer and chairperson of the Damascus Church Men's Retreat, finds his wife dead not far from the front door of their home. Anne is the Damascus Church secretary and beloved in the community. Bruce calls Allen Belcher who serves with him as an elder on the Damascus Church Council. Belcher notifies Dr. Preston and the Sierra County Sheriff Department's Medical Examiner, Dr. Mayes before he makes his way through the honeycombed passages with Hector Flores and Alex Temecula, unemployed lumbermen, who work for Belcher Mortuary as cemetery gardeners, crematorium attendants, and gravediggers. When they reach Dean's home, Dr. Silvia Preston is finishing her examination of Anne. She takes pictures of Anne's body from various angles, as well as pictures of the tunnel ice walls and the maze of passages leading to Anne's residence.

The position of Anne's body leads Dr. Preston to believe Anne collapsed suddenly, as if from a stroke or heart attack. The fact that Anne's clothing isn't frozen and her joints are flexible indicates Anne has been lying in the snow for an hour or two. She estimates Anne died around eight o'clock, when she apparently was shoveling snow inside the tunnel.

Monday, January 3, 11:06 a.m.: Dr. Preston permits the body to be removed. Allen carefully rolls Anne to her back and straightens her clothes. Hector and Alex place Anne on the gurney.

Instead of having Anne taken to the mortuary, Dr. Preston instructs Allen to take Anne to the town morgue. Allen nods and does not question her decision. With the body removed Silvia takes more pictures. She especially focuses on the shovel that was trapped under Anne's body. With gloved hands she carefully removes the shovel. She takes more pictures.

Silvia records every event taking place at the death scene, including comments made by Bruce, Allen, Alex, Hector and herself during the removal of Anne's body. Dr. Preston and Bruce watch Anne wheeled along the passageway, disappearing around the corner in the darkness. They remain silent until the sounds of the mortician's voices vanish.

"Bruce, I am so sorry for your loss. Anne was loved and appreciated by everyone in our community. I can guarantee you she didn't suffer and the end was quick and peaceful."

"Thank you Dr. Preston. I don't understand why the Lord took her. She was so young."

"I know. The good news is her spirit is with us. Once through your grief, you will remember the good she accomplished in her allotted time on earth."

Unabashedly crying, taking a deep breath to calm his emotions, Bruce nods in accord with Dr. Preston's words of comfort.

"I know you're right Dr. Preston. I feel so much pain in my heart, it feels like my chest is about to explode."

Sobbing deep breaths, he hugs Dr. Preston. She hugs him back before returning to the office. At the corner, she looks back and waves good-bye. Standing shrouded in darkness, Bruce waves back.

Dr. Preston arrives at the medical clinic by noon. Florence has closed the office for lunch, which gives Silvia ample time to load Anne's pictures and notes into the computer. She sends them by confidential security transmission to the county medical examiner in Downieville, Dr. Jeffrey Mayes. Dr. Preston and the county forensics team will consult via teleconference, during the autopsy and exhaustive medical examination of Anne, later in the evening.

Monday, January 3, 3:30 p.m.: Abbeville's Volunteer Fire Department begins to open the town's drives and streets. Having barely adequate equipment, their progress is slow. Removing the first portable street cover they clear the snow from Second Street. Then, turning the corner onto Salmon Creek Road, the fire engine's six-foot road scraper runs into Ellen's mini cab snow blower.

Ellen Jackson appears to be frozen dead at the wheel inside the cab. Dr. Preston and the county medical examiner's office in Downieville are immediately called by the firefighters. Dr. Preston arrives within five minutes. She notes her time of arrival at 4:00 p.m. and estimates the time Ellen was found by the firefighters at 3:40. She follows the same medical and forensic protocol she did with Anne Dean earlier in the day. Dr. Preston preliminary determines Ellen death was caused by asphyxiation. Determining the estimated time of death poses more of a problem.

Dr. Preston calculates, "Given New Year's Eve weather reports indicated the rate of snowfall being 13 inches an hour. If Ellen was trapped in her tractor cab at or before 9:00 p.m. on December 31, the cab must have been completely snow covered by 1:00 a.m. on New Year's Day." But how could Ellen have possibly allowed herself to be trapped in the cab?"

The volunteer firemen wait for Dr. Preston to complete her examination.

She thinks, "Before nine o'clock in the evening, the walkway from the salon to the snow-blower allowed Ellen plenty of room to open wide the snow-blower's cab door. Evidently, when Ellen drove away, the cab doors were only inches away from the ice walls along Second Street."

Dr. Preston surmises the mini-snow blower must have stalled, trapping Ellen in the cab around seven or eight o'clock in the evening. Looking along the ice walls next to the blower's cab door, she searches for evidence to support her theory. As she thought, there are marks, gouges in the ice where it appears Ellen was trying to open the cab door multiple times. Dr. Preston takes numerous photos.

"It certainly appears Ellen was trapped inside her cab by the snow and ice," she reasons, "If Ellen continued slamming open the door to get out, she might well have expended lots of energy and depleted oxygen faster, hastening her death."

Volunteer fire Captain Edward Forbes asks Silvia whether she wants Ellen removed from the snow blower.

"In a minute Ed," Silvia gives the situation more thought, "Given the freezing temperatures ranging from 16 to 25 degrees according to official weather reports, it might have taken Ellen four to six to eight hours to die from the cold. But, given the combined affects of the heater being on and oil and gas fumes emissions from the tractor engine, plus her struggling to get out of the cab, Ellen death was caused by asphyxiation, not the cold."

The evidence is consistent with someone dying a calm and peaceful death, slowly letting go of life. After considering the factors, including Ellen's medical history, Dr. Preston sets the time of Ellen's death between 7:00 a.m. and 9:00 a.m. on New Year's Day.

Dr. Preston instructs the firemen to pull the mini-blower onto Second Street where the cleared road is wide to fully open the snow-blowers cab doors. Watching Ellen being pulled past her, Dr. Preston can't get the thought out of her head that if Ellen hadn't missed the turnoff down John Drive, she would have probably been back home and alive.

On Second Street, Dr. Preston easily opens the cab door and takes more pictures. She touches nothing, knowing any item may be valuable physical evidence. Dr. Preston visually inspects the entire inside of the cab and closely examines Ellen's topography—her clothes, hair, exposed skin areas, socks, and shoes. She observes a cut on the left frontal part of Ellen's forehead that runs into her hairline.

She reasons, "In the process of banging open the door, Ellen probably hit her head against the inside of the cab door. That would explain the cut high on her forehead."

Dr. Preston touches Ellen's body, which appears to be frozen solid, having been entombed in snow since Friday evening. She calls Belcher Brother's Mortuary and talks with Christopher Jenkins, head gardener and landscaper for the Abbeville Cemetery, who also works as a part-time embalmer, handyman, and hearse driver. Twenty minutes later Christopher and another unemployed lumberman turned gravedigger, Richard Aguilar, arrive. Dr. Preston directs them to remove the body to the morgue. She takes photos of every step of the removal process and notes the time of removal at 6:00 p.m.

Monday, January 3, 6:30 p.m.: Christopher and Richard push Ellen along side Anne in the refrigerated room in the town morgue, a converted meat locker of the old meat company across from the Preston Medical Clinic. Dr. Preston crosses the street to her clinic and sends her photos and reports to the medical examiner.

Five years ago the 100-year-old Sierra Meat Company went out of business, after Fred Masher, the owner and last of the Abbeville Masher's, died. Dr. Preston petitioned the town council to buy the building to use as a town morgue, which she would be willing to operate. At the time the meat company was purchased, the Sacramento Courier carried the story. The Abbeville town council president was quoted, as saying:

"When the Sierra Meat Company went out of business, we got the building, a refrigeration unit, a sink, and some stainless steel tables," Whitman said. "This is about being prepared for the worst. Dr. Preston needs the space where she can do what she needs to do," Whitman concluded.

One may not think there's much business for a morgue in a small town, but the Abbeville Town Morgue houses a dozen or so bodies a year, as the morgue is often used by surrounding towns and the Sierra County Sheriff Department. When a tour bus crashed down at Bassett's Station last year, seventeen bodies were housed in the morgue. Dr. Preston's farsightedness serves the county and Abbeville well.

Monday, January 3, 7:30 p.m.: Notifying Mo Jackson is not an easy task for Dr. Preston. As objective and professionally distant as she can be, her business is working to save lives. Breaking the news about death to the family is difficult. Beneath her tough, evidence-based exterior, she is a cupcake. With clear streets, she makes the short trip across Second Street, through Meadow's parking lot to the garage. Mo is under a truck when Silvia enters.

"Mo," Dr. Preston calls in a soft voice.

Knowing who it is calling and what the call is about, Mo rolls from beneath the truck and without getting up from his mechanic's creeper responds to Dr. Preston.

"It's Ellen isn't it Dr. Preston? She's gone isn't she?"

"Yes Ellen died peacefully inside the snow blower, not too far from the beauty shop."

As he creeps back under the truck continuing to working, tears well in Mo's eyes.

Dr. Preston says, "Are you going to be alright, Mo?"

"Sure. I need some time to get a hold of myself. I do that best when I'm busy."

"Okay," Dr. Preston says, "You know how to get a hold of me. Please call. I do want to talk with you more later today or tomorrow."

Clearing his throat Mo says, "Don't worry Doc. I'm fine, and I will call you tomorrow. Thanks."

"I'll be expecting that call Mo, good-bye."

Monday, January 3, 9:12 p.m.: Dr. Preston works late teleconferencing with Drs. Mayes and Brown and the forensic team of Jensen, Gastineau and Curry. Bright halogen lights flood the autopsy table where fixed cameras focus at all angles on bodies under examination.

"Can you hear me now?" Dr. Preston tests the sound system in the morgue, "Testing, testing, embalming is the art and the science used to prevent the natural decomposition of the dead human body . . ."

"Yes Dr. Preston we hear you and you look well too," says Dr. Mayes, Sierra County's medical examiner.

Dr. Preston removes the sheet covering Anne Dean and describes her to the medical examiner and his forensic team.

"This is Anne Dean, blond, five foot five inches tall, slender, a thirty-five year old married woman who died of a heart attack. As her primary physician, I know. She had a history of congenital heart failure. Viewing her outward appearance, no unusual or suspicious marks appear on any part of her body."

"What an extraordinarily beautiful woman," Dr. Mayes comments.

"Yes," agrees Dr. Preston, "And she had an inner beauty to match."

Automatically streaming photos to Dr. Mayes and the forensic team in Downieville, Dr. Preston slowly moves her portable 10x Zeiss Observation Camera along the surface of Anne's body. At the receiving end of the camera Mayes and his forensic team study the pictures and listen to Preston's comments on their specially designed, high-resolution 106-inch plasma display panel and sound system.

"She really has nice skin," comments Mimi Gastineau, a forensic technician, "Not one blemish; her skin is crystal clear."

"If anything was suspect, it would stick out like a big black beetle on a white wedding dress," Dr. Brown contributes.

Dr. Preston probes through Anne's hair focusing the camera closely on Anne's scalp.

"No signs of nothin'," observes head technician Hopper Jensen.

"Well stated Hopper. Didn't they have English courses at the college where you earned your EMT?" Quips forensic technician Curry.

Dr. Preston slowly runs the camera over Anne's face, neck, shoulders and breasts. Special attention is given to Anne's fingernails, pubic area, and toenails. As Silvia swings past Anne's feet to shoot Anne's other side, she bumps into Ellen's morgue table, which lies in the shadows.

Dean Curry jokingly exclaims, "What was that Dr. Preston, an earthquake?"

"No Dean, only a tired, clumsy doctor doing her job," replies Dr. Preston, as she continues to closely examine Anne's body through the camera's zoom magnification lens.

"And who's your friend, Dr. Preston, the one standing behind you?" Mimi inquires.

"Very funny Mimi. Your sense of humor seems to have been emotionally arrested somewhere in the third grade, I'd say."

Supporting Mimi Dr. Mayes says, "No Silvia, in the fixed camera shot there really is someone behind you."

Dr. Preston stops, slowly turns, and faces a shrouded figure that stands head and shoulders above her. Throwing her arms in the air, she screams at the top of her voice, crashing her hand-held zoom camera into the halogen lights above the morgue room table. Dr. Preston lurches backwards, peddling as fast as she can away from the gray apparition, which sends Anne and her morgue table rocketing across the old meat company's refrigerated room.

"Holy Kripes! Ellen! You're alive!"

Seeing Ellen falling from the morgue table, Dr. Preston regains her composure and rushes across the room to catch Ellen before she hits the floor. The camera keeps on filming the bottom half of the action, enough to glue Mayes and the rest of the forensic team to their display screen.

"It's a miracle!" exclaims Dr. Brown.

"Are you alright, Dr. Preston?" inquires Dr. Mayes.

"Fine . . . fine, I've never had a corpse spring back to life. It's a first for me."

Waking in the morgue does not shock Ellen as much as feeling the bone chilling cold and the pain of thawing tissues. Dr. Preston loosely wraps her patient in a sheet and covers her with a blanket. She avoids rubbing Ellen's arms, legs and body, which would only cause further tissue damage.

Monday, January 3, 11:30 p.m.: Dr. Preston phones Florence, waking her with the news of Ellen's return to life. She asks Florence to go to the clinic, activate the whirlpool and ready exam room three to receive Ellen for treatment and bedside care. Twenty minutes later, Florence has heated the pool to forty-two degrees, adding a measure of mild antibacterial soap to fight infection. Dr. Preston wheels Ellen along the tunnel between the morgue and the clinic, positioning Ellen beside the gently circulating whirlpool. Ellen's thawing body is placed in the Hoyer lift and slowly lowered in the tub of cool water. Over the next forty minutes, Florence keeps a close eye on the distal ends of Ellen's fingers, toes, nose and ears for signs of blood coming back to the once thawed areas.

"It's going to be tough sledding for Ellen over the next few months Florence. We need to keep her under constant watch."

Florence understands.

"Call Gary French, Yolanda Richardson and Maxine Williams. See if they're willing to work a second shift after working their jobs at the Coyoteville Convalescent Home."

"It's past midnight. I may not be able to reach them, but I will leave a message."

"Good. And, give a call to Dr. Richard Barrington for an immediate consultation. See if he can come out tonight. I want him to take a look at Ellen and our efforts at debriedement. Tell him we'll need a long-term management plan respecting continued removal of Ellen's dead, damaged and infected tissue. Plus, I'll need to know if amputation and skin grafting are necessary."

Florence hops right on Silvia's directions and returns to her with the good news that Barrington is on his way and Gary, Yolanda, and Maxine have consented to work at the clinic. Yolanda will take the day shift, Gary is on graveyard, and Maxine will accept the swing shift.

"Excellent. After the debriedment process is completed, make sure we have at least three sterile sheets to wrap Ellen. I need two hundred capsules of eight hundred milligram Ibuprofen available at her bedside and low molecular weight dextran to prevent erythrocyte clumping in her blood vessels. Give her a five percent dextrose, twenty percent saline I.V. for the next eight hours."

Florence asks, "What dosage of dextran is needed?"

"Five hundred milliliters of dextran for administering when we arrive and set up for slow continuous intravenous infusion of 500 milliliters dextran over six hours for the next three days."

Florence is out the door quick as a bunny, taking care of business.

Tuesday, January 4, 1:15 a.m.: Dr. Barrington arrives in time to help Silvia and Florence move Ellen from the bath to her bed, elevate her feet, and debried clear blisters to prevent thromboxane-mediated tissue injury. They leave hemorrhagic blisters intact to reduce the risk of infection. Fortunately for Ellen, Barrington is a Professor of Medicine, Emeritus, at the College of Physicians and Surgeons, Jasper Medical Center, New York, where he directed the Durhan Burn Unit. After examining Ellen's body Barrington gives his medical assessment.

"These areas will probably heal or mummify without surgery. I'd suggest low-dose infusions of heparin to prevent microthombosis.

Dr. Preston nods, while Florence takes notes.

"Have you conducted scintigraphy at your clinic?"

Dr. Preston informs Barrington that she has ample radiopharmaceuticals in lead storage units for such a procedure and quips, "So long as we have novices trying to climb the Buttes in walking shorts, we'll stock pile enough meds to meet the challenge."

Barrington smiles and continues, "I'd suggest a thallium stress test to see if the amount of thallium-201 in the heart tissues correlates with her tissue blood supply. I don't see any immediate need for amputation. Although, I would suggest you combine your intravenous heparin with the intravenous tissue plasminogen activator, which should improve her outcome given she has frostbite of the digits."

Preston listens attentively and allows Dr. Barrington to finish. Ellen sleeps peacefully and only hears Barrington's comments from a far distance through pain medications and a fog only a morphine drip can produce.

"Although the efficacy of bupivacaine is unclear according to the medical research, we may want to use it for cervical or lumbar sympathetic blockage to decrease sympathetic tone and relieve pain. But, if everything else we've done is working, we may not have to go there."

Barrington's consultation went as Dr. Preston had hoped. Florence and Silvia closely monitor Ellen's vital signs.

Tuesday, January 4, 3:00 p.m.: Gary arrives, taking over for Dr. Preston. Before she crawls into bed in examination room one to go to sleep, Dr. Preston calls Mo with the news about Ellen.

"Hello Mo, this is Dr. Preston. This is going to be somewhat of a shock for you, but Ellen is alive."

"Alive!"

"Yes, alive.

"A miracle," Mo exclaims.

"Evidently her body temperature dropped and she sustained life, as if she were in a state of hibernation. She is resting and her prognosis for recovery is excellent."

"Thank God, Dr. Preston. I'll be over as fast as I can."

"Florence will let you in when you come to the clinic. Understand, Mo, Ellen's recovery will take months. Your being here will give her more incentive to get well."

"Thank you doctor. I'll be there as fast as I can."

Silvia's first appointment is 9:00 a.m. Five hours sleep is a luxury under these circumstances. Mo arrives at 4:00 a.m. and is set up to be by Ellen's bedside. He will be there constantly until she is fully recovered. Shortly before eight, Florence greets Yolanda to the day shift and waves good bye to Gary who is on his way home.

Tuesday, January 4, 10:30 a.m.: Before the news of Ellen's recovery hits the streets, Abbeville's gossip mill grinds out another rumor.

Loud enough to attract the attention of everyone within earshot at the

Abbeville General Store, Edna exclaims, "Oh! What is this town coming to Bunny?" then, lowering her voice, she says, "Did you hear the scandal about Anne and the Reverend?"

"No, I haven't heard anything, Edna," the distracted Bunny says hopping down another trail of thought, "Edna, look at the price on these doilies! Edgar knows the price of these things. He's trying to gauge us again, screw his friends and neighbors!"

"Bunny," Edna tries to reign in the Bun, "You promise not to say a word to another living soul?"

"Of course not Edna, go on."

"Reverend Henry and Anne Dean were having an affair and when Bruce found out he beat poor Anne to death with a shovel, right on the door step of their home. Imagine that!"

Bunny, her eyes and mouth open wide with no sound coming out, almost drops the two orange wash clothes she's about to buy.

"No!"

"Quiet Bunny, I don't want everybody to hear us. Try to get a hold of yourself girl. Yes, I heard it from a reliable source, Fredrika."

"No!"

"Yes."

At the library about the same time that Edna is talking to Bunny, Fredrika is with Jenny in one of the glass walled, soundproof study rooms. Jenny's thumbing through a Cosmopolitan magazine, when Fredrika begins talking.

"Poor Anne, I told you about what happen to her, didn't I?"

Jenny nods.

"Well, did I tell you they found poor Ellen yesterday?"

"No, Fredrika what happened."

"The way I heard it from a reliable source, whom I can't divulge to you at the moment, is that Mo Jackson came home drunk from the Blue Goose Tavern."

"No!"

"Yes, and poor Ellen and Mo got into a big argument over how much time Mo spends at the tavern."

"No!"

"Yes, and when they were in bed, he smothered Ellen with his pillow!"

As her Cosmopolitan magazine slips off her lap to the floor, Jenny's eyes and mouth fly open wide with absolutely no sound.

"Quiet, Jenny, I don't want everybody to hear us through the soundproof glass. Try to get a hold of yourself girl. Yes, I heard it from a reliable source, Holly, but don't tell anybody."

Signaling not a word will be mentioned, Jenny nods her head yes and puts her finger to her lips.

Wednesday, January 5, 10:15 a.m.: The news of Ellen's miraculous recovery spreads through town like wildfire. Midmorning, Fredrika and Jenny have walked downtown and are having coffee at the Knead-2-Feed Bakery.

Jenny appearing upset says, "Fredrika! I must have told twenty people that Mo Jackson smothered his wife to death because she complained too much about his drinking. How do you think Ellen being alive makes me look to everybody?"

"I told you not to say a word about Ellen didn't I?"

"Yes, but you don't really expect me to keep that old promise, besides I had my fingers crossed."

"You did not!"

"I did so!"

Joyce opens the door of the Knead-2-Feed Bakery for Edna, who strolls into the bakery, smiles at Jenny and Fredrika and orders a cup of chocolate and a pumpkin scone. Pulling a chair over from another table, Joyce joins Freddie and Jenny, who look like they have their panties in a bunch!

"Good morning ladies. How are you all doing?" Joyce cheerfully greets the two.

Reversing faster than the Dow Jones Averages, Fredrika leans forward, "Girls, Ellen's not dead. Mo didn't kill her!"

Leaning forward Joyce says "No!"

Jenny says, "I know that Fredrika!"

"Yes, Ellen is pregnant with Bruce Dean's baby and is over at Preston Medical Clinic until she gives birth."

"No!" Joyce says.

"Where did you get that information, Freddie?"

"From a very reliable source, Jenny."

With a serious look on her face Jenny says, "I thought Ellen looked a little frumpy when she cut my hair New Year's Eve day."

Edna, who has changed her order to a chamomile lemon tea and a crumpet with three pads of butter, brings another chair to the table, squeezing between Joyce and Jenny.

"Did I miss anything girls?"

The girls sing out "Nothing Edna."

Joyce laughs, "That will be the day, Ladies."

Thursday, January 6, 8:14 a.m.: Another potential grizzly set of events begins to surface, when townspeople noticed the Abbeville's Farmer's Market isn't opened. Jeremy works hard during the winter preparing for the springtime. He's always puttering around repairing or building food stands, painting stalls, white washing the back fence, and fixing potholes in the parking lot. He is busy ordering fruits and vegetables from reputable organic farmers in the area. With other farmers, he negotiates new contracts to get the best foods at the lowest prices for Abbevillians. Jeremy, a fanatic ice and fly fisherman, thinks nothing of back packing into some wilderness area for a week or ten days. Customarily, he leaves word about his ventures with Edgar, Alma or with Nick Simmons at the Blue Goose. But, no one knows Jeremy's whereabouts.

Friday, January 7, 1:17 pm: Sadly, when the area around Packer's Lake is cleared of snow, Jeremy Paxton's body is uncovered. Dr. Preston takes all the photos and notes she needs, when Alexander Belcher and Juan Aquino—the last of the unemployed lumbermen that work as gardeners, gravediggers, and limousine drivers—arrive to remove the body.

All physical evidence and the results of Silvia's on-the-scene examination indicate natural death due to exposure. Preston allows the body to be taken to the mortuary, although she can't get the thought out of her head that Paxton, frozen like Ellen, might still be alive.

She thinks, "What are the chances of two frozen bodies coming back to life in the same week?"

From the looks of the body Silvia determines the time of Paxton's death to be ten days to two weeks ago and settles on the date of December 28th to record on the death certificate. To double-check her medical opinion however, Silvia sends her notes and photos to the Downieville medical examiner for confirmation. But, she is fairly certain of her pronouncement.

Sunday, January 9, 7:30 a.m.: Reverend Henry arrives at church early as usual on this very unusual Sunday morning.

With the rumors flying around the tunnels about his love affair with the dead church secretary, he is depressed and breaks into tears every so often. Maybe two weeks of snowing without seeing the sun adds to his anxiety. Maybe living in close quarters underground has made the whole town crazy. Although there is no substance to the rumors about Anne and him being lovers, he has lost hope all the same.

Henry wants to chuck the whole thing and run away. Taking time to pray he asks God to take this miserable burden from his wounded soul. He randomly flips through the Bible, which somehow stops on page 1631. He scans the page for something, anything that will lift the heaviness from his heart. Then, there it is. God's words seemed to jump from the page.

"No temptation has overtaken you except such as is common to man; but God is faithful, who will not allow you to be tempted beyond what you are able, but with the temptation will also make the way of escape, that you may be able to bear it."

Instantaneously, his despair and complete abandonment of the hope of salvation vanishes. The dark pall of melancholia stifling his heart lifts. When he teaches the message God gave him from chapter ten, verse thirteen of First Corinthians; Reverend Henry knows the blanket of gloom that also covers his congregation will be lifted, too. He takes the pulpit. He looks out over the congregation at the first service, sweeping his eyes in search of Mo Jackson, Bruce Dean, and Bruce's twelve-year old son Curtis. Then, Henry's eyes lock on Fredrika, Bunny, Edna, Jenny, and Joyce, who collectively squirm to avoid eye contact with him. He pauses until the eyes of the whole of the congregation are focused on the five gossipers, wriggling in the front row of Damascus Church.

"If we call on HIS NAME, The LORD is faithful," the Reverend begins, "He will never leave our sides in a moment of trial. He will never leave us in the depths of despair. Our hearts go out to Bruce, Curtis, and the friends of Jeremy for their loss. Although we may not see clearly on this side of the mortal veil because of our sorrow and grief, God is faithful. He will not allow us to remain inconsolable. He will not allow us to flounder and drown in melancholy seas. For God through Jesus Christ protects us from all that Satan and his demons can throw at us. Praise be the name of God! For God through Jesus Christ guarantees us a safe passage through this world into the glory of God's presence. Praise be the name of the Lord!"

The congregation echoes the phase, "Praise be the name of the Lord."

Reverend Henry echoes back the congregation, "Praise be the name of the Lord."

"Praise be the name of the Lord."

"Yes," Reverend Henry echoes the last refrain, "Praise be the name of the Lord."

At this moment, the spirit of the assembled congregation changes from sorrow and sullenness to hope and euphoria. To all who believed Reverend Henry that day, the Lord performed a miracle. The sunshine of the Lord swept away the somber skies from Abbeville, bringing new hope to all, who listened and were opened to the Word of God.

"Reverend Henry continues, "The storms of this winter have take sister Anne and brother Jeremy from us. The Dean family has asked me to announce services celebrating Sister Anne's life will be held at the Damascus Church on Thursday, January 13th at 10:00 a.m. Jeremy's friends have asked me to announce the celebration services for Brother

Jeremy's life will be held at the Abbeville Cemetery Chapel on Saturday, January 15th at 10:00 a.m."

Coming as no shock to the assembled, Reverend Henry announces that Ellen is not dead, but alive and doing well convalescing at Preston Medical Clinic. Many in the congregation believe Ellen's return from the dead was a miracle; and, without hard evidence to the contrary, who can say otherwise?

This Sunday's services are the shortest and the best Reverend Henry has ever delivered. In one short sermon, Henry completely placed his faith in the word of God and served as God's instrument in raising the people's hopes and spirit and overcoming his first crisis of faith.

Reverend Henry renews his commitment to trusting in the word of God and not leaning on his own understanding. But, he has a long way to go before he feels comfortable in his own skin.

Chapter 2

❦

Wednesday, January 12, 11:15 a.m.: Abbeville's gossip mill is fearless. Fredrika, Bunny, and Holly huddle in the far corner of Fabrics Plus by the yarn and fabrics' sales table and the specially marked down rack of dresses.

"Fredrika look. What do you think of this dress for Anne's funeral? I think it's a bit too fancy, but with a little black lace around the neckline and on the bodice, here and here?"

"Bunny you'll look adorable at the funeral," says Freddie.

Holly agrees, "Bun you'll be the bell of the ball."

"Did you hear about Jeremy Paxton?"

"No," reply Bunny and Holly in unison.

"Jeremy sells drugs, you know."

"Ah my word, no I didn't know," says Bunny fluttering her fake eyelashes and patting her hand on her chest feigning shock.

"Really Bunny," remarks Fredrika, showing she's not going to buy into Bunny's fakery.

"I didn't know either," says Holly.

Rolling her eyes Fredrika continues, "And when he couldn't pay the drug cartel, he ran deep into the mountains."

"No."

"Yes. And they found him and staked him out in the snow storm."

"No."

"Yes. And, when he was still alive, wolves and foxes came along and ate his face!"

"No."

"Yes. I heard it from a reliable source that I promised never to disclose."

"Possibly Edna?" Holly says.

"How did you know Holly? Did Edna tell you too?"

Bunny emphatically interjects, "Yes! I will buy this dress and the black lace. Together it only costs $13.35!"

Rumors rage about Anne Dean's affair with Henry. How her husband is a big contributor and chairman of the upcoming men's retreat. Gossip spins out of control. Salacious, but false details about the supposed affair depict Reverend Henry and Anne making love in the choir loft, in his office, and in the church pews, after Sunday services.

"How could this man of God ravage one of his flock?" is the question the rumor mill tries to plant in the minds of Abbevillians.

Conferences that Pastor Henry legitimately attends are twisted into erotic outings, dripping with lewd details that titillate prurient minds. As the week goes by, Fredrika and the girls stir the pot harder and harder.

"And all of this happening right under the nose of her husband! How revolting! How absolutely revolting is that?" swirl the lies.

Reverend Henry walks in the Abbeville General Store to buy groceries. His cheery greetings to several of his congregation are met by stony faces and short replies with little or no eye contact. No one wants to be seen talking to Henry. He looks for Edgar.

"Bridget, is Edgar in the store today?"

"Edgar's in the back room shelving deliveries. Michael has a doctor's appointment."

Thanking Bridget he walks to the back of the store. Edgar is shelving a shipment of pickles and beans.

"Edgar," Henry calls, "do you have a minute to talk with me?"

"Sure thing," says Edgar, "While we talk, could you hand me the cans of baked beans from the open carton?"

Reverend Henry grabs cans from the box and starts handing them to Edgar, who carefully stacks them on the storage shelves.

"Edgar, I don't really know where to begin. My life is crumbling before my eyes. What is going on? I thought last Sunday's sermon cleared the air, but . . . I just don't know what to do. "

Edgar stops for a moment and takes a hurried look at the Reverend before taking several more cans of beans out of Henry's hands. He methodically, slowly stacks the cans on the shelf.

Edgar thinks, "This man of the cloth is asking me for advice?" Pausing, Edgar then says, "Henry, this probably isn't the best place to carry on a conversation about topics like this. The walls have ears. Do you have time this evening to have dinner with Alma and me?"

"That's exactly what I hoped for you to say, Edgar. I would like a little privacy."

"Good. Say about seven?"

Henry happily accepts the dinner invitation and continues helping Edgar unload the boxes of beans and pickles before returning to Damascus Church. The rest of the day continues to move agonizingly slow. Ground to dust by the rumor mill, shunned by his congregation, which is virtually the entire population of Abbeville, the euphoria he felt from what he thought was the best sermon of his life slides into doubt, then self-pity, and finally, gloom. Back in his office, Henry drops to his knees, as he has done many times. He prays for God to lift the burden he carries. He asks God to show him His purpose in allowing such calamity to visit his doorstep. But, Henry hears no answers to his questions.

Soon, events will place his feet on a path that will lead to better understanding. For now, he doesn't get it. Dejected, he sits in his chair and pulls his favorite version of the Holy Bible from small library behind his desk. Thumbing through the pages, nothing seems to jump off the page to save his soul.

Henry makes his way from church to Alma and Edgar's cabin. He's absorbed in the nightmarish thought that tomorrow he will stand before his congregation falsely convicted of adultery with the woman whom he will eulogize. He feels like someone punched him in the gut. The knot in his stomach won't go away.

Wednesday, January 12, 7:00 p.m.: It takes all the energy Henry can muster to walk the steep stairs at Alma and Edgar's cabin and knock on the door.

"Henry, good to see you; we have the perfect dinner for you. Winter pot roast, an endive radicchio and lemon vinaigrette, toasted hazelnut noodles, gorgonzola, and pudding pears."

Alma steps across the entry and gives Henry a much-needed hug. Henry melts in Alma's affirming embrace. He chokes with emotion, almost sobbing his words between short intakes of breath. Deep down, he is starved for affection. Alma holding him makes him feel much better.

"We all need a little good comfort food from time to time," Alma says.

"Alma, you're too kind," is all Henry can say through his shuttering sobs and deep sighs."

Henry has always found it difficult to express deep emotions.

Fenway eagerly accompanies Alma to the door excited to see who is coming for dinner. When he sees it is Reverend Henry, her tail stops wagging; she turns and walks to Edgar's room, jumps on the bed, and goes to sleep. Not everyone is pleased to see Henry. Looking him directly in the eyes, Alma gently releases her embrace and smiles warmly. She holds on to his shoulders, then, lets her hands run down along his arms.

Holding onto his hands, she says, "Please, Henry, come in."

Beginning to retighten his strings, he starts breathing. Regaining his composure, he walks into the cabin. Edgar is the first person he sees. Then, he sees Bruce Dean, standing in the front room, smiling, and ready to greet him. Henry doesn't know what to think. Bruce steps forward and shakes Henry's hand.

Giving him a brotherly hug, Bruce, his voice quaking with emotions, says, "I know these past days have not been the best for you Reverend."

Henry is speechless.

Bruce holding Henry tightly continues, "I want you to know I love you, my Christian brother; and, I have confidence in you as my pastor."

Bruce puts his arm around Henry in friendship and turns toward Alma and Edgar.

"And tonight my dear friends, "Bruce continues," we are going to plan how to reverse things in our tiny community that have gotten a little twisted by these false rumors going around town about my beloved Anne and you, Henry."

Reverend Henry stands astounded by what he has heard. Never in his wildest hopes would he have ever expected to meet Bruce and explain to him how sorry he is about Anne's passing and the terrible things being said about this fine Christian woman let alone the chances of forming a united front against the forces of evil.

After a deep breath and a long sigh Henry says, "I don't know whether I have the words to adequately express my gratitude for inviting me to your home," Henry stops to quickly take in and exhale a deep breath so as not to breakdown, "And—and—I don't know, if I have the right words to express the depth of sorrow and sympathy I feel for you, Bruce and for little Curtis' loss of his mother. She is greatly missed."

"I know Reverend, you do not have to say any more," Bruce reassures Henry.

"I know, but I must ask your forgiveness for not contacting you, when I heard about Anne's passing. I felt shamed by the rumors and did not have the courage to talk with you."

"I understand Reverend Henry. I know you better than you think, Henry. If Anne were alive, she would tell us to stop feeling sorry for ourselves and twist some ears to straighten things out."

Laughing Henry responds, "Yes, she sure would have. She never was one to wallow in self-pity."

On the way to the dinner table, Edgar shakes hands with Reverend Henry. Feeling a handshake is not enough Edgar turns and gives Henry a big hug.

"Thank you Edgar for understanding me and having Bruce here. It means more than I can say."

Edgar whispers, "Bruce coming to dinner was Alma's idea, Henry."

The news that Alma contacted Bruce and set this whole thing up catches Henry completely off guard. In the instant, like the blind man at the well, Alma follows the principles Jesus taught. He is stunned by the thought that this Alma, a naturalist, a spiritualist, who supposedly lives an enchanted life in the forest, could be so Christ-like in action.

Henry utters, "I never . . . I never would have thought that."

Edgar replies, "Henry, sit here at the head of the table. Tonight is all about you and how we can band together to face adversity. I have a feeling after we're finished here, life in Abbeville will never be the same."

Overwhelmed by the evening's events, a puzzled-looking Reverend Henry sits at the head of the table. Alma opens a bottle of Biltmore Chateau Cabernet Franc she selected to pair with the pot roast. She pours the first glass for Henry and asks Bruce to open the dinner with a prayer.

"Dear Lord and heavenly Father, we are blessed to be in Thy presence and ask you to bless this meal for our use and to your greater Glory. We ask that you put your hands on Henry's shoulders, guide him, lift him Lord to serve you. God, Jesus Christ, we ask you to bless the hands that prepared our meal and bless, Edgar, who brought us together in Thy Presence. Amen."

The initial moments of the dinner are silent.

Henry repeats part of Bruce's dinner prayer to have it sink in, "Yes Lord, I ask you to put your hands on my shoulders. Guide me. Lift me up to better serve you."

Food passes around the table. Bites of the succulent lean round steak meat slow cooked in the porcini mushrooms; garlic, thyme, bay leaves and sautéed onions melt in their mouths.

Fortified with a good meal, good friends, and the help of God, the gathering begins to address the hard issues. Bruce is clear that he and Henry need to be shoulder-to-shoulder at the funeral. The solid show of mutual respect and friendship is not geared to show a united front to weather the storm of gossip. No, justice demands that Anne's goodness be honored and that the actions of the gossips, which dragged her name through the mud, be emphatically turned around. For good to triumph on this earth good people must stand and confront evil.

Henry is fast to translate Bruce's words, "The way to vanquish evil is to follow Jesus' words spoken in the Sermon on the Mount."

"You mean kill them with kindness?" Bruce comments.

"Yes, kill them with kindness." Reverend Henry agrees.

Edgar speaks, "The decent people of Abbeville are entitled to a defense of the town's sound moral principles. Because we have not confronted evil our town has become inhospitable. Abbeville has change to a place where neighbors backbiting neighbors has become the rule. These canons of evil must be challenged.

Alma does not believe good must annihilate evil. But, she does understand the destruction evil brings sets the stage for goodness to abound.

While twirling and looking at his fork, Bruce says, "Alma, Henry, I know you both very well. And, although I have seen you meet in town on many occasions, I've noticed you two seem like distant strangers. You never linger to enjoy each other's company."

The comment brings a smile to Edgar's face, while Alma slowly leans back in her chair and closes her eyes for a moment. Henry strokes the side of his face with his fingers, appearing lost in thought. Of course Bruce is correct and Henry well knows the responsibility is on his shoulders to make amends, as he is the one who harbors hatred in his heart for Alma.

Edgar is the first to respond, "You are right. You should hear them go after each other every Sunday afternoon. I have to pull them apart so I can beat Henry at chess."

This brings a smile to Reverend Henry's face. Alma sits calmly, quietly, and takes in everything.

"What's that all about?" Bruce pursues his point.

Seemingly endless moments pass; still no one else responds. Henry is not refusing to answer, rather he has never seriously addressed why he feels the way he does about Alma. They always hug, but never in public. At the cabin, after they do hug, sparks begin to fly, as if the hug was the opening bell of the first round of another boxing match.

Bruce continues, "I know both of you well and know you have deep spiritual and moral convictions. You treat everyone in town with the same gentleness and kindness, understanding and acceptance, and compassion— everyone, that is, except for each other. Why is that?"

"Bruce, I think the word that comes to mind, when I hear your description of my behavior is hypocrite. I have become as hypocritical as were the scribes and Pharisees of Jesus' time."

"And you Alma?" Bruce says, pursuing his belief that both are at fault and need to make amends.

"I have no hatred in my heart against Henry. I love Reverend Henry."

Reverend Henry responds, "Alma is right. I have felt nothing but love and compassion from Alma. I remember when she said my sermons were as dry hot winds blowing across the Sahara desert. She has never been to one of my sermons, but she was right. She was a mirror, reflecting the truth. I didn't realize that until now."

"The door is opening, my dear brother."

"Maybe it is, Alma. I'm not quite sure, yet," Then looking at Alma Reverend Henry, says, "I confess to you Alma, my dear sister, I have wrongly judged you. I allowed myself to listen and believe the gossip about you: the tales of magic, the supposed spells, enchantments cast on nature. I allowed myself to believe you are a witch; a Godless person and I hated you for it. I am sorry Alma and ask for your forgiveness."

Alma with eyes water-filled says, "There's nothing to forgive, Henry. You have merely taken a few more steps in your journey and have a ways still to go."

Henry does not speak. Alma is right. He still has enmity in his heart. He rocks back in his chair swirling the wine in his glass to release its bouquet and methodically takes a sip. Before speaking, he watches through his wine glass the flames from the fireplace dance, as gravity resets the wine to the bottom of his glass.

"You're right. Alma, the truth is I have disgust for those who do not believe Jesus Christ is God and Lord of their lives. Though I know this is wrong, I have harbored hatred toward you, hidden in the deepest recesses of my soul. I can't help it, Alma, that is the way I feel."

"Yes, I know how deeply rooted are your beliefs. I do understand. Henry, some day you will realize we do believe in the same God, the *Agnostos Theos*, that Saint Paul talks about in the Book of Acts. The God we know is beyond all things, lives in unapproachable light, and is the creator and destroyer of all things. God creates and recreates."

Henry recoils at Alma's words and thinks he's not going to sell out on Jesus Christ so easily.

"Yes Alma, my God is an awesome God. He is the creator of all things and destroyer of evil. He is . . ."

In that moment Henry becomes aware he is talking about "his" God, Henry's creation of God.

His thoughts reveal, "Idolatry of Idolatries!"

Alma smiles, "Yes, the God of the universe is an awesome God, everyone's God, yours and mine."

"But Alma," Reverend Henry says despite his self-condemnation of idolatry, "You do not believe Jesus Christ is the Son of God, the savior, the only way back to God the Father."

There he said it, straight out to Alma; the Reverend won't be compromised. That he will never do, for Alma or anyone else.

"How do you know I don't believe, Henry?"

Henry doesn't know how to respond.

With Christ's words "judge not" spinning in his head, he says, "I am sorry, Alma, I have no right to question your beliefs. All these years I thought I was doing God's will the way God wanted . . ."

"You appear to me to have been striving to do God's will as you understand it, Henry. We have human frailties, flaws that interfere with our spiritual development. When I'm in nature, I taste god's ambrosia. I hear the creator speaking through the natural spires, in the tree tops."

Henry finally gets it.

"You're right. I have judged you from my beliefs. I forgot there is One greater than me, the sole fountain of goodness. It is not my place to judge you Alma, only to love you, as Jesus taught us to love."

Bruce pops up, "Since we have that settled, let's give this town a good lesson they will never forget."

The group plans every step of the morrow's church celebration for Anne Dean. Reverend Henry's funeral sermon is written based on the group's collaboration. While they are not so naive to think the old destructive habits of some townspeople will stop, they believe this is the time to start rebuilding the moral fabric of the community, first starting with themselves. The rest they will leave in God's hands, as they understand God.

The evening ends with everyone joyfully hugging and encouraging each other for the challenge of the next day. Fenway comes to the door and rolls over at Henry's feet. Henry sits on his haunches and scratches Fen's tummy.

"Good girl, Fenway, good girl," Henry keeps saying with a big smile on his face.

Thursday, January 13, 9:45 a.m.: The weather on Anne's funeral day is gloomy and unwelcoming. In sharp contrast, the church is bright and inviting. Anne's closed casket is draped with a carpet of beautiful red roses, surrounded by a sea of standing sprays—white and pink rose wreaths, lily and eucalyptus open hearts, double heart of orange roses and peach carnations with alstroemeria, gerbera daises, and more. Damascus Church is packed. People are standing solid in the side aisles along the walls, which circle behind the pulpit along the church stage. The church is quiet, respectfully waiting for Anne's service to begin.

The grand, magnificently beveled glass doors to Damascus Church open wide. Five hundred plus mourners watch Reverend Henry, Bruce Dean, and a sobbing Curtis Dean walk through the doors and down the center aisle toward Anne's coffin. When the crowd sees Alma and Edgar follow into the church, a murmur emanates from the throng of onlookers. As the five principal mourners gather at the casket, the hush settles. Reverend Henry walks the steps to the pulpit, as Alma, Bruce and his son, and Edgar walk and stand before their chairs on the church's front stage.

"Please, be seated." Reverend Henry announces.

Before making his comments, Henry pauses and looks at the richly grained ash wood casket, containing Anne. Then, after appearing to study the congregation he opens the service.

"As we gather this morning to honor the memory of Anne Dean's life and acknowledge her passage from life to death, we understand death is life flowing into the boundless ocean of God's eternity. Anne has entered immortality and is with God."

The mourners settle back in their pews.

"Not striving for greatness, Anne, like the river's water, gave nourishment to everyone she touched. To those in pain and suffering she gave great comfort. To those confused, like Mo Jackson, she gave the directions to his Bible study class."

Damascus church's congregation laughs because they know Reverend Henry is accurate about his church secretary, who graciously, unassumingly tended to the needs of the flock, always in good humor. He is spot on about Mo, who can get lost in a paper bag when he's at church.

"She always brightened our days, didn't she, Mo?"

Mo nods with a big grin, as the congregation nods sympathetically.

"If it couldn't be done, Anne would do it. If you couldn't be helped, Anne would help you. If it couldn't be found, Anne would find it. Isn't that true, Bruce? Right Curtis?"

From on stage, Anne's husband and Curtis smile and motion affirmatively.

"Isaiah has said, 'though the mountains be shaken and the hills be removed, yet my unfailing love for you will not be shaken nor my covenant of peace be removed, says the Lord, who has compassion for you.' Anne received God's compassion and was a model of compassion, here on earth. Her compassion extended to everyone in Abbeville. Anne had a kind word for everyone, including Fredrika Handley, Bunny Grimmer, Edna Pinkney, Holly Spears, and Jenny Hobbs. Isn't that true? Right Edna? Didn't you feel her love Fredrika? She always had a kind word for you, Holly. Before Sunday services, Bunny, didn't you always manage to talk with her? Jenny, you asked Anne to visit your mother and comfort her in her last days?"

Reverend Henry had named the front line of Abbeville's gossip mill. There were many more he could have named, but he stopped with the top five, letting the words sink into the hearts of he town's gossipers. Convicted by Henry's words and the measure of their consciences, a third of the town's gossipers never again spread rumors. But, the rest of the gossipers were furious at being called out in public. How dare he point a guilty finger at them? The sting of a guilty conscience does not set well with Fredrika, who seethes with anger under her composed exterior.

"Anne's compassion for people was great." Henry continues, "Every day, she petitioned God's mercy for the sick, the poor, the down hearted. She made it a point to remember a few of you in her prayers, each night. Month after month, year after year, you were in Anne's thoughts and hearts. Her kind thoughts and acts were done in private. She was an exceptional person who followed in the footsteps of Jesus. Our hearts go out to Bruce and Curtis. The depth of their loss is unimaginable. The Psalmist has said, 'Weeping may remain for a night, but rejoicing comes in the morning.' So we celebrate Anne's life today and may weep for our loss, knowing tomorrow brings us a new day."

Tears are seen to flow from the eyes of Curtis and his father, as Henry's words break apart and release and lessen the heart-stifling pain they feel.

"'God is our refuge and strength, an ever-present help in trouble. Therefore we will not fear, though the earth gives way and the mountains fall into the heart of the sea.' This was one of Anne's favorite verses. The road she traveled was as difficult, as any of our roads; yet, she was not fearful. She was an eternal optimist at every turn in her life. We were blessed to have known Anne Dean and to have been touched by her kindness. Rest in peace Anne."

The congregation responds, "Amen."

Reverend Henry gives his benediction, "'May we be blessed as we go on our way. May we be guided in peace; may we be blessed with health and joy; and may the wings of peace shelter us. Keep us in safety and in love. May grace and compassion find their way into every soul. May this be our blessing, Amen.'"

Coming from the wings, Allen Belcher takes stage center, above the coffin.

"On behalf of the family, I thank you for being here to express your sympathy for Anne and to support the family. Your kindness is greatly appreciated. This ends the celebration of Anne Dean's life. The graveside service is for the immediate family and close friends. Thank you."

Walking out arm-in-arm, Fredrika whispers in Jenny's ear, "You would think if Anne was so compassionate to the world, at least she could have invited us to the graveside services."

Jenny looks Fredrika honestly in the eyes and says, "Freddie, you've never gone to anyone's graveside service. You don't like getting your shoes dirty."

Jenny unarms herself from Fredrika and walks home. Bunny is all too happy to hook arms with Fredrika and continue railing about how terrible Reverend Henry was, speaking foul untruths from the pulpit.

Family, invited friends, and Reverend Henry fall behind the funeral hearse, carrying Anne's casket. They follow the slow moving hearse from Damascus Church down Matthew Drive then along Salmon Creek Road. Belcher Brother's Mortuary staff has cleared Cemetery Road and the spot beside where Anne's grave will be dug in the spring. The mourners gather around Anne's future gravesite. Alma says the final words.

"That which is done is what will be done. Remember your Creator before the silver cord is loosed or the golden bowl is broken or the pitcher shattered at the fountain or the wheel broken at the well. Then, the dust will return to the earth as it was and the spirit will return to God who gave it."

Watching the snowfall, the group talks quietly beneath the graveside tent. A lone wolf howls, as they disperse and walk back to town in groups of twos and threes.

Down the street from Damascus Church, a group of townspeople, who couldn't or didn't want to go to church, gather in front of the Blue Goose Tavern. They watch the mourners traipse by them on their way back from the cemetery. They take off their hats, as Anne's hearse passes the tavern on its way back to the meat lockers at the town morgue, where Anne will be kept until the spring thaw. Having paid their respects outside the Blue Goose, they file into the tavern to drown their sorrow and remember Anne.

"If you are here to lament the passing of Anne Dean," the owner of the Blue Goose announces, "except for the calling whisky and mixed drinks, the drinks are on the house."

Not counting Fenway, who Edgar left with Helen Simmons for safekeeping until Edgar's return, the band of mourners' number a dozen or so. They take their seats at the bar and at tables to be served the beverages of their choices. Kelly Watson works the tables, while Helen takes orders at the bar. Patrick O'Reilly, Jack Thompson, Juan Aquino, Alex Temecula, Daisy May Canak, and Fred Barns take their usual bar stools. Conrad Corbett, Robert Winston, Peter Sanders and Cannon Monroe take their usual table. McWhinney Thurston and Auggie Castro steal away by themselves to a table at the far back of the tavern.

"Okay, Ranger Pat, what do you want?"

"I'd like a Belfast Car Bomb, Helen."

Fenway has her paws on the bar, helping Helen serve the customers.

"You want a Car Bomb? That's going to cost you, Pat."

"My Irish heritage demands it, Helen. Where I come from it's an essential part of the mourning process."

Actually Ranger Patrick O'Reilly really has only a drop of Irish blood running through his veins, but he milk's every bit of Ireland from that single drop as he possibly can. Making matters worse, Ranger O'Reilly was born in Lake Gonzalez, Texas where nary an Irishman can be seen for a thousand miles in any direction.

"That will be five dollars and fifty cents, big spender."

Jack Thompson, the part-time auto mechanic down at Meadows Garage, has never heard of a Belfast Car Bomb and watches Helen build the drink. After pouring equal parts of Bailey's Irish Cream and Jameson and Son's whisky in the shot glass, Helen pours a pint-sized beer glass three quarters full of Guinness stout.

Jack says, "What a terrible thing to be doing to that Guinness."

Holding the shot glass full of cream and whisky over the stout beer, Helen says, "Okay, Patty my boy, are you ready?"

"Yes my lassie, let it fly."

Helen drops the shot glass like a bomb in the Guinness. Slow on the up-take, Pat's hands fumble along reaching the car bomb before chugging it down. Jack takes a look at the cream curdling on top of the beer and turns his head.

"Ugh, Don't tell me O'Reilly, you're really going to drink that puke?"

O'Reilly turns toward Jack with a curdled cream mustache and says, "Ah my boy, that hits the spot. Jack, the dastardly deal is done!"

At the bar, everyone leans over for a better look at O'Reilly. They see Pat with a big smile on his face and curds of cream on his upper lip. Fenway jumps on the bar and pokes her face into Pat's face and licks the curdled cream from his upper lip.

"OOOEH, disgusting . . ." is the collective response from the rest of the residents at the bar.

Helen shakes her head, "I thought I've seen and heard everything. Oh brother! Now, what will the rest of you be having?"

Juan says, "Not that crap. Give me a Corona."

"Me too," echoes Alex.

Daisy May and Fred Barns both order well whiskeys. Unruffled by the drama at the bar, Kelly takes the gentlemen's orders at the table.

Kelly asks, "What do you gents want?"

"My dear, do you know how to make a Duck Fart?"

"Is this one of your stupid jokes, Mr. Sanders?"

Sanders replies, "You put your hands on its sides and push real hard."

"I thought so. Hilarious Mr. Sanders, remind me to laugh later. What is it you want to drink?"

"Kelly would you ask Helen to mix equal parts of Crown Royal, Irish Whiskey and Baileys on the rocks please?"

"You've got it, Mr. Sanders. It will cost you extra for the Duck Fart."

Sanders smiles agreeably.

"Mr. Corbett what's your pleasure?"

"Scotch and tonic please."

"Mr. Winston?"

"I'll have a brandy with a milk chaser. My stomach's been acting up again."

"Very well Robert. And, Mr. Monroe?"

"I'll have a glass of that wonderful Mourvédre you have from Salmon Creek Winery, Kelly."

"What a surprise."

With that Kelly travels over to the two lovebirds at the back of the tavern; they order two glasses of red house wine.

With the first round of drinks down the noise level inside the tavern escalates a few decibels and spirits begin to be resurrected at the Blue Goose. The second round of drinks sets the stage for some oratory. Through the tavern doors, Edgar makes his grand entrance. Fen rushes to her life long friend and rolls at his feet for loving strokes and is accommodated by Edgar. He stands and addresses the tavern.

"I have gone to the mountain and beheld the hand of God at work!" Edgar announces to his compatriots, "Nick I need a Manhattan."

Nick quickly throws Edgar's Manhattan together and hands it to him. Edgar holds the fluted glassed Manhattan to the light.

"Perfect, maestro, perfect."

The clarity and color of Edgar's drink signals Nick has concocted another magnificent Manhattan. He takes a sip and begins to tell the tavern faithful every detail of Anne Dean's departure from this earth—the grandeur of the entrance; Reverend Henry's glorious eulogy; the stunned expressions of the cabal of gossipers after being struck down from the pulpit; the solemn grand walk to the cemetery; and, Alma's words at graveside. After his second Manhattan, Edgar waxes lyrical about the finality of death, the cold ground, and the town morgue meat locker, which he was instrumental in procuring for the town when he was president of the town council, before sitting down. Conrad is the next to take the stage.

"Thank you Edgar. You have brought a resplendent vision of Anne's tribute to our souls. A toast!"

"A toast!" responds the tavern's entirety.

"To our beloved Anne, no finer lily of the valley has ever graced our presence, to our Shoshana!"

"To our Shoshana!" echoes the assembly; and they seal the toast with their drinks.

Peter the town's lawyer, his duck fart gone and done, stands and calls for glasses of Champaign to be served to the gathering. Raising high his glass, looking around the tavern, Peter waits for all to be served.

"To Anne, the purest of hearts."

Repeating the refrain, "To Anne, the purest of hearts," the congregation drinks their Champaign.

Cannon, who is no stranger to lifting a few glasses in honor of others, raises his glass in praise of Anne.

"God is drawn to the humble and opposes the proud. Humility and pride cannot coexist. Anne is in heaven, drawn close by God to his side. To Anne."

"To Anne."

Robert, the town's librarian, is the last to salute beloved Anne. After several rounds of brandy and milk, he is feeling no pain. Unsteadily rising to his feet, he sings one of Yeats poems that are truly a song, *Wandering Aengus*.

Though I am old with wandering
Through hollow lands and hilly lands
I will find out where she has gone
And kiss her lips and take her hands
And walk along long dappled grass
And pluck till time and times are done
The silver apples of the moon,
The golden apples of the sun.

Trying to fathom the tribute to Anne through the dappled grasses and dreamy words of Yeats, most in the tavern sit befuddled. Who is Wandering Agnes anyway? Winston raises his glass in memory of Anne.

"lóca hwǽr go Anne."

Only slurred approximations of Winston's toast echo from the tavern patrons. Edgar leans over to Peter and asks what Robert said. Peter, probably the brightest person in the group, tells Edgar it's something like "here is to wherever Anne goes." That satisfies Edgar and the rest of the table listening.

By the end of the tavern services, Fenway is the only sober breath in the house. Somber and with emotions spent, the Blue Goose Tavern empties its contents into the night, one-by-one. They have honored Anne in ways most of Abbeville would not find acceptable. But their hearts are in the right place; they are sincere to the bone about their feelings and praises. Edgar enters an empty cabin and retires to bed along side Fenway.

Friday, January 14, 9:13 a.m.: The day after Anne's funeral, life in Abbeville goes on in slow motion. The day moves especially slowly for Edgar, who is working off his celebration of Anne's life at the Blue Goose Tavern. Alma was awake early in the morning and is meeting with sisters in Snow Clearing, a mile or two above Yuba Pass. The day moves even slower for the townspeople of Abbeville, as tomorrow is Jeremy Paxton's memorial service at the cemetery chapel. Abbeville is in mourning the loss of two friends and neighbors.

Saturday, January 15, 7:42 a.m.: Today opens with a profound dreariness that has never been experienced by Abbevillians. Jeremy's death makes a more saddening impact on the town than did Anne Dean's passing. To be sure both deaths were tragedies. They were young, loved, and respected by the townspeople. But somehow Jeremy's passing is most pitiful.

Jeremy had lingered in the snow; he died so young—younger than Anne Dean—so alone and without family. Anne's passing was a celebration of her life in which virtually all of Abbeville participated. For Jeremy's funeral, circumstances are very different. No roads to the cemetery are cleared for Jeremy and his mourners. There are no overflowing crowds at the Damascus Church, waiting in reverence for Jeremy's family to walk to his casket. There will be no solemn procession to the grave; and there will be no mournful song sung about Jeremy by Bob Winston at the Blue Goose Tavern.

Walking up Cemetery Road is difficult, but manageable for the handful of Jeremy's friends, who are in their twenties and early thirties. Ted Michaels and Bridget Silver are the first to arrive and quietly take seats in the first row of chairs. Hector Flores and Reverend Henry come through the door from the crematorium.

Hector places an exquisite forest green cloisonné urn containing Jeremy's ashes on the draped table at the front of the chapel. He centers the urn and leaves. Henry greets Ted and Bridget and sits along side of Ted. Several minutes of silence pass until Carol Belcher, Noreen Correra, Kelly Watson, Angela Jackson, and Terri Sanders file in the second row behind Ted, Bridget, and the reverend.

Within minutes of the service's scheduled time, Alexander Belcher walks to the front of the chapel.

"Good morning. Welcome to you, friends of Jeremy Paxton to this memorial service in his honor. Jeremy's family is unable to be here with us. His father has sent us a letter to be read to you in behalf of the Paxton family."

Noreen, who had hoped one day to marry Jeremy, begins to cry. The thought of Jeremy being separated from his family for several years and his family not able to be with Jeremy is too hard for her to bear. Mr. Belcher takes the letter from his pocket and begins reading.

"Dear Friends of Jeremy,

Our beloved son is gone from us, forever. His mother and I will never see him again. Our lives have been empty, since he left home, promising to return to us soon. But that promise can never be kept. It is devastating for us, knowing how Jeremy died. His death opens a wound in our hearts that will never heal. This is why Martha and I have written a letter to you, Jeremy's friends, who love him, had good times with him, and who are with him to the end of his life. He wrote to us often about hunting with Ted and hiking and swimming in the Sierra's with the "gang" as he called you.

Noreen, he loved you so much and sent us pictures of you and him cross-country skiing. I know you would have made a wonderful daughter-in-law. Thank you for being there with Jeremy.

God bless you all.

Love,

Christina and Craig Paxton."

Mr. Belcher concludes and takes a chair at the far end of the front row. Reverend Henry avoids the podium and simply stands, facing the small group of Jeremy's friends.

"Jeremy's parents would have loved to have met you and hugged each of you. The letter conveys the deep affection they have for you, who have loved and stood by Jeremy, since he came to Abbeville two years ago.

In his heart, Reverend Henry wonders what, if anything, can possibly said to Jeremy's friends who are so deeply distressed and sobbing uncontrollably.

"There is not a single thing we can say or do here today that would have any effect upon the destiny of Jeremy Paxton. I saw him every Sunday at church. He was a good honest man. He was respected in Abbeville for his hard work and friendly ways. If Jeremy was a Christian, he would tell us to wipe the tears from our eyes and rejoice with him because he is in heaven with God the Father, Jesus Christ, Holy Spirit, and all the Saints, who have believed and gone on before him.

When we cry for Jeremy we are crying not for Jeremy, but for our loss of Jeremy. We will miss him. We are grieving our loss of Jeremy. If Jeremy is a Christian, he knows God, while we only dimly see God. Jeremy is meeting the Saints, while we can only imagine that happening. So stop crying for Jeremy because he is in a better place than we are, if he has accepted Jesus Christ as his personal savior."

Carol Belcher raises her head to take a closer look at Reverend Henry. She is surprised and is becoming more upset at his comments. The shock of hearing the reverend words, telling them to stop their crying because Jeremy doesn't need their tears, brought most of Jeremy's other friends to their senses. That Reverend Henry is ambivalent about whether Jeremy is a Christian or not disturbs the group. It is evident to them that Henry didn't know Jeremy well enough to give a sermon at his funeral. Henry too feels uneasy about the words coming out of his mouth, but he feels compelled to continue to drive his point home.

"When such calamities rain down on us, we have to leave such matters in the hand of a God, who knows and does all things well. In the Book of Acts, after Stephen professed Jesus and was stoned to death, the believers lamented. While Scripture tells us it's not wrong to sorrow, we do not have to drown in sorrow, like those who have no hope. For we have hope and live daily in the hope of salvation, a salvation that Jeremy may have claimed before coming to Abbeville."

Jeremy's friends incredulously stare at Reverend Henry. Noreen and Ted are Christians in the traditional sense. Carol and Terri attend Damascus Church, but are closet atheists in the predominantly Christian community. Angela and Bridget are hedonists, party girls if you will. Kelly has been around the religious block a few times—a Jehovah's Witness turned Pentecostal, turned Mormon then turned loose. She believes in a power beyond herself and not much more.

Reverend Henry knows Kelly and these young ones. His words are designed to shock some sense into them. Carol Belcher gets up and leaves the chapel. Knowing full well how Reverend Henry grates on his daughter, Carol's father watches her leave.

"Who knows whether Jeremy, in his last hours found the Lord, Jesus Christ?" Henry begins to wind up his sermon, "We pray he did. For with that final choice Jeremy chose to be with God in heaven. So, it is dust to dust and may God, who is all-powerful, have mercy on Jeremy's soul and the souls of his friends. Amen."

Everyone leaves for the walk back to town with Reverend Henry's words rolling through their heads. Carol and Alexander Belcher walk with Reverend Henry, but it's Carol and Henry that talk all the way back to Belcher Mortuary. By the time Henry parts with the Belchers, it's late afternoon. Shades of night have enveloped the town as he reaches his house behind Damascus Church. Henry feels he has made a positive impact on Carol Belcher. Her leaving the service early indicates to Reverend Henry, Carol Belcher's soul is under conviction. He certainly gave her something to think about, the status of her immortal soul. Still nagging in the back of his head is the dark thought that he was judging Jeremy and his friends like he had judged Alma.

Couldn't he have gotten God's message across without making harsh judgments about Jeremy? The question gives him a restless night. Henry knows he has wrongfully made a judgment about the soul of another person. He knows Scripture plainly says God is merciful, God's ways are not our ways and only God knows for certain what is in our hearts. Why do I make judgments about people like that?

Sunday, January 16, 6:00 a.m.: Henry wakes Sunday morning with a question that's a prayer.

"God will I ever learn?"

He realizes that he went back into his little bubble of thinking he can judge people and save their souls for Christ. He vows to change his sick thinking. Today, no winter storm warnings are in effect. The sun brightly shines on Abbeville. For Reverend Henry, who has had an emotionally exhausting week, his personal storm passes grudgingly. Still, he continues struggling to turn a new leaf in his life. His sermon on "Faded Love" is well received by his congregation. More importantly, he presented God's word without singling out and making judgments about people.

Reverend Henry is back at the pulpit teaching God's word. He carefully scripts examples about himself, his foibles, stories with which his congregation can easily relate and apply to themselves. Henry does not have to point an accusatory finger at anyone. Again, the townspeople of Abbeville are drawn to Henry, as the insightful, easy-going, non-judgmental, fine young pastor of Abbeville's Damascus Church, that he is.

With Sunday services over and the church secured for the rest of the weekend and the Martin Luther King, Jr. Birthday holiday, Henry sprints the road to Alma and Edgar's cabin for his game of chess and lunch. The afternoon sun beats down on ruminants of snow and still wet drives, streets, parking lots, and school grounds. Water vapor rises like steam from the pavements. Abbeville is returning to near normal. New life is about to flourish in Abbeville.

Chapter 3

꙳

Tuesday, January 18, 1:00 p.m.: Alma convenes the last of her bicentennial committee meetings with a sense of urgency. In recent years, festival attendance has dwindled to a pathetic trickle. No one is interested in same-old-same-old potato salad picnic and pie-eating contests that have driven a stake through the heart of the once thriving town festivities. Something, anything needs to be done and done fast to resuscitate this summer's celebration.

As the town council is notorious for its foot-dragging antics, the purpose of Alma's final meeting is to hammer out a sure-fire festival plan and find someone competent and enthusiastic to keep the town council's feet to the fire, until the job is done right.

Alma opens the meeting, "Everyone here knows our town needs a booster shot to keep from dying on the vine. This is a critical year for our community. To start, we need one of you to accept the position of grand marshal for the Abbeville Bicentennial Summer Festival. We need someone who is willing to finalize the plan we develop today and make sure our Bicentennial Festival is the success we all want it to be."

She looks into the eyes of her committee members and smiles. Martin Lawrence the banker has his eyes glued to a spot on the dining room table. Robert Winston the town librarian looks at Alma with a forced smile and an expression begging not to be the chosen one. Alma understands that Samantha Cross, Abbeville's only retired teacher, while having the contacts and respect of the community is probably too old to take on a job, as demanding as she has in mind. Obviously Reverend Henry Johnston and Emma Torrance, Abbeville's schoolteacher, and Dr. Silvia Preston will be a great supporting cast; but they too are busy to take on a task of this magnitude.

"Bill, Bill Silva you're a very busy man, Chairman of the town council and the economic backbone of the Blue Goose Tavern," states Alma.

No one, I mean no one smiles at the least part of Alma's comment. Bill is a retired truck driver who spends a lot of time at the Blue Goose, but the "economic backbone of the Blue Goose Tavern" line doesn't crack the stone faces of most of the committee members.

"Mr. Silva, it's the busy people who get things done. Bill, will you consent to being grand marshal of this year's festival?"

"I was hoping you'd ask me Alma. Yes, I'd be proud and pleased as punch to serve as this year's grand marshal."

Except for Dr. Preston, who, sitting back in her chair, appears amused by the unfolding drama, the burst of pent emotional tension mixed with out-and-out jubilation of the committee erupts with the explosion of a blown-out tire. A little flushed and dizzy from holding their breaths for so long, the committee's exuberant congratulations almost beat Bill to death, wishing him the best and good luck as the new Bicentennial Festival Grand Marshal. The irony is Bill really wants the job and happily accepts the accolades of his friends and neighbors.

Alma calls for Bill's appointment to be formalized by committee vote. The motion by Martin Lawrence, seconded by Samantha Cross is met with a resounding, "Aye!"

"Bill," Alma continues, "I am confident you will do a great job for Abbeville. As the newly elected grand marshal of the festival do you have anything to say to the committee?"

"Thank you, my dear friends. You have made this day one of the happiest in my life."

Witlessly the committee listens to Bill's comment. They nod like kiwis birds, staring wide-eyed at each other with big smiles painted on their faces. They find it incredible that Bill is so enthusiastic about his appointment.

A grateful Reverend Henry listens to Bill and sits easy in his chair alleviated from the burden of additional responsibility, which Alma could have cajoled him to do. Even though he has the upcoming Damascus Men's Retreat to plan for in April, Henry never could have the heart to refuse Alma anything. Taking charge of the Bicentennial Festival would have about killed-off the young, congenial perfectionist. Alma and Dr. Preston thoroughly enjoy Bill's genuine expression of thanks and happiness and the elation of the rest of the committee.

Bill immediately carries on wearing his new mantle of authority as if he had been knighted by Alma and the Knights of the Round Table, which of course, he has.

"I'm looking for a motion to hold the Abbeville Bicentennial Summer Festival on the weekend of the forth of July," Bill states, taking charge.

Robert Winston literally springs from his chair to make the motion, "By that time most of the snow around here will be melted and the summer's sun will not have had a chance to turn uncomfortably hot. So, I move we hold the Abbeville Bicentennial Summer Festival on the weekend of the Fourth of July."

Samantha seconds the motion and the group settles down to business enthusiastically nodding consensus approval.

Martin rises, "I move we recommend the town council approve carnival rides take place as part of the festival down in North Yuba River State Park: a Ferris wheel, a carousel, a flying jungle ride, submarine ride, dragon-faced roller-coaster ride, and a fun house."

Reverend Henry seconds the motion, which is again enthusiastically approved by nods of consensus.

"We need something for the little kids too," Emma Torrance urges, "I move the town council provides continuous entertainment throughout the three-day festival suitable for toddlers and three and four year olds. Pin-the-tale-on-the-donkey, a piñata, a ping-pong ball toss, ring tosses, squirt gun horse races and a petting zoo. This will be all non-competitive; everyone getting participation prizes, everyone a winner."

Martin seconds the motion, which passes unanimously.

Emma volunteers her seventh and eighth grade students to run the little kid games and entertainment.

After thanking Emma, Bill divides the committee into three teams— one to plan the parade route, another to decide parade activities and the third to plan the after-parade opening day activities. Shortly before lunch, Dr. Preston presents her team's ideas:

"On Saturday morning, the parade will start at 11:00 in front of the speaker's stand that will need to be built on 10th Street behind the library and town hall. The parade will line up along Switchback Road, behind the speaker's stand. The parade route will go down Matthew Drive, continue along Salmon Creek Road, cross under Highway 49 onto River Road, and to the Yuba River Park parking lot, where the parade will disband at the site of the carnival."

Bill calls for the parade route plan to be approved and seconded. The group unanimously approves the Preston committee's suggestion be recommended to the town council.

Robert Winston is the next to report on suggestions for the parade events.

"The 11:30 parade kickoff will start with a short speech by the grand marshal who will welcome everybody and acknowledge those responsible for planning and contributing to the festival. He introduces Edgar who is the only male descendent of the Abbe Family to say a few words."

Bob puts his finger over his lips to alert the committee to keep their voices lowered, as Edgar is in the next room and Bob doesn't want Edgar to hear.

"Then, after Edgar's comments, Bill will quickly move to the microphone and announce the surprise that it's Edgar's sixty-fifth birthday, making the Bicentennial Festival a real celebration of Abbeville and those that founded it. Edgar will be invited to ride in the VIP horse drawn wagon at the front of the parade."

After finishing the hushed part of his report, Bob signals the committee that it's all right to speak in normal voices.

Bob continues, "When the last group in the parade passes the reviewing stand, the crowd at the town hall and library parks will be invited to fall in behind the parade when the last marching band passes them. By the time the last marching band enters Yuba River State Park, everyone watching the parade will be in the park, where the food stands, Farris wheel, and carnival are.

A few questions are asked and answered to the satisfaction of the entire committee. Bill calls for the parade activities to be approved and seconded. Again the committee votes in accord approving Bob's committee recommendations, which will also be reported to the town council for final approval.

Martin Lawrence is called next to present his team's ideas.

"With the parade taking about two hours, festival activities won't begin until around two o'clock. People will be hungry and the kids will want to go on the rides and have fun at the carnival. We suggest the first day of the festival be entirely spent at the state park where the food stands, carnival and logrolling contest will be held at Indian Point. And, we plan to keep the carnival opened until midnight."

"What kind of food stands would be there, Martin?" asks Samantha.

"Nothing matching Alma's gourmet standards needless to say," Martin says with a smile, "But plenty of crowd pleasers like hotdogs, corn dogs, hamburgers, Philly cheese steaks, cheesecake, cotton candy, pop corn, snow cones, sandwiches, beer and wine and other foods and beverages that should satisfy a crowd's lusty appetite."

Martin's subcommittee report is approved by the entirety of Alma's committee.

With the first day planned and the aroma of fresh bread, garlic and baked something wonderful wafting in the air, Alma calls a lunch break and invites her friends to enjoy the buffet table she's prepared. She has a tantalizing spread of cool veggie pizza, toasted crescent dinner rolls topped with cream cheese and a mayonnaise-garlic-dill-weed with an assortment of fresh vegetables: broccoli, green onions, bell peppers, mushrooms, carrots, and tomatoes.

Alma's next offering is an egg-dipped breadcrumb coated Blackberry Brie that is deep fried to golden brown and served with a semi-sweet blackberry sauce, garnished with fresh blackberries, and a sprig of mint.

Third is a large plate of hors d'oeuvers: baked red potato halves stuffed with chervil Dijon mustard tartar sauce, topped with a lemon-broiled scallop.

Peach-apricot ice tea, ginger pineapple punch, and sparkling apple cider complete the committee's lunch menu. Yummy!

In the blink of an eye the mood of the committee changes from formal and business-like to relaxed and social. Everyone mingles well. Emma and Samantha talk shop about how they will work the schoolchildren in the Bicentennial Festival.

Bill approaches Martin for a bridge loan so everything the town council approves for the festival can be purchased without delay. The banker has no problem loaning the council $50,000.00 for six-months at the low rate of 5.4% for the Council's purposes. He's committed to support his community and makes $2,700.00 in the process.

Pardoning himself, as he reaches past Emma and Samantha to get the last piece of veggie pizza, Reverend Henry inadvertently interrupts their conversation. Emma drifts across the room and begins talking with Silvia. Samantha looks around before engaging Alma in discussion.

Robert taps Henry on the shoulder and indicates he wants to have a little chat. Sensing Bob wants to talk in private, Henry moves to the side of the room next to the window overlooking Abbeville.

"Reverend, I learned so much from your sermons. I understand why the town of Abbeville has confidence in you. I may have been in your church a dozen times over the last ten years and have come away with the same feeling. I do believe something or someone beyond this world created everything. At my age I will be facing that unknown sooner than later."

"Yes please go on Bob."

"Thank you Reverend. Let me ask you straight out then. Is there a God that I need to do something about before I die?"

"It seems to me Bob, the fact you're raising this question signals a need to take care of what your conscious is telling you."

"Well my conscious may be acting on a fluke idea, Reverend. How am I supposed to know whether what you people have been saying and I've been hearing all my life is absolutely true?"

"Bob, let me let you in on a little secret. I am not absolutely certain there is a God. But, not absolutely knowing doesn't stop me from believing God exists. My heart is convicted of that fact. Otherwise, I would not have become a pastor."

"You doubt there is a God, Pastor!"

"In the beginning, yes, I had my doubts. When I was considering the ministry, yes I doubted. No matter how much I tried to get the idea of God out of my mind, God kept coming back to me. He was inescapable. Now, I have no doubts. The question of God's existence has been settled for me. I live according to the teachings of Jesus."

"Hum."

"Bob, all I know is if God exists, you'd better pay the tab before you leave or there might be hell to pay!"

They suppress their laughter not to draw the committee's attention. It's too late. Although not one head turns, nothing escapes the eyes and ears of the committee. Neither are Henry and Bob laboring under the illusion their conversation and behavior is unnoticed. Appearing to keep the conversation light and respectfully social, Bob asks Henry an odd question before picking the last stuffed red potato half from his plate and popping it in his mouth.

"Why is it, Reverend that you've never married?"

Taken aback, Henry nonetheless answers, "I don't know."

Both laugh at the irony that throughout the whole course of their exchange Henry keeps admitting he doesn't know anything for certain.

"You don't seem to know much this afternoon Henry."

"No, no Bob I take your question seriously. I don't want to answer cavalierly, however.

"Take your time Reverend."

"Okay, I've had a little time to think about it Bob. I'd say I always seem to have other important matters on my mind."

"That's it? Like what?"

"Graduating from college, settling on a vocation, finding a place to work. You know the usual things most of us do before we invite the responsibility of raising children into our lives."

"So what's stopping you now Henry?"

"Good question. I guess I haven't found the right person to share the rest of my life with. I haven't quite settled down, yet."

"I guess all the town gossip about you doesn't help matters much."

"Yes, all the gossip, all the deaths, and quite frankly, I've got a lot to think about, Bob. But, let's get back to you. Is there anything further you wanted to discuss?"

"My life style's a little unhealthy. I spend as much time at my job at the library as I spend at the Blue Goose and I'm not getting any younger."

"I see. You're wanting to get your thinking straight before you meet the unknown."

"That sums the ideas rather well, Henry."

Bob and Henry's chat continues until the committee's intermission ends. Bob seems satisfied, as if Reverend Henry has taken some of the weight of the world from of his shoulders. Henry is satisfied too. He's given Bob honest answers that will help him take the next steps he needs to deal with whatever Bob's facing.

Reverend Henry's admission that he really isn't absolutely certain God exists gnaws at the back of his mind. He has never before put that acknowledgement into words. Although Henry spoke as if the issue of doubt was in the past, he knows that isn't exactly true. Why did he confess that intimate fact to Bob, of all people, at a social gathering, of all places?

Alma taps Henry on the shoulder.

"Are you and Bob ready to join the rest of us? The committee is about to start."

"Sure Alma," Reverend Henry says, "I guess I got lost in my thoughts for a while."

"You sure did reverend," Bob affirms, "Our conversation seems to have kicked off a lot for us to think about."

In no time, the committee is back to business. With only a few more issues to decide, the time goes by quickly.

Planning day two of the festival is the key to enticing the first day's large crowds back to Abbeville. After lengthy discussion, Alma's committee agrees to submit the following fun-filled pack of activities to the Town Council for consideration.

10:00	Turkey Shoot behind Spring Creek Park
	Carnival opens until midnight at North Yuba River State Park
12:00	Fly-fishing for Accuracy Contest at Salmon Creek Winery Pond
2:00	Chili Cook Off at Spring Creek Park
3:00	Free Hot Dogs and Soda or a Beer at Spring Creek and Yuba River Parks
4:00	Log-rolling Contest at Indian Point on the Yuba River
5:00	River Rafting to Downieville (Shuttle Bus back to Abbeville)
7:00	California Sierra Style Big Ranch Barbeque at Spring Creek Park
9:00 to	Midnight: Jazz Band Concert and Dance on the grass at Spring Creek Park
12:00	Hold your Admission Tickets Folks! The Bicentennial Raffle $10,000 in prizes at the Ferris wheel in North Yuba River State Park.

The final day has to be the crowning jewel of the Bicentennial Festival. But, what can possibly top the first two days of fun and frolicking? Reverend Henry comes to the rescue.

"We've seemed to have forgotten Monday, the last day of the festival, falls on Independence Day. Let's end the Bicentennial Festival with a bang! Fourth of July fireworks at Upper Sardine Lake would be a big draw. The fireworks display will be spectacular for those making the climb. Those not wanting to climb up to Upper Sardine Lake can see it from the Lower Sardine Lake."

Bob Winston makes the motion to strike the old fashion country-dance from the last night's events and have a wiener roast in its place plus the July 4th fireworks at Upper Sardine Lake for the Bicentennial's finale. The motion is seconded and passes. Working back from one half an hour after sunset for the fireworks to the weenie roast the committee works out the rest of the final day's program.

9:00	Abbeville Bicentennial 4th of July Fireworks at Upper Sardine Lake
6:00	Fourth of July Big-Time Weenie Roast at Sand Pond
4:00	$1 Tickets Folks! For the 2nd Bicentennial $10,000 Raffle by the Ferris wheel
	In North Yuba River State Park.
12:00	Picnic along the Shores of North Yuba River State Park
11:00	Yuba River Rafting to Downieville (Shuttle Busses back to Abbeville)
	Logrolling Contest at Indian Point on the Yuba River
10:00	Carnival opens until 4:00 p.m. at North Yuba River State Park
	Turkey Shoot behind Spring Creek Park
7:00	Fly-Fishing Trout Fishing Contest behind Spring Creek Park

Alma asks Emma and Samantha to write out the committee recommendations for the town council and give them to Bill for his February meeting.

Their mission accomplished, Alma thanks the committee's for their fine work and officially disbands her group. She graciously accepts the committee's appreciations for her hospitality. All the committee members leave in plenty of time to be home before another predicted snowstorm hits Abbeville.

After the last person leaves Edgar asks, "How'd everything go Sis?"

"Very well Edgar. You primed Bill perfectly. A Fly-casting contest is planned for the second day of the festival and a fly-fishing contest on the last day of the festival."

Ecstatic with Alma's remarks, an otherwise clueless Edgar rolls to a more comfortable position in his chair and falls asleep with Fen, while Alma cooks dinner.

Chapter 4

❦

Thursday, February 19 -24: Abbeville's rumor mill roars full bore with tidbits leaked by Alma's committee members. But for a change, the rumors are positive. There's almost no time for or interest in the rumor mill grinding out the usual who said what about who after church, at the fabric store, tavern, the barber shop, hairdressers, or the general store and cafe. Bill Silva has done a fine job keeping Alma's hopes for a successful bicentennial festival this summer and has bowled over all obstacles, standing in the way of Alma and her committee's wishes.

Thursday, February 24, 7:30 p.m.: The town hall meeting agenda is packed with financial recommendations to spruce-up Abbeville for the Bicentennial Festival. Abbeville's town hall is filled to capacity and then some. Council members can't remember when it faced a more critical and complex task of this immensity. Even if they could remember, the council is a rubber stamp for whatever Alma and Edgar want. Most of the townspeople don't know for sure who is on the town council; but everyone knows and respects Alma and Edgar and Fenway.

Bill Silva looks at Edgar who nods, giving Bill the signal to start the meeting.

"Good evening friends. I'm pleased as punch to be this year's grand marshal for the Bicentennial Festival. I know everyone is as excited as I am about the festival, so let's get started. First, I'd like to introduce the members of the town council, then review tonight's agenda, hear our financial and housing reports and maybe even act on a few recommendations."

Laughter breaks out on the comment that the council possibly could make a decision. Bill smiles and breaks out in a short nervous laugh, banging his gavel on the table to quiet the energetic crowd.

"I'm sure everyone knows Edgar Whitman, who owns the Abbeville General Store, restaurant, post office, gas station, and lodge. Our Bicentennial Festival commemorates the founding of Abbeville by Edgar and Alma's great-great grandparents. Mr. Whitman will be summing everything up at the end of our presentation. So let's make it a really big show."

The crowd applauds Bill's announcement. Edgar, who prematurely reaches the microphone thinking he was going to give a speech, returns to his chair, and sits down by Fenway.

Bill continues, "Councilman Ranger Pat is no stranger to you either. He'll give us a report on the number of people we can expect to be camped down in North Yuba River State Park. How much mula that will bring to our town treasury, Ranger Pat?"

"Point of order, point of order Mr. Chairman," someone from the first row calls out, "You forgot the secretary-treasurer's report."

"Oops. I forgot to introduce Maureen Belcher, our town council secretary, who will read the minutes from our last meeting. Sorry Pat. It will be a couple of more minutes before you can say your piece."

"Thank you Councilman Silva. There are no minutes from our last meeting because we didn't have a last meeting. But I can tell you we have nine hundred forty-three dollars and sixteen cents in the town's treasury."

"That starts us off with a big bang doesn't it Bill!" someone from the audience shouts.

A roar of hardy laughing ignites the town hall.

"All right, all right and thank you whoever the goofball is in the audience that made that comment. Let's move on. Thank you Mrs. Belcher for your report. Councilman Pat O'Reilly, please give the park report."

"Thank you Councilman Silva. North Yuba River State Park has one hundred seventy-two camping sites. On average, each site serves four people, which means, if all sites are occupied, we should be able to house about six hundred ninety people per week. The town council's share will be around $61,000 dollars with the rest of the funds collected going to the State."

"That is a good start. Thank you for your report Councilman. Are there any questions or comments from the community? Hearing none I'll ask Councilwoman McWhinney Thurston to report on the number of people we can expect to be in town for the festival and the expected income from our Spring Creek Park and Campgrounds."

"Townspeople, members of the town council, and President Bill, "We have one hundred fifty-two campsites that should generate seventy-five dollars a campsite each week. And, as you know, Abbeville town council receives all of the proceeds from Spring Creek Park. With occupancy at zero percent from January through the end of March or April, about twenty percent at spring time and ninety-two percent during the summer months, which begins around June 15th here, about $103,512 dollars will be generated for our town treasury this year."

"So far, so good Councilwoman," Bill encourages McWhinney.

"Yes Siree," responds McWhinney, "Last year's festival was an economic failure to be sure, so I contacted the town councils of Coyoteville, Sierra City, Downieville, and Loyalton to drum-up business. It looks real good. I think they are going to give our town a good look-see. I think people will be pouring in from Truckee and Grass Valley! I expect four thousand people a day at our festival, that is, if the first day is a real draw and the second day is even more attractive and the third day of the festival holds its own. Figure thirty dollars spent per person per day pouring into our fair town would be my guess."

Bill observes. "That amounts to over a cool half-a-million dollars. Not bad for a little town carnival."

McWhinney adds, "If we charge an admission fee of $1 per person, per day in every car driving into town, we might add another $12,000.00? That money could be use for raffle prizes. People could use their admission tickets as raffle tickets for daily cash drawings."

"Thank you for that report and the idea about daily cash drawings,

Councilwoman Thurston," Bill continues, "I would like to add one more thing before the Honorable Bronco Brown speaks. The Council was able to get a start-up loan from the Abbeville Savings and Loan for the festival. The loan would cost us $2,700.00 for six-months. But, I understand our esteemed banker, Martin Lawrence, will forgive the loan fee costs, if we impose on his largesse as a community leader. Right Martin?"

A huge roar of approval goes up from the crowd. Half the townspeople stand and give Mr. Lawrence three hip-hip-hurrahs for his generosity. Mishearing Bill call the banker an imposing large ass shocks the other half of the audience. They only clap half as loud. Bill's strategy works as Martin stands and accepts the accolades of the citizens of Abbeville.

"You got me on that one Bill," Martin says under his breath as Bill sits down.

"Look at it as advertising for the bank, Martin," Bill says smilingly, then addresses the crowd, "Okay, Councilman Bronco swing away."

And swing away Bronco did to the delight of the audience. Bronco Brown starts the town businessmen's donations off in a big way.

"Howdy folks."

"Howdy Bronco."

"Y'all know I own the Bar-B Ranch in these parts. And, I want to supply the town of Abbeville with all the beef hamburgers, corndogs, hotdogs, sausages, steaks, and chicken parts we'll chow-down for the festival and that includes hotdogs for the free hotdog event—all free of charge to the town council, of course."

"At-a-Boy Bronco you've got the ball rolling now. That's the way to put new lipstick on our town festival!"

Bill's comment sets waves of chortles and giggles moving across the audience. Bill has never been known for his tact and blurting out the way he did leaves people laughing and shaking their heads.

"Thank you Bronco. The town hall meeting is now open for community comments," proclaims Chairman Bill.

But another delay holds up the meeting. Someone in the front row of the audience catches Bill's attention to point out he's forgotten to let Edgar speak.

Fenway sits alert at the sound of Edgar's name and watches Edgar take hold of the microphone to summarize the financial picture for the Bicentennial Festival. Fen's tail wags from start to finish of Edgar talk.

"There is no question in anyone's mind that the festival will be a lot of fun and put a lot of money in everybody's pockets," Edgar opens, "So far by my figuring the town's treasury can expect about $716,512.00, not counting Bronco's generous contribution of meats and Martin forgiving the interest on our advance from the bank."

After the standing ovation for Edgar's announcement, a kid in the third row reminds the Council, "You forgot the 943.16 in the town's treasury Mr. Whitman."

Another wave of hearty laughter roars through town hall.

"You're right son. Make that $717,455.16. Do I hear more?"

The town hall meeting takes on the energy of a red-hot auction house. On a motion from Councilman Brown, the town council conservatively sets a spending limit of 300,000.00 dollars for its Bicentennial Festival. That will rake in over $600,000.00 for the town treasury, if everything works out as planned. All that money will set the town up pretty for years to come. The motion passes 5-0. The townspeople roar their approval, which startles Fenway to her feet, as fast as a ninety pound, laidback golden retriever can move.

Council Chairman Silva opens the meeting to public input and invites people to line behind the microphone to make their comments and contributions or ask questions.

"My name is Jane Brown, and I own Fabrics Plus. I couldn't be more excited about our Bicentennial Festival, and I think the council has done the right thing appropriating the money for the event. I would like to offer my services and the services of my ladies to make banners and flags for the festival. My workers and I can easily enlist scores of Abbeville's women to pitch in."

"Jane, what a kind and generous offer you're making. The council is delighted and honored to receive your donation. Thank you."

"Good evening Mr. Bill. My name is Peggy Elgin and the kids at the school want to volunteer to help people find their way around the festival."

Inspired by the school's very creative offer, Councilman Bill thanks Peggy and the rest of the students for their offer, and acknowledges Ms. Emma Torrance, Samantha Cross, and the rest of the Abbeville school staff for encouraging the children to get involved in the festival. All assembled nod their heads in support of the councilman's comments and feel proud to have their children volunteer to help with the festival along side of their parents and the community.

"Conrad Corbett here your Worship."

Before speaking, Conrad waits for the waves of laughter to lose energy, running through the onlookers and council members.

Bill with a big grin nods like a bobble-head doll, as Corbett continues, "Barely fifty meters from the carnival rides and games is Indian Point. I have met with the Kitwa Tribal Council and Chief Silver Squirrel. They have agreed to construct an authentic Kitwa Village at Indian Point. They will be in authentic Native American dress, tell their stories of creation, hunting party stories, dance to honor the Great Spirit and perform Ghost Dances that honor those who have passed on. Oral histories, dating long before the founding of Abbeville and the gold rush, will be shared. American Indian arts and crafts, including pottery and jewelry, will be displayed, and there will be demonstrations of how to design and make authentic replicas of Kitwa art."

Clearly the townspeople are moved by the offer the Kitwa Chief and Tribal Council. What a unique and meaningful contribution to the Bicentennial Festival. Councilman Bill and the rest of the council ask to meet with the Kitwa Council to personally thank them. The only concern is that someone may spike the traditional peace pipe tobacco with wacky weed. It's been done before as a prank, spiking the peace pipes. Precautions will be taken this time not to have that happen in Abbeville.

"Hi Bill. To make sure no one goes thirsty, the Blue Goose Tavern will supply the festival's beer requirements and all the beer needs for the free hotdogs and beer on the second day of the festival."

Tavern owner Nick Simmons gets a standing ovation from the audience, which again excites Fenway, who starts running around the council table before coming to rest on Edgar's feet. Her exhibition delights the crowd.

Cannon Monroe, owner of Salmon Creek Winery, not to be outdone by the Blue Goose Tavern, stands and matches Nick Simmons offer by supplying all of the wine the festival can use plus free wine tasting at his winery for every day of the festival. The audience stands, giving Cannon a variety of whistles, hoorays, and applause.

Fenway can't be contained any longer. She bolts down the Town Hall center aisle. Hands from every side of the aisle extend to touch and pet the golden retriever, as she dashes faster and wilder around Town Hall spurred on by everyone's laughter and chants of "Fenway-Fenway-Fenway!"

Charging back through the center aisle to the front of the meeting, Fenway is in seventh heaven. Then, Timmy Jackson stands in the front of the dog, romping down the aisle. The crowd gasps! Fenway dives on Timmy's feet bowling him over. She rolls on her back and happily takes in all the love Timmy delivers, as he scratches her underside and pats her tummy. Timmy's mother steps in the aisle and takes Timmy back to his seat so the meeting can continue. The audience loudly cheers their approval. Reveling, it seems, in the crowds' adulation, Fenway takes her time and returns to Edgar's feet. After the crowd calms, Councilman Bill signals the next speaker.

As prizes at the Abbeville carnival, Mo Jackson, owner of Meadows Garage Service, donates fifty free oil changes. Dr. Preston will keep Preston Medical Clinic open for the entire three-day festival to care for anyone sick or injured. Washington Reyes, the town's blacksmith, offers an assortment of silver bridles and fancy Stübben Siegfried saddles for horses used in the festival parade. The Knead-2-Feed Bakery offers to supply thirty-five cakes and run the cakewalks at the Bicentennial. Cassandra Blake, the new operator of the Abbeville Farmer's Market, pledges all the corn and candy apples the townspeople and festival can use.

Belcher Brothers announce they will donate and install a sound system throughout the entire festival, from the town square through the whole town of Abbeville, Spring Creek Park, Salmon Creek Winery, and the whole of North Yuba River State Park. Everyone, walking about the streets and drives of Abbeville or enjoying the festival activities wherever they are taking place, will be able to clearly hear music and important announcements.

The Sierra County Sheriff-Coroner Department authorizes Ranger O'Reilly to tell the council they will have deputies volunteer to ensure festival security. They'll also line the parade route from Town Square to the carnival at North Yuba River State Park.

Bronco Brown volunteers his ranch hands to do all the Bar-B-Q cooking, as well as judge the chili contest and the turkey shoot.

Abbeville explodes with enthusiasm for the festival. Which triggers the fact the Loyalton Fire Department will have its Old-Timers' Fire Truck and Bucket Brigade act perform at the Abbeville festivities. Taking on all comers, the Sierra City Volunteer Fire Department will hold a Tug-O-Rope contest at Salmon Creek Stables and a Log Rolling contest in the North Fork of the Yuba River.

Although it seems like the town meeting has just begun, the meeting is over. Everything and more that the community had hoped for has been accomplished by nine o'clock. Heading outside in the blustery weather most of the townspeople assemble on the frozen town park lawn and mingle joyfully past ten o'clock that night. No one wants to let go of the exciting moments, when the whole of Abbeville came together. What a night to remember. A small contingent of townsfolk slip unnoticed down the street to the Blue Goose. They will continue rehashing the glorious meeting of the century well past midnight. Fenway is the last one seen entering the tavern.

Thursday, March 17, 6:00 p.m.: Chairman Bill has put in hundreds of hours at the Blue Goose arranging the details for the Summer Festival and has a big red nose to show it. He spends hours at his office speaking to everyone who volunteered something at the February town council meeting. Unofficially, Bill plans to unofficially unveil the final details of the Bicentennial Festival to the public at the Blue Goose on the evening of Saint Patrick's Day.

Saint Patrick's Day and the wearing of the green is usually a non-event in Abbeville, as the town turns to a sea of orange on the 17th of March. Strange as it seems, however, Nick Simmons and Bill Silva figure it's still a good night to plug the Bicentennial plans and get feedback from a unique sampling of the Abbeville community. Not to mention, it's a great idea to build-up business on an otherwise dead night at the Blue Goose Tavern. Simmons cooks a pot of corned beef and cabbage and offers a free meal along with a free beer.

Patrick O'Reilly, the Irishman with a single drop of Irish blood in his veins is the first one in line, piling his plate high with food and sloshing generous portions of horseradish over the top of his corned beef. McWhinney Thurston who is actually one half Scotch on her father's side and one half Irish on her mother's side is right alongside Pat, doing the same thing.

Chief Silver Squirrel and several Native American's named Loadstone, Broken Arrow, and Half Moon are next and take small portions of the corned beef and cabbage, as this is the first time they have tried anything like it let alone celebrate Chief Saint Patrick's Day.

Calvin "Cal" Wharton and Fred Barns, two custodians who usually clean up after everybody, delight in the free food and drinks. Allen, Alexander, and most of the Belcher Brother's Mortuary staff—Hector, Jack, Alex, Richard, and Juan—wouldn't miss Saint Patrick's Day any more than they would miss pozole, beans, and Mexican rice on Cinco de Mayo.

Conrad, Robert and Cannon, big enthusiasts of corned beef and cabbage, stand and toast Nick's generosity and wonderful hand at making the best corned beef and cabbage they had ever tasted. Mo. After hearing the food and drink endorsements, Bronco and couple of wrangles from the Bar-B Ranch, known only as Buckshot McGregor and Joker, pile their plates high with food.

Edgar and Fenway were the last in line. Edgar is a big fan of corned beef and cabbage. Fen turned out to be a bigger fan. When Edgar went to the bathroom, Fenway ate Edgar's plate of food, horseradish and all! Laughter rocks the tavern on Edgar's return.

"Well, at least he left my beer," Edgar said when he saw what had happened.

Legend has it that Bob Winston christened free corn beef and cabbage event with the name it has to this day: The Green and Orange Festival.

Shortly before the first Green and Orange Festival ends, Buckshot and Joker clang their glasses of beer with their forks to gain the group's attention, as they go to the middle of the tavern.

"Thank you and thank you Nick, for the good Irish grub," Shotgun starts, "Joker and I have been talking it over with Bronco and we think the boys at the Bar-B would like to give anyone who wants to the opportunity to break a wild horse or ride a Brahma bull at the festival. What do you think of that idea Bill?"

"Since the majority of the town council is passed out and can't violate the Brown Act, Bill shouts, "I think it's one hell of an idea boys!"

Bill proclaims, "That's the icing on our cake. All I can say is a big hoorah for Bronco and the boys down at the Bar-B Ranch for helping us."

Nick's Blue Goose closes about three o'clock in the morning. Except for Fen everyone seems to be dazed like bugs shaken hard in a paper bag. How anyone found his way home that morning is a mystery. Few recall being guided home that night by the hands of friendly silhouettes in the pitch-black night. Abbeville's gossip mill spreads more good news about the Blue Goose meeting. Information about the Brahma bull riding and wild horse breaking events electrifies the town, the Kitwa Nation, and cowpokes throughout the Sierras. Sacramento Courier picks up the beat of the good news, with the headline: BIGGEST DEAL IN ABBEVILLE SINCE THE 1849 GOLD RUSH!

Book Three

❦

Spring Break

Chapter 1

⟡

Monday, April 4, 8:30 a.m.: With families on vacation, Abbeville becomes one of the most serene places in the Sierras. It's time for the older folks to take care of personal business, which they've have pushed aside during the winter. Bob Winston slips away from the library long enough to have Dr. Preston give him a much-needed physical. Coming from her meeting with Alma and the Sisterhood, Florence barely beats Bob through the door before his appointment. Bob is seventy-six, feels tired and has had sever stomach pains for five months. He has avoided seeing Dr. Preston, fearing something is really wrong.

As usual, Bob is greeted by the bouncy, uplifting voice of the ever-vivacious Florence. She has worked as the receptionist and nurse practitioner at Preston Medical Clinic since graduating from nursing college, twenty years ago.

"What's happening with you today, Bob?"

"Oh, I feel a little more run down than usual Florence. Guess my age is catching me."

"That will be the day Bob! You haven't slowed down, since the first day I met you."

"Well, that was then and this is now, Flo. I haven't been feeling the same."

"I know Dr. Preston is ready to see you. Let's go back to examination room two. Sit on the table or chair, which ever you like and Dr. Preston will be with you shortly."

Dr. Preston enters the room and exchanges pleasantries with Bob, who appears to be in some pain. She has Bob's weight and vital signs that Florence recorded during his intake.

"Florence tells me you're feeling run down, and, I can tell you're in pain, Bob. On a scale of one to ten with ten being unbearable, how would your rate your pain?"

"I'd call it a solid eight, doctor."

"Where is the pain coming from?"

"Right here doctor," Winston indicates the area of discomfort by placing his hand over his upper abdomen. "My pain's in here," he says patting his hand on the spot for emphasis.

"Can you lay down on the table or is the pain too severe?"

"I think so," Bob says, although stretching out on the examination table appears to cause him considerable discomfort.

Bob winces as he scoots himself in position on the table.

"How long have you've been experiencing sharp pain, Bob?

"About two weeks or so."

"Have you been eating?"

"I'm pretty sick to my stomach. I can't hold much down especially meats."

"You have indigestion or a burning sensation where you're holding yourself?"

"Yes."

"Do you experience bloating after you do eat a meal?"

"Sometimes."

"Has anyone in your family died from an aneurysm, Bob?"

"No aneurisms, Doc. but heart attacks, yes," answers Bob.

"Hum."

Silvia reaches over and pulls Bob's chart. She notices a fifteen-pound drop in his weight since his last annual check up and continues her questioning.

"Do you have blood in your stools?"

"I don't stand around looking at my dump in the toilet, doctor."

"What color are your stools Bob? Dark or light?"

"I guess dark. Where is all this heading Dr. Preston?"

"You appear to have blood in your stools. I can't say for certain whether you are bleeding from the upper or lower intestines or esophagus. I don't know why you are bleeding. From what you've told me, Bob, my best guess is the bleeding is coming from the upper intestinal tract. To be sure, however, I'm going to order a blood test for you."

"What does that mean doctor?"

"It can mean anything from peptic ulcers to tears in the stomach or esophageal walls to cancers to inflammation of the intestines. I need to immediately pin down the cause of your bleeding, though. Do you feel up to a trip by air ambulance to the University of California Davis Medical Center?"

"Doesn't sound good to me Doc."

"Bob, too early to tell. That's why I need you to be checked out at Davis. Do you have any objection?"

"I guess not," Bob replies with a grimace.

Dr. Preston dials Redwood Empire Air Care Helicopter to transport Mr. Winston to Davis Medical. REACH lands at the Abbeville Volunteer Fire Department helicopter pad about a half a mile up highway 49. Bob is quickly placed on the helicopter and under the care of a flight nurse. Winston is connected to cardiac, oxygen and blood pressure monitors. In no time flat, he is airborne and on his way.

The remainder of Dr. Preston's morning appointments is routine physicals and run smoothly. Dr. Preston likes her appointments scheduled forty minutes apart, so she can spend more time with her patients— asking questions, tending to their physical, as well as social and emotional needs. She leaves twenty minutes between appointments, which she uses to complete her notes, prepare for the next patient, and make a few phone calls.

Between twelve thirty and two o'clock Dr. Preston's clinic is closed for lunch, allowing Florence and Silvia to go for a power walk; talk about the day's events; and order a quick sandwich and drink from the General Store. Today, they find Conrad having a late breakfast. Dr. Preston can't resist commenting.

"Edgar would you fix me the heart-stopper special like you rustled-up for Conrad and hold the defibrillator!"

"And a good morning to you Miss sunshine. I take it you don't like good grease?"

"A little grease is good, Conrad. Your organs need oils to slide around comfortably inside your body. Your skin needs oil to avoid wrinkling, like one of those mummies you find on your archeological digs. But, you abuse the privilege, Conrad. Too much fat in your diet, Conrad, way too much fat."

Conrad laughs. "Florence is your laugh-a-minute doctor always in such rare form?"

"Always," Florence wryly answers.

She orders a glass of water and turkey on wheat toast, lettuce, tomatoes and hold the mayonnaise and pickles.

Conrad inquires, "Did you, Florence, and Alma run around the forest last night?"

"As a matter of fact we did spend some time together and a very nice outing it was.

"What time did you guys end your pow-wow?"

"Cute, cute Conrad, we ended when you were sawing logs this morning to answer your question, Mr. Corbett. What do you have planned for the rest of your busy day?"

"If Ranger O'Reilly is in a good mood, I'm spending the afternoon at Indian Point in Yuba River State Park. There are plenty of abalone pendants, cut-shell beads, charm stones, and fishhooks. We need to figure out which artifacts belong to which tribe—Kitwa, Maidu, Nassian or Piaute or a few artifacts from all tribes? At one time or another, different tribes roamed around here, claiming the same hunting grounds. Plus, my archeological buddies think they've may have found the remains of a Kitwa hangi."

"A 'hangi?'"

"Yes. A hangi . . . It's an earth and bark covered round-house for worship, a place where Native American's dance, giving thanks and respect for everything the earth mother has provided. It would be the first hangi found in this area."

"Have you ever found human bones in the forest, Conrad?" Florence inquires.

"Not around here. Native American burial grounds are sacred. No one talks about those who pass to the great beyond. But, the area around the Buttes and parts south of Plumb Creek Road haven't been explored. It would be something to run into a stack of old bones out there."

"That would be something," remarks Dr. Preston smilingly.

Pointing to her watch, Florence nudges Silvia.

"Got to go," Dr. Preston comments.

After wishing Conrad luck in his search for a hangi, Florence and Sylvia walk back to the clinic. Preston's clinic reopens at two o'clock on the dot. Unlike the morning, when Bob Winston's ordeal caused quite a stir, the afternoon appointments are uneventful.

Thursday, April 7, 2:00 p.m.: The warm spring, sun shinny day bring out the fragrances of wild flowers on the mountainside. The ground where Anne's coffin will be buried has thawed enough for backhoes to dig her grave. Without public fanfare, Bruce, Curtis, Alma, Edgar, and Reverend Henry watch Anne lowered to her final resting place. Later that afternoon, Jeremy is interred on the edge of the cemetery, in an area reserved for special memorials for those having no community or family ties in Abbeville. Only Carol, Noreen, and Reverend Henry attend.

Monday, April 11, 8:30 a.m.: Bedlam breaks out at the schoolhouse. Abbeville's only schoolteacher didn't show up, after spring break on the first day of school. Twenty-six school children—ages seven to thirteen—run wild through the streets of Abbeville, Library Park, and the playground. For them, spring break isn't over; school is still out! At eight thirty-five, Edgar begins getting phone calls about the school situation. He leaves the General Store in Bridget, Michael, and Daisy's capable hands and makes his first phone call to Conrad Corbett.

"Conrad, the ferrets are out of the cage."

Retired British commando turned amateur archeologist, replies, "Get a gun and shoot them. Why bother me?"

"Of course, you've heard the news!" Edgar exclaims.

"New? What news are you talking about?"

"The news that Abbeville's future leaders are running amok?"

"Gee, that's too bad. Thanks for informing me; good bye, Edgar and good luck."

"Don't you hang up on me, Conrad, this involves you too!"

"How do you figure that, Edgar?"

The kids are running wild in the streets, Conrad! It's your civic responsibility to help me regain the controls of civilization. You've got to help me, Conrad! Please!"

"Yaow! One of the little vermin just ran past my window, screeching his little head off. That sounded like Curtis Dean."

Conrad is more than capable of keeping people, including kids, riveted by his stories and historical perspectives until the cows come home. He is finally persuaded by Edgar's desperation. Conrad dressed and walks to the school, picking up students like the pied piper of Hamelin. Soon, all the ferrets are corralled and back in their cage and under the spellbinding influences of their substitute teacher: Major Conrad Corbett—archeologist, former British commando, and all-round storyteller extraordinaire.

Edgar walks out of his store onto the wooden walkway and takes a deep breath.

"Good morning Edgar," a cheery voice calls out.

"And, a good morning to you too Reverend Henry."

"I saw all of the children running around the church parking lot this morning, but they seem to have returned to school."

"That's good. Conrad is their teacher today. I think our schoolteacher and the custodian ran away to get married and avoid scandal."

"That's why I'm here Edgar."

"You're going to marry the two of them Reverend?"

"No, I'm not here to talk about marrying Cal and Emma, although that would be nice. If Cal and Emma were to get married, I'd do the ceremony. I'm here to talk to you about the possibility of Fred Barns, my church custodian, taking over Cal Wharton's custodial job at the school. He's interested. I can highly recommend him to you Edgar."

Edgar accepts the pastor's offer. Thanking Reverend Henry, he goes back in his store. Edgar still has quite a mess to clean up. He calls the county office of education to hire a new teacher. The county office of education makes things easy for him. There is only one substitute teacher available in the county, a Mrs. Desiree Parker and she is interested in the Abbeville job."

Monday, April 11, 12:30 p.m.: Desiree Parker arrives for her interview with Edgar at the General Store. She is an attractive, well-dressed woman in her early forties. Desiree walks into the Abbeville General Store, as if she were walking down the lobby of the Mark-Hopkins Hotel San Francisco.

"Very classy, maybe too classy for Abbeville," is the first thought that races through Edgar's mind.

"Good afternoon, young lady. Are you here to interview for our teaching position?"

"Yes I'm interested in teaching school in your fine town. You must be Mr. Whitman."

"Yes I am."

Edgar leads Mrs. Parker past the can goods, hunting and fishing equipment, office and school supply, the liquor and frozen foods aisles into the restaurant to a booth next to the window, overlooking the town.

He pulls the white, slightly soiled terry-cloth towel from his shoulder and wipes the table and benches. Though beads of water still delineate the path of his washrag, Edgar stands proud over his work and invites Desiree to take a place in the glossy yellow oak booth.

"Please, please sit down and relax. Do you want a cherry coke or something to eat?"

"Thank you Mr. Whitman. I've already eaten lunch at North Star. However, I would like a glass of water, please."

Whitman hurries behind the counter. He pulls the last pitcher of near icy-cold water, which sat all night next to ice encased coils, from the back of the refrigerator. Mrs. Parker regally sits in the dining booth and crosses her legs. Edgar, in a kind of running shuffle, makes his way to the window table and pours Mrs. Parker a glass of water. She nods a polite thank you. The water has the faint aroma of deli meat. Desiree takes a sip and smiles.

Daisy, leaning against the oak paneled wall next to the magazine rack, and Fenway, from her favorite position under a far table, watch. They don't know quite what to make of Edgar's bizarre behavior. A while passes before Daisy May continues cleaning the counter and tabletops. Fenway returns to doze-mode.

"What a picturesque town, Mr. Whitman, quite charming. How long have you lived here?"

"My whole life. Abbeville was founded back in 1839 by my great-great-grandfather Matthew Abbe and his two brothers, Mark and John."

"I suppose they were married, Mr. Whitman?"

"Oh yes, yes, Mrs. Parker, they were married, Mark and Mary, John and Jane and my great-great-grandfather Matthew and his wife Carol Ann. The Abbe brothers built this store and restaurant in 1842 before the gold rush. There's still gold to be found in these hills."

"Interesting."

"Yes Ma'am, we're in gold country, you know."

"Yes I know, Mr. Whitman."

Lead by Desiree's questions, Edgar runs out of small talk. He is oblivious to the fact that Desiree is conducting the interview of Edgar, rather than Edgar conducting the interview of Desiree. She invites Edgar to sit, as she continues to guide the conversation.

"The teaching position, Mr. Whitman, what are your expectations?"

"Oh yes, my expectations. I . . . I expect you to show for work on time and not run off with the custodian."

"I have always been punctual Mr. Whitman, and as for running away with the custodian, I don't make it a habit to abandon my duties to the children. No, I won't run off with the custodian Mr. Whitman."

Edgar looks at the wedding ring on Desiree's finger.

"Widowed Mr. Whitman. My husband died recently, that's why I need to go back to work."

News that Mrs. Parker is widowed strikes a pleasant note with Edgar, who blurted out, "Well, I guess you have the job Mrs. Parker."

"There are a few of questions I'd like to ask before I accept your kind job offer, Mr. Whitman. How many children will I be teaching? What grade levels?"

"You will have twenty-six children in your class from grades one through eight."

"That's a perfect class size. How much does the job pay? What are the health and welfare benefits? How many days am I contracted to teach, Mr. Whitman?"

"Our teaching position pays thirty-eight thousand dollars for teaching one hundred eighty days from September 15th through June 15th. You will have fourteen holidays, a two-week spring break and summers off, of course. And, you'll get Kaiser Health Plan Benefits and Delta Dental. I guess that about does it, Mrs. Parker."

"One more question, Mr. Whitman. I currently live in Carnelian Bay, North Star. Driving to Abbeville is quite a distance and, at times, impossible in winter. I expect to tutor the children that need extra help and provide challenging work for Abbeville's more gifted children. I would be working long hours. Is there any way you could help me with lodging, Mr. Whitman?"

"Yes, you could move into the spare bedroom at my home. I live with my sister. She will love your company. I'll throw in meals too."

What is Edgar thinking, as he offers his home to a stranger? He isn't thinking is the answer to the question. Edgar takes the bait, as only a big mouth bass can—hook, line, and sinker. Who's the expert fisherman, now? Desiree is more than mildly delighted with the offer of a job and free room and board, quite a job perk for an afternoon in Abbeville.

"How kind of you, Mr. Whitman. I accept your offer. May I start teaching tomorrow?"

"Absolutely, Mrs. Parker that is fine with me. I'll introduce you to the class tomorrow morning."

"And, I insist on cooking dinner for you and your sister this evening," Mrs. Parker presses Edgar.

"Thank you ma'am, that would be fine with me and Alma. Then, you'll be staying the night with us?"

"Yes, I've brought enough clothes to stay here several weeks."

With that, Desiree stands and extends her hand to Edgar. He mirrors her motions, extending his hand. They shake, sealing the deal.

"Mr. Whitman, when will I receive my teaching contract?"

"Tonight. I'll draw up the contract this afternoon and take it around to the town council members for signatures. And, that will be that."

As Desiree drives out of the parking lot and turns onto Matthew Drive to the cabin, Whitman begins his paperwork.

Chapter 2

M *onday, April 11, 4:23 p.m.:* Edgar feels like he's landed the biggest fish in the lake and can't wait to tell his buddy Conrad about the new teacher in town.

Hello Conrad, I hired a new teacher. You're off the hook for tomorrow Pal."

"That was fast Edgar. My teaching wasn't that bad was it?"

"No Conrad, from the reports I've heard, the kids loved you and learned a lot about world history and current events, especially the navel tactics during the South China Sea Blockade."

"Good, good, Edgar. I was worried that I wouldn't make the grade," Conrad laughingly says.

"Not to change the subject Conrad, but now listen to this! Mrs. Parker, the woman I hired as the new teacher, she's a real keeper. I'd like for you to meet her tonight at my house for dinner. She's cooking! Can you believe that?"

"How will that sit with Alma, a stranger taking over her gourmet kitchen? "

"Alma isn't like that Conrad. She'll enjoy the company; and you, my friend, will have a chance to tell Desiree all she needs to know about her new students before she meets them tomorrow."

"I don't know about Alma and Mrs. Parker hitting it off that well. Women are one strange and unpredictable breed of cat. I can't figure them out to this day. But, I'm not turning down a free meal either. What time is dinner served?"

"How about five-thirty?"

"I'll be there for cocktails at five."

To the delight of Bridget, Michael, and Daisy May, Edgar closes the general store early and hops into his car to take Desiree's teaching contract around town for signatures. He arrives home in time to find Alma and Desiree preparing dinner in the kitchen.

"I'm glad you two are getting to know each other. I've invited Conrad Corbett for dinner around five-thirty. He'll be arriving at five for drinks. What are you two cooking?"

Desiree looks at Alma.

"We'll call it Chef's Surprise and leave it go at that Edgar. You my dear brother stay out of the kitchen."

Edgar hands Desiree her teaching contract, settles in his recliner, reads the newspaper, and promptly falls asleep.

Monday, April 11, 5:00 p.m.: A knock is heard at the cabin door. Alma greets Conrad and welcomes him with a big hug and begins to introduce him to Desiree, when Fenway dives at Conrad's legs and slides on his feet pinning him to the ground, almost knocking him over. She rolls on her back inviting Conrad to pet and scratch her undersides. Conrad enthusiastically complies.

"Good dog Fenway. You're such a good dog. Yes such a love, good girl, good girl."

Conrad really gives Fenway a good belly rub and scratches her with both hands while talking to her.

Alma suggests Conrad and Desiree move onto the deck to get better acquainted. Fenway is more than happy to curl on her pillow and eves-drop on their conversation.

"So you're Desiree. I've heard so much about you from Edgar that I feel I know you already."

"What has Mr. Whitman been telling you, Mr. Corbett?

"It's not so much about what he tells me; it's how he talks about you. Underneath that country bumpkin exterior Edgar is one bright cookie. Given his high regard for you, I can tell you have impressed him greatly."

"Kind of you to say so, Mr. Corbett. So far Edgar doesn't know too much about me. Does that bother you, Mr. Corbett?"

Conrad is caught in his own banter, which is designed to make a good impression on Desiree, he almost lets Desiree's odd question slide by without comment. Desiree is not about to open herself to this gentleman, a stranger whom she's met for the first time. She probes his comfort level and goes to school on his response.

"Not so much of a bother as a mystery. Please call me Conrad."

Desiree is satisfied with the idea of being a mysterious woman in Conrad's eyes. That's as close as she wants to be to him.

"Conrad, obviously you weren't born in Abbeville. What is your story?"

With her eyes closed Fenway heaves a big sigh, as Conrad drops the whole bail of hay on Desiree. Born in Germany, traveled the world over and became a citizen of the United States at the peak of the Tianjin Conflict. He joined the military, was transferred to the diplomatic corps and attached to General Theodore Morrison's Pacific Command for six years. He retired from the military and lived in Turkey for another six years. Conrad is a man of the world: mature, sophisticated, cosmopolitan. Abbeville was an unexpected, unscheduled stop in his life.

Desiree seems to be cut from the same cloth, except Desiree stays in 5-star hotels instead of living in pup tents; eats caviar instead of leaves and twigs served in the military; and drinks champagne instead of sweet fragranced mao-tai from a communal pot with natives in some back water village in China. Abbeville was not a planned stop on her schedule, either.

Conrad rolls on for an hour or so of fascinating monologue about himself with Desiree appearing to be intensely engrossed in every word Conrad articulates. Word by word Desiree builds a romantic construct based on Conrad's exotic exploits.

"What delicious fantasies we weave," she thinks.

Cued by Desiree's allure—her ability to show a man she is truly listening to him, rooting him on to run further than he has ever been rooted before—Conrad continues to fire full volley's of information non-stop. Their intellectual-emotional connection deepens to a primal level. Fully entranced, they fall in love with the reflections of themselves each seems to see in the other's eyes. Far from the electric crackle of flirtation, Fenway is still, sleeping like a stone.

"Dinner's served," Edgar breaks in on the conversations and comments, "Conrad you missed cocktail hour. The drinks were free Pal." Desiree and Conrad laugh.

"Well you snooze you lose old boy," Conrad retorts.

Edgar escorts them to the dining room where Alma's first course of the meal greets them, a mouthwatering display, exquisitely presented. The prospect of living in this house is turning out to be a reality far beyond Desiree's expectations.

"Sis really knows how to throw a little soirée don't she?" Edgar awkwardly hits the nail on the head.

Desiree says, "Alma, I had no idea your so into gourmet cooking. What do we have here?"

"A red bell pepper and tomato salad," Alma describes, "halved grapes and cherry tomatoes with cubes of red pepper on a bed of red and green lettuce, a little extra virgin olive oil, white wine vinegar and a pinch of ground cumin accompanied by a hard, caramel colored crusted, artisan French bread."

Edgar most formally pronounces, "You may be seated and let the feast begin."

Before the group begins to chow down, Edgar, who doesn't pray, is moved to pray.

"Thanks for the potatoes. Thanks for the meat. Thanks for everything. Good God, let's eat."

Instead of a chorus of amends, silence ends the prayer, as Alma serves the first dish to her guests. Her salad is light, refreshing, and well paired with a crisp white grassy Sauvignon Blanc from Cannon Monroe's Salmon Creek Winery.

"Alma, you are unbelievable in the kitchen; and, from the fresh aromatic of the Sauvignon Blank, it is certainly the perfect choice," Desiree complements her hostess, revealing her knowledge and taste for pairing wines.

Alma returns the favor, "Desiree is simply marvelous in the kitchen. Tonight's salad wouldn't have been possible without her." She toasts her guest, "To Desiree our teacher, *Regazza benvenuta.*"

A bit embarrassed Desiree turns red, but politely accepts Alma's compliment. Alma acknowledging her this way, when all she did was chop the red and green lettuce, triggers questions in Desiree's mind: Why is she going out of her way to share her spotlight with me? Is this the way Alma treats every new guest? Or, is there something more that doesn't meet the eye?

Throughout the night, Alma does continue to open doors for her guests to be the center of attention. Desiree closely observes Alma's behavior and provisionally concludes Alma is sincere in her compliments. But, Desiree's skepticism is not completely erased.

"You two seemed to be getting along quite well," Alma says, opening the door for Conrad and Desiree to comment.

Having clearly heard Conrad and Desiree's conversation though the kitchen window and observing body language, Alma has formulated what the answer to her question might be. Conrad answers true to form.

"Yes it seems we have known each other forever. I find Desiree's ability to comfortably discuss a wide range of topics refreshing. She is an interesting woman."

Testing the waters of male observation, Alma asks, "And, Conrad, what did you learn about Desiree?"

Conrad has a puzzled look on his face. Alma's question quickly reveals Conrad knows nothing more about Desiree than what he heard from Edgar. Alma's question does not escape Desiree's attention. She knows Conrad is clueless about her, as she intends him to be. Desiree, who also knows the art of questioning others to tease out information, knows what Alma is doing.

"Alma, I can't exactly put it in words. I feel I have a better understanding of her. Does that make sense?"

"Sure does to me," Edgar pipes in, "I knew she'd be a fine addition the school faculty!"

Playing Edgar's comment, Desiree replies, "Thank you Edgar. Since, I'm the only member of the Abbeville school faculty, I'll take that as a compliment."

After a moment of a dazed silence on Edgar's part, laughter rings out from the dinner table across Abbeville. Desiree succeeds in diverting the conversation. Fenway continues sleeping undisturbed by the antics of humans.

Hardly able to catch his breath Edgar says, "Laughter is good for the soul right, Alma?"

"Yes, my only brother," is all Alma can wheeze out between laughs, which set another chain of bursting laughter.

In time, the group calms and finishes their salads. Alma sets her fork aside and describes the main course: pesto encrusted salmon fillet with sautéed broccoli and mushrooms with roasted Cascabel chilies. Alma justifies her choice of wines, explaining that the rich, tropical and pear fruit taste of the Sonoma Loeb Chardonnay stands well against the pesto encrusted salmon.

"Another excellent choice of wine, Alma!" is all Desiree could say.

"Incredible! You are magic in the kitchen Alma," Conrad reports with a true sense of awe.

"Yep, Sis whips up stuff like this every night for me when I come home from a hard day at the store. Like you city slicker folks, I like eating high off the hog." Edgar adds.

No round of laughter cascades, after Edgar's statement. Desiree and Conrad are truly amazed at Alma's culinary skills, letting Edgar's vacuous comment fall dead on arrival. Alma inhales her guests' compliments and exhales a sincere thank you. She serves the salmon entrée hot from the kitchen. A meal beyond belief, large succulent salmon flakes fall with a touch of a fork, the flavor exquisite. Alma's homemade champagne sorbet cleanses their pallets, clearing the way for dessert—hand picked wild blackberries from her back yard topped with a semi-sweet amaretto whipped cream.

"Where does this woman's talents end," thinks Desiree pondering the depths of the woman she's only met this afternoon.

After dessert Alma presents her guests and brother with glasses of chilled white port wine and tonic water over ice with mint leaves and a slice of lemon.

Raising her glass Desiree toasts Alma, "To the perfect hostess, Alma."

Conrad and Edgar join in the toast, "Hear, hear to the perfect hostess."

"Thank you. Your praises are very much appreciated. While Desiree and I take care of things in the kitchen, why don't you gentlemen retire with your portonics to the deck for cigars and conversation?"

Like sheep, Edgar and Conrad follow Alma's suggestion. They and their portonics move outside. The gentlemen light their Bolivar's under the canapé of mountain stars, waxing philosophical. Desiree clears the table, as Alma washes the dishes.

"Desiree, how do you feel about living in Abbeville?

Alma opens another door. Taking a moment to think, Desiree decides to reveal herself a little more to Alma.

"At least, for a short while, I believe I'm going to like it here. I'm too much of a butterfly to land in one spot too long. Although, after meeting you, Alma, I might have to reconsider my wandering ways."

"Then, we will enjoy our moments together, Desiree. You see I too do not stay in one place for long. *Alma liberada*, dear sister."

Desiree vaguely understands and offers a comment testing the water, "Alma, your soul wanders inward, my soul outwardly wanders."

"We are meant to use our outward visions to illuminate our inward journeys and to use our inward visions to enlighten our outward voyages, Desiree."

"You speak in riddles Alma. What is your meaning?"

"A walk through Abbeville's Cemetery may answer your question?"

"Possibly, cemeteries tell their own stories," Desiree responds and adds, "When do you want to go?"

"Tomorrow. Say around six o'clock? We can meet at the cemetery gate. Do you know how to get there?"

Because, when she drove into Abbeville, she saw the gate to the cemetery,

Desiree answers yes and accepts Alma's invitation. The night's conversation wanes to other topics, like the best seasons for growing vegetables and herbs in the Sierra's; what's going to happen with the farmer's markets; gourmet meals; and especially Abbeville's gossip mill.

"You will be fresh meat for our town's gossip mill. News of our dinner has already traveled from here to the other end of town.

"How can that be, Alma?"

"Forest eyes see and ears hear. The news carries on the wind."

Hearing a familiar soft knock, Alma walks to the front door and greets Dr. Silvia Preston. Silvia is a close friend of Alma. She often drops in on the Whitman's at odd hours, usually after making her home visits. Silvia is invited in, introduced to Desiree, and offered a glass of port, which she eagerly takes after her long day.

"I'm glad to meet you Desiree. I've heard so much about you."

Desiree surprised by Preston's opening comment replies, "Thank you, but how..."

Alma interjects, "Forest whispers."

Silvia counters, "More like reports from townsfolk's observing you and Edgar at the general store. Abbeville's gossip mill works at full tilt, at all times. Besides your party is echoing, no, actually broadcasting across Abbeville tonight. Walking here I could hear every word spoken. Sounds like Edgar and Conrad have solved the world's problems over a KWAB talk radio station."

"Still forest whispers, as I've know them to be."

Silvia drinks a good bit of her portonic, leans against the kitchen wall and gives a long sigh.

"Ah refreshing, quenches the yearnings of the soul, doesn't it?" She half jokingly poses a rhetorical question.

Silvia is not a pretty face, but is a strikingly irresistible woman, a virile beauty with the arresting qualities of being direct, dominant and magnetic. She is more comfortable around men than most women and loves to engage in intellectual discourse. She is fully capable of and delights in disarming and disemboweling any man silly enough to underestimate her intelligence and toughness.

Silvia is all facts and no unfounded speculations. She and Desiree are interesting portraits in contrasts and similarities. Desiree, although she is a pretty face is no pushover.

As is her usual *modus operandi*, Desiree begins her line of soft, but probative questioning.

"What brought you to Abbeville, Dr. Preston?"

Alma observes, staying in the background.

"Desiree, please call me Silvia. A need to cut out middlemen and run the whole shows myself to answer your question. And you?"

"Your answer fascinates me Silvia. What does cutting out the middlemen mean?"

"Life's too complicated to suffer needless interference. I have a seven hundred patient practice. For the most part, the life style people live is very healthy—nutritious food, plenty of exercise and clean mountain air makes my job easier. Florence is my receptionist and colleague, a nurse practitioner. We know our patients well. Except for an occasional outside consultation, my work is a one-man operation. I like it that way."

Dr. Preston pauses for Desiree's response, but silence fills in the gap.

"Desiree, why have you come to choose Abbeville? I'm sure you could have been hired in almost any other school district and received much better pay."

"I'm quite content to be here. Alma is a perfect example of why I think I'm going to enjoy teaching here."

"Excuse my persistence. So far you have only answered my questions with questions and vagaries. Is there some reason why you keep deflecting my questions?"

In a more formal social setting Silvia probably would have stopped pursuing someone ducking questions. In Desiree's case, it's different. Desiree has gotten under Silvia's skin; and, she's not going to let Desiree easily wiggle off the hook.

Desiree automatically fires a defensive round across Silvia's bow, "I'm not trying to divert conversation, Silvia. I sincerely want to know why you choose to stay in Abbeville. I understand you are a professor of histology at the prestigious Holmen College of Medicine in Davis."

Laughingly Silvia continues pursuit, "Desiree, you're still dodging my questions. I'm convinced you don't want to reveal anything about yourself to me, at least for tonight. Maybe some other day, when you feel more comfortable in your surroundings, then maybe not? Then again, I'm may get tired of putting more energy into conversations going nowhere."

Desiree is skewered rather well by Silvia's comments. She is well aware of the hole Silvia has torn in her veil of concealment. Questions loom. What is Desiree hiding and why? Or, is she simply a private, shy individual? Alma who hasn't missed a trick cuts through the hostility crackling through the air.

"A little more port ladies?"

Returning to their neutral corners, the women allow Alma to fill their glasses. Alma has seen enough to know Desiree and Silvia are two of a kind. Bright, strong willed, determined to do things their own way, and always be in control of the situation. The clashes of personalities attest to these facts.

Edgar and Conrad surface from their conversation on the deck to join the ladies in the kitchen.

"Silvia, what a pleasant surprise!"

Conrad, obviously happy to see Dr. Preston, kisses her on the cheek and gives her a huge hug. A slight turn of head and click of Desiree's glance toward Conrad communicates volumes to Alma and Silvia. Was that a twinge of jealousy displayed? Unaware of the dynamics, Edgar gives Silvia a big hug and a kiss too.

"What have you girls been talking about?" Edgar innocently reopens the door to conversation that Alma had successfully shut.

"Girl talk, which you gentlemen wouldn't in the least be interested." Alma replies.

Silvia and Desiree smile and sip their wine. The evening's conversation turns to safe talk and more laughter.

Monday, April 11, 8:12 p.m.: Desiree is the first to leave, as the morrow brings twenty-six young supple minds to her doorstep. She thanks Conrad for the information about the class and bids everyone good night, as she retires to the spare bedroom Alma gave her. Conrad, looking puzzled because he doesn't remember talking about substituting for the wayward Emma, who he hadn't, waves good night to Desiree.

Silvia subtly probes what Edgar and Conrad know about Desiree, which is, of course, next to nothing. Around midnight Conrad takes his leave. Tuesday, he'll sleep in, as substitute teaching, meeting Desiree, and partying through the night has drained his tank. Edgar follows suit, leaving Alma and Silvia to their time, which had been preempted by Desiree's impromptu welcome dinner.

"Alma, what are you thinking Alma?" Silvia asks.

"A good question, Silvia. You really scared Desiree."

"She's lucky to still have a head on her shoulders," Silvia replies.

"Desiree scared you too," Alma adds.

Silvia ponders Alma's remark.

"Yes, she did. I guess that's why I went on the offensive so fast."

"Um-hum," Alma pauses.

"Oh no. You're trying to pull more information out of me than I want to give right now. I'd rather talk about Desiree's reaction, when Conrad hugged and kissed me. Priceless?"

"Priceless, you say."

"Priceless the way Desiree reels him and Edgar in like the poor fish they are. Men are such suckers for wily women. Desiree's artfulness, playing with them like a cat with a mouse before biting off their heads, is priceless. You have to defang men before seducing them, which does make them look stupefied."

"Maybe that is the way nature intended our species to be," Alma acknowledges.

"But, why did I get so upset?" Silvia wonders out loud.

"Possibly," Alma suggests, "because Desiree only allows Conrad to see his reflection in her eyes. Love of one's self is the most fetching, but shallowest love of all. It seems the way to a man's heart isn't only through his stomach."

"You mean Desiree is using male vanity to entrap Conrad?"

"Or, maybe she mesmerizes men to keep them at arms distance?"

"I flat out don't trust the woman, whatever she's doing!" Silvia exclaims.

"At one time, you had designs for Conrad," Alma remarks.

"That was so long ago. I'd almost forgotten."

"Silvia, your protective instincts are showing."

Alma hit the nail on the head.

"Oh, that's what is going on, yes. I don't want to see Conrad hurt. That is it, Alma. I'll be able to sleep better tonight with that problem solved." Silvia admits.

"Desiree may genuinely like Conrad, but keeps him at bay by playing with him?"

Silvia thinks out loud, "Could be. Desiree may have been so hurt in another relationship that she's only protecting herself."

"According to Edgar, Desiree is a recent widow."

"Maybe I was too harsh with her."

"Desiree weathered your storm of questions and accusations very well. She seems to have the toughness to give the wildest of Abbeville's children a run for their money. Before she leaves Abbeville, I think she may give a lot of people a run for their money."

"You're considering her for the Sisterhood! So far she's done nothing, except try to obfuscate and frustrate attempts to know her. I don't trust Desiree any further than I can throw her."

"Are not all women candidates for the Sisterhood?"

"Yes, all women are candidates," concedes Silvia, "Will you be meeting Florence at Sand Pond?"

"Do you want to join us?"

Silvia feels the allure of the forest spirits and sees the dancing shadows.

"Tempting, but no. I have a busy day planned for tomorrow. Patients start coming in around nine o'clock. Don't keep Florence out too late. I need a fresh partner in the morning."

"Oh Florence will be her usual, energized self by the time your first patient arrives."

"True, she has never failed me yet."

They embrace for a time and part without further words.

Tuesday, April 12, 12:37 p.m.: Alma meets Florence at Fog's Clearing, two miles into the forest from the old snag tree on Wild Plumb Road. Alma never exactly discusses what Silvia said to her that evening. Nevertheless, Florence senses Desiree's presence in Alma's thoughts.

"Alma, what are you thinking about the new school teacher?"

"Her guardedness is a drawback, but in time, when she feels more comfortable in her new surroundings, her true colors will be revealed."

"Yes, we have many in the Sisterhood with drawbacks; the whole purpose of the Sisterhood is to be the crucible that melts our drawbacks and purifies our souls."

"She is a perfect candidate for the Sisterhood. She will be a good test for our sister, Silvia, which may melt down some of her rough edges too."

"That will be fun to see."

"Oh yes, fun it will be."

"How did Desiree wear on the men in your life?"

"Very well with Edgar and Conrad. Desiree is a sophisticated, entrancing woman."

"And, with you, Alma?"

"I find Desiree cautious, as well as a keen observer. Beneath her protective armor, I sense a deeply spiritual, moral woman. A sure candidate, as we have discussed, for the Sisterhood. And possibly someone you and Silvia will pair up with, when I'm gone." Alma says hopefully.

"Is Silvia planning to be with us tonight?"

"No, she wants to be fresh in the morning and wants you at work on time."

"Figures. So, how did Silvia and Desiree get along?"

"Silvia would be your best source on that question." Alma comments.

"Good point, I'll ask her when I get to work."

Silvia and Florence leave Fog's Clearing before sunrise. Their lives return to normal, as they greet the new day, in much the same ways that you and I greet a new day, after a solid eight hours sleep.

Chapter 3

❦

Tuesday, April 12, 8:45 a.m.: School bells ring, signaling students have fifteen minutes to be seated at their desks and ready for work. Rising to their feet, greeting the town's patriarch and their new teacher, Edgar and Mrs. Parker enter the presence of twenty-six engrossed students.

"Good morning Mr. Whitman." Students, ages seven to thirteen say, sitting as quietly as they can.

Edgar smiles in return. Beloved, old Mr. Whitman, the nice man who gives free candy to them at the general store dressed in familiar attire—hunting boots, jeans and a brown fishing shirt with pockets for hooks and worms, his hair rather disheveled. Having never been that close to a beautiful and beautifully adorned woman, the children's eyes are as big as saucers. Mrs. Parker's style and makeup are perfect. Mrs. Parker is wearing a Jones New York tweed three-button jacket and matching skirt, accented with gold button earrings, an etched gold bead necklace, and quilted black and grey checked pump shoes.

"Good morning girls and boys," Mr. Whitman begins, "I'm here to introduce you to Mrs. Parker, your new teacher."

Edgar, who loves being the center of attention and who especially loves performing in front of the children, doesn't notice all of the students' eyes fixed on their new teacher throughout his presentation.

"What happened to Mr. Corbett? Did you fire him?" asks Jimmy Brown, a fifth grader and noted class clown.

No one laughs. Eyes hold on Mrs. Parker who is unruffled, her eyes communicating calm.

"No Jimmy," Mr. Whitman continues," Mr. Corbett was not fired. He was substituting until the new teacher was hired."

Curtis Dean stands and smarmily asks, "Did Mrs. Torrance run off with the custodian to get married?"

Curtis looks at his classmates for an endorsement. He sees the class's eyes, watching the teacher and melts back into his seat.

Mr. Whitman waits patiently and when Dean deflates he continues. Edgar's confidence soars, as he believes he has magically controlled the situation.

Girls and boys your new teacher, Mrs. Parker."

The class stands and more or less in unison says, "Good Morning Mrs. Parker."

"Thank you boys and girls and a good morning to you," responds Mrs. Parker.

Edgar goes on to explain the rules of the school and his high expectations that the class will pay attention to their new teacher and make her feel welcomed in Abbeville. He leaves the class with a final warning that Mrs. Parker will be reporting to him after school and will let him know who was good and who was acting badly on this first day of school.

"Yes Mr. Whitman," is their seated response.

On Mr. Whitman's exit, Mrs. Parker surveys the class before speaking. "Jimmy."

Silence falls like a sludge hammer. One can feel the tension in the air as Jimmy laughs in the crook of his arm, pretending not to hear the new teacher.

"Jimmy your father is one of Abbeville's town councilmen and your mother runs the town's fabric store. Would they be pleased that you didn't speak when I called your name?"

A sheepish Jimmy answers, "No ma'am."

"Sara Simmons your parents expect you to graduate from Loyalton High School, attend UC Davis, and graduate with a degree in animal biology?"

"Yes, Mrs. Parker."

"Tim, Tim Jackson your parents want you to be a lawyer. But you have other plans?"

"How did you know that, Mrs. Parker?"

"You might say a little bird told me. You wouldn't buy that or would you Tim?"

"No, Mrs. Parker, I don't believe a little bird had anything to do with you knowing I don't want to be a lawyer. I want to be a farmer."

The class wisely holds itself in check.

"A fine line of work Tim. You'll make a great farmer, if you set your mind to it."

Quietly commanding the attention of the class, Mrs. Parker walks the length of the classroom, looking through the large wooden framed windows to the playground.

Stopping at the window she says, "Boys and girls, I am new to Abbeville. But, Abbeville is not new to me. Last night, I called each of your parents and discussed what they expect from you for the rest of this year. I bet you know the answers your parents gave me. I will be calling Jimmy's mother tonight to report on how he progressed today. I intend to keep in close contact with each of your families because your education is important to me."

Mrs. Parker turns from the window and looks at her class.

"Grades one through three open your arithmetic books to chapter ten, subtraction word problems. I would think you older students would want to help the younger students with their work rather than solve two hundred word problems. Helping your classmates with their subtraction word problems will be a good review for you."

"Curtis, I think you will work well with Karen Jones. Is that acceptable?"

He looks at the teacher; then, he averts his eyes to the corner of the classroom and down to the floor before answering.

"Yes, Mrs. Parker."

Tim, "Would you work with Mary Cunningham."

"Yes, ma'am."

"Sara, I think you will do well with Billy Sutton."

"Yes, Mrs. Parker."

"Peggy, would you like working with Bobbie Crane?"

"Yes, Mrs. Parker.

After the last of the students are paired, Mrs. Parker informs the class the parings will be the same for the rest of the school year.

"At ten o'clock, I will quiz grades one through three students on their answers to the subtraction word problems. Remember how you went about solving the problems because getting the right answer is good, but remembering how you solved the problem is better. You will earn three points for explaining your thinking and one point for getting the right answer. Those students and their tutors, who pass the quiz, will go out to the ten-thirty recess. Those students and their tutors not passing the quiz will stay in from recess and figure out what went wrong. I'd like to meet with Jacob, Nancy, Elroy and Camay at the back table for reading. Questions?"

There are no questions. Mrs. Parker had made herself plain as plain can be. The school carries on spinning like a top.

Mrs. Parker is a naturally gifted teacher, credentialed to teach grades kindergarten through fourteen. She is eminently qualified in mathematics and literature and is more than capable to masterfully educate the children in Abbeville's K-8 elementary school. This is a teacher the class will not swallow whole. This is a teacher her students will never forget.

Her gentle touch is as effective when laying down the law as it is when treating and bandaging a student's scraped knee. She genuinely respects her students and believes if a child can find their way to school, the child can learn anything she has to teach them. Her travels around the world bring the dazzle of adventure to the doorsteps of Abbeville's elementary school— quite a luxury in the remote Sierras. In a short time, her students come to love their new teacher, Jimmy and Curtis in particular.

Shortly before recess, a woman enters the classroom. The children smile, some waive. Mrs. Parker takes a mental note of the degree of excitement expressed by her students at the sight of this woman. She walks over and greets the lady.

"Good morning, may I help you?"

"Oh, no one told you about me? My name is Shanice Jackson. I'm your teacher assistant. Surprise!"

"No, I wasn't told Mrs. Jackson, but I am pleased to meet you. How long have you worked as a teacher assistant?

"Going on four years, Mrs. Parker. What do you want me to do?"

"What have you done in the past?"

"Take the children out to recess. Supervise them at lunch time and help them with their school work."

"I wouldn't change a thing Mrs. Jackson. Will you continue to do as you have been doing?"

"Happy to, Mrs. Parker."

Mrs. Parker asks Shanice to take the children to recess."

Shanice says, "Boys and girls, you may put your pencils down and sit straight for me."

Her soft, melodious voice charms the students into following her direction.

"Mrs. Parker says you all have earned recess today. Good work boys and girls. Jamie, will you lead the class to the tetherball courts."

"Yes, Mrs. Jackson."

Jamie stands and quietly exits the classroom and is followed by the student sitting behind her and so forth, until the class is orderly outside.

Mrs. Parker steps in the privacy of the small office and lunchroom adjoining the classroom. She slips out of her high-heel pumps, takes off her jacket, blouse, and skirt, laying her earrings and jewelry on the desk. She slips into her sweats, a tee shirt, a pair of Nike Shox Turbo's, slaps on her Aztec baseball cap, exits the schoolhouse, and jogs across the playground. Mrs. Parker's transformation flabbergasts her students.

"Anyone wanting to play softball over to the baseball diamond," she yells and blows her whistle.

The boys look at each other for a second and run as fast as they can to the diamond, laughingly hooting and hollering all the way. Mrs. Jackson and the rest of the class follow. Mrs. Parker's windmill fast-pitch screams past the heads of the eight grade boys, who immediately fall in love with their new teacher. Curtis Dean swings the bat so hard he almost screws himself in the ground, falling down in the process. His classmates laugh hysterically. Mrs. Parker chastises the class for poor sportsmanship. They immediately stopped laughing. From the ground Curtis looks at Mrs. Parker.

"That's okay ma'am. I did look pretty silly."

As the game continues, Curtis jumps to his feet and gives high-fives to his classmates on the way back to the dugout. Mrs. Parker runs bases, throws a ball, and hits the ball out of the playground better than any of her students. She gives her students pointers on how to improve their game. Not one to boast, Mrs. Parker never tells her students about playing softball at Palos Verde Peninsula High School before pitching down south for the Aztec's.

Standing on the sidelines with the rest of the students, Mrs. Jackson says, "My word, your new school teacher really knows how to play ball!"

Yes, Mrs. Parker establishes herself well with her students from the first moment they laid eyes on her. At school's end, half of the mothers tired of waiting for their kids to come out of school, get out of their cars and go into class to retrieve their children. They find their children lingering after school to do extra credit work and be with Mrs. Parker. Nothing like this had ever happened in Abbeville. The positives about this new teacher, Mrs. Parker, quickly spread through Abbeville.

Late that afternoon, Mrs. Parker stops by the general store to shop for the night's dinner. Throughout the day Edgar is bombarded with rave reports about the new teacher he hired. Virtually every parent in Abbeville thanks him.

"You've made quite a hit in this town, Mrs. Parker, and I might add, you have boosted my image in the eyes of the townspeople. Good job Desiree, good job."

"Why thank you Mr. Whitman you're too kind. I simply was doing what you hired me to do. Thank you for the opportunity to work with Abbeville's young people. They are exceptional."

"What can I get you today Desiree?"

"Some basics, Mr. Whitman. Do you have agemono, nagemono or shashimi?"

With this incredulous look Edgar says, "I don't think so." After thinking, he comments, "You're kidding me, right?"

Mrs. Parker smiles and pulls out her shopping list, which has a variety of fresh vegetables, a pork loin, eggs and bacon, five-grain bread, and a few personal sundries for her to buy. Edgar trips over himself to take care of Desiree's order. Standing alert with her tail slowly wagging, Fenway watches Mrs. Parker's every movement.

"Mrs. Parker don't you worry about a thing. I have everything on your shopping list and will take them home, after I get through here. And the bill's on me."

Mrs. Parker thanks Edgar for his generosity and leaves the store. With about an hour to freshen up, before meeting Alma at the cemetery, she walks up the hill to the cabin. Today was a stunning success for the new schoolteacher—game, set, and match for Mrs. Parker.

Chapter 4

Tuesday, April 12, 6:00 p.m.: By four o'clock Alma has finished walking her figure-8 route around Upper Sardine and Lower Sardine lakes. Precisely at six o'clock p.m., she arrives at the gate to the Abbeville Cemetery. Looking into the cemetery, Alma sees Silvia, walking passed the crematorium.

"Good evening, Desiree. You found the trail from the cabin to the cemetery, I see."

"Yes, that's quite a short cut. Beats going through town."

"And, the walk gives one an unparalleled feeling of peace and serenity most townspeople don't understand."

"Strange, that's exactly what I felt, too, making my way from the cabin through the cemetery."

Abbeville Cemetery grounds are green, beautifully landscaped and impeccably maintained. Tombstones are polished, cemetery sections logically laid out and the floral tributes fresh, a spiritual place where people want to be. Crowning the greenery is the Abbe Family Mausoleum atop serene grounds overlooking the cemetery and the town.

John Abbe (1800-1868) was the first to be buried in Abbeville. Later, when the Abbe Family Mausoleum was constructed, John was the first to be placed in the family crypt. Alma and Desiree walk the black asphalt path, which winds through the graveyard, up the hill to the Abbe crypt.

"Eight hundred fifty-five people reside in these graves, more people than the population of Abbeville. What does that tell you about life in our town?"

Desiree takes several thoughtful steps along the path and answers, "This community is close knit. Life has rolled on unhurried for the two hundred years, allowing people to know one another, at a deeply personal level. The grounds testify to how much the dead are cherished by the living. The past is eternally cared for and respected in Abbeville."

"An astute observation and exceedingly accurate more than you know. Abbeville's history can be told through the lives of those resting here with more stories to tell by the shadows in our graveyard."

Although Desiree didn't quite catch what Alma meant by more stories from graveyard shadows, she nods knowingly. Desiree is always prepared for solving mysteries. Alma has piqued her curiosity. They reach the rain forest green marble steps leading to the Abbe Family Mausoleum, a striking edifice. Each of the five steps, leading to the mausoleum's Christ at Heart's Door entrance, is inscribed with gilded lines of ancient thought.

"Should the guilty seek asylum here," Desiree reads the gilded inscription on the first step.

Standing on the second step, Alma gives voice to the next inscription, "Like one pardoned."

Desiree moves to the third step and reads aloud, "He becomes free from sin." Alma looks at her and asks, "What do you think?"

Desiree responds, "I think we are told everyone who come to this place can expect to be protected and freed from blame."

"I think so too, Desiree."

Joining Desiree, Alma climbs step four and reads.

"Should a sinner make his way to this mansion," Alma continues to read the fifth step, "All his past sins are to be washed away. What meaning does this have for you, Desiree?"

"By the time we travel this far through life and allow God's forgiveness to enter our hearts, we realize our sins are forever forgotten," Desiree ventures.

Alma looks into Desiree's eyes and says, "It is so."

"I seem to remember something like this spoken by Emperor Shah Jahan, describing the Taj Mahal. Only he finished by saying, 'the sight of this mansion creates sorrowing sighs; and the sun and the moon shed tears from their eyes. In this world this edifice has been made to display thereby the creator's glory.'"

"Dear sister. The essence of this earthly jewel is the same, the glorification of the Creator."

Alma and Desiree walk along on the terrace that surrounds the magnificent gorora stone, octagon shaped earthy jewel and stop in front of Christ at Heart's door, which is the entrance to the mausoleum and stand in the outer luminescence of the afternoon sun, streaming through the translucent portal.

"Astonishing, I've never felt anything like this, Alma."

"The mausoleum was designed facing east, ensuring the sun's radiance continually floods the interior of the crypt from before dawn until the sun sets beyond the western horizon." Alma explains.

"I would have never guessed the splendor of the Creator ever existed on earth, as strongly as I feel it here.

Alma continues to describe the details of the architect's vision, "Desiree, there is no outside knob or latch on the mausoleum door."

"Then, how does one enter?"

"The secret is Christ's door can only be entered through one's heart— an act of will."

"Oh," Desiree says wonder filled.

Christ's Heart's door is so perfectly balanced Alma only touches the door for it to open wide.

"Oh," Desiree says with less wonder.

The deep green Indian marble steps and terrace flow into the inner atrium of the mausoleum. Alma and Desiree stand in the inner luminescence. As if standing in the radiant presence of God in heaven, light streams through the Heart of Christ's door, from the oculus glass ceiling above and through the stunning resurrection depiction of Jesus etched in the westward wall-window.

"Lumen de Lumina means light from light," Alma translates the inscription carved in the center of the mausoleum's dark, almost black emerald marble floor.

Desiree says, "This tomb is an amazing structure designed to symbolize the mystic strivings, the universal experience, testifying to the Light of God that is present in this world."

"Yes," Alma affirms.

"Indeed amazing," Desiree continues, "But how can darkness exist in the radiance of God? Darkness vanishes in the light? Why is the same dark emerald marble used on the steps and terrace of the mausoleum allowed to dominate the interior floor?"

"The idea of eternal light and eternal darkness coexisting is a spiritual principle found in all major religions of the world. A literal translation of the Hebrew from the Book of Isaiah says, 'I form the light and create the darkness. I make peace and create evil. I the LORD do all these things.'"

"Are you telling me the dark emerald marble represents the evil God created?"

"I believe the architect's intention was to communicate that notion."

As she moves on with her tour of the family mausoleum, Alma leaves the thought to linger with Desiree.

"You're right. Even agricultural fields are burned to make way for new crops. Interesting." Desiree replies.

"There are fourteen burial chambers surrounding us, eight on the north wall, six on the south wall. Abbeville's three founding brothers head the north wall and their wives are paired across from them on top of the south wall."

"There are twenty-four total burial spaces in the mausoleum and with fourteen filled spaces, why aren't the remaining burial spaces filled?" Desiree asks.

"Good question. Why indeed are ten spaces vacant?"

"That wasn't the end of the lineage. Weren't there more descendants to bury? You and Edgar are descendants and so were your mother and father and so on?"

"More pieces for your puzzle, Desiree."

Desiree takes in what Alma says and mentally verifies each of Alma's statements against the standard of her own logic and common sense. But, with so many pieces of the puzzle missing, the answer is not clear.

Desiree simply replies, "Who would have the slightest notion that hidden in this valley in the Sierra-Nevada mountain range, one would find a royal burial vault that rivals the Valley of the Kings? This is Abbeville's version of the El Escorial?"

Alma smiles and moves on.

"Across from John Abbe are the remains of his wife, Jane Franc Abbe (1815-1875). They were childless, which accounts for the vacant burial spaces below their names."

"You said Jane's name was "Jane Franc." There's no "Franc" carved in her crypt."

"True. The question is why isn't Jane's full name placed on her tomb?"

"Another puzzle piece, I presume. I don't quite know the answer to your question, Alma. So, let me ask you another question. What are the full names of the other women married to Abbe's?"

"Natasha 'Tasha' Gorbi, Mary Sand, Susan Smith, Jeane Lyon, and Carol Ann Paul."

"Then, the answer to your question is, I think, only the "Abbe" name is allowed in the Abbe Family Mausoleum."

Alma awards high honors to Desiree, "You are an "A" student."

"Why, thank you, Alma. Coming from you, I take that as a high compliment."

"You are a quick study Desiree. In a short time, you figure out the puzzle."

Studying all the crypts more carefully, Desiree begins to make more connections about the history of Abbeville's founders.

"I see Mark (1802-1870) and Mary Abbe (1802-1870) occupying the center column burial spaces across from each other. I presume their child Jeff (1862-1925) married Tasha (1903-2000), when she was only sixteen and they immediately had Jeff Junior (1919-1944)? He died so young?"

"Yes Mark was fifty-seven when he married Tasha Gorbi and had Jeff Junior, who died young, fighting in the Second World War. Tasha died at the age ninety-seven and is the last of the Abbes to be buried in the family crypt."

"John Junior? Was that John and Jane's grandson who also died in the Second World War?"

"No since John and Jane never had children, the eldest brother Matthew Abbe decided to name one of his sons after his brother. John Junior is the grandson of Matthew and Carol Ann Paul Abbe.

"Interesting." Desiree says moving on, "Matthew (1797-1878) and his wife Carol Ann (1840-1945) lives span three centuries! Wow!"

"Yes one hundred forty-eight years from Matthew's birth to Carol Ann's death, quite impressive."

"She was the arch-matriarch of the family."

"She was my great grandmother, a woman of great vision and a greater sense of social justice."

"Hum, you have five relatives that died within two years?"

"That was a very intense period for the Abbe family. Matthew Abbe Junior, his son John Abbe, his grandson John Abbe Junior and Mark Abbe's grandson Jeff Junior all died around the end of the Second World War. My grandfather Edgar died around that time too. The Abbe family absorbed quite a hit in the short span of three year."

"I'd say. The walls of the mausoleum tell quite a story, especially the empty vaults," Desiree comments.

"Yes, and we haven't talked about Jeane Lyon, Josie Mark, Jane Franc, Francis Bell and Carol Ann Abbe Whitman."

"It's getting late and I'm getting overwhelmed by all the puzzle pieces," Desiree points out," I need to be getting my night's sleep. I have to be sharp for my students tomorrow morning. Do you mind if we head back to town?"

"It is getting late; and, you've have had quite a history lesson to digest."

Standing on the terrace in the light from the set sun flowing through Christ's Heart door, the name Carol Ann Abbe Whitman finally registers in Desiree's mind.

"Matthew and Carol Ann Abbe's daughter isn't buried in the family crypt?

"My great grandmother, Carol Ann Whitman, was barred from the Abbe Mausoleum."

"Your mother and grandmother aren't in the mausoleum either."

"According to Abbe family tradition, neither will Edgar nor I be buried here. We're Whitman's. Besides, dear sister, my bones will never see the grave."

Desiree tucks Alma's astounding piece of the puzzle away, until she has time to assess the whole evening's walk.

"What an injustice, Alma. How can you live with the unfairness, especially when there is room to bury everyone?"

Alma looks across the cemetery and says, "Another curiosity, Desiree, is the Abbe men are separated from their wives. The Abbe family only allows their male descendents to be buried in the family mausoleum, wives are only permitted to tag along at a distance on the south wall, stripped of their maiden names."

"The crypt is a men's club. Your mother, father, Edgar, and you will not be buried in the Abbe family mausoleum. But you are the last of the line?"

"Edgar and I are the last of the Abbe Family lineage. But, in the eyes of the Abbe brothers, it was important only to keep the Abbe family name going. The last of the Abbe Family died out when Matthew Abbe Junior died in 1946. The final chapter, though, hasn't been written. In time, injustices will be righted."

More to tuck away for another day Desiree thinks.

Changing the subject Desiree says, "Alma the sun has set below the western horizon some time ago, yet we stand her talking with plenty of light. How does that work?"

"Although the mausoleum was built in 1870, improvements have been made to the Eye-of-God glass ceiling that improves ventilation within the building and, more to your question, that captures and intensifies the sun's radiation from below the horizon."

"I've read or heard something about that several years ago," Desiree replies.

"Yes, they call it 'glass skin.' Five years ago, a glass skin was installed over the Eye-of-God glass ceiling, which enhances the sun's first available light and magnifies the sun's last fading light. The Abbe Family Mausoleum is plainly visible for miles around and remains lighted to the naked eye hours before sunrise and hours after nightfall . . . Watch your step going down the steps at night can be tricky," Alma cautions.

"Alma," Desiree whispers, "I thought I saw something in the trees. Yes over there beyond the statue of Saint Francis."

Alma stops and looks for a long time in the direction Desiree is pointing, "I don't see anything unusual Desiree. It's only the shadows playing tricks on us."

"I must say Alma this cemetery lay out and the family mausoleum are as impressive a memorial park and gardens as I have ever seen. You know so much about the architecture too. Interesting. Who designed the cemetery and the mausoleum?"

"The park, gardens, and mausoleum were designed by a young architect, Sam Whitman, Carol Ann Abbe Whitman's husband."

Desiree is struck dumb, motionlessly standing on the cemetery path. The idea that Alma's great-grandfather designed everything and built the mausoleum, knowing his remains, the remains of his wife, and the remains of his children and his children's children will never rest in the mausoleum flabbergasts Desiree. Even after several minutes, Desiree finds it hard to pick the right words to express her shock.

"Your great grandfather built the cemetery and the Abbe Family Mausoleum," is the whole of what Desiree can utter.

"Yes, great grandfather Whitman was a talented and forgiving man. Someday you may bump into him out here. Wouldn't that be interesting?"

"You're kidding?"

"Let's say that's another puzzle piece for you to solve the mystery, Desiree."

Desiree laughs out loud, her laughter echoing from the cemetery hillside across the town.

"You sure know how to lay the puzzle pieces down Alma."

"And we haven't yet talked about the real legacy of the Abby family."

"I don't know if I can take anymore, Alma. My systems are on overload."

"Let's leave this topic with one last piece of the puzzle. I have many sisters and soon to be brothers that will carry on the true legacy of our creation into the future."

This makes no sense to Desiree. Alma has no sisters; she has no children; and, she has only one brother, who is old and not likely to marry and have children. Future legacy? Desiree thinks not . . . certainly, not on this side of the mortal veil.

"Desiree, how do you find Dr. Preston?"

"You are so full of surprises Alma. Where did that question come from?"

"Curiosity."

"Do you mind if I hold my answer. I haven't quite formed an opinion about Dr. Preston. I haven't deconstructed our first encounter."

In choosing not to answer, Desiree knows she has revealed the analytical, slow to judge side of her to Alma. For Desiree the walk to the cemetery gates is awkward, as she does not know what else she's revealed to this very insightful woman by not directly answering her question.

"Desiree, we'll take the short way back to the cabin without going through town. If that is all right with you?"

By ten o'clock they reach the fence that separates the cemetery from the cabin.

"Desiree, see over there, the lights shining? That's the cabin. Head along this trail and you'll be home soon. The moon and starlight are bright enough for you to easily find your way.

"I know I haven't answered your question Alma. All I can say is be patient with me. I've never really opened myself to anyone, but if I do it will be with someone like you."

"You will, when you are ready. I understand."

They hug and part ways. Desiree follows the trail as Alma instructed, which is the same way she traveled earlier that afternoon. The trail looks different at night; the moonlight casts an otherworldly feeling in one's bones. She stops several times along the trail, sensing she is not alone. But, seeing nothing, she continues on her way to the cabin.

Climbing the steps part way, she is compelled to turn and look back on the trail she walked so she can use the short cut again. Desiree is amazed to find the trail she traveled has disappeared. The stars and the moon brightly shining on her do not penetrate the dense forest from which she came.

Desiree thinks to herself, "I didn't think twice when Alma suggested I walk alone from the cemetery only guided by moon and star light. But, only darkness exists where I walked. How can that be?"

Entering the cabin Desiree hears Edgar snoring away in his favorite chair, newspaper splayed over his lap as usual. She tiptoes to her room, readies for bed and in no time flat she is asleep.

For Alma the night is far from over.

She rides her Vespa almost to the end of Wild Plumb Road and parks along side of Florence's car. Moonlight shining on the snow covered Buttes is spectacular. High winds blowing snow from the mountain heights add to the wonder and mystery of the evening. Alma turns and disappears into the forest and soon joins her sisters.

Alma greets each of the sisters with a hug and a kiss before sitting down. Stella May is the first to speak.

"The rumor mill is working hard to undermine Reverend Henry. Why is that so?"

"He's shown a bright light on the cockroaches and they're angry and scurrying to avoid the light of truth," Emma Jane Walter's observes.

"I'd like to see them scurry out of Fabrics Plus into the streets. They're driving away business," laughs Jane.

"It's no laughing matter. Mo still hasn't got over the drubbing they gave him about killing me!" Ellen quips.

Florence comments, "Their deeds need to be brought out in the open. I'm afraid that Reverend Henry is not suited for such a battle. He's too principled, too morally upright. I think his days are numbered at that church."

"That is a shame," Emma Jane laments, "Our town needs more good hearted, moral people, like Reverend Johnston. I hate to think that Fredrika and her gossip mill have the power to drive him from the pulpit."

"Fredrika is a formidable force. She has driven hundreds from Abbeville," Alma remarks.

Many sisters nod their heads in agreement.

Florence continues, "Reverend Henry is perplexed. I can see it in his sermons. He's leaning away from the power of his beliefs to take matters in his own hands, which is a sure path for self destruction."

"Sisters, "Alma speaks, "Evil will fall on its own accord, in its own time. We do not have to directly confront it. We do need to continue in our good works and expand the reach of our Sisterhood. That alone will hasten the destruction of evil."

"You're considering Desiree for the Sisterhood Alma?" Silvia poses the question to Alma.

"I am considering Desiree. I believe Desiree will fit well into the Sisterhood. It's too early to tell. What is your thought, dear sister?"

Silvia answers directly, "Based on my observations of the evidence, Desiree is not cut out to be one of the Sisterhood."

"Your emotions seem to cloud your vision. Use your scientific intuition. At first glance, all is not clearly observable. Hold your judgment still, dear sister, until all the facts are in."

"Fair enough, dear sister."

The group sits in a circle around the small fire. The shades of night appear and disappear in the fire's light. They sense the presence of sisters past. Anne Dean's presence is most real, as animals watch from afar.

Early the next morning Florence is at the office.

"Reverend Henry's leaning away from God? What's up about that, Florence?"

"I said that Reverend Henry is leaning away from the power of his beliefs."

So, what's the difference, Florence?"

"I do not know what God thinks in this situation; but, I do attend Damascus Church, I do know Reverend Henry's persona well enough to be aware of a shift in his spiritedness, his animation. He's lost the spark of passion he once had."

"Good empirical reasoning. I don't know the man that well to say; but your observations and conclusion seem to have merit."

"Speaking of empirical reasoning, Silvia, what was all that about Desiree? I know you reserve such moments of passion for rare occasions. Do you want to talk?"

Before Silvia can answer, the first patient of the day walks in the door early.

"How are you doing this morning, Mrs. Sorenson?"

I'm doing very well, thank you Florence. I'm here to see how my baby's doing. Tell me, how's your week been going?"

Dr. Preston smiles and goes to the back of the clinic, disappearing in her office.

"I've been a little busy, things are going fine now. How have you been feeling with your pregnancy?"

"No problems, as of yet. Been feeling good, so far."

"Okay Abigail, are you ready to see Dr. Preston?

"Yes I am."

Florence leads Abigail into the examination room. She takes and records Abigail's weigh and vital signs. Florence asks Abigail to remove her blouse and under things, slip into the medical gown, and lay on the examination table. Abigail anxiously waits to hear good news about the development of her second child, a baby boy who will be loved and taunted by his two-year old sister, Rachael.

"Good morning Abigail. How are you and your baby feeling today?"

"I'm a little tired, Dr. Preston."

"That's to be expected in the late term of a pregnancy. Otherwise, you feel well?" Preston asks.

"Yes doctor. I have been taking my vitamins as prescribed and have been taking my walks to ensure my baby is healthy.

Florence asks Dr. Preston if she is needed anymore. Silvia shakes her head and Florence returns to the front desk to ready the file for the next patient.

"Are you eating well Abigail?"

"I have had a recent loss of appetite doctor."

"Are you craving any foods in particular?"

"No cravings. Is that a bad sign?"

"Not really, it's an individual matter. Some women experience lack of appetite near the end of a pregnancy. You are about a month away from delivery. Abigail, how are you feeling about your second child?"

"Very excited, doctor, I can't wait for the moment to see my new baby."

"Good, it's time for your vaginal examination. I'll be as gentle as possible. Remember try to relax and breath deeply.

Silvia knows some women are not happy to have a pelvic examination, especially when pregnant. However, she insists on visually and tactilely examining each of her pregnant patients. Her histological training and experience gives her a distinct edge over most obstetricians. Checking for signs of cervical anomalies like early dilation, signaling a possible miscarriage or effacement are trademarks of Silvia's thoroughness. She continues Abigail's examination via sonography, which allows the doctor and patient to share in real time their observations about the health of Abigail's developing fetus.

"How does everything look?"

"Look at the ultrasonic projection for yourself, Abigail. Everything seems to be going well. Baby's heartbeat is strong. He's appropriately active, there doesn't appear to be any obstruction in blood flow and his internal organs seem to be functioning normally. Your uterus and ovaries seem in the pink of health too."

"When do you think I'll deliver?"

"I would say expect Manuel to arrive between twenty to thirty days from now. Do you want Florence to help you dress?"

"Thank you, no Dr. Preston, I can do it."

"Very well. Please schedule an appointment in the next ten days to two weeks. I want a better idea about the timing of your delivery. I wouldn't want you to miss that?"

Laughing, Abigail answers, "No doctor, I wouldn't want to miss that either."

Dr. Preston closes the examination room door and goes back to her office. Bob's completed lab work was delivered to the clinic at nine thirty. Preston begins her careful review of the histology report. Florence interrupts with the news that Peggy Elgin broke her arm while climbing the monkey bars at school. Her mother reports they will be here momentarily. Dr. Preston acknowledges Florence and continues reading. Bob's results aren't good, but there seems to be a fault in the analyses. Rocking back in her chair Silvia mentally reviews the possibilities.

Florence sticks her head in the door and says, "They're here and Peggy's mother is more distraught about the arm than Peggy."

"Hum. Examination room two Florence," Silvia says preoccupied with Bob's biopsy report.

Nervously Mrs. Elgin prattles on about Peggy, "Dr. Preston, I don't know what I'm going to do about her. Yesterday, she was doing cartwheels and walkovers and handsprings and today she ran over to a maple tree and climbed out on a limb, when plop she fell out of the tree onto the dirt road. I can still see the dust poof in the air; what am I going to do with her. She's such a tomboy."

Mrs. Elgin is a part time teacher assistant and takes over for Shanice on occasion. Silvia smiles and turns her attention to Peggy.

"Peggy let me look at your arm. Tell me what happened?"

While listening to Peggy's explanation, Dr. Preston topographically examines Peggy.

"So when you fell from the bars did you put your left hand out to stop the fall?"

"Yes doctor."

"Peggy can you rotate your left wrist like this?"

"Yes doctor. See?"

"Do you feel any pain in that wrist Peggy?"

"No doctor."

Dr. Preston gently holds Peggy's hand and firmly presses on the wrist bones and lower end of the ulna. Peggy reports no pain. Preston presses firmly around the thumb joint. Peggy exhibits and reports no pain.

"How old are you now, Peggy?"

"I'm eleven years old, doctor."

Dr. Preston holds on to Peggy's upper arm with one hand and with the other hand takes hold of Peggy's forearm and pushes the arm parts together.

"Ouch that hurts Dr. Preston," Peggy responds.

"Pretty tender at the ends of your bones. Peggy, I'm sure you've bruised or fractured the end of your arm bones. The good news is the fracture will most probably heal without any problems. I need to see an x-ray of your elbow to be sure nothing else is broken."

Peggy's mother wants to know whether she should take Peggy to the hospital in Loyalton for the x-rays. Silvia shakes her head and says that wouldn't be necessary because she has a portable x-ray machine in the clinic that will do the job.

Dr. Preston calls for Florence to make ready the office's Quantum Imaging System with film digitizer and full screen display for Peggy and her mother. The process takes less than ten minutes.

In a little while, Dr. Preston, Peggy and Mrs. Elgin are viewing the results of Peggy's x-rayed elbow. Dr. Preston explains her diagnosis of Peggy's lateral condoyle fracture and classifies Peggy's injury as a type-1 Salter-Harris fracture.

Peggy's mother asks, "Where do we go from here doctor?"

Dr. Preston gives Mrs. Elgin the worst-case scenario regarding the suspected transverse fracture of the growing zone of the physis. Once the medical obligation to explain the worst-case scenario is complete, Dr. Preston discusses Peggy's treatment for the injury, explaining to Mrs. Elgin that if Peggy follows her directions, Peggy's injury has a good prognosis. Peggy is in examination room one where Florence is placing a splint on Peggy's elbow.

Dr. Preston emphasizes, "When Florence has finished splinting Peggy's elbow, be sure Peggy immobilizes her arm the best she can so the injury can heal faster. The elbow should be iced several times a day to reduce the swelling and soreness."

"What happens at school, doctor," Mrs. Elgin asks anxiously.

"When she is at school and home she needs to keep her arm elevated as much as possible to keep swelling at a minimum, plus elevating her arm will reduce throbbing pain."

"Peggy, did you hear what the doctor said?

"Yes, mother."

I am scheduling an appointment with Dr. Fredrickson, an orthopedic surgeon in Loyalton, for a re-evaluation of Peggy's injury in two weeks."

Seeking assurance Mrs. Elgin asks, "Are you sure Peggy's arm will be alright and will grow normally?"

In a reassuring tone Dr. Preston repeats, "Mrs. Elgin the growing zone of the physis is probably not injured badly. To be safe I'm treating her as if the growing plate was fractured. Growth disturbances for this injury are uncommon. That's why I want to periodically check and make sure things are going well."

Peggy with her arm in a splint and elbow held high by the ice bag in her other hand walks back to the car with her mother. Mrs. Elgin appears to be relieving her own anxiety by issuing a continual stream of warnings about Peggy being careful, raising her arm, and icing her elbow.

Peggy can be heard saying, "Yes mother. Yes, mother," until her mother closes the car door.

As the Elgins leave the parking lot, Florence notifies Silvia that Dr. Ichikowa is on the phone with information about Bob Winston.

"Paul Ichikowa, it's been a long time. I understand you're doing well at Davis."

"Yes. Thanks to the greatest histology teacher on the face of the planet."

"Why Paul, you still know how to get those A+ grades. You can stop with the compliments, you've already caught the bus!"

"Thank you doctor. It looks like Mr. Winston dodged the GIST bullet. Magnetic imaging scans show a six and a half centimeter sized tumor below the lining of the upper GI tract that has not broken the lining. A fine needle biopsy and immunohistochemical tests show no presence of KIT proteins; and, the PDGFRA related protein was present. Our people feel this is a benign tumor posing no problem for Mr. Winston at this time.

"Paul, Bob's blood tests shows a BUN to creatinine ratio of 58, having a sensitivity of 93% and a specificity of thirty percent. That worries me. I think the tumor has possibly metastasized to his liver or somewhere else."

"Interesting doctor. I'll have that checked out. I will personally get the information back to you ASAP."

Dr. Preston is confident that her former student will get back to her as he indicates. Less than three hours later Paul texts Dr. Preston with the news that Mr. Winston has pancreatic cancer and has a twenty percent to fifty percent chance of living six months. She will make a home visit tomorrow to personally deliver the unfortunate news to Bob.

Without so much as a word about their morning conversation about Desiree, Dr. Preston leaves closing the clinic to Florence and heads for home. Florence knows the questions she raised that morning will stick in Silvia's head. By nature, unanswered questions keep Preston occupied like a dog gnawing a bone.

Chapter 5

Tuesday, April 12, 4:45 p.m.: Dr. Preston bumps into Desiree coming out of the Abbeville General Store.

"Desiree, how nice to see you again."

"Dr. Preston, I am happy to see you too. It's been a busy day for both of us. Peggy Elgin looked like she was back to herself after leaving your office."

"Yes, Peggy's a very energetic and resilient child. Some kids are born that way. The rest of us have to work for it."

"She said her arm wasn't broken like we thought?"

"That's right. She bruised the cartilage at the ends of her arm bones, which is painful, but it shouldn't hamper her school work."

"True, it didn't seem to phase her today. She told me about the doctor's orders and, as far as I could tell, the patient exactly followed them. She is such a sweet child."

"Other than Peggy falling out of the tree, how was your second day in class, Desiree?"

"Wonderful, these kids are so attentive and eager to learn."

"You must be an excellent teacher. According to Florence, Mrs. Elgin was very impressed by you. She said Peggy's mother couldn't stop singing your praises."

"That's good to hear, I do so want to make a good impression on the community. By the way I need to apologize to you for the way I avoided your questions last night."

"No you were right, I was pushy and should have respected your privacy. Please accept my apologies."

"No apologizes needed."

"You are new to the community and need to be cautious. I understand completely."

"I'm glad we had this time to talk. I look forward to seeing you in the near future. Goodbye for now."

"Yes, we should get together more often. After all we do work with the same clientele."

Although the meeting is cordial and both try to undo the first impressions they made on each other, they are still a little wary of each other. On impulse, Silvia turns and calls to Desiree.

"Desiree, would you care to have tea with me sometime?"

Desiree, as startled as Silvia is surprised by her actions, says, "Why, yes, a conversation over a cup of tea would be fine."

"Let's make it tonight behind the mausoleum. I've heard you had a tour of the cemetery and know its history well?"

Desiree is completely blown away by Dr. Preston's suggestion.

Desiree thinks, "Alma must have discussed our meeting in the cemetery with Dr. Preston. Ah, they met after Alma showed me the trail back to the cabin. Strange events and getting stranger by the minute."

Very much the adventurer, Desiree accepts Preston's offer.

"Tonight behind the mausoleum. And, yes, I know the place."

"I have a few home visits to make. Say around nine o'clock this evening?"

Nine o'clock is usually past Desiree's bedtime, but this is one party she doesn't want to miss.

"Yes, nine is fine. I'll see you then."

"I'll bring a thermos of tea. Do you want sugar and cream?"

"Sugar and a little lemon works for me."

"Till then, Desiree."

Desiree walks back to the Whitman cabin. Should she tell Alma about meeting with Silvia? She decides not to say anything.

Dr. Preston stops in at the Knead-2-Feed to get a cup of coffee before heading over to Samantha Cross' home. Florence and Alma are sipping glasses of lemonade with chocolate chip oatmeal cookies.

"Fancy meeting you two here." Dr. Preston says with a smile, "I'll have a cup of your African roast and one of those strawberry iced almond cookies, Stella."

"Hard day at the office Silvia?" Alma asks.

"The usual aches and pains mortals have to bear," Silvia replies.

"How well I know," Florence jokingly laments, "My job is settling the patients down before meeting Dr. Preston and smoothing Silvia's rough edges before she sets eyes on her first patient. The care and feeding of Dr. Preston is a tough business these days."

"Very funny, very funny Florence."

"We've been talking about you and Desiree. Have you decided how to deal with that situation?" Florence inquires.

"As a matter of fact, I have. Desiree and I are having a little chat tonight behind the mausoleum."

Florence and Alma fain surprise. Silvia takes a bite out of her cookie and drowns it in a sip of coffee.

"You really work fast doctor, when you want to." responds Florence

"You could knock me over with a feather." Says Alma.

"Stop it you two. You know I can't simply ignore anything you say. I respect your judgment too much. Besides, that woman is a complete mystery to me. I got so riled about her and don't know why. That's not like me to take things so personally."

"So, you're giving Desiree another fly by," Florence observes.

"I need to be more objective about this. After being confronted by you this morning, I couldn't walk away feeling tight as I am. I don't know what exactly is going to happen, but I will be there to listen and understand, not close my ears and judge."

"Good. You know your opinion is indispensable to our deliberations about who is accepted into the Sisterhood. When the time comes to make a decision about Desiree, your voice will need to be heard." Alma says.

Silvia breaths a heavy sigh.

"I know."

"You can bet Desiree knows something's going on too. This is her second jaunt through the cemetery in two days," quips Florence.

"I'll make this meeting as painless as possible," Silvia comments, as she finishes the last of her cookie and coffee, "I have home visits at Samantha and Bob Winston house, then I'll meet with Desiree."

Bob stoically takes the news about his twenty to fifty percent chances to live six months. He takes the news so well that Dr. Preston knows Bob has come to terms with life's end long before he sought her services. When she leaves Bob's house, dark has fallen on the town. The moon is high in the southern sky, as she walks behind the glowing mausoleum, to wait for Desiree.

Minutes later, Desiree is moving up the steps to the terrace level. She re-reads the inscriptions carved in each step, as she goes and moulds the message of steps into one thought: Seeking, I am pardoned, washed clean, free to walk this mansion. Walking alongside the crypt, she repeats this thought like a mantra. Rounding the corner, Desiree sees Dr. Preston in the soft glow of sunlight, emanating from the tomb. She is sitting on the edge of the terrace with her legs dangling off the walkway, looking at the moon. Without a word Dr. Preston pours Desiree a cup of tea. She adds one lump of sugar and leaves a slice of lemon standing in the saucer. Desiree sits and dangles her feet from the terrace walkway too. Dr. Preston offers a cup of tea to Desiree, which she takes from the doctor's hands.

"Nice evening for a winter's night," Desiree opens.

"Perfect. I love this cemetery. The road below us is Old Gold Lake Road. The faint sounds we hear come from Gold Lake Road, which is cut into the mountainside above us. We are quite secluded here."

"Rather eerie, if you ask me Silvia. I guess you're used to it?"

"Oh yes, quite used to it. There is an otherworldly dimension here, but no sinister or evil undertones. Sitting in the wilderness somehow completes my existence. There is nothing to fear in a cemetery. You weren't scared, when you were here with Alma, were you?"

"I had no sense of fear being here with Alma. Matter of fact, the evening was fascinating, exhilarating."

"Alma is what I like to call a beast-queller. There seems to be nothing to fear within a fifty-foot radius of that woman," Silvia agrees.

"Based on my experience, I can't argue with you. Has she always been that way?"

"Ever since I've known her, she's always had an allure about her."

"Now, you're making her sound like an enchantress."

"It's beyond me," admits Silvia.

"So, the girls have been talking about me?" Desiree comments.

"Yes, the girls have been talking about you. How does that make you feel?"

"I expect women to check out the new girl in town. On the other hand, I am ever vigilant. I can't escape past experience, where women seem to be threatened by me and tried to eliminate the competition."

"Did you feel that way about Alma?"

"No."

"And, what did you feel about me?" Silvia says getting to the point of the meeting.

"Hostility?"

"Not at first, but later, I was confrontational."

"Because I avoided answering your questions directly?" Desiree says knowingly.

"Yes, because you ignored my questions and turned new questions back at me."

"That irked you?" Desiree says identifying with Silvia the best she can.

"Yes, game-playing annoys me."

"You are not the first person to tell me that. I know I danced around. I realize it is annoying. But, like I told Alma, it takes time for me to trust people."

"Trusting people a little bit doesn't mean you have to spill your guts to them. Or, in your case does it? Are you hiding a deep dark mystery inside you? Trust me, Desiree, you have nothing to fear from me."

"Of course, with Alma, Florence, you, and the rest of the Sisterhood sharing information about me."

Desiree fears her life is being split open like a watermelon and shared with the whole town. This is exactly what she's run away from her whole life. What a nightmare!

"I don't know if you can believe me, but Alma has never discussed anything with me or the Sisterhood about what you two have discussed. Alma doesn't show and tell. She holds sacred the trust of those confiding in her."

"I kind of sensed that, but it's all new to me."

Silvia does not say a word and stays attentive.

Desiree takes a step of faith, "Okay Silvia, we all have deep dark secrets. Mine is at one time I was married to Jeremy Paxton."

Silvia does not look surprised or show emotions of any kind. She appears empathetic and attentively listens to Desiree's story unfold.

"He was my husband, until he got mixed up with the wrong people. When I read he had passed away in the Sierra's, I wanted to be with him. By chance, the teaching position fell in my lap and everything else simply fell in place, when I arrived."

"People say your ex is or was dealing drugs." Silvia honestly discloses.

"I've heard the rumor about Jeremy's drug trafficking. He is no more a major drug dealer than you or me, Silvia. He never used or sold the hard stuff and only sold marijuana to friends, and then only when they hounded him. Two years ago, he stopped using and selling marijuana."

"I know his death was an accident," Silvia interjects, "I was the attending physician and thoroughly examined your former husband. Toxicology came back without a trace of narcotics of any kind. Jeremy's blood was as pure as spring water."

Desiree acknowledges. "I know. He had turned his life around before leaving Boston and was committed to living a more simple, healthy life— one close to nature. That's why he fell in love with the farmer's market he opened and operated."

"You and Conrad were hitting it off rather well." Silvia moves to the next subject on her agenda.

"Actually yes. I like Conrad. But, you see I still have feelings for my ex-husband even though we did not match up well. I was more than a few years older than Jeremy. I was more of a mother or older sister to him. Now Conrad, that's a different story," Desiree confides.

"Now, here's my deep dark secret," Silvia admits, "Conrad and I were an item at one time."

"Lovers?"

"Yes."

"And now?"

"He's all yours, if you want him, and with my blessings."

"What's wrong with him?"

"Nothing. He's a fine catch, but I'm married to my profession."

"Thank you. I think I will take advantage of the opportunity. Let's get back to this networking among the women in this town. What's going on?"

"Alma, Florence, I, and most of the women in this town are part of the Sisterhood."

"What's that, a women's club?"

Silvia laughs, "Oh where do I begin? Let's just say the Sisterhood is a group of women committed to making themselves and the town the best it can be."

"A service club, like the Soroptimists?"

"I can see the similarity, but no, the Sisterhood is not like the Soroptimists. It's a much more deeply grounded group Spiritual at its core. There will be more time to get into the Sisterhood later. Besides, you are living with the heart and soul of the Sisterhood, Alma. And I work with Alma's equal Florence," Silvia responds.

Desiree agrees, "I've only been in Abbeville for two days and it seems like I've lived here a lifetime, everything is spinning past me so fast. I haven't had time to adjust to all the changes. I need time to settle in and analyze the situation. Do you know where Jeremy is buried?"

Silvia rises to her feet, takes a large flashlight out of her bag and leads Desiree to the plot where Jeremy is laid to rest. Desiree sits on the cold ground besides the marker and remains rooted on the spot for some time before standing.

"You are a very kind soul, Silvia."

"I can be. I've seen a lot of life and death in this town and elsewhere. Given the circumstances I understand your wanting to keep things to yourself. I'm privileged that you've begun to trust me, Desiree. We've come a long way."

"I think so too."

They walk to the back of the mausoleum and sit for a while.

"I feel I could talk with you for hours, Silvia. I don't especially feel the need to talk, but having you here is comforting. Being with you in the wilderness somehow dispels the unfairness I feel about Jeremy's death and all. I haven't quite figured out exactly what's going on yet? Do you know?"

"It's complicated. The gossip mill, the Sisterhood, and the happenings at Damascus Church are part of a grand plan, a design that is still unclear to me. So, let's wait on the answers to your questions."

"Oh no," Desiree insists, "what's going on? I've been straight with you haven't I?"

"Yes, you've been straight with me."

"Well, go on, Silvia."

"Do you believe there is anything beyond this world?"

"Don't tell me you are one of those Jesus Freaks?"

Silvia laughs.

"Not exactly a Jesus freak, but there's a lot that goes on around here that's beyond me."

"Go on."

"Do you know anything about mysticism?"

"Oh no, you're not a member of a wacko cult are you?"

"We are very much alike, you and I, very practical, very much the realist. No wacko cults, but I can't scientifically or rationally explain everything I see and experience around here either."

"Now you have my curiosity aroused. What exactly are you talking about?"

It's Preston on the ropes now. How can she accurately explain the workings of the Sisterhood to someone who may have never had a moment of spiritual ecstasy?

Desiree pushes further, "A little while ago, you told me that being alone here in the wilderness somehow completes your existence. What did you exactly mean by that?"

"I can't exactly explain that very well either. It's a feeling I have."

"You're not making a pass at me, are you?"

"No more than you're making a pass at me, Desiree."

"Well that's good to know. Then, what is it?"

"How do you feel being around Alma?" asks Silvia.

"Interesting question. Like I said, There's an absence of fear. Peacefulness, I suppose."

"There are a lot of women in Abbeville that follow a peaceful path. They are called the Sisterhood."

"I see, but I don't see."

"In time you will not only see, you will know all there is to know."

"Oh no. You can't leave me without being more specific than that. Please go on."

"I am a scientist, so my explanation is grounded in what I consider to be the real world. Anything beyond my abilities to test and understand, I find hard to swallow. However, it's a biological fact that women are connected by their biochemistry, hormonal secretions, if you will. We are connected in ways men can't imagine."

"Our hormonal secretions tie us together? Just how does that work?"

"Our hormonal secretions connect us in ways only understood by women. Until a better explanation comes around, that's about it." Silvia restates her case.

"Let's see if I have this right? We are not talking metaphysics. We are talking about biology and hormonal secretions? And that's why most of the women in Abbeville are Soroptimists?"

Silvia gives a short chuckle before giving it another try.

"From my perspective, we are talking about the biological differences between the males and females of our species, which lead to the different ways males relate to males and females relate to females. That's why males and females view the world differently."

"Yea but what's your point?"

"That's how we are created. It's fascinating that so much is determined by whether one has an "x" chromosome or not."

"Interesting, yes, but so what?" Desiree pushes.

"In Abbeville, most of the women know they are the glue that keeps their families together and are the glue that keeps this town together. They are the glue that has the potential to keep cultures and our species together to ensure the survival of our species. Historically, the warrior-hunter class—the males—have been the leaders, which has served us not so well to a point."

Desiree asks, "The Sisterhood is a feminist group?"

"Absolutely not. The Sisterhood is not trying to upset the balance of nature. We need the warrior-hunters, but we need them to stop killing our species and battle against war, plague, starvation, and death through science and technological innovations. This is the new battlefield for men. Women are biologically better suited to lead, collaborate, and problem-solve in non-violent ways, which sustains the survival of our species. The fact that there is a Sisterhood does not in any way diminish the importance of the males in our species."

"I'm sure that will bring some relief to most of the men I know. One question though. How did women allow the leadership of our species to fall into the hands of the men in the first place?"

"Men hit harder!" Silvia explains, "But, in the long run, physical threat and violence cannot defeat the nurturing power of women, especially as more women get into world politics and exercise their rights to vote."

"Good point," Desiree concedes, "Are Alma and Florence in agreement with your views?"

"This is my view as a physician and a woman who sees things realistically. Alma and Florence understand the Sisterhood from a Spiritual outlook. Spiritual outlooks are different than scientific outlooks. But I believe we are describing the same event from different perspectives."

Desiree restates her understanding, "The Sisterhood is on a mission to reset human evolution."

"That captures my thinking exactly. The Sisterhood is about changing the course of human evolution by changing our behaviors so men will get the picture over time—the same way an orthodontist gradually tightens braces to straighten out teeth."

"The Sisterhood is the pool of orthodontists that gradually change the behaviors of men, which somehow improves the human gene pool."

"Exactly. We hope to give our genetic material a booster shot to keep pace with the rapid technological and scientific changes happening. I'd hate to see our species extinguish itself any faster than it's doing."

"Extinction! The Sisterhood is trying to save humankind from extinction?" Desiree concludes.

"Yes that's my take on things, but I could be wrong."

"You said the Sisterhood includes women, but not all women?"

We are all flawed, some more than others. Not all women are created equal. Not all women are raised in healthy environments. Not all women make good choices in their lives that ready them for the Sisterhood. There are societal overlays that extinguish some women's natural biological instincts. Many women try to become dominant in the ways nature evolved men to be."

"Like the early feminist movement in the United States."

"Exactly," Silvia affirms, "Then, there are the effects of society, which changes the natural order of things. Everything from the shape of a woman's body, the shape of her eyes, the color of her hair, and the way she thinks. When procreation and motherhood play second fiddle to the whims of market advertising, business, and Wall Street, the natural order of their biology goes out the window. Women of the Sisterhood are more in tune with what nature intended."

Desiree comments, "Yes, I've noticed women like Alma, Florence and Shanice do share certain common characteristics. They seem to be shaped by the ideal of a womanhood, rather than be shaped by market forces, advertising, public opinion or religion."

"That's an excellent observation. Women in the Sisterhood do strive to live according to a high moral code. They are known by what some call fruits of the spirit."

"Fruits of the spirit?"

"They are known by their love of humanity, joy of living, peacefulness, longsuffering. They are kind and good and gentle and faithful and exercise self-control."

"Alma is all of that." Desiree observes.

"So is Florence, Shanice, Ellen, and so was Anne Dean." Silvia adds.

"Anne Dean?"

"Yes. Anne Dean was the secretary at Damascus Church who died of a heart attack in January. You would have liked her."

Desiree follows up, "And you, Silvia, are you are also known by the fruits of the spirit?"

"I'm working on it. That's why I'm here with you, making amends for being so harsh the other night. I was hardly an example of self-control, kindness or gentleness; the way I treated you."

"You're striving to be more kind, gentle and in-control by making amends with me?"

"Yes I'm striving. In all honesty, I am not yet truly part of the core of the Sisterhood."

"I think some day you'll get there, Silvia."

"Kind of you to say so. Someday, I think I will come to understand the shadows and the Sisterhood, as well as Alma and Florence. But being one that believes only what she can observe and prove, it's an up-hill battle."

"I'm really out of my depth on this one, Silvia. I'm a novice at all this." Desiree confesses.

"Here's my observation that you might want to tuck in the back of your mind. Except for Alma, Florence, Shanice, and Ellen, all of the women exhibiting the full measure of spiritual gifts have passed on. The rest of us are in the state of becoming."

"I will keep that in mind for sure. But what about the rest of us down here on the ground?"

"My guess is we are all in a state of becoming, learning how to control our impulses and be truly kind and patient.

Desiree keeps Silvia's observation in mind and mingles Silvia's thoughts with pieces of the mystery Alma's given her. None of the Whitman women are buried in the family mausoleum. She sits for a long while without speaking. She mentally replays every word Silvia spoke. It makes eminent sense to her. Still, there is a lot to digest, much to understand, and tonight is not going to be the night everything falls into place.

"Silvia, you're making a lot of sense. This is all so new to me. Coupled with all the changes I've been through, I need time to get my bearings."

"Yes, you have been through a lot. You're still probably grieving the loss of Jeremy. You must feel free to allow yourself the time to recover from the shock of your loss. You know Alma and I will be here for you. You will be working with Shanice. When you are better acquainted with Florence, I know you will have another ally."

"I feel much better. When we first met you scared the hell out of me. You saw the screen I set in front of me and sliced straight through it to the bone. I wasn't ready for that. You are formidable."

"Yes formidable, but I was wrong. I felt you were one of the damaged women of the world and wouldn't have the slightest notion of what the Sisterhood was, even if it ran over you like a Mac truck. I was wrong, I'm sorry I misread and misjudged you."

"I wasn't much help to you, exercising my arts of deception the way I did. I understand your apprehension. Thanks for the second chance and the vote of confidence."

"You are sincerely welcome. We will have other times to talk."

Silvia's flashlight beam bounces along the ground, as the two women walk back to town along Cemetery Road to the top of Matthew Drive. Silvia gives Desiree her flashlight and says goodnight. They hug again. Silvia walks a well-lighted 10th Street to her home in Abbeville Estates. Desiree continues up Switchback Road and turns on the narrow unlighted gravel drive to Whitman's cabin. With each step, Desiree gradually loses her edge as an animal of superiority.

Sierra nights present a soundless world of things living in the darkness. Desiree's sharp daytime vision is no longer of any use. Nightfall in the Sierras causes one to lose orientation. Only the sound of gravel crunching beneath her feet gives evidence of human existence. Solitary human existence without the sound of another human makes Desiree feels most vulnerable.

Ever so often she stops and listens, but the deep quiet of the forest engulfs her. She flashes her light in the grasses along the trail, in the trees, and into the forest. She sees only the momentary retinal reflections of animals. Shining her light down the road the flashlight beam ends at a point beyond which an impenetrable blackness continues.

Desiree's heart is pounding almost out of her chest. Within the soundless dark, she is alone, as if lost in the mouth of a great beast.

"Oh, if only Alma was here to quell the beasts," she thinks.

More flashing her light around only excites her imagination, mounting anxiety. Her breathing becomes more rapid and shallow, but she keeps on trudging. The sight of cabin lights gives her a glimmer of hope, but she feels at any moment she could be snatched and devoured without leaving a trace of her body and soul.

When Desiree at last arrives at the top step of the cabin she finds Alma standing on the deck, looking at the Buttes bathed in moonlight. Instantly Desiree's forest madness vanishes.

Alma comments, " You know about the Sisterhood?"

Desiree responds with a smile, "Silvia says it's like joining the Soroptimists."

Desiree bids Alma good night and goes to her room. Amused, Alma remains on the deck before retiring.

Book Four

❧

Fall from Grace

Chapter 1

❧

F*riday, April 15, 6:00 a.m.:* Reverend Henry Johnston spends three hours researching material for his Sunday morning sermon. He'll spend two hours writing before reading his sermon into his hallway mirror. Driven by his passions, lost in the excitement, hours pass like seconds. Saturday, he puts the finishing touches on his Sunday sermon. As always, Reverend Johnston's three Damascus Church services will fill to capacity. His sermons are, by far, the best show in town, interesting and entertaining. He reveals the life and teachings of Jesus clearly, in down to earth ways that allow people to easily apply the Christ's teachings to their lives.

He is a teacher, not a preacher. Reverend Henry does not spoon-feed his congregation church dogma. He wants Christians to think critically, test what is given from the pulpit, and above all, make their own decisions about what they believe and how they are going to put what they believe into practice. His thirty-seven years on earth have taught Reverend Henry there are many valid interpretations of Scripture giving rise to many valid ways of believing. His openness gets him in trouble from time to time with his congregation and his Council of Elders. But, Reverend Henry continues to be intellectually honest, as well as faithful to the Word of God.

In high school Henry was an excellent student, quiet, a loner. When he attended church, he was filled with the Holy Spirit, adrenaline coursing through his arteries and veins. Wednesday night prayer meetings and Sunday morning services fired him up; he felt alive. As a teenager ignited by his passion for the Lord, Henry Johnston knew his calling was the ministry. Admitted to Cornell University, Henry earned his undergraduate degree in the classics, followed by his graduate degree in religious studies from Stanford. His doctorate of divinity degree was earned at Cambridge University, where tradition places the Doctor of Divinity above the Doctor of Laws and Medicine. Boasting over one hundred fifty Nobel Prize winners, Henry walked where Milton, Wordsworth, Byron, Tennyson, Newton, Harvey, Cromwell, Darwin, Bertrand Russell, Jane Goodall, and Stephen Hawking walked. So how did the Reverend Henry Johnston manage to land in Abbeville? Blind chance? No, Reverend Henry believed like Tennyson that "nothing walks with aimless feet, that not one life shall be destroyed, or cast as rubbish to the void, when God has made the pile complete." Reverend Henry believed he was destined for Abbeville, as God ordained it to be before the beginning of creation.

Sunday, April 17, 6:00 a.m.: Easter Sunday morning, Reverend Henry readies himself for the first service, which begins at nine o'clock. Walking across the parking lot he stops to muse on the message he has placed on the electronic billboard in front of the church, *Christ Is Risen! What In The World's Come Over You?* Henry thinks, "The old song title says it all," he thinks, "Indeed, what in this world will come over us?"

In this Easter morning's keystone sermon, he will again draws the battle line between opposing groups—those who believe Jesus is the risen God that created the universe and holds salvation out to humankind; and, those who believe random chance created the universe and human salvation is in the hands of humankind. Everything needs to be exact for his daring half-hour sermon on Intelligent Design, the Christian's ultimate weapon against godless science.

Reverend Henry plans forty-five minute breaks between services, allowing his congregation to reflect on his words and socialize over coffee and donuts. During breaks, he mingles among the faithful, answering questions, while assessing their responses. To personalize and add humor to his oration, Reverend Henry often quotes members of his flock in subsequent sermons. His final service is fully polished, his words, body language and humor exceptional, his timing perfect.

Nine o'clock rolls around quickly this Easter morning. After half an hour of inspirational music, melodious prayers to God, Reverend Henry takes the pulpit.

"Today we celebrate the miracle of our faith. *Christ is Risen!* And all of God's people said?"

"Amen," responds Reverend Henry's congregation, right on cue.

"In the 18th century, the influence of philosophy and science increased and belief in God through Jesus Christ diminished. The French, Haitian, and American revolutions had liberated the human spirit from the tyranny of government and religion. The Age of Enlightenment that was born in France and spread through Haiti and the United States of America is alive today and sets itself against the people of God. It's proponents—godless scientists, secular humanists, and naturalists—dream about a world without the influence of Christianity. The Age of Enlightenment places the will of humans above the will God. *What In The World's Come Over You?* The answer is worldly arrogance has come over us—arrogance, not seen since God banished Lucifer from heaven, tossing him into the bottomless pit. God will not let the blasphemy of this generation's arrogance stand for long either."

Many in the congregation nod in accord with Reverend Henry's words, as others shout "Amen" to the truth they believe Reverend Henry speaks.

"As many of you know, Charles Darwin was a classmate of mine."

A burst of appropriately measured laughter breaks out from the congregation.

"As an early pioneer, I respect the contributions Darwin made to the field of evolutionary biology. To this day, many of his evolutionary principles have stood the test of time exceptionally well. That an animal descends from common forerunners, that only the fit survive, and that animal biology gradually changes over time to flourish in select environmental nooks and crannies are viable biological concepts. But Darwinian theory as a whole is suspect."

As the reverend pauses for his words to sink deeply, a smattering of throat clearing and a mild cough or two is heard from the congregation. The affable mood of the people begins to tighten. Acknowledging anything positive about Darwin is a red flag that enrages the faithful.

"It is true that Darwin did believe human descended from primates and that intermediate primate-human species should be evident. To date, at least thirty examples of these so called 'missing links' have been discovered, which arguably support his evolutionary notion. But, it is also true that many in the modern scientific community have re-evaluated the physical and biological facts and developed a new scientific theory, which states the universe and everything in it was created by intelligent design. Now, Christians have a scientific theory about the creation of the universe that places God in the center of creation, in the center of humankind."

Henry musters another pause for his listeners to process and evaluate the information given them. Some in the congregation appear to have moved from mere throat-clearing behavior to outright squirming in their seats. Hearing that godless Darwinian evolution is competitive with the Bible and its teachings does not sit well with most of the assembled. What do evolution or ID have to do with what the Bible says happened on Easter?

"I understand many of you are anxious for me to drop the hammer on Darwin."

A smaller, strained break of laughter emanates from the congregation.

"Fair is fair. Charles Darwin first conceived his theory of evolution two hundred years ago, when the theory of spontaneous generation prevailed in the scientific community. Spontaneous generation theory held life simply popped out of balls of mud dredged from the bottom of the sea, a theory Darwin rejected, favoring his actual observations of nature, which indicated life slowly develops over time and changes over time to adapt to its immediate surroundings."

Henry's congregation is familiar with riding the emotional waves Reverend Henry makes in his sermons. As far as most of Reverend Henry's congregation is concerned, the reverend has crashed and burned this Easter.

"Science has advanced dramatically since Darwin's time. Today's science renders Darwinian evolutionary theory obsolete. That's progress."

Instantly, part of the congregation that was tightening cautiously begins to relax, while those relaxed begin to tighten. For the conservative Christians, Reverend Henry has committed the unforgivable sin, for which they will give him no redemption.

"With the advances of modern science and technology, there is a better answer. Today, more and more microbiologists and geneticists agree with biophysicist Dean Kenyon: 'with the new scientific knowledge, we have a clear picture of the immense submicroscopic complexity of even the simplest of cells. No longer is it a reasonable scientific proposition to think that a simple chemical event could have any chance at all to generate the kind of complexity that we see in the very simplest living organism, so we have not the slightest chance of a chemical evolutionary origin for even the simplest of cells.'"

A smattering of coughs and throat clearing runs through the congregation.

"Dr. Kenyon received his Ph.D. in biophysics from Stanford, was a research scientist at Ames Research Center and a professor of biology at San Francisco State University, had theoretically described the causal chain of life from the elements existing in warm seas on early earth to types of monomers that self-assembled themselves into living cells, which eventually developed all life on this planet. After further study, this eminent scientist changed his mind. Yes, he denounced his own theory! And, from that point forward taught Intelligent Design Theory in his classes at San Francisco State University, for ten years. Currently, he is a Fellow at the Discovery Institute, a non-profit public policy think tank that advocates Intelligent Design."

Except for the conservative element in his congregation, Reverend Henry has the congregation's full attention. They are amazed to find credible scientists challenging modern theories of biological evolution on scientific turf.

"God created humans and breathed life into their immortal souls. Through Christ's death and resurrection, we celebrate the complexity of the human body and soul, which could have only come from the mind of God, the super intelligent designer, not from the chance product of primordial soup."

Reverend Henry again pauses, as many of the congregation's heads nod affirmatively.

"At the end of this month, in the most beautiful conference setting you will find in this world—the Lookout Tower Conference Center is perched eight thousand ninety feet high in the Northern Sierra Buttes—the Damascus Church Men's Retreat offers you the opportunity to delve deeper into the core principles of Intelligent Design. Sign-up for the Men's Conference before you leave church today and be with us at the Lookout Tower Conference Center, April 29 through May 1.

Christ is Risen! May God bless you and keep you this Easter day."

The congregation remains seated until Reverend Henry comes down from the pulpit and walks to the front center of the church, as is his custom.

Dr. Preston is the first to come forward and compliment Reverend Henry on his sermon. She offers to continue her services as the retreat's doctor, as she has done for the past several years. She will be the only female at the retreat and always gives the men a run for their money in small group discussions. Reverend Henry thanks Silvia for her kind words and enthusiastically accepts her offer.

Outside the church there's a big commotion. People gathering around someone like a rock star draw Reverend Henry outside the church. The crowd parts for him, as he moves to the hub of the action and sees a very healthy Ellen Jackson standing, accepting admiration from the congregation.

"Ellen!" Reverend Henry calls out, "You look wonderful, you're fully recovered, thank God."

"Reverend Henry, I feel better than I have for years. I'm going back to work next Tuesday."

"Praise God Ellen, you are back with us. Whenever you feel better let's meet over a cup of coffee at the bakery some morning?"

"I would like that reverend. Would Tuesday morning be too soon?"

"Perfect. How about meeting at Knead-2-Feed about seven o'clock?"

"That's a date reverend! See you then."

As Reverend Henry leaves through the rally for Ellen, people close ranks and continue swarming Ellen as if she came back from the dead. The women of Abbeville are so excited, they clamor around her to make hair appointments for Tuesday.

Reverend Henry continues to greet and talk with the last members of the congregation. Many lingered to shake his hand and positively comment on his sermon. In the back of his mind, Reverend Henry ruminates on Ellen using the word "date." He fears the rumor mill will stoke the fires about his date with Ellen. His fears are answered. The word on the street Monday morning is the Reverend and Ellen are dating behind Mo Jackson's back and with Anne Dean barely resting in her grave. Today, however, Reverend Henry earns an A+ on his report card from most of his followers and enthusiasm for the Damascus Retreat is stellar. He almost feels back to his old form—confident in his understanding of the Word of God and esteemed by the community. But, somehow he fears the ground he regains will slip away. He remembers how his popularity plummeted, when those ridiculous rumors about Anne Dean almost brought his house of worship down.

Re-entering the church he thinks, "All these negative thoughts come from a place I don't want to go. Get thee behind me Satan!"

He walks to the front of the church and sits in the first pew and petitions God.

Trying to reign in his crazy thoughts, Henry prays, "God give me the wings of an eagle to sore high close to thee."

Reverend Henry struggles with his pride and daring. This is not the first time he prays to God for the wings of an eagle, only to fly toward the sun, have his wings melt apart and he falls into the sea. Like the children of Israel, Henry is continually lifted by God's grace and mercy, only to be dragged down by his arrogance, pride, and selfishness. Will Henry ever tire of being salvaged by God?

As the last car pulls away from the church parking lot, Reverend Henry gathers himself and rings the church bell, alerting Edgar to set the chessboard for their Sunday afternoon match and praying for Alma to prepare one of her mouthwatering leftovers for lunch.

As usual, the lunch is delicious. The one thing Henry is sure about is the friendship of Edgar and Alma. Then, why does he feel pulled away from God? Questions flood his mind, and he loses three chess games in a row, which is unusual.

"Henry, your mind doesn't seem to be on the game today."

Reverend Henry hesitates to tell Edgar, but Edgar is persistent and Henry delves into his feelings.

"I feel the presence of evil in this house. I feel separated from God."

"Oh?" Edgar says. "We've played enough chess today. Do you want to tell me more about what you're feeling?"

"I'd like that." Henry says feeling less intense.

Indeed, what in the world's come over Henry? Edgar is not offended by his friend's comments. He understands human nature and generally understands the dynamics of why people project their fears and anxieties on objects and others.

"Henry, I believe you do feel evil in this house. Why do you feel evil resides here?"

"You think all this is in my head?"

Henry pauses to draw Edgar into an argument, but Edgar waits him out.

"The more I think about it," Henry continues, "Maybe so. Today, I launched a brilliant sermon. I wish you were there to hear it Edgar. But, after seeing Ellen Jackson at the church, I was unnerved for some reason."

Edgar listens attentively.

Maybe I'm afraid the rumor mill will start again with greater furor than ever. Remember when I nailed Fredrika and her friends from the pulpit two times? Fredrika hasn't been to church since. "

"That bothers you," Edgar responds.

"I shouldn't have done that, Edgar. It was wrong of me to strike out in my anger against those who gossip. I cast stones at these people. It's not my place to judge others, it's God who makes those kind of judgments."

"Henry, we've been over this many times and it's still with you. If you can't let go of your negative feelings, you give those past rumors legs to run on."

"Yea, my fear has legs alright and it's running around in my stomach."

"I've known you for a long time, Henry, and I've always been a good friend to you."

"Yes, you have, Edgar, and I deeply appreciate your friendship."

"Let me be honest with you. It's only been three months ago, when you were despondent and came to me for help. Remember what Bruce said to us during dinner?"

"He said that he understands me better than I do myself and if Anne Dean was alive she'd be telling me to stop feeling sorry for myself."

"Yes, and you said Anne would never allow you to wallow in self pity."

"I remember."

"Do you see any patterns?

"What do you mean, Henry?"

I say this as a friend, Henry. Since January, your mood swings have seemed to intensify. You swing from euphoria to depression and from supreme self-confidence to self-deprecation. Three months ago you were full of anxiety and self-doubt over rumors being spread about you and Anne Dean. Alma's dinner was a Godsend for you that set you back on track. This morning, you feel at the top of your game because you delivered a great Easter Sunday sermon; this afternoon you're berating yourself for being judgmental and feel this house is full of evil."

"I've been like that my whole life, Edgar. That's just the way I am. I sin and ask forgiveness and get back on track."

"I see. Henry, whatever it is you are doing, it's not working. Most people do emotional flip-flops in the same day, every few weeks, every few months, or every few years without something being seriously the matter. You have many unresolved issues, Henry, that you can't overcome by doing what you've been doing."

Reverend Henry sits quietly, replaying Edgar's words through his mind. He is convinced he is okay and is being tormented by Satan because he is a man of God. Not for one moment does Henry think his problems are due to unresolved matters. He is normal, God-fearing and not delusional or paranoid. The voices he hears are real. Satan is real and goes about this world stealing souls away from God's hands.

"You are my best friend, Henry. I hear what you are saying. I know what this looks like from the outside. What you are observing is the battle going on between the Devil and God over my soul. It may look crazy to you, but the spiritual battle that rages inside me is real."

"Okay. This may not be my place to say anything Henry, but what does the Bible say to someone feeling the way you do? Or, to put it another way, what advice would you give a parishioner who feels the way you feel?"

Henry's response is rapid, "Go to that person and confess your wrongs, ask for forgiveness and pray to God to help turn from your sinful behavior."

Alma comes into the room to see if her boys want some refreshments. She recognizes the sensitivity of the moment.

"Gentlemen, do you want some tea or lemonade?"

Henry leans back in his chair, scratching his out stretched arm.

"I think lemonade will do me fine, Alma."

Edgar says, "Me too Sis."

"Lemonade it is."

Alma exits the room to make the lemonade, leaving Henry and Edgar time to finish business.

"Henry, you believe you sinned when you singled out Fredrika and her friends from the pulpit. You know, everyone to whom you confess your wrong doings like Fredrika and Bunny may not have a forgiving spirit."

"Scripture is clear about what I need to do; and, God's forgiveness does not rest on whether Fredrika or Bunny forgives me or not. When I honestly confess my sins and ask for forgiveness with a sincere heart, the monkey jumps from my back onto the backs of Fredrika and Bunny."

"That Bible is full of good stuff, isn't it Henry?"

"Absolutely and it appears to me that you know more about Scripture than you've let on to me in the past, Edgar."

"Alma used to read the Bible to me when we were kids. It made a lot of sense to me then; and, it still makes good sense now."

Reverend Henry receives a bit of a revelation from Edgar's comments. Alma read the Bible to Edgar! That's food for thought.

"Here you go boys."

"You've spiced the tea with something good, Alma?"

"Henry, are you trying to peek at my secret recipes?"

"Yes."

"Ginger-cranberry-pineapple straight from the witches pot," replies Alma jokingly.

"Witches' brew!" laughing exclaims Henry, "Not bad, not bad at all. Witches' brew on Easter."

For the moment, Henry enjoys his oxymoron.

Chapter 2

❧

Monday, April 18, 10:15 a.m.: Fredrika's gossip mill cranks out the news that everyone at Damascus Church is not happy with Reverend Henry's sermon. The reverend's Easter message was more about his friend, Charles Darwin, than it was about Jesus Christ! Like Darwin, Henry started out a Christian; they both went to divinity school at Cambridge; and they both lost their religion because they believe more in scientific discovery than in Christ. Along with the new whispers about Henry's blasphemy from the pulpit, Fredrika, Bunny and Edna mix remind the good people of the affair Reverend Henry had with his beautiful church secretary, Anne Dean and Mo Jackson's wife, Ellen.

Faced with this new barrage of falsehoods, Reverend Henry makes his way to his first stop to make amends and ask forgiveness. He has rededicated himself to the Word of God and is impervious to the arrows shot to bring him down.

Fredrika opens her door, "Reverend Henry, you are the last person in the world I expected to come knocking on my door!"

"I know. May I come in?"

"Yes, Reverend Henry, come right in."

"It's been a long time since I've been here, Fredrika. I shouldn't have stopped making home visits. As church attendance grew home visits were pushed aside. I intend to correct my error and have decided to make you my first call."

"The last time you were here, Reverend Henry, was when my husband passed away three years ago. Do you want a cup of tea?"

"That's very kind of you, yes please."

Henry is directed to sit in the big overstuffed chair that faces the window. He waits patiently with his fingers in a steeple position, his elbows on the armrests, and his thumbs resting on his chest. Fredrika returns and gives him a cup of tea in a blue flowered China cup on a matching saucer. She sits in the chair across from him.

"Tell me Reverend, what is the nature of your business?"

"I'm here to confess to you that I was wrong to call your name out from the pulpit. I was wrong, singling you and others out in public. I ask your forgiveness for the hurt I caused you and will confess my sin to the congregation at next Sunday's service."

"Well, I should say so reverend. You certainly acted foolishly and greatly embarrassed me in front of the community. I must say I do not have forgiveness in my heart to give to you today. It will take time for me to consider whether you mean what you say. I don't know."

After Fredrika's response, Reverend Henry sips tea.

"I understand completely, Fredrika. I know my being here after so many years is a shock. Please take the time you need before letting me know your decision."

"Is it your intent, reverend, to say the same thing to Bunny, Edna, Holly, and Jenny?"

"Yes Fredrika, I intend to speak to all those I have wronged with my accusations. I will also talk with Joyce Lawrence, whom I offended along several others I mentioned at a previous church service."

"I remember that dreadful sermon too, reverend. I certainly hope you make things right to all of our satisfaction."

"I will sincerely do my best to give you and the others full satisfaction, Fredrika."

"I certainly hope you keep your promise to apologize to the whole congregation, Reverend Henry. Is there anything else you would like to say?"

"That covers it all, Fredrika. Thank you for your kindness hearing me out and thank you for the refreshments."

Reverend Henry did keep his promise to humbly grovel at the feet of the gossipers and sincerely ask for forgiveness. Only Jenny Hobbs quickly forgives Henry that day and reverses the tables, asking Reverend Henry's forgiveness for her part in spreading rumors about Anne and him. Henry is quick to forgive Jenny. Not everyone is as forgiving as Jenny. Resentment against Henry continues to build, as the gossip mill efficiently grinds truth into lies as efficiently as ever.

Tuesday, April 19, 6:00 a.m.: For the first time in a long while, Henry wakes happy and eager to meet whatever comes his way. Confessing his sins in public has cleared his troubled mind and simplified his life. Simply doing what he believes the Lord is directing him to do becomes his purpose from morning to night. He dresses and after his morning prayers, Reverend Henry arrives early at the Knead-2-Feed Bakery for his meeting with Ellen Jackson. He pays Stella May in advance for whatever Ellen may want for breakfast. A minute after seven o'clock, Ellen walks up to the bakery counter and is surprised.

"Thank you reverend. I'm planning to have breakfast on you several times a week from here on out," she jokes.

"That sounds like a plan to me, so long as you start tripling your church offering each Sunday," Reverend Henry replies.

Each begins to drink their beverage and take bites from the delicious fresh baked pastries they selected from the display case.

"What are we here to talk about Ellen?" inquires Henry.

"Dr. Preston and Florence nursed me back to health from the edge of death. My recovery moved wonderfully in the right direction thanks to your visits and words of encouragement. I wanted to have the opportunity to personally thank you for the care and support you've shown to Mo and me, during our ordeal."

"That is good to hear, Ellen. Don't discount your indomitable spirit for bringing you back, either. You listened to the Words of God we discussed. We both know it was your faith in God that brought you back."

"Yes, Mo and I are grateful to God and to you, Dr. Preston, and

Florence for being there for us. We see you as our guardian angels. God certainly used you as instruments in my renewal."

"Interesting that you should describe your miracle of life as a renewal." Reverend Henry remarks.

"I'm not the same person I was before I almost froze to death. I'm better than what I was. Mo even thinks so."

"Near death experiences sometimes have that effect, a second chance works wonders."

"Both Dr. Preston and Florence have commented how young I look. I see my face in the mirror and, if being frozen didn't almost kill me, I'd recommend it, as a beauty treatment."

"You seem to be so full of life, too. You radiate energy."

"I feel wonderful and I do beam from within. I look forward to reading Scripture every day before and after work. My near-death experience gives me a different perspective on what Scripture is telling me. Before it was all about sinning and getting out of a hole. Now, it's all about continual self-rejuvenation and doing what's right. I don't have time to be negative or feel sorry for myself. I'm just happy to be here and have a second chance at life."

"You have a wonderful story to tell. Would you be interested in giving your personal testimony at church?"

"It's an old, but good story of death, rebirth, and living a blessed life. Thank you, Henry. When I'm ready, I will take you up on your offer."

"You are welcome. You sound ready to me. Your story is God-centered and compelling."

"Yes but . . . there I go with the "buts" again. This time though it's for a good reason though. I want to finish reading the Bible from cover to cover to see if my re-interpretations of Scripture are on the right track. I would love to have you come over every week or so and lead Bible discussions for Mo, me, and other members of our church. I think our house can easily accommodate fifteen or so people."

"It was only yesterday that I said the same thing to another church member. I need to get back to making more home visitations in our community. Ellen, I think starting a Bible study at your home would be a good start."

Reverend Henry listens to Ellen speak about her personal restoration experience, which she feels illustrates Jesus' promise to give life and give life more abundantly.

"Reverend Henry, I feel renewed and others around me notice my renewal. They keep asking me what happened? What's your secret? All I know is that in those last moments before losing consciousness I prayed, as I never have prayed before, that I would be saved from death. When I woke, my prayers had been answered. I'm not the same person I was. I'm better."

Your story reminds me of an Old Testament verse, "Those who are wise will shine like the brightness of the heavens, and those who lead many to righteousness, like the stars for ever and ever."

"Kind of you to think so Henry, but it's my nature that has been changed that's doing the shining."

"You are wise to recognize God's work in your heart and mind."

Although rumors fly about Ellen and Henry's supposed affair, they are too engrossed in Ellen's story about her near-death experience and reawakening to care about the new wave of rumors. They finish their coffee klatch shortly before nine and walk out of the bakery exchanging their good-byes.

Henry has a rare unscheduled space in his calendar. His next appointment isn't until the Elder's meeting at seven o'clock in the evening. His first impulse is to return to the office and prepare for the Elder's meeting. Instead, he walks across the street and for the first time enters the Blue Goose. Henry figures it's time to rub shoulders with the town's outcasts and, like Jesus, not worry about what the Scribes and Pharisees have to say.

Henry takes the open barstool between Edgar and McWhinney Thurston.

Reverend Henry orders, "Nick my friend, I'd like a coke please."

Startled, Thurston jumps off her bar stool, knocking her drink over.

Edgar exclaims, "It's about time you visited the real people of Abbeville!"

Even Fenway seems to say, "Huh?"

"You said a coke, Father?"

"Yes Nick, a coke would be fine."

Kelly walks over with the coke and says, "There you go reverend and Nick says the drinks on him."

"What does that mean?"

"You don't have to pay, Reverend Henry."

"Oh yes I see. Thank you Kelly and thank you Nick."

"Don't mention it, Father," Nick says from behind the bar.

Edgar leans over to Henry and whispers, "I don't think Nick knows your a protestant minister, he's never seen one come into his bar, ever."

"Thanks Edgar, I get it now."

The doors to the Tavern swings open and in walk Conrad and Ranger Pat. Both freeze where they stand upon seeing Reverend Henry.

Ranger Pat says, "Faith and begorrah is this the end of the world or what! Hello Reverend Henry, what brings you to our humble abode?"

"I thought it was about time I learned how to mingle with my fellow sinners."

"Time long overdue pastor. Glad to have you aboard."

"Thank you, Pat."

"I don't believe I've had the pleasure of meeting you Reverend Henry, although our mutual friend here has told me a lot about you. My name is Conrad Corbett."

"I've heard good thinks about you Mr. Corbett, happy to met you too."

Conrad suggests the party move to a table, which everyone does, except for Thurston McWhinney who walks past the table and out the door.

McWhinney in passing by says, "I don't have time to sit around in a bar and drink like some folks. I got to get back to the campgrounds and get some work done."

McWhinney's comment brings smiles to Edgar and Conrad's faces, Reverend Henry looks puzzled. Pat looks hard at the table.

Pat says, "I think that shot may have been meant for me."

Pat's comment cracks everyone up, except for the still puzzled Henry.

The barroom discussion takes Reverend Henry places he's never been before. He finds mixing with all types of people a refreshing experience. Most importantly, Henry realizes he does not have to compromise his beliefs to be respectful and friendly with people, who do not hold the same views he has.

Every once in a while, when some comment is made that grates against his beliefs, Reverend Henry feels righteous anger rising deep from within his viscera. Like when Conrad comments that recent archaeological discoveries prove the three thousand-year-old water shaft that the Bible says was used by King David to take Jerusalem from the Jebusites, was not in use at the time David was king, Reverend Henry feels a twinge of anger and a knotting in his stomach. Although he wants to lash out in defense of the Bible, Reverend Henry recalls the advice given in the Book of James. "With your tongue we bless our Lord and Father and curse people who are made in the likeness of God! These things ought not be so. Not many of you should become teachers, my brothers, for you know that we who teach will be judged with greater strictness." He decides to hold his tongue, smile, and nod his head attentively. Henry is learning to smile and laugh a lot, which are great newfound tools he uses to keep the lid on a boiling pot. He learns how to breathe and not take himself so seriously. Reverend Henry learns how to relax and enjoy himself for a change.

The mid-day sun almost strikes Henry blind, as he walks from the darkness of the Blue Goose.

He quips, "Now I know how Paul felt when God struck him off his donkey on the way to Damascus."

Laughter explodes from the small band of men.

"You're okay," Pat says to Henry.

"Thank you," replies Henry.

Each go their way, shaking their heads and laughing as they remember pieces of the conversation they shared in the Blue Goose.

Tuesday, April 19, 6:45 p.m.: Reverend Henry is the first to enter the conference room for his meeting with the Elders. He places an agenda attached to a folder, containing all of the backup materials, on the table before each of the thirteen chairs placed around the conference table. Elder Elroy Jones is the first to arrive.

"Good, I see everything's ready. I love reading the back-up material before the meeting starts. Reverend Henry, is there a reason why we can't receive the agenda and backup materials a few days before the meeting?"

Elroy is a stickler for detail and a methodical thinker. He hates being rushed about anything.

"I'll have next month's agenda and materials sent to the elders' homes on the Monday before each meeting."

"Perfect. Thank you."

Elroy sits in his chair and goes to work reviewing the night's agenda and prepared materials.

"Good evening reverend. Elder Jones, good to see you," greets Canter Cunningham.

Elroy informs Canter, "In the future, Reverend Henry will send the agenda and meeting materials to our homes a couple of days before council meetings."

"Great, good idea."

Henry deflects the praise and gives Elroy full credit for the idea.

"Yippy-yi-yo-ki-yay gentlemen. Bronco has arrived. Let the fun begin."

Bronco Brown's entrance loosens the stodginess of any meeting. He's a welcomed sight in Henry's eyes.

"Welcome friends," Bruce Dean, the head elder of the church greets everyone, "I have bad news. Elders Jacob Richmond, Mark Correra, and Harvard Elgin called to say they couldn't make this evenings meeting and hope everyone understands."

Everyone does understand because the three men rarely miss elder council meetings and are fine, upstanding Christians, well known for their charitable work in the community. A couple of minutes before the seven, the meeting starts, as Allen Belcher, Larry Sherman, Malcolm Simmons, and Martin Lawrence enter, greet everybody, and take their seats.

Martin announces, " Robert is running a bit late, but will make it to the meeting as soon as he gets off work."

Reverend Henry counts heads and declares the eight, soon to be nine, elder quorum sufficient to start the meeting. Elder Simmons opens the meeting with a prayer asking for God's will to shine through the decisions the Council makes tonight.

Reverend Henry begins, "Here's the final draft schedule for the retreat take some time to look it over before I take it to the printers."

Henry takes ten minutes, allowing the council a chance to take a last look at the program schedule, which they have reviewed several times before.

LOOKOUT TOWER CONFERENCE CENTER
DAMASCUS CHURCH MEN'S RETREAT

Friday, April 29

8:30 -10:00 a.m.	Registration, Conference Packets and Refreshments
10:15 -11:15 a.m.	Dr. Matthew Taylor, Biochemist, University of California, Davis "Earth's Make-up at the Time of Creation" (Tower Lecture Hall)
11:30 -12:30 p.m.	Small Groups w/Matthew Taylor (Conference Rooms A-M)
12:45-2:00 p.m.	Lunch and Talk w/Dr. Corwin Plum, "Why Believe Anything?" Professor of Philosophy of Science, Cornell University
2:30- 3:30 p.m.	Mr. Samuel Jackson Cantrell, "Clear Evidence from God's Hand" Senior Curator, Stanley Museum of Natural History
3:45-4:45 p.m.	Small Groups w/Samuel Cantrell (Conference Rooms A-M)
5:45-7:00 p.m.	Dinner and Talk w/Dr. Jim Swift, "What Have Atheist's Missed?" Professor of Theology, Sam Hill University
8:00-10:00 p.m.	Discussions Around the Campfire

Saturday, April 30

8:30 -10:00 a.m.   Breakfast

10:15 -11:15 a.m.   Dr. Kenneth Wellman, Mathematics, Stanford University "Let's Do the Math!" (Tower Lecture Hall)

11:30 -12:30 p.m.   Small Groups w/Ken Wellman (Conference Rooms A-M)

12:45-2:00 p.m.   Lunch and Talk w/Dr. Nate Cummings, "Why Believe Anything?" Professor of Geological Sciences, Nebraska University

2:30- 3:30 p.m.   Dr. Gene McIntyre, "Irreducible Complexity" Professor of Microbiology, Michigan State University

3:45-4:45 p.m.   Small Groups w/Gene McIntyre (Conference Rooms A-M)

5:45-7:00 p.m.   Dinner and Talk w/Dr. Jim Swift, "Directed Natural Selection?" Professor of Microbiology, University of Virginia

8:00-10:00 p.m.   Discussions Around the Campfire

Sunday, May 1

8:30 -9:30 a.m.   Breakfast

9:40 -10:30 a.m.   Dr. Joel Stevenson, "(Tower Lecture Hall) Professor of Constitutional Law, California Liberty University

10:30-10:45   Stand Up Break

10:45 – 11:45 p.m.   Brunch and Discussion with Joel Stevenson (Tower Lecture Hall)

11:45 – 12:00 noon   Wrap-Up, "Have We Heard Enough About Bacterial Flagellum?" Dr. Ezekiel Gates, the Senior Pastor, Middleton Covenant Church

"Henry, you have done a magnificent job organizing the men's retreat. But, why is Ezekiel Gates closing the Conference and not you?" Elder Brown asks.

"I need time to re-evaluate myself. I need time to consider whether the ministry is for me or not? Having Ezekiel share pastoral responsibilities for a while will give me time to step away and reflect, pray, and meditate on God's Word."

"Sounds like you're burnt out Henry?" Elder Elroy observes.

"Maybe so. I need to take a break. You know Pastor Gates. He's a fine man. Experienced at the pulpit and someone I implicitly trust."

Elder Jacob says, "I heard you have been talking to some of our congregation about mistakes you've made. Your visitations have cause dissentions within our flock."

"I have confessed wrongs that I have committed from the pulpit by chastising members of our assembly. As Christ directs us to do when we have harmed others, I visited their homes to apologize and ask their forgiveness."

"I've received calls too, Henry," Elder Cunningham contributes.

"I intend to make a public confession and ask for forgiveness from our congregation at next Sunday's services. I have asked Ezekiel to give Sunday's sermon, so the congregation will feel they know him before the Men's Conference."

"You've done this without the approval of the council!" objects Elder Lawrence.

Dean steps in, "According to the by-laws of our church pastors have the latitude to petition the Council for a leave of absence or adjustments to his contract for personal reasons."

"He's taken action before consulting the Council! That's a slap in our faces. I won't stand for that," protests Elroy.

"When I inform each of you about Henry's intentions, I made it clear why he wants us to consider allowing his service contract to be modified to give him the personal time he requests. You all agreed. No one objected. I suggest we continue our discussion in closed personnel session," Head Elder Dean Curtis reminds the group.

"Elder Dean, that's not the point. Matters of this importance need to be brought before the council as our charter requires," insists Elder Cunningham.

"Gentlemen, one other thing," Reverend Henry injects, "I had breakfast with Ellen Jackson this morning. She said something I needed to hear. I need to get back in touch with individual members of the congregation. I'll be starting a Bible study group at Ellen's home in May. Having Ezekiel give an occasional sermon once a month or so will allow me focus on home ministry. Also, Ezekiel taking on the leadership of this year's men's retreat will give me a chance to be on equal footing with the men in our congregation at the conference. I believe God is leading me in this direction for his own purposes. I must follow."

Reverend Henry's actions stole the thunder from the Elders dissatisfaction with his performance as pastor. They wanted to call a closed personnel session to fire him. They feel cheated and suspect someone tipped him off about their plans. Reverend Henry is totally unaware of their plans to discharge him, however. His choice to follow where he believes God is leading was made after meeting with Edgar, long before hearing rumblings from the elder's council.

Robert Crane sheepishly enters saying, "Sorry for my tardiness, Reverend Henry and my apologies to my fellow elders. I hope I haven't missed anything important?"

Crane quickly takes his seat and listens attentively, as Reverend Henry continues with the agenda item on the table.

"So, how does the council feel about the conference schedule for the retreat?"

All the elders are pleased with the schedule and have no questions. They thank Reverend Henry for the hard work he has done, putting together what looks like a very fine church event. With no further agenda items to discuss, Elder Cunningham makes a request.

"In light of what Henry has told us about his need to regroup, I think we need to meet in closed session to discuss Henry's comments."

It takes a majority vote of the Council of Elders to hold a closed personnel session on a pastor, a fact that Canter Cunningham knows well. Elder Cunningham has counted eight elders present at the meeting and asks the head elder, Bruce Dean, to call for a vote. Dean calls for a motion to hold a closed personnel session.

Martin Lawrence says, "I move the Council of Elders hold a closed personnel session to discuss matters pertaining to Reverend Henry Johnston."

"Hearing the motion is there a second?" Dean proceeds.

"I second the motion," volunteers Elder Crane.

Dean continues, "All those in favor of the motion signify by saying 'Aye.'"

Most of the elders say, "Aye."

Dean runs on, "Those opposed thereto say 'Nay.'"

A weak scattering of "Nays" is heard.

Dean declares, "The motion for a closed personnel session fails."

He gavels the meeting closed. Reverend Henry looks like he's in a state of shock. He had requested the elder's council meet in private to consider his requests. But, for some reason head elder Dean is reluctant to convene the personnel session?

Lawrence stands, "Point of order Elder Dean, there were more 'Ayes' than 'Nays' cast. I would like to have roll call vote."

Dean sits and calls role.

"Elder Allen Belcher"

"Aye."

"Elder Arthur Brown."

"Nay."

"Elder Canter Cunningham."

"Aye."

"Elder Elroy Jones."

"Aye."

"Elder Larry Sherman."

"Nay."

"Elder Malcolm Simmons."

"Aye."

"Elder Martin Lawrence."

"Aye."

"Elder Robert Crane."

"Aye."

Dean concludes, "The chair counts 6-Ayes and 2-Nays. The motion fails for lack of a majority of the seven votes of the twelve council elders necessary to hold a closed personnel session. This meeting is adjourned."

Martin objects, "I differ with the interpretation of the chair. You know there are other issues relating to Reverend Henry we need to discuss in private."

Dean responds, "Your objection is noted, Elder Lawrence. Will you lead us in a closing prayer."

Lawrence knows when he's been out foxed and closes the meeting with an appropriate prayer.

On the way out, Dean whispers in Reverend Henry's ear, "Close but no cigar, and I don't think the council can muster seven votes, even if all twelve Elders were here, even if you went to the Blue Goose every day. Have a good night's sleep, Henry. Leave the church politics to me and you keep on with what you're doing. Good night."

Henry smiles at Elder Dean's comments. He waits until the last elder leaves and locks the church doors. He somberly walks to his cottage at the back of the church and turns in for the night. Lying in bed, he wonders if the twelve apostles had these kinds of problems? His answer is swift. Christ's life was full of scheming, trickery, and double-dealing. Christ was doubted, his apostles disloyal, turning their backs on him when he needed them most. Henry is no Christ and the council is not his apostleship, but the lesson is clear. Henry's decision will steer him through rougher waters from here on out. Trusting Jesus' teachings, Henry has a clear conscience, turns everything over to God, and sleeps like a log.

Wednesday, April 20, 8:00 a.m.: The gossip mill fed by disgruntled church elders spreads the news Henry is on the frying pan. Why? He's having another affair, this time with Ellen Jackson, and moreover, Reverend Henry has a drinking problem. He no longer has the moral character to be pastor of Damascus Church. The news stings Henry's ears, but he is secure in knowing the gossip is untrue. He has placed his faith in the rock of Jesus love and teachings. Henry is confident in the fact he is doing the right thing.

Sunday, April 24, 9:00 a.m.: From the pulpit Reverend Henry makes good on his promise to Fredrika and the other ladies.

"My brothers and sisters in Christ, I have a confession to make to you today and I ask for your forgiveness. Several weeks ago I wrongfully mentioned names from this pulpit and hurt members of our congregation. For this I am heartily sorry for offending God and members of this congregation, and I ask your forgiveness."

Except for Fredrika and her group, who sit up straight, basking in Henry's public humiliation, the congregation silently forgives Henry and prays for him.

"Thank you Lord Jesus," Henry praises God, "Today, I have a treat for you. I have asked my friend and colleague, Dr. Ezekiel Gates, the Senior Pastor of the Middleton Covenant Church to give today's message. I have also asked Reverend Gates to lead the Lookout Tower Men's Retreat this coming weekend. Ezekiel has graciously consented to do so and brings his pastoral staff in support of our Retreat."

The congregation is taken aback by Henry's announcement. They have heard the rumblings, but didn't expect Henry to step away from the pulpit this soon.

"Let's give a warm welcome to Reverend Dr. Ezekiel Gates."

As the congregation applauds its welcome, Henry and Ezekiel shake hands and embrace.

"Having Pastor Ezekiel here allows me to begin my home ministry in our congregation. I will be starting the first home Bible study on Tuesday, May 24. You may sign up for the Bible study in the patio kiosk after church. Thank you Pastor Gates, my friend and brother in Christ."

As Henry descends the pulpit and takes a seat in the congregation, Reverend Gates begins his sermon, "Are we the light of the world, the city on the mountain top that other's see at the first gleam of dawn? Do we shine with our testimony of Christ even brighter in the full light of day?"

Reverend Gates is an accomplished preacher and administrator and deftly weaves Jesus' words into the tight fabric needed to refashion the hearts and minds of the people in Abbeville. Reverend Henry could not have made a better choice.

Chapter 3

꩜

F*riday, April 29, 8:30 a.m.:* Lookout Tower Conference Center draws over five hundred Christian men to the retreat hosted by Abbeville's Damascus. Fired with enthusiasm, attendees listen to dynamic speakers present their scientific beliefs about intelligent design, which some refer to as ID; natural history; the origin and nature of the universe; and conservative Christian theology. The evening's pinnacle events are discussions "Around The Campfire," where those attending the conference meet and engage in conversation all of the day's speakers.

After attending different sessions throughout the morning and afternoon, Reverend Henry, Dr. Preston, Mo Jackson, and Robert Winston have decided to attend the Around The Campfire session given by the Senior Curator of the Stanley Museum of Natural History, Mr. Samuel Jackson Cantrell. His topic for the night is "Clear Evidence From the Hand of God."

"What a beautiful night under God's sky." Dr. Cantrell opens the discussion, "I love sitting around the campfire, enjoying Christian fellowship, and discussing one of my favorite topics: the hard scientific evidence supporting the theory of intelligent design. I want this to be as informal as possible and have as many of you as possible ask questions and comment on the topic. Who would like to start?"

"My name is Howard and I enjoyed your remarks immensely this morning. I would like to have you clarify one of your statements for me."

"Sure Howard."

"Have any of the hundreds of thousands of specimens at the Stanley Museum of Natural History ever been created from the elements in the seas?"

"Good question Howard. Atheist scientists have never been able to biochemically create life from chemicals in simulations of the warm seas God created. Chemicals can't assemble themselves into living things. Only God can create life, which He did in His workshop at the beginning of time. Secular scientists have no idea of how to produce life from scratch."

"Jasper Parker. But, scientists have cloned sheep and other animals in their laboratories."

"Yes, but they are only copying what God has already created."

"Tom Safer here. It all fits. Our human biological systems are too intricate to have come from simpler, primitive, or less complete animals."

"You are absolutely correct, Tom. It's unbelievable to think our human brains and body systems happened through a series of chance mutations over five billion years. Darwinian evolution is an incredibly false theory. The gentleman in the blue shirt."

"Thank you, my name is Richard Castro. Mr. Cantrell, I read where the chances of finding intelligent life evolving from a single cell over four billion years is less than 1 divided by 10 times 340 million. The only way humans could have possibly come into being is by the design of a super intelligent being, one who grasps all the complexities and is able to create a living, breathing, flesh, and blood man and woman."

"Well stated Richard. You show how ridiculous are the claims these secular scientists make about our human origins. You've studied your Bible well and know science only reaffirms what the Bible tells us."

Silvia can no longer sit on her hands. Every year she volunteers to be the attending physician at the men's retreat; and every year she jumps in their discussions, as if she was one of the guys. While some men find her presence annoying, most find her comments intelligent and her questions interesting.

"Mr. Cantrell, my name is Dr. Silvia Preston, I'm honored to be here as the conference physician. If God made all the specimens you have in the natural museum at one time at the beginning of creation, why are there so many different kinds of animals roaming in, on, and above the earth today?"

"Good to have you here Dr. Preston. We haven't found the diversity your speaking about. A spider from four hundred fifty million years ago looks like a spider today. A ten thousand year old human still looks like a human today, and a frog yesterday is still a frog today."

"How many eyes did that four hundred fifty million year old spider have?"

"Eight."

"Today we know many spiders are found with no eyes, two eyes, four eyes, six eyes, and eight eyes arranged in various and, at times, bizarre ways. What accounts for this diversity we find in the number of eyes and arrangement of eyes in spiders?"

"Those changes are superficial. A peppered moth changes color to blend in with its environment. It's still a pepper moth. You don't see a pepper moth evolving into a frog?"

"Darwinian evolutionists would agree with you, Mr. Cantrell. A moth doesn't evolve into a frog anymore than an a chimpanzee evolves into a human because what you are saying doesn't follow what the modern theory of biological evolution suggests."

"Thank you for your information, Dr. Preston. I see others wanting to join our conversation. Let's move on."

"One final statement and two more questions, then I will sit and be a good girl."

Henry leans over to Mo and whispers, "That's never going to happen!"

"Yes Mr. Cantrell, I promise."

"Here we go," Reverend Henry says under his breath.

Ignoring Henry's comment, Silvia smiles and continues, "High end estimates place the number of cells in the human body at 100 trillion, where as the total number of foreign microorganisms living in the human body are estimated at 10 x 100 trillion. Given ID scientists hold human beings haven't changed over time, how do they account for all those microorganisms? Did the Hand of God put four pounds of microscopic bugs and plants in our systems on the sixth day of creation?'"

"That's a whiz-banger of a question Dr. Preston," Mo comments.

"Interesting. I'm a curator at a museum of natural history. Your question is better asked of a professor of microbiology or parasitological. Thank you for your sharing."

"Oh my, the man cut and ran, interesting," Bob observes, "I hope we get out of here alive."

This year half of the Damascus Church Council of Elders view Dr. Preston's comments as provocative and disturbing. Reverend Henry feels her questions and the exchanges with the speaker are healthy and thought provoking. When Dr. Preston participates in discussions at men's retreats, she only sees testosterone in full bloom.

Saturday, April 30, 7:00 p.m.: Next evening, the fireworks around the campfire are even better.

Henry, Bob, Silvia, and Mo walk the path through the pole pines to join Dr. Gene McIntyre, Professor of Microbiology from Michigan State University, who is leading the discussion on "Irreducible Complexity."

After the professor welcomes the group, he calls on the first person he sees raising his hand, which happens to be Bob.

"Good evening Dr. McIntyre. I thoroughly enjoyed your presentation this morning. And, I have a question about what one of last night's speaker said about scientists not being able to create life in the laboratory."

"Thank you. And your name is?"

"Bob Winston, I am the librarian in the town of Abbeville. Yesterday, Mr. Cantrell said because secular science hasn't reproduce life in a laboratory, the theory of biological evolution is proven wrong."

"Yes, he did make that point."

"What laboratories proof do Christian scientists have that differs from proofs found in secular laboratories? Have ID scientists placed God in their labs and observed human life being formed?"

McIntyre responds, "I could say the complexity of life we examine implies an intelligent designer the magnitude of God. But I don't believe my former student sitting there would let me get away with that, would you Dr. Preston?"

Mo, Henry and Bob's heads swivel to Dr. Preston, who sits with a big smile beaming across her face. Silvia knows Dr. McIntyre from her university days. Dr. McIntyre's lectures and lab shaped her thinking and gave her the depth of understanding in microbiology she needed. Dr. Preston keeps on the cutting edge of microbiology by reading articles written by Dr. McIntyre in the Journal of Clinical Microbiology.

"To answer your question, Bob, you are spot on," McIntyre continues, "We have not observed God creating life in our laboratories. You are also right, in my opinion, about man's inability to create life not disproving modern-day theories of biological evolution. Biological evolution is, however, being scientifically challenged. The principle of *Irreducible complexity* I discussed this morning is a key concept in ID theory.

Bob presses McIntyre further, "It appears to me, Professor McIntyre, Christian and secular scientists follow different sets of rules for scientific exploration? One presumes there is a God that created nature. The other presumes God has nothing to do with nature. Why is that?"

"Whether one is a Christian or a non-Christian has nothing to do with science, which has one set of objective methodology to explore the universe. I say this with full knowledge that some of my secular and Christian colleagues unfortunately try to mix the two. The result is bad science."

"So, what are the scientific rules ID scientists play by?"

"They must play by the same scientific rules set for secular scientists. ID theory must be as clear and simple as possible; ID theory must agree with and explain all existing observations; and above all ID theory must withstand the probing of independent testing. If ID theory does not meet these standards, it is not a credible scientific theory."

"Don't most of your ID colleagues differ with you? They challenge the modern scientific methods, where theories are based on observation and measurement, some type of practical experimentation and independent verification?"

"I differ with many, but not all of my ID colleagues on this point. There are some creationists and ID theorists that believe their theories can be proven on the empirical grounds that you describe. I believe there is no need to drastically change our modern scientific methodologies that have stood so well for over two hundred years."

Bob thanks Dr. McIntyre for his honest answers. Rather than sitting down on the ground next to Henry, Mo, and Silvia, he walks over to a fallen log at the edge of the clearing to rest. Silvia observes Bob's unsteady gate. She asks Mo and Henry to keep an eye on him.

"Dr. McIntyre, I'd like to continue where Bob left off. Isn't it fair to say ID and evolutionary scientists may never discover the origin of our species? I see no incontrovertible evidence supporting either the theory of evolution or the theory of intelligent design."

"And your name is?"

"Sorry, Brannon, Al Brannon."

"While I'm optimistic that science will eventually explain what we call mysteries of life, Al, I doubt that it will be in our life time. Biology is chaos in action because of the mine-boggling numbers of various minute particles at play and the dynamics of biological interdependence at work. Our mathematical models are difficult to work out given the trillions times trillions times trillions of calculations needed to be made about biological and cosmic events."

Brandon modifies his question, "Okay. I understand that. But, certainly working with simple organisms can't be that difficult."

"Even when we come across the simplest of animals and their evolutionary changes, things get exceedingly difficult," McIntyre elucidates, "Example, specifically why and how do moths biologically change their colors to camouflage themselves in different environments? Specifically why and how do crickets biologically change their signaling acoustical systems? Specifically why and how do human genetic materials biologically change to produce cystic fibrosis, hypertension, stroke and possibly developmental delay, heart rhythm problems, and, or blindness? No one exactly knows the scientific answers to these questions."

"You're making my point, Dr. McIntyre. There is no incontrovertible evidence supporting either the theory of evolution or ID."

"You may be correct, but I take a different tact. Our history shows not knowing is only a temporary state for us humans. It wasn't that long ago scientists thought the universe was filled with aether and the Newton's laws of Motion were constant throughout the universe. Modern science is in its infancy. In time, we will figure out God's creation, as I believe God intended. Why else are we so dang curious?"

McIntyre's response sparks laughter. Still not satisfied with McIntyre's explanation, Al remains standing.

Leaning over to Dr. Preston, Henry says, "This professor of yours certainly isn't the dogmatic type of ID scientist I'm used to hearing."

"Professor McIntyre is a scientist and a believer who is comfortable keeping the two belief systems separate. He is a rare bird. He treats his opposition with kindness and respect."

Al continues to pursue what he thinks is a weakness in Dr. McIntyre's argument, "You admit your ID theory is fuzzy science!"

"Al, let's remember science begins with questions no one can answer. Our preliminary answers to these questions may be, as you say, fuzzy, but our scientific methodologies aren't fuzzy and will lead to better theories. Intelligent Design Theory is a viable scientific theory about the origins of our universe and the origins of life found in that universe. We are still in the early stages of our scientific inquiry."

Al holds on to his opinion; but Al can't find a way to pick apart the reasonableness of Dr. McIntyre's position. He thanks McIntyre for the enjoyable discussion and sits down.

"Professor McIntyre I have a question for you."

"Dr. Preston, my esteemed former student and colleague, your comments about the 10 x 100 trillion microorganisms making homes in our bodies precede you. You are the talk of the conference, you know?"

"You really know how to turn a girl's head, professor."

"Only out of self-defense, doctor. What is your question?"

"Correct me if I've misunderstood something. For a biological unit to be irreducibly complex it has to be 1) composed of several well matched, interacting parts, 2) the parts must contribute to the biological unit's basic function, and 3) the removal of any part causes the biological unit to stop working."

Professor McIntyre comments. "Yes, that's a stripped down version of Michael Behe's definition. Go on."

"Would Professor Behe hold each one of those 10 x 100 trillion microorganisms living in the cells, tissues, and organs of the human body is an example of irreducible complexity?"

"I can't speak for him, but I would guess the answer to your question is yes."

"Each of those thousand trillion microorganisms is the creation of an intelligent designer?"

"Yes."

"Then, it follows that changes produced from the interaction of the microorganisms and the humans in which they reside are also the creation of the intelligent designer?"

"I wouldn't put the question that way because it leads us away from science into philosophy and religion. I would ask two questions: 1) What are the long-term effects of symbiotic relationships among protists and microorganisms and humans on humans?" And, 2) What are the long-term effects of symbiotic relationships among protists and microorganisms and humans on protists and microorganisms?"

"Good scientific questions, Dr. McIntyre. Only time will tell."

"Yes, Dr. Preston. Only time will tell."

McIntyre next calls for a question or comment from a man who looks half asleep and about ready to fall face-first into the campfire.

Harold Smoots wakes and asks, "According to Behe's principle of irreducible complexity, what are the essential parts of a human, which if removed, would make him not a human?"

McIntyre responds, "Ah, finally a question directly on the topic I talked about and a difficult question at that! Harold, let me first say, in one sense, there is nothing that could be taken away from a human that would make him not a human. Having said that, I would answer your question this way. There are animals that genetically resemble humans that are not human, which we identify as gorillas, orangutans, and chimpanzees. Some argue porpoises and whales also are similar to humans in key respects. But, taking any genetic or anatomical part of a human being away does not reduce the human to a gorilla, chimpanzee, or porpoise. Taking away genetic or anatomical parts from humans result in malformed humans, not simpler species."

"So, humans cannot be reduced any further?"

"I believe that is true. Humans are irreducibly complex, as is every other animal on the face of the earth."

McIntyre entertains a half a dozen more comments and questions before closing the evening's session in prayer. Silvia works her way over to Gene. They only have time to exchange a few pleasantries and their cards, as everyone wants to talk with Dr. MacIntyre.

Everyone stands, slowly stretching to get the kinks out and the blood flowing. Bob stays seated on the log and appears to be drained of energy. Henry and Mo steady him between them and head back to the lodge. Bob's pallor accentuates his frailty. Every few steps he groans and asks to stop for a while. Forest shadows gather and disperse with the winds over the Buttes.

Each stop along the trail, dancing leaves and forest shadows seem to refresh and comfort Bob. Silvia catches the group that has moved only a couple of hundred feet from the campfire with about a hundred yards more to go to the lodge. She senses the end is near for Bob and marvels at his ability to withstand what has to be excruciating pain. She notes Bob's will to negotiate his finale on his own terms is strong; and, despite his weakness, he appears in good spirits. For the past two weeks Dr. Preston has had Bob on a regiment of sustained-release doses of up to 200 milligrams of oral morphine up to three times a day.

In his room, Silvia tucks Bob in bed. She asks Henry and Mo to take turns periodically peeking into to Bob's room to check his breathing. She checks his vitals from time to time. When Mo and Henry retire for the evening, Silvia preps Bob for continuous intravenous morphine infusion giving him the option to self-administer larger doses of morphine to control breakout pain.

Looking into Silvia's eyes Bob weakly smiles, as if to say he knows Silvia is doing everything she can in a losing cause. Miraculously, he makes it through the night.

Sunday, May 1, 7:30 a.m.: The next morning Bob is too ill to remain at the conference. Silvia and Henry decide to take Bob back to the Clinic. Mo stays behind to collect everyone's and personal belongings. He will bring them to town later in the day.

Taking the curves slowly, Silvia avoids the potholes and rocks, making the ride home as smooth and comfortable as possible. She knows every jarring lurch and pitch causes pain. Bob's stare out the van window fixes deeply in the forest. He dies quietly in Henry's arms.

"Silvia, Bob's gone," is all Henry can say.

Dr. Preston is not immune to the intensity of loss she feels with each patient's passing. Dryness in her throat and the sting of tears welling in her eyelids indicate her compassion for the sick and dying. She has never been able to completely emotionally distance herself from her patients, a sign of the superb physician that she is. The bounce of the van releases a tear that runs down her cheek and drops from her chin. She, Henry, and Bob reach town where the living lift and carry the dead into the town morgue. Gently placing Bob on a morgue table, they cover him with a clean sheet. Dr. Preston contacts the Sierra County Sheriff Department Medical Examiner's Office and reports Bob's cause of death, as pancreatic cancer.

By the time Reverend Doctor Ezekiel Gates gives the final benediction on the last day of the conference Bob is at peace. Although some Christians attending the conference are hot under the collar, most see the conference as a positive uplifting experience. Both ID advocates and evolutionists appreciate their opportunities to hear some of the most distinguished proponents of ID and were invigorated by the nightly discussions around the campfires. Many of the conference attendees are highly motivate to re-read their Bibles in search of what Scripture has to say about the issues surfaced at the conference.

In spite of the conference's success, Abbeville's mountain top experience further divides the warring factions in Henry's former congregation and fuels the town's gossip mill. At the next elder council meeting, Bruce Dean is unable to stop the seventh vote from being cast, which allows the closed personnel session to dismiss Henry to proceed. In closed session, the council votes seven to five on a motion to retire Henry from the pulpit without pay. A second vote to outright fire Henry holds at seven to five, falling short of the ten of twelve votes required to fire a senior pastor.

Wednesday, May 4, 8:30 a.m.: A sub-committee of the council, supporting Reverend Henry—Dean Curtis, Bronco Brown, Larry Sherman, Harvard Elgin, and Allen Belcher—calls on Henry at home to give him the results of the council's vote. Henry is pleased with the news, but tenders his resignation. His need to regroup his personal resources and re-evaluate his life without the responsibilities that come with the pulpit outweighs his need to remain in the leadership of the church.

"I've asked Ezekiel Gates to give the sermon on this coming Sunday, Mother's day. He is willing to rearrange his duties to cover Damascus Church until another minister is appointed by the Council to take my place."

The subcommittee tries to change Henry's mind by asking him to take a leave of absence and not resign. In the end, Henry convinces the committee he needs to completely sever himself from the church to focus his entire attention on what God wants him to do."

Bronco speaks for the group, "Alright Henry, if you're going to be stubborn in you conviction, we'll have to accept your decision. Anytime you change your mind, the door is open to you."

Reverend Henry smiles. His body language communicates he'll keep Bronco's idea in mind.

Although nothing could be further from the truth, the Abbeville gossip mill runs hot with the news of Henry's defrocking by the unanimous vote of the Damascus Council of Elders. Henry hears the rumors, but he is immune to their poisonous stings.

Wednesday, May 4, 2:15 p.m.: In accord with Bob's last wish, Allen and Alexander Belcher do the work required to bury Bob in the most clandestine way possible. Reverend Henry, Edgar, Mo, and Ellen, Dr. Preston, Florence, Nick and Helen Simmons, Kelly Watson, and Conrad Corbett witness Bob's cremation and watch his remains interred next to Jeremy Paxton's resting place. As he wished, Bob Winston is buried with no public fanfare.

Book Five

❦

Earthly Miracles

Chapter 1

❧

Sunday, May 8, 10:15 a.m.: With nothing to do Sunday morning Reverend Henry arrives earlier than usual at the Whitman's cabin. He seems to be back better than ever and wins three straight games from Edgar. Alma prepares Dagwood sandwiches for lunch that hit the spot.

"Ah how strange," Henry sighs, "This is the first time I've not been in church on Sunday morning in my entire life."

Edgar and Alma wait.

"Stranger yet, I feel pretty good. I didn't think I could turn this page of my life so easily. I'm really looking forward to the opportunities the future brings my way. This time, I'll pay more attention to how I feel, than to what I think."

Henry is energized. He feels and believes he is doing exactly what God wants him to do. For ten years he was busy, busy, busy with church business and the needs of his flock and sermon preparations. All the Scriptures and the lessons he taught were exclusively for others. This time around, he'll pay more attention to himself. He is reminded of the Book of Exodus where Moses was leading his flock of sheep to find green pastures among the Horeb Mountains when he saw the burning bush on Mount Sinai. Now, it's Henry's turn to go the mountains and listen for God to give him direction, starting immediately.

"Do you want to go for a walk this afternoon?" Alma suggests, "A hike to Upper Sardine Lake would be great way to work off lunch."

"That sounds like a great idea Alma. Are you coming Edgar?"

"I don't think so, Henry. Fenway and I intend to spend our time hanging around the house puttering, until you two return."

By the time Alma and Henry return to the cabin, Edgar and Fenway are fast asleep. Henry enjoys his time with Alma. They walk and talk about nature and things spiritual. Henry wonders why he was so against those who love God's creation.

For the next two weeks Alma and Henry, sometimes with Edgar and Fenway, walk to a different spot in the Sierras. When Edgar and Fenway tag along, they show Alma and Henry streams, rivers and lakes where fishing is best.

Sunday, May 29, 11:45 a.m.: Alma suggests they leave before lunch and hike unbeaten paths to avoid the Memorial Day masses of people who will be milling around popular spots like ants.

"Where are we going today, Alma?"

"With so many people around, I think somewhere on the east side of the Buttes would be open range for us."

Edgar wants to lounge around the cabin with Fenway and maybe do some fishing in Salmon Creek on the cabin property.

"Edgar, would you be willing to drop Henry and me on Butcher Ranch Road?"

"Sure Sis, that's a great area, but where along Butcher Ranch Road? You know that road goes on forever?"

"Below Tamarack Lakes."

"Good fishing, Tamarack Lakes. Yea, I can do that."

Twenty minutes or so later, Edgar and Fenway drop Alma and Henry on Butcher Ranch Road below the lakes.

"What time are you planning to get home?"

"Nightfall." Alma says, "You won't need to pick us up. We'll hike below the Buttes and take Bolder Trail down from Upper Sardine Lake to get home."

The dust from Edgar's truck doesn't last long in the mountain breeze.

Soon, they are alone in the quiet of the forest. Alma takes Henry to the large outcropping of granite west of the road that she knows will be a good place for lunch. Perched above the floor of the forest, below the Buttes, the aroma of their spicy tuna sandwiches invites ants for a bite to eat.

"Holy Mackerel Alma! I'm sitting on an ant farm. Ouch! Those little suckers can bite!"

Henry jumps to his feet, beating his clothes. Parts of his sandwich fall to the ground, where ants begin to converge for a feast. Amused, Alma watches Henry's performance.

"I haven't seen anyone do the jitter-bug in years, Henry. I didn't know you had so much rhythm. You could have worked that into your Sunday services." Alma wryly observes.

Henry sits on the other side of Alma. They watch huge black ants dismantle the remains of Henry's sandwich, taking bits of tuna and bread back to their nest.

"Someday, Henry, I'll take you up one of those steep trails you see above us, to the fire tower at the top of the Buttes."

"I know that area; that's where we held the men's retreat. But, getting there, climbing up the Pacific Crest Trail, is another story," Henry replies.

"I like the climb from lower Upper Sardine Lake to Lookout Tower because you experience the full Sierra scenery, the lakes, and summit vistas. In a few months you'll be ready, Henry."

"I hope so, looks pretty tough to me."

"It is. Today's hike back to the cabin will help toughen you for the tower trip. Trust me."

Throughout the day, Alma gives Henry a geological history of the Northern Buttes. How they were probably first formed three hundred fifty million years ago by ancient volcanic eruptions and shaped by successions of uplifts and tilting caused by more volcanic activity, during the Permian and Jurassic ages.

Henry thinks all this is bunk because he knows the creation of the earth happened within the last six thousand years, but he listens attentively to Alma, who is quite informed about these things. He becomes more fascinated in what Alma is saying and memorizes key phrases and terms Alma mentions about the "accretionary prism being represented by the Shoo Fly Complex," which is gobbledegook to him. But, he'll Google it as soon as he gets home to more fully understand what she said.

Talking nonstop about the rocks, the plants, animals, life, and death, Alma and Henry's time seems compressed into seconds. Stopping in the forest, observing nature take place as if they the only humans in the forest, take on dream-like qualities. Henry feels the forest's spirit, hears soft winds rustling, and believes God is whispering to him. The moments are timeless.

Working their way down Salmon Creek, Edgar and Fen fish into the dusk before returning to the cabin. He doesn't give a thought to Alma and Henry not being home. But, after night has fallen for sometime, he wonders why they have not returned. Even though it is commonplace for Alma to stay out all night, Edgar worries because she is with Henry and hopes Alma will be sure to get Henry off the trails and home before nightfall. They've been gone for nine hours. In that amount of time, they could have walked to Look Out Tower and come back to the cabin. Edgar calls Conrad, Desiree, Florence, and Dr. Preston to see if they know the whereabouts of Henry and Alma. When it's clear no one knows what happened to them, Edgar asks the group to meet at Packer Lake Road. By the time the group convenes, it's pitch black.

Sunday, May 29, 9:45 p.m.: As Florence and Silvia lead the way, Fenway stays close to Edgar and the group. They visit several camping areas around Sand Pond and ask questions. It is clear. No one has seen Henry that afternoon or evening. The only way to Upper Sardine Lake is a narrow bolder-covered trail, which only high-clearance 4 x 4 wheel trucks can negotiate, if they are expertly driven.

Into the black of night, Fenway lopes ahead as the party carefully picks their way among the boulders in the light of a lantern light they brought to see their way in the dark. Before long, they see small bright headlamp beams haphazardly scattering light through the cool inky air, as three people are rapidly bounding down Boulder Trail from Upper Sardine Lake. The closer the bouncing lights get to the searchers, the more the bouncing lights appear to be on the heads of three hikers returning after a day's climb in the Buttes. Edgar can't get a word in edgewise to ask his questions about Henry and Alma, as the excited climbers are incoherently jabbering away.

Dr. Preston calms the group of hikers, "Whoa, whoa, settle down. We want to understand what you're saying. Take a few minutes and catch your breaths and wits."

Meribella Swenson speaks first, "There are two bodies at the bottom of the lake. You can see them there as plain as day, the water's so clear."

Sam Jaffe adds, "We first saw them before the sun went down They were walking above the lake on the sheer granite, and then, the next time we looked, they were gone."

"We thought they had moved out of our line of sight and were continuing along the south side of the lake until we saw the bodies," Dave Farnum adds.

"Is there any chance they are alive?" Edgar asks not really hearing the finality spoken by the hikers.

"None, I'm afraid. It took us ten minutes to hike part way along the north side of the lake. When we looked back with our field glasses, the water was as still as glass, no ripples and no one in sight," reports Jaffe.

As if his legs folded under him, Edgar falls to the ground, sobbing. Desiree and Fen go to his side and try to comfort him. Edgar is inconsolable.

Conrad tells the hikers, "There's a land phone at the resort at Lower Sardine Lake. Can you contact the Sheriff's department and tell them about this?"

"Yea, we know our way around this place and that's exactly what we plan to do," Dave responds, as he and the other hikers continue bounding down Boulder Trail.

Silvia and Florence tell Desiree and Conrad to stay and wait to direct the Sheriff. Conrad wants to go to the lake with Florence and Dr. Preston, but they convince him to stay with Desiree, who is not familiar with the area. Florence reminds Conrad that Edgar is too distraught to be left alone and

Desiree will need help, if Edgar goes into shock. Conrad nods agreement. Silvia gives him the lantern. Conrad and Desiree settle Edgar in a small pine needle covered area aside the trail that is not strewn with rocks.

Florence and Silvia quickly pick their way along the road and soon reach the upper lake dam. Water bubbling from the spring feeding Sardine Creek below the dam is the only sound heard at the edge of the lake. Based on the hiker's information, the bodies should be directly across the lake from them. To save time, they run around the easier trail on the south side of the lake, their flashlights scanning the lake's bottom as they go. Soon two bodies are caught in the lights. Shadows embracing the bodies take flight up the granite walls of the Buttes.

The incessant wailing sirens, which have sounded constantly for the last half an hour, finally stop. Desiree and Conrad see bright flashing red and blue lights inundate the outer parking lots, the restaurant entrance, and the water's edge of the resort at Lower Sardine Lake. They and Fenway watch sets of revolving yellow, red, and blue lights atop one Sheriff's off-road vehicle slowly crawl the bolder strewn trail. Shrouded in darkness, a large black and white vehicle stops beside them, glaring lights reflecting on the hillside and trees. A brilliant white spotlight shines in their eyes.

"Who are you?" a friendly but official sounding voice calls from the towering cab.

"Conrad Corbett with Desiree Parker and Edgar Whitman, officer. Dr. Preston and Florence de la Rosa have gone ahead to find Alma Whitman and Reverend Henry."

"Okay, stay here until we retrieve the bodies."

The sheriff deputy's matter of fact words cut like knives through Edgar's heart. As the sheriff's van lumbers away to the lake, Desiree and Conrad decide it is best to help Edgar down the hillside and wait in the resort bar and restaurant.

On the other side of Upper Sardine Lake, Florence and Silvia see the faint glow of flashing lights above the dam. They know sheriff deputies and detectives will soon be coming their way. Not wanting to have possible forensic evidence disturbed by humans treading, Dr. Preston makes a command decision. To preserve the possible crime scene, she tells Florence to wait with the bodies while she intercepts the Sheriff deputies at the dam and tries to delay retrieving Alma and Henry until morning. Dr. Preston arrives in time to plead her case. Sheriff's Detective Lieutenant Milo Freeman, who is in charge of removing the bodies and conducting the investigation, agrees with Dr. Preston and radios the news to Detective Sergeant Dirk Jacobson. Desiree, who is taking calls for Edgar, receives the sergeant's message to wait until morning before continuing the retrieval process.

Ghastly thoughts of Alma at the bottom of the cold alpine lake crushes Edgar's soul, leaving him feel dead, empty inside. Desiree thanks Detective Jacobson in Edgar's behalf. Eventually, Edgar resigns himself to accept Dr. Preston's decision, but he will not sleep soundly that night and many nights to come with the thought of his beloved Alma lying at the bottom of Upper Sardine Lake.

Sunday, May 29, 10:30 p.m.: The Sierra County Sheriff Department Medical Examiner and his forensic team are the next to arrive at Lower Sardine Lake. They are informed of Dr. Preston and Detective Lieutenant Milo's decision to halt the forensic investigation until morning.

Drs. Mayes and Brown, Hopper Jensen, Mimi Gastineau, and Zack Curry file into the resort restaurant and sit at the bar as Conrad, Florence, and Edgar are leaving for home. In all the commotion, Sydney Cameron, a reporter for the Sacramento Courier slips in the bar unnoticed. She has the eyes of an eagle and the ears of a bat, detecting anything and everything that can be reported to the public faster than lightening. That night the resort houses the medical examiner and his team. Sheriff's deputies bivouac at Sand Pond and Sydney sleeps in her car. Back at the Whitman cabin, Desiree and Conrad feed Fenway and stay the night to watch over Edgar. Fen sleeps warmly by Edgar's restless side.

Monday, May 30, 6:15 a.m.: By sunrise, using yellow tape, Florence and Silvia have cordoned off the trails and mountainside above the area where Henry and Alma lay at the bottom of Upper Sardine. No foot traffic is allowed to destroy any evidence. They have staked out one small trail for Sheriff deputies, medical examiners, and forensic personnel to travel in and out of the area. Dr. Mayes and his forensic team conduct a thorough foot-by-foot search for physical evidence. Their investigation finishes at three o'clock in the afternoon.

Doctors Mayes and Preston allow Alma and Henry's bodies to be carefully removed from the lake and transported to the Abbeville Town Morgue. Upper Sardine Lake is sealed from public use for the next week to allow experts from the University of California to arrive and conduct another sweep of the area. For additional expert assistance Dr. Preston also puts in a call to her old teacher Gene McIntyre.

As Alma and Henry are placed on stainless steel metal tables, the county forensic team immediately sets to work on Alma. She is photographed and autopsied by the doctors. Henry is next. Physical evidence found on their bodies is collected, bagged, identified, and placed into the custody of Dr. Mayes. Examinations complete, the medical examiner authorizes the bodies to be taken to the mortuary. By nine o'clock that evening, Alma and Henry are picked up, delivered, and placed side-by-side on separate porcelain embalming tables at Belcher Brothers Mortuary.

Florence and Silvia arrive at Whitman's cabin around nine thirty to inform Edgar of what they found at the lake and think happened. They meet with Edgar, Conrad, and Desiree.

"You understand everything I disclose to you must be held in the strictest confidence. You realize that technically you are all suspects in the deaths of Henry and Alma. Please understand standard police practice dictates the family and close friends are considered suspects in these circumstances until proven otherwise." Silvia opens as sensitively as possible.

A bit surprised by Silvia's opening they, nonetheless, agree to hold what they hear in confidence. While Silvia carefully observes the body language of everyone, Florence takes the lead, explaining what Silvia and she believe took place.

"First, there is no evidence of foul play. According to the hikers who saw Alma and Henry, everything looked normal. Within a window of thirty minutes to an hour, however, both bodies are at the bottom of Upper Sardine Lake."

Edgar says, "However, you are not ruling out foul play?"

"Correct, death by foul play is still a possibility. Unless someone was tracking them or someone was laying in wait for them, the other possibilities boil down to these," Silvia answers, as Florence observes, "Accidental death, double murder, murder-suicide, or double suicide."

Conrad says, "I can't believe anything like murder or suicide had anything to do with their demise. Accidental death is the possibility, I'd consider."

"I don't have sufficient evidence to draw that conclusion, Conrad, but it is one possibility. What makes this case difficult is both of them died at or about the same time."

Desiree speaks up, "I know I've only been here a month, but from all my talks with Alma and being in the house with Reverend Henry, the relationship between the two was close. They both thought fondly of each other and held each other in high esteem. I don't see any possibility of murder. They were happy to be alive. I can't see murder or suicide as a possibility either."

Florence responds, "That is the way I see the event too. Both death certificates will show the cause of death to be accidental, unless other evidence is found to the contrary."

"Two accidental deaths in the same time frame, how does that work?" Questions Edgar.

"Either Alma accidentally fell into the lake and Henry, trying to save her, fell. Or, the reverse could have happened." Florence answers.

"Or," Silvia interjects, "and I apologize for how this may sound to everyone, both may have wanted to die together. Or, one may have accidentally fallen in and the other, in an act of despair, committed suicide."

Edgar says, "I don't think Alma or Henry would take their own lives. They were looking forward to doing so many things together."

Silvia continues, "If that was the case that would have been motive, showing why one or the other would have taken their life with their own hand struck, if struck with the loss of that future together."

Florence says compassionately, "I know how that must sound to you. Please understand we have to consider all the possibilities."

Conrad says, "Who would have laid in wait to kill either or both of them?"

"Who had a reason to kill either or both of them? Answer that question and we are well on our way to solving the mystery." Silvia comments.

"Which brings us to another point." Florence interjects, "Detective Lieutenant Milo told us he could find no information about a Henry Johnston or a Reverend Henry Johnston on the Police National Computers or COFEE. Their searches of public records show nothing as well. No high school diploma, no degrees from Cornell and no degree from Cambridge University! Henry's existence appears to have started ten years ago in Abbeville."

"COFEE?" asks Desiree.

"Yes," volunteers Conrad, "Computer Online Forensic Evidence Extractor. It's a computer device that digitally captures evidence live at the scene of the crime and downloads it into a flash storage unit. Handy, just insert the USB device into the computer when you get back to the lab."

Silvia and Florence appear astonished by Conrad's knowledge about COFEE. They know there are variations of the computer forensic technology that are supposedly top-secret projects at Langley and Los Alamos National Laboratory.

"Remember, I retired from the military."

"Thanks for refreshing my memory Conrad," Silvia replies, "I had forgotten because you never mentioned what you did in the military, except being an attaché for some general. Now that you let the cat out of the bag, what does all this intrigue mean to you?"

Before answering Silvia's question, Conrad pauses, while looking around the room at each person.

"I've seen this scenario many times. Henry may have been a former CIA agent. Or, he is in a witness protection program. Or, he is ran away from something and chose to disappear in Abbeville. I'm sorry to say, maybe who or whatever he was hiding from caught up with him."

Edgar's eyes fill with tears.

"Alma may have been killed as an innocent by-stander?" Edgar comments.

"Possibly," replies Conrad, "Silvia, have the toxicology reports come back?"

Silvia and Florence's heads shake side-to-side, signaling no.

"I would wait to turn that stone over, rather than wander in aimless speculations," responds Conrad.

Exhausted by the ordeal and emotions spent discussing the forensics and possible reasons for Alma and Henry's deaths, Conrad, Desiree, Florence, and Silvia agree to stay over night at the cabin. Hugging each other, they retire to their rooms. Edgar rests more easily surrounded by the people he loves and trusts, the people who loved Alma. But, no one is close to solving the mystery surrounding the deaths of Henry and Alma.

Tuesday, May 31, 7:00 a.m.: CHURCH ELDERS OUST PASTOR, PASTOR FOUND DEAD IN LAKE blares the banner headline across the morning edition of the Sacramento Courier. Sydney Cameron's feature story reads like a paperback novel. Based on sources in the medical examiner's office, sheriff investigators believe there is a connection between Reverend Henry's mysterious death at Upper Sardine Lake and disgruntled elders of the Damascus Church. Cameron writes, "Investigators suspect some resentful elders from the church may have conspired to have Reverend Henry removed from the pulpit by extreme measures."

Strangely, no mention is made of Alma in the front-page article of the Courier. Alma's story, BELOVED TOWN MATRIARCH DROWNS AT UPPER SARDINE LAKE, is found on page eight. But, Abbeville's morning edition of gossip has Alma and Reverend Henry plunging hand-in-hand into the icy waters of Upper Sardine Lake, a lover's suicide pact.

Tuesday, May 31, 8:30 a.m.: As planned, Allen and Alexander Belcher arrive for breakfast with Edgar to arrange Alma's funeral services. Alexander hands Edgar the morning edition of the Sacramento Courier. To stop salt being poured into Edgar's wounds, the Belcher brothers decide not to tell Edgar about what the town gossips are saying. Edgar takes them to the dining room where an old country breakfast is laid out on the dining table, compliments of Florence, Silvia, and Desiree. After greeting each other, Conrad, the three cooks, Edgar, and the Belcher brothers take their seats and begin eating. As he is reading the front-page article about the stir at Damascus Church and sees the names of his friends mentioned, Edgar is occupied with town events and neglects to eat.

"Cameron's news story doesn't do Damascus Church any favors, "Edgar comments, "Listen to this, 'One elder, who asked his name not be used, accused Pastor Henry of doing harm to Scripture because, the elder claims, the pastor deliberately misinterprets Scripture to suit his own purposes,' end of quote. I bet Dean Curtis will love reading this article."

Turning to page eight, Edgar twice reads the article about Alma and makes no comment, handing the article to Silvia, who reads the article out loud in its entirety.

Florence remarks, "The article did a fine job honoring Alma and lamenting her loss to the community. What do you think Edgar?"

"Yes, it was a fitting tribute to Alma."

After breakfast everyone is served coffee. Edgar is first to break the silence.

"I'll come right to the point. According to the newspaper the townsfolk want a big funeral for Alma, but Alma wants to fade into history without making a ripple. I would like Alma cremated and have my sister placed next to her great grandmother, Carol Ann Abbe. Can that be worked out?"

Allen Belcher replies, "Absolutely Edgar. Leave all of the details to us. We'll prepare a newspaper article for your approval, expressing your gratitude to the town for their kind words and thoughts for Alma."

"Good, that's settled," Edgar says impatient to move past painful moments as quickly as possible.

The rest of the breakfast conversation turns to fishing, backpacking, and the new archeological site being excavated at Indian Point. After breakfast, Allen and Alexander politely excuse themselves from the company of Edgar and his friends.

Before they reach the door, Florence points out that Henry's final affairs have not been settled. The brothers return to the dining table.

"My brother and I have tried to contact Reverend Henry's family, but so far we haven't found anyone." Allen reveals.

Conrad speaks, "I think you'll find we are the only family Henry has."

"I see," Alexander responds, "I had a feeling Henry was a loner. All these years, I have never heard him mention family or anything to tie him to the past. We could give him a quiet burial and put him in the cemetery next to Bob Winston and Jeremy Paxton."

Allen Belcher is an elder at Damascus Church who supported Reverend Henry and expresses his concerns about a quiet burial for Henry.

"Alexander, usually I agree with you. But this time I think we should consider other factors before we make our decision about Reverend Henry. I believe Edgar is well aware of what Henry was embroiled in at the church."

Edgar concurs.

Allen continues, "If Reverend Henry quietly takes the backdoor out of life, some malevolent individuals in our church and community will gloat and say they were right to have wanted to remove Henry from the pulpit. They will use Henry's demise and slinking exit from this world to aggrandize themselves.

"Why make a spectacle, when the man is dead," Alexander argues.

"Because no one should be allowed to use Henry's death to promote their evil agenda," Allen counter argues, "Henry deserves a better legacy than that from our church and community. He was a sensitive and a good man who went about doing good for others. I know the church will pay for Henry's casket, burial site, and funeral expenses."

Alexander changes his tune, "You're right Al. Most of the church and community does feel the way you do. I think between the church and our services everything will be taken care of."

"We would like to contribute to Reverend Henry's funeral expenses too," Edgar says speaking for Henry's friends, "I have just the cemetery plot in mind where Henry would like to be buried."

Edgar's ideas for Henry's funeral and burial meet with everyone's approval.

Desiree asks, "One more time, what's the plan?"

Allen responds, "With Edgar's permission, we will prepare Alma for cremation on Thursday morning, June 2nd at 7:30 a.m. and hold closed services for Alma afterwards in the atrium of the Abbe Family Mausoleum."

Edgar agrees, "Yes, the closed services will only include the people in this room."

"Wednesday, June 8, Henry will be honored at Damascus Church and buried under the oak tree above Salmon Creek on the hillside overlooking his church.

Everyone nods in assent.

With both funeral service arranged to everyone's satisfaction, the Belcher brothers again pardon themselves and leave with their tasks clearly assigned. They walk down the hill to their mortuary to prepare Henry and Alma for their final journeys.

Wednesday, June 1, 7:32 a.m.: After an early morning emergency meeting of the Damascus Council of Elders, head elder Bruce Dean phones Louis Jones the editor and chief of the Sacramento Courier. He objects to the newspaper article connecting Henry's death to members of the elder's council.

"You must be kidding Lou! How could you print such libelous garbage in your newspaper? I thought you had more integrity than that! Our lawyers advise us to sue you, Cameron, and your newspaper chain over this outrage."

"Bruce, hold your horses. The information came from a reliable source in the coroner's office. It's no secret that you have some crazies on that council of yours. You know they have been shooting their mouths off all over town about how much they despise Henry and want him removed from his church pastor position."

"Lou, let me put it in terms you understand. Damascus Church has over seven hundred God-fearing members. They all read your newspaper. If they feel you're attacking their church, you will be in for the fight of your life. In all fairness, you have to do something to take away the stigma you've placed on our doorstep."

Lou tells Bruce he will discipline the writer and print an apology for having the article written in such a way that paints everyone at the church the same color. Lou's suggestion is acceptable to Curtis who texts the agreement to the elders.

As for the editorial written in the afternoon edition of the Sacramento Courier, Lou did apologize for the upset Sydney Cameron's article caused the good members of the Damascus Church. But the damage is done. Lou lightly rakes Sydney Cameron over the coals for the fiasco, but she is not fired because after her story broke, the Sacramento Courier's readership shot up thirty percent.

Chapter 2

Tuesday, May 31, 9:45 p.m.: Edgar receives a phone call from Allen Belcher.

"Hello Edgar?"

"Yes Allen?"

"I don't know exactly how to explain this to you."

"Go on."

"Alma and Henry's bodies are missing from the morgue room."

"What!"

"Someone has stolen your sister's body and the body of Reverend Henry from the mortuary."

Edgar shakes his head in disbelief and tells Allen to wait and not notify anyone until he arrives at the funeral parlor. Allen agrees. Twenty minutes later, Edgar arrives at the mortuary with Dr. Preston and Florence who retraces the day's events with Allen and Alexander and check through the entire mortuary for physical evidence of any kind. Alexander hands Dr. Preston the video security tapes, which show the bodies in the morgue room one minute. Then, after six and a half minutes of what appears to be an electrical blackout or something being held in front of the video camera in the morgue, the bodies are gone.

Dr. Preston phones Detective Lieutenant Milo's office and has him paged. When he calls back, she informs him of the situation. Sheriff deputies and the county forensic team occupy the crime scene within the hour, allowing Florence and Silvia to move out from the mortuary to search the surrounding area.

"Silvia, over here . . . in the parking lot."

"What do you think, Silvia?"

Silvia sees what looks like a broad, luminous trail of glitter, coming from the back of the mortuary, across the parking lot, and across Spring Creek Drive. The glitter continues up the side of the mountain, across Spring Creek, then behind Abbeville Estates. Florence and Silvia pick up their pace and follow the glowing trail up to Lower Sardine Lake. Along the way, they notice the grass and flowers look awakened, as if they were receiving the full rays of the sun.

"I've never seen anything like this before, Florence. Have you?"

"Yes, Silvia. When Alma and I traveled these mountains at night, she would often take the lead, dancing along the ground, illuminating the vegetation for yards around her."

"Then, Alma came this way?"

"The evidence seems to be telling us so."

The path of glowing glitter follows the edge of the lake and half way up to Boulder Trail, where it stops.

"Where's the luminescence?" Silvia puzzles.

"It's fading from view. Soon, the glittery substance will disappear completely from mortal view, leaving no trail of evidence," Florence confesses.

"You're telling me, you see evidence of the glitter continuing beyond the place I see the trail stop? You still see the luminescence?" Silvia questions Florence.

"That's my reality, Silvia, a reality that you cannot yet see. Evidence of Alma passing by here and following the trail back to Upper Sardine Lake is still visible to me."

Silvia can only take what Florence says with a large grain of salt, as Florence's testimony does not square with Silvia's observations and has not been validated scientifically.

"If what you are saying is true, Florence, Alma and probably Reverend Henry were whisked away from the mortuary by someone or something, came this way, and are probably somewhere up the Buttes," Silvia surmises.

Looking further up Boulder Trail, Florence replies, "That's a good guess, Dr. Preston."

Silvia laughs, "A good guess, but only a guess," she says, "We'll keep this our little secret, until I can objectively verify your perception."

"Of course, Silvia, as is our usual practice. You're piling up quite lot of mysteries to scientifically unravel, aren't you? " Florence responds.

Silvia smiles and nods her head. They walk back around the lake and rejoin the sheriff and forensic team still searching for evidence at the mortuary.

"Find anything?" Lieutenant Milo inquires of Dr. Preston.

"Not a thing, Lieutenant. Have you turned up anything?"

Milo concedes not one bit of physical evidence has been found, after hours of searching.

Thursday, June 2, 7:00 a.m.: Again, the headline in the morning edition of the Sacramento Courier shocks the town: LAKE BODIES MISSING FROM MORGUE. Cameron reports, "Police baffled by bodies stolen from Belcher Brother's Mortuary." The article sends shivers through the spines of Abbevillians.

From the general store to the bakery to the library, revolting gossip that Alma and Henry's dead bodies were stolen by unemployed lumbermen and sold to medical schools spreads from one end of town to the other. The gossip shakes the town to its knees, as many Abbeville residences fear random abductions will next happen to them, sending a wave of panic through the town that causes a few people to move out of Abbeville.

A patron of the Knead-2-Feed Bakery asks of Stella, "What's going on with this town?"

Stella says, "I really don't know what to tell you. I've never seen the town in such turmoil."

From his geezer table, Rich Castro quips, "Looks like the wheels are coming off the happy wagon!"

Rich expresses the sentiments of most townsfolk. Abbeville, the once friendly, unassuming small town nestled in wildflowers below Northern

Buttes is a war zone where factions of townspeople battle among themselves. Like ant armies fighting to ensure their way of life survive, church elders clash with church elders, townspeople assail the town council, and gossip continues to tear apart the social structure of the town.

Thursday night's Damascus Church Elder Council meeting becomes a hotbed of controversy as elders struggle to control the church. Led by Elder Jacob Richmond, who fervently believes Reverend Henry consorts with Alma and her witches' circle, he and his group of church elders wants to take on the Sisterhood for once and for all. They believe Satan is using the Sisterhood to bring down the church and attack Christians. But, council debate does not directly confront the Sisterhood because the wives of these elders are either sympathetic to or are actually one of the Sisterhood. So, Elder Jacob's focus turns to the selection of the deceased pastor's chosen successor, Ezekiel Gates.

Robert Crane objects, "I believe allowing the pastor to leave his flock at Middleton Covenant Church to pinch hit here sends the wrong message to our congregation. This elder council is responsible for the selection of church pastors. Reverend Henry exceeded his authority when he picked Reverend Gates as his successor. What do we know about Ezekiel Gates? For all we know he's in covenant with the Sisterhood too?"

Canter Cunningham agrees, "Pastors usurping the authority of elder's undermines the church. Reverend Henry's fingerprints should not be on the new page about to be turned at Damascus Church. We need a clean start, one we as elders agree upon by vote of the members of council."

Elder Jacob suggests, "The council should direct our head elder to write an appropriate letter to Reverend Gates, thanking him for his kind offer and informing him we wish to move in another direction. Within our church community we have ample talent to maintain the ministerial wing of the church on our own."

Elder Elroy Jones, "I move our head elder, Bruce Dean, write a letter to Dr. Ezekiel Gates thanking him for his willingness to temporarily take over the ministerial duties of this church, but that his services are no longer required."

Elder Mark Correra, "I second the motion that head elder Bruce Dean write an appropriate letter of thanks to Dr. Ezekiel Gates for his willingness to stand in for Reverend Henry."

The motion passes seven to five.

Allen Belcher, "I move Bruce Dean temporarily take over the ministerial duties of this church and with the approval of the council invite guest pastors or members of our church to preach Sunday sermon until a new pastor is appointed."

The motion is seconded by Elder Bronco Brown and passes by a vote of eight to four. With no further business placed before the council, Elder Dean adjourns the meeting.

Friday, June 3, 7:18 a.m.: Rumors start early at the Knead-2-Feed Bakery. With coffee and scones in hand customers hear Fredrika and Bunny, who are quite animated and purposely loud, spin yarns straight from the Damascus Church elder's meeting.

"Bunny, I've heard the most awful news coming from our church."

"No!"

"Yes, poor Alma and Reverend Henry were walking along the lake shore, when a band of forest witches swarmed over them like bees and drown them in the depths of the lake!"

"No!"

"Yes."

"But wouldn't the witches drown too?" Bunny asks with the most serious expression on her face.

"No silly, witches don't drown. They have magical powers."

"Oh. But I thought Alma was one of the forest witches. Why would they kill her?"

"Bunny, this is straight from our church elders. Please don't tell a soul."

"May my eyes be burnt out with red-hot pokers if I say a thing, Freddie."

"When Alma put a magical spell on Reverend Henry making him love her, the witches became jealous and killed both of them. They're such a bunch of lesbians."

"No!"

"Yes!"

As improbable as it seems, the forest witches' story gains traction in the community. According to local folklore, the forests and hills around Abbeville have always been haunted. No one can walk the forests at night without having snippets of witch folklore play with their minds prompted by forest sounds and forest shadows. The town is jittery, as Abbeville is becoming a place to avoid in the Sierras.

Bill Silva has spent a lot of time promoting the Abbeville Bicentennial Summer Festival and is nervous, as he reads the newspapers and listens to the town gossip. As president of the Abbeville Town Council, he calls an emergency council meeting to figure out how to stop the bad press and gossip from killing the prospects of a successful festival. Flyers declaring "Time We Confront Our Fears" are circulated door-to-door throughout Abbeville, calling all citizens to attend the emergency council meeting.

Saturday, June 5, 10:00 a.m.: Since Edgar has been given a leave of absence, Bill Silva calls the town council meeting to order with four members attending.

"May we have a moment of silence in remembrance of our beloved friends Alma Whitman and Reverend Henry Johnston."

The audience of about a hundred and fifty people bows their heads in a moment of silence.

"Thank you, my dear friends. Fear is settling in Abbeville, fear of the unknown, fear of death, and fear the life of Abbeville is coming to an end. Today, we need to confront our fears and get hold of ourselves. Abbeville has been around for two hundred years, and we are going to have one hell of a Bicentennial Festival."

The audience remains still. Bill, who is all fired up to fight demons, doesn't notice the crowd is not with him, as he continues to build public confidence by opening the meeting to public comment.

"We have an open microphone for you. Who would like come up and express what's on their mind about how to face our fears and turn things in a positive direction in Abbeville?"

From the back of the town hall a familiar figure walks to the microphone.

"You all know me, Elder Jacob Richmond of Damascus Church. Last evening the council of elders voted to take back our church and our town. We are placing our faith back in God's hands. The elders of Damascus Church will share the responsibilities of running our church to serve the townspeople of Abbeville. Abbevillians need to do the same. God bless you and God bless Abbeville."

Half way back to his seat, Elder Jacob turns around and returns to the microphone.

"I know this may upset some people, but it needs to be said. I know Reverend Henry Johnston murdered Alma and buried her body in the hills above Sand Pond before he committed suicide because he was under the influence of Satan."

Bronco stands on stage, interrupting Jacob.

"Jacob Richmond, you know nothing of the kind. I'm ashamed to say we are elders on the same church council. If I wasn't a Christian, I'd come down from here and knock your block off."

Bill gavels the meeting to order and calls for civility.

"I know we are under a lot of stress, but let's try to keep things in perspective."

But Jacob will not settle down and raises his voice louder to be heard over Bronco's admonishment.

"What I say is the God's truth. Alma and Henry bodies lie decaying where they fell with the rest of the miners who lie buried in the mineshafts above Sand Pond. Everyone knows they didn't like each other. We all heard them fighting and calling each other names. When they fought over the gold they found in one of those abandoned mines, Alma's blood was spilled and Henry couldn't stand to face this community."

Ranger Pat and McWhinney Thurston jump from the stage and take a hold of Jacob, who's struggling with them and raving all the way down the main aisle and out the door.

Bill Silva pounds the gavel to get the audiences' attention, "I'm sure something snapped in Jacob's head. I've never heard anything so absurd. We have been friends and neighbors of Alma and Reverend Henry for years and know nothing Jacob said makes any sense."

As Pat and McWhinney come back to take their seats, Jacob's screams are heard clear as a bell from the jail cell under the town hall.

"Listen to me people of Abbeville!" Jacob continues ranting, "We all know there are hundreds of abandoned gold minds in the hills above the lakes and Sand Pond. Prospector's Trail connects all of those mines. The hills are full of dead miners. Miners who couldn't keep their mouths shut about the gold they found and were murdered by claim jumpers and bushwhackers!"

Gradually the town council begins to lose its audience, as one-by-one and two and three people at a time get up and leave.

"Go up and search the collapsed tunnels! Look between the boulders!" Jacob continues screaming, "You'll find the bones of dead men and when you look hard enough, you'll find the bones of Alma and Henry too! You'll see!"

Soon, the Abbeville Town Hall is empty.

"The mines are haunted! Everybody knows the covered-up trails are haunted too!" Jacob is heard saying.

Bill gavels the meeting closed to an empty house. The council leaves Jacob screaming in jail and walks down to the Blue Goose to sort things out. That evening Ranger Pat goes back to the town hall jail and lets Jacob out. Far from calm, Jacob is madder than a wet hen and runs into the night, screaming like a mad hatter.

Sunday, June 5, 7:45 a.m.: Abbeville's morning gossip train steams down the track with news that Elder Jacob was attacked by the Abbeville Town Council and is being tortured in the dungeon beneath the town hall for expressing his religious beliefs. You can hear the property values falling in Abbeville. The sad state of affairs compels more people to move out of town. The only good new is no reporters from the Sacramento Courier cover the town meeting. But, unfortunately for Abbeville, the nightly KTRC News airs its prime time special on the deaths of Alma Whitman and Reverend Henry: MYSTERIOUS SIERRA DROWNINGS.

More unfortunate for Abbeville, the program features Elder Jacob Richmond as Abbeville's spokesperson interviewed by KTRC-TV investigative reporter Slam Houston. The KTRC camera zooms in on a full head shot of Elder Jacob, whose hair looks like it's been combed by an egg beater; whose grizzled stubble beard gives him the appearance of a frantic, desperate man; and whose wildly dancing eyes sunk in the deep, dark sockets tells the tale of mental instability. Elder Jacob from Abbeville is quite the sight to have coming into your living room at night with the kids watching.

Those watching in the greater Reno-Truckee area are used to seeing crazy in the Sierras, but this wretched soul from Abbeville, gazing into the camera is too much to bear. Most turn their televisions to another station. But the damage is already done. The rest watch the spectacle with morbid curiosity, in disbelief that KTRC is treating this loony-tunes Elder Jacob, as a credible spokesperson for the town of Abbeville.

In a most respectful radio voice Slam begins, "Elder Richmond you're a long time member of the Damascus Church and an upstanding member in the community in Abbeville. What really happened to Reverend Henry Johnston and Alma Whitman up in Abbeville?

"Thank you Mr. Houston for you kind words. The truth is God struck Alma Whitman and Reverend Johnston dead for their sins and cast them to the bottom of Upper Sardine Lake. Then God resurrected their bodies and threw them to the bottom of an abandoned mind above Sand Pond to rot there until judgment day."

Slam Houston is thinking, "Oh my god! Who did the preliminary interviews with this screwball and certified him credible to answer questions on my program?"

Stunned by Jacob's opening, Slam hesitates and inadvertently allows Jacob's rant to continue.

"Mr. Houston, we will live with fire on the land. The fire that is God Almighty has come to slash and burn with pillars of fire the town and evil forests surrounding Abbeville because of the sins of Reverend Henry, the servant of Satan, and Alma Whitman, the high witch of the Sisterhood. I looked and behold a whirlwind was coming out of the north, a great cloud with raging fire engulfing itself and lightening was all around it, radiating out of its mist like the color of amber, out of the midst of the fire came the likeness of four living creatures . . ."

KTRC cuts to a Smoky the Bear's safety tips commercial that blows away their audience. What is going on in Abbeville? At this point no one needs to know anymore than steer clear of Abbeville. Slam Houston is never again seen on KTRC Television. Not a trace of Slam's hide or hair appears in public ever again.

Abbeville's townspeople fear Elder Richmond or one of his followers will soon burn Abbeville to the ground. They envision waking one morning in a blazing forest fire set by one of the kooks at Damascus Church. They are more than a little nervous about living in a town with all the horror stories, demonic preachers, crazy elders, deaths, witches, stolen bodies, and fanatics running around. Constant rumors about murder-suicides, conspiracy murders hang in the air. Abbeville seems hell-bent to become another Sierra ghost town.

Monday, June 6, 7:45 a.m.: Sacramento Courier's morning headlines help counteract some of the bad news coming out of Abbeville: COUNTY CORONOR DETERMINES CAUSES OF DEATH ACCIDENTIAL. Sydney Cameron's reporting is straightforward and factual.

"The deaths of Alma Whitman and Reverend Henry Johnston are the result of accidental drowning. The evidence is clear in this matter. There is no need to convene a coroner's inquest," states Dr. Jeffrey Martin Mayes, Chief Medical Examiner for Sierra County.

But, Abbeville is far from having its shirttail out of the wringer. While the coroner's office has shelved the case, Alma and Henry's deaths and missing bodies are very much an open, active investigation.

Based on interviews with possible suspects and persons of interest, Detective Lieutenant Milo Freeman and Detective Sergeant Dirk Jacobson have developed three conspiracy theories.

The front-running theory has Edgar Whitman murdering his sister in a fit of passion. The theory is predicated on Edgar's perception that Alma loved Reverend Henry more than she loved Edgar. They believe Edgar had accomplices help him kill or plan to kill Alma and Henry.

The second murder theory involves Fredrika Handley. Substantial evidence—phone calls, leaks to newspaper reporters and Fredrika's conversations with townspeople—has been accumulated, showing Fredrika harbors deep hatred for Reverend Henry. Because of her age, sixty-seven, Fredrika would need others to help her commit murder. Again, Jake Langdon's name surfaces in association with Fredrika.

The third conspiracy to commit murder theory focuses on Elder Jacob Richmond. Jacob's religious fervor and his public ranting against Henry and Alma are well documented.

Lieutenant Freeman and Sergeant Jacobson have presented their conspiracy to commit murder theories and evidence to the Sierra County District Attorney, Marcus Chao.

"No sale, gentlemen. All we have so far are two missing bodies, a lot of hunches based on hearsay evidence from a lot of people. We have no hard-evidence supporting any one of your theories that will prove anyone conspired to murder Alma Whitman or the Reverend Henry Johnston."

"Motives, Marcus, we have suspects that have clear motives to kill Alma or Henry. Elder Jacob hates Reverend Henry. The evidence is clearly found in the records of Elder Council meetings and in the newspapers. Fredrika hates Reverend Henry; all of the gossip undermining Henry is easily traced to her doorstep," Milo argues.

"Convictions don't ride on the backs of motives. Convictions ride the backs of hard evidence, gentlemen. Who murdered Alma? How was she murdered? Where's the evidence putting Fredrika or Jacob at the scene of the crime? If they hired for murder, who did they hire?"

Lieutenant Milo and Sergeant Dirk have no answers for Marcus' questions. At this point, all they have are creative and unsubstantiated speculations based on the transcripts of their interviews of Edgar, Conrad, Desiree, Florence, Elder Dean, Elder Jacob, and others on the Elder Council of Damascus Church, Fredrika Handley, Bunny Grimmer, Edna Pinkney, Jenny Hobbs, and Holly Spears.

"Sorry gentlemen, I can't go to court and convict on what we have. But . . ." Marcus holds out one hope for the investigators, "go back and pull together what you have supporting each of your theories and call for a coroner's inquest on your suspicions there was foul play and you may be able to convince a coroner's jury."

"How will that help?" Dirk asks.

"I'm allowed more latitude to question witnesses at an inquest than at a criminal trial. I don't have to look out for the rights of defendants because there are no defendants. The purpose of an inquest is to probe into the manner and cause of someone's death. Who knows what might pop out of one of your suspects or persons of interest, when they are placed on the stand under oath and asked questions?"

"But the county medical examiner is satisfied with the causes of death being accidental," Dirk continues.

"But you guys have reasons to doubt their deaths are accidental. That's what coroner's inquests do—get all the information on the table and let the jury decide. Inquests are not adversarial they are fact finding in nature."

Milo and Dirk thank Marcus and go back to the office intent upon getting their ducks in a row to present at a coroner's inquest. But, they do not want to contradict the medical examiner's public statement. They decide to meet with Dr. Mayes to work something out.

Book Six

✣

Bicentennial Festival

Chapter 1

❧

Saturday, July 2 6, 7:45 a.m.: For some inexplicable reason, the Abbeville Bicentennial Festival opens with record-breaking crowds. Maybe the fact most of the month of June is relatively quiet in Abbeville allows people to forget the crazy people, deaths and missing bodies? Maybe all of the April and May hoopla are attracting droves of curious people to Abbeville? Whatever the reason, Abbeville's Bicentennial Festival is off to a rip-roaring start.

Shouting, musical instruments tuning and the beating of drums, which seem to be right under his bedroom window, wakes Edgar. Fenway, on the other hand, sleeps soundly as only a big old golden retriever can sleep. Below the cabin, the parade groups are lining up on Switchback Road. He looks at the clock by his bed.

He thinks, "It's too early to get up. I don't have to be to the speaker's stand until eleven o'clock. Plenty of time for a couple more winks and time to get ready."

Edgar rolls to his side and shuts his eyes. It sounds like dueling bands. The Downieville High School Marching Band is playing John Phillip Sousa's *Stars and Stripes Forever* verses the Loyalton High School Marching Band's version of the *Michigan Fight Song.* In the background, he hears the mysterious sounds of exotic drums booming and banging.

"Those strange loud drums," Edgar's ears hear in a distance haze, "those drums. Where in the world did we get those drums?"

Edgar forgets the Northton Chinese Drum and Bugle Core and Japanese Tako Drums of the Sierras were invited to march in the Bicentennial Parade and perform throughout the festival. No way can Edgar fall to sleep with the racket going on below his window. Resigned to his fate, he bounces out of bed and into the shower. He can't get the *Stars and Stripes* out of his head. He unconsciously hums and dah-dee-dahs the music until he becomes aware he is back to his happy-go-lucky self. At first, he feels guilty.

"Why am I happy and having fun, when Alma is gone and can never feel the joy of living?" flashes through his mind.

His breathing becomes shallow. He puts a hand against the side of the shower and begins to cry. It was a good cry, one that releases Edgar from the hands of suffocating emotion.

Then, it dawns on him, "This is Alma's day; today is the day she planned for and promised the town."

He begins to breath again, to restart life. He is turning the corner, heading back to normalcy. His grief-stricken heart is beginning to accept the fact life must go on. Edgar realizes living and enjoying life is not disrespecting Alma. She would want him to live and live well.

Edgar starts laughing, "Here I am singing and standing with my head in the shower crying. No one would know I'm crying because the shower water and my tears are all rolled into one. What a mess I've become!"

He turns off the water and looks at Fenway. She is watching him with those deep brown eyes in the same way Fenway always looks at him.

"Well girl, that's the end of that. I should cry more. It's a great therapeutic release."

Edgar dresses. He feeds Fenway and eats a bowl of cereal before heading down the driveway toward Switchback Road. Looking at the parade line, he waves to Chief Silver Squirrel and the Kitwa Tribal Council. Edgar goes over to them to personally greet and welcome them to the festival. Watching the little kids from Coleville's Dance Studio, running around in their mice and cheese costumes, brings a smile to Edgar's face.

Over the omnipotent sound system installed by the Belcher brothers, Edgar is summoned to the speaker's platform. Bill Silva stands behind the podium on the specially built large oak speaker's platform arching over Matthew Drive on 10th Street. Bill and the town council chomp at the bit to get Edgar on stage quickly, so the parade can begin on time.

Half walking, half trotting along Switch Back and down Mathew Drive, Edgar crosses 10th Street, under the speaker's stand and stops to talk with members of the Loyalton Marching Band. He shakes the hands of the student bandleader and drum major. Edgar thanks them for taking the time and effort to be in the parade. He waives to the high school principal and music teacher as he walks from under the speaker's stand. Emerging in front of the oak grandstand, the throngs of people, who have been standing for hours in library and town hall parks, spontaneously erupt in wild cheering. He waves to the crowd and, then, runs back and shakes hands with Conrad who's poised at the head of the parade in the four-in-hand Landaus VIP carriage, to lead the parade down Matthew Drive.

To the dismay of the town council members leaning over the platform railing to see what's taking him so long, Edgar stops to pet and talk with the team of four black chestnut bay brown Morgan horses decked out in silver bridals and fancies, including red, white, and blue parade plumage that will pull the VIP carriage. Fenway's tail wags faster than usual she is so excited to see the horses.

Again, Edgar pauses looking at the crowds. His spirits are uplifted, as he is witnessing Alma's dream for the town coming true.

"If only Alma were here to wear the cotton sweetbrier teal blue dress she made for the bicentennial parade, "Edgar wishes, "but, that was never meant to be," he admits to himself.

Edgar climbs the steps to the speaker's platform. On the platform, Edgar shakes hands with Bill and the rest of the town council. Overhead, a large red, white and blue banner flaps lustily in the wind proclaiming, ABBEVILLE 200 YEARS OF PROGRESS WELCOMES YOU. The banner can be seen by thousands of people lining Mathew Drive and upper parts of Salmon Creek Road.

"It's about time you rolled out of bed and got here Edgar, " Grand Marshal Bill jokes.

"Yea, I almost didn't make it except for all the noise you guys were making! I couldn't get back to sleep through the drumming," Edgar humorously rejoins.

"Alma would have been so pleased to see the town come to life again," Ranger Pat says.

"Alma would have enjoyed the parade and probably is enjoying the parade," replies Edgar.

"We wouldn't be here, except for the vision she had for this bicentennial festival," Bill says.

"Probably not, Bill, nice of you to remember Alma that way. I bet she is looking down and enjoying herself immensely. She is certainly with us in spirit. Look at that crowd!"

Looking from the platform straight down Matthew Drive, banners with the words "Abbeville Bicentennial Festival" span across Matthew Drive at each street intersection. Edgar and the town's dignitaries have a spectacular view of the red, white, and blue banners, reaching down Matthew Drive into Yuba Park and the thousands of people lining the drive and streets, looking up at them.

Edgar leans over the back rail of the speaker's platform and waves to the parade lines ready for action. Gold nuggets along side of the Abbeville Elementary School Gold Rush Float wave back at him, as do the Sierra City and Abbeville Volunteer Fire Departments and members of the Abbeville Veteran's League and Damascus Church Choir. As promised, the Loyalton Fire Department Old-Timers' Fire Truck and Bucket Brigade brings up the rear of the parade.

At the Grand Marshal's signal the Loyalton High School Marching Band stops the music. The people overflowing library and town hall parks quiet, sending a wave of silence through the streets and drives of Abbeville.

"Good morning friends and neighbors and welcome to the 200-year celebration of the founding of Abbeville this wonderful Fourth of July weekend," the Grand Marshal greets the masses of people standing in the parks, sitting on the hillsides, and standing along the drives and streets.

The broadcasting system strung from the library and town hall parks through the streets and drives of Abbeville, Spring Creek Park, Salmon Creek Winery, and through the carnival grounds at Northern Yuba River

State Park and Indian Point is so clear, the crowds of people hear every word Bill says.

"I will keep this short. We would not be here, if it weren't for the efforts of our beloved Alma Whitman, whose vision and leadership made this day possible."

Because of all the media coverage about the demise of Alma Whitman not one person is unaware of who Alma is and what she means to Abbeville. Everyone stands and cheers loudly.

Grand Marshal Bill tightly grips the microphone and thanks the Sierra County Sheriff's Department for the security provided at the festival, Bronco, Cannon of Salmon Creek Winery, and the Blue Goose for all the food and beverages. He gives special thanks to Belcher Mortuary for the sound system, Jane Brown owner Fabrics for the decorations, the banners and streamers. Bill praises Cassandra Blake operator of the Abbeville Farmer's Market for the candy apples and Stella May Fields for the cakes. By the time Bill finishes about everyone in Abbeville has been thanked right down to the town blacksmith, Mo's free oil changes and the deviled eggs prepared by Emma Jane Walters at her Wog Farm.

Bill is so smooth and entertaining, the crowd wants to hear more. Then, Bill stops and invites a startled Edgar to the podium.

"Let's hear it for Alma's brother and the last of the Abbeville founders, Edgar Samuel Whitman."

The crowd roars their approval, as Edgar stands dumbfounded.

At Bill's signal, the principal of Loyalton High School leads a beautiful, spirited Grey Lusitanian Stallion fitted with silver bridles and Washington Reyes Stubbed Siegfried saddle in front of the VIP carriage. The town council walks down from the platform to the VIP carriage. Bill stops Edgar from getting in. Edgar looks confused.

"Edgar," Bill says, "You're leading the parade, my friend; the Grey Lusitanian is for you."

Edgar mounts the Grey to the delight and cheers of the crowd and heads down Matthew Drive waving at the multitude. Fenway struts and barks along side her master's side. Bicentennial Marshal Bill takes the front seat of the VIP carriage next to Conrad Corbett, while the rest of the town council pile in the back seat of the carriage. Conrad brings the Morgan horse drawn carriage a safe distance behind Edgar. In a VIP car, Chief Silver Squirrel and the Kitwa Tribal Council attired in authentic Native Indian dress pull up behind the town council's carriage in a presidential touring car, rumored to be Franklin Delano Roosevelt's 1939 open top Lincoln convertible. The sight of the Native Americans riding in a presidential touring car amazes the throngs of people and steals the show. The Loyalton High School Marching Band, moves behind the Lincoln, striking up John Philip Sousa's 1931 The Aviators March.

Everything is so well organized that each group in the parade falls in the exact spot they were designated to fill. The Gold Rush Float follows Peggy Elgin and the elementary school kids with bright orange vests volunteering to help people find their way around the festival follow the gymnastic team, the Chinese Drum and Bugle Corps follow Buckshot and Joker driving a truck with one of the bulls for the bull rides and so on to the Old-Timers' Fire Truck and Bucket Brigade that signals the crowd to fall behind the parade, as it passes through town to the North Yuba River State Park to the carnival and the parade's end.

Edgar, Fenway, and the Grey stallion named Charger pass the Damascus Church. The parking lot is stacked with people cheering, whistling, and whooping. Edgar sees Bruce Dean and Curtis in the crowd, waving feverishly beside a woman who resembles Anne Dean. Edgar waves enthusiastically, as the lady smiles and waves back at him. A few yards down the drive, Edgar looks back, but Anne—if it was Anne, but of course it can't be Anne—is lost in the crowd. Passing the Blue Goose scores of people shout to catch Edgar's attention and exchange comments.

"You look great on that Grey, Edgar!" one enthusiast calls out.

"Easier said than done," Edgar replies, waiving all the while, "my rump's sore and we haven't gone a third of a mile yet!"

Laughter roars in response to Edgar's comment.

"Hang on to the saddle, Little Beaver," calls another from inside the Tavern.

"Little Beaver," Edgar Shouts, "Right-on Red Ryder," Edgar shouts to the crowd's delight.

Hundreds of people are in the parking lot at the Abbeville General Store. The high-spirited crowd applauds as Edgar goes by. Edgar's eyes find a blue dress with black lace on a woman he notices in the sea of people. Again, a second glance does not recapture what he thought he saw. Then, over by an oak tree, Edgar catches a glimpse of what appears to be a young man with a book of some kind under his arm. He knows it is impossible, but the man resembles Reverend Henry.

The psyched throngs lining Salmon Creek Road, enthusiastically greeting the parade keeps Edgar so busy waving and talking that he pushes the images of Anne, Alma, and Henry to the back of his mind. Then, while passing Wog Farm, he looks uphill toward the farm and sees a solitary man standing on the road waving. It's impossible, but the guy looks an awful lot like Bob Winston! That was it. Edgar stands upright in his stirrups, both of his hand waving above his head. The parade stops. Charger parts the onlookers, as Edgar rides toward to the solitary man and greets him.

He dismounts Charger, "I couldn't resist coming over when I saw you."

"Wow! You could have blown me over when I saw you stop the parade and ride up here. My name is Jud Nelson. I came all the way from Grass Valley to be here, and now I'm glad I did."

"You look so familiar, Jud. I couldn't resist coming up here and saying hello. Sorry for embarrassing you." Edgar sincerely apologizes.

"No embarrassment at all. You're Edgar Whitman, I saw your picture on television. Happy to meet you." Jud gushes excitedly.

"I'm happy to meet you too, Jud."

Edgar remounts and wheels Charger back to the front of the parade.

"I'm glad I checked out my hallucinations. Seeing Alma, Henry, Anne, and Bob like that . . . I think I'm losing my mind. Simply cases of mistaken identity, I suppose." Edgar thinks to himself; then, while patting Charger on the neck and turning to Fenway, Edgar says, "Fenway, old girl! Did you see anything out of the ordinary?"

Fenway wags her tail and runs on ahead.

Edgar thinks, "Neither did I, Fen, neither did I. I think you're the only link I have with reality girl."

Crossing under Highway 49 to River Road the hoots and shrieks from the crush of people echo like thunder booming through a canyon, deafening the ears. At the parking lot at the end of River Road Edgar dismounts and pats Charger for a job well done and thanks him for not tossing him. Washington Reyes pats Edgar on the back, takes the reigns from his hand and walks Charger over to drink from the river. Washington fits Charger with a bag of oats he brought from Salmon Creek Stables.

Edgar goes over to the carnival food stand and buys a beer, while he waits at a table for the rest of the parade to end. He still can't believe the size of the multitudes, attending the festival. He figures five thousand people at least. After ordering a round of beers, the rest of the town council joins Edgar. Pat brings over a couple of pitchers to make sure nobody runs dry with the temperature in Abbeville in the mid-90's.

"What was that run up Wog Hill all about, Edgar?" McWhinney inquires.

"I thought I saw someone I hadn't seen for a while, but it wasn't him," Edgar nonchalantly replies.

"For a while you looked like a man possessed," observes Conrad.

"For a while I was," Edgar agrees.

"What's next on the agenda," asks Bronco.

Bill says, "The carnival is scheduled to go all afternoon and into the evening. The feature events for today are the Turkey Shoot at Spring Creek Park, the cake walk back in town, Logrolling in the Yuba River and out at Indian Point the Kitwa Native Americans are demonstrating their Ghost Dances in honor of those past." Edgar responds, as Bill nods in accordance.

Conrad suggests everyone go over to Indian Point and watches the Kitwa ghost dances and listen to Native American folklore. Except for Edgar, everyone agrees. Edgar has something to take care of before joining the group. He visits the first aide station manned by Dr. Preston.

"How's business, Silvia?"

"Thankfully slow, Edgar. The festival looks like a big success so far."

"I think Alma would be proud."

"Alma would be in her element. Like Bill said, we wouldn't be having this bicentennial festival if it weren't for Alma. I think of her a lot these days."

"That's what I want to talk to you about. I saw Alma today. I also saw Anne Dean, Henry, and Bob Winston. What do you think about all that Silvia?"

"I think you want to believe you saw the people you love so much and were with for so many years. You know the gene pool isn't that large, especially around here. Lot's of people look like people we know. It doesn't take much to see similarities among people, especially when you wanted to see these people."

"Yes, that sounds about right. That's why I had to see whether I really saw Bob up on Wog Hill."

"I wondered why you stopped the parade and tore up that way. You're clear enough to do a reality check when you need to. Not many can say that."

"That's exactly what I did. I'm thankful I have most of my marbles at this age. The guy was about the same height and stature as Bob and I guess I let my wishful imagination do the rest."

Silvia agrees.

"An excellent self analysis, if I do say so myself. I'm going over to Indian Point to see the ghost dances. Want to come along?"

"I have to wait for Florence to relieve me, but I'll be over later."

Edgar walks about a hundred yards from the first aide station toward Indian Point. He can hear Chief Silver Squirrel telling the history of Kitwa ghost dances, as Loadstone, Broken Arrow, and Half Moon put the finishing touches on the authentic Native American village complete with hangi. Edgar stands quietly, watching the Kitwa ceremonial dance. Everyone seems to be enjoying the folklore and dancing.

"The Mandoo people lived along the coasts and in the central valley of California and were among the first to hear about the ghost dances," Chief Silver Squirrel recounts, "Wodziwob, a Northern Paiute prophet, dreamed of the time when the white invaders would be driven from their lands and the land and buffalo restored. The first ghost dances faded, as the white people conquered the Native Americans."

Loadstone, Broken Arrow, and Half Moon emerge from the sweat hut they reconstructed at Indian Point. In special Native American dress, painted with magic symbols, they dance short sidesteps in a circle, as they face the fire.

Silver Squirrel speaks, "Wovoka was a powerful Paiute medicine man, who studied Christian theology and understood the stories in the Bible. He testified that he was taken into the spirit world where he saw the dead ancestors alive. 'The ancestors prosper,' he said, and are 'happy and lived in a restored world, free from their oppressors.' Wokoka prophesied that, in time, the dead and alive will join hands and become one on the face of the earth."

Immersed in the Ghost Dance and the words and worlds spoken of by Chief Silver Squirrel, the onlookers at Indian Point are swept into the past, when magic was in the air and Native Americans ran like the buffalo.

"Do my white brothers and sisters have any questions?" Silver Squirrel asks.

Tommy Freeman poses the first question, as only a child can, "Are there bad ghosts?"

"There are good and bad ghosts. The good-hearted ghosts follow the path of the Milky Way to Heaven Valley. Bad ghosts are turned into rocks and bushes."

Tommy's eyes get big at the thought that bad ghosts get turned into rocks and bushes.

"Do your people's burial rites differ from your ancestors?" asks Conrad.

"Good question, my friend. Our burial rites are the same as those of our ancestors. We bury our dead in bearskins with their belongings. They are faced to the west. When one of our clan dies away from the village, he is cremated and his remains brought back, later to be buried in the village."

Dr. Preston poses the next question, "Your burial grounds are found in Kitwa villages?"

"No, 'buried in the village' is an expression we use. Our sacred burial grounds are hidden and protected in the mountains."

Silvia probes further, "How are the hidden burial grounds protected, Chief Silver Squirrel?"

"By birds of prey from above and wolf packs below. The locations of our sacred grounds are never whispered. The names of those who hearts are gone are never spoken. It has been that way since the days of our ancestors, long before Wounded Knee.

"You believe the dead, both the buried ashes and the buried dead are alive and well in Heaven Valley and some day will be entirely restored?" asks Florence.

"There are many beliefs about restoration. Some say we should avoid mourning the dead, as they will be resurrected in a short period of time. Those believing in quick resurrections pray, chant, and dance, like we have today."

The question and answer period holds the people's attention into the evening, when Chief Silver Squirrel and the Kitwa council members take one last question, promising to return the next day with more Kitwa tales, dances and magic charms and jewelry to sell.

"Chief Silver Squirrel."

"My friend, Edgar. You have the last question of the day."

"Alma . . . Will Alma be resurrected soon?"

"My friend, Edgar, your sister is a great spirit and is already with us."

Calliope music mixed with screams from the roller coaster ride, the haunted house, and the laughter of children at play linger in the air as the session at Indian Point ends. Carnival lights and sights and sounds fill the forest and mountains. To make a buck, carnies look for mooches to scam and avoid sharpies, wise enough to know their carnie scams. The hustle and bustle of the midway is a welcomed window of excitement for the townspeople of Abbeville.

Edgar and Silvia walk from Indian Point to the Ferris wheel and wait for the blue seat to reach them before boarding. Desiree and Conrad follow and get in the seat behind them. Everyone wants to see the view from atop the wheel and pays a little extra for the carnie to hold them atop for a good while. The wheel turns slowly, as everyone has paid the price to stop and watch the best view of Abbeville anyone can imagine.

"What did you think of Chief Silver Squirrel's show?" Edgar asks.

"Impressive. I wasn't aware of the short resurrection aspect of their religious beliefs," responds Silvia.

"Indeed, quite impressive."

"You're thinking about Silver Squirrel's answer to your question?" Silvia inquires.

"If only it were true," yearns Edgar, thinking about Alma.

Desiree interjects from the seat below. "Death is such a bolt from the blue. We humans may need something like religion to soften the blow of mortality. I wish I viewed death more like the animals, who don't seem to worry about such things,"

"I think Christianity may have influenced the Kitwa culture somewhere back in the 1800's," Edgar hazards a guess.

"Around 1832, to be more exact," Conrad contributes.

"If anyone knows, that would be you, Conrad," responds Silvia.

"I heard that to win against overwhelming odds, some Native Americans believed the dead, who fought bravely in battle against the white invaders, were quickly resurrected, recycled, and sent back to battle, increasing the number of warriors?" Desiree shares.

"Sounds a little far fetched to me." Dr. Preston assertively declares.

"Desiree is not far off base," interjects Conrad, "Consider this interesting historical tidbit about the spiritual leader, Wovoka, that Chief Silver Squirrel didn't mention. Wovoka created the idea of ghost dancing and was known for his magic bullet catch. Someone would fire a gun at Wovoka and he would catch the bullet. Somehow news of the bullet catch was weaved with the idea of ghost dances, which made the shirts of ghost dancers bulletproof. Sadly, on the morning of December 29, 1890 the belief of the Lakota tribe in the invincibility of their "ghost shirts" proved wrong, when U. S. troops opened fire on unarmed Lakota people, killing 290 men, women, and children in a matter of minutes."

"That was the Wounded Knee Massacre Chief Silver Squirrel mentioned today," responds Desiree.

"Still, maybe quick resurrection for some purpose worked out for Alma." Edgar thinks to himself.

Looking from the top of the Ferris wheel Edgar sees Anne Dean.

"Silvia! That woman by the cotton candy machine, that woman looks like Anne Dean!"

Edgar's voice is loud enough to be heard by the people below them. One couple doesn't care because they are from out of town and haven't heard of Anne Dean. They simply think the guy sees someone he knows. Conrad and Desiree peer at the woman, as does Silvia.

"Yes, Edgar, I see the woman by the cotton candy, but it's hard to tell who she is from this angle. How many times have you seen the top of Anne Dean's head from a Ferris wheel?" quips Silvia.

"You're right, Silvia, I'm seeing what I wish to see again. I think I've had enough excitement for the day."

Fenway and Edgar ride the shuttle from Yuba Park to town hall. They hoof it the rest of the way to the cabin. Everyone else parties at the carnival past one o'clock in the morning. Then the carnival shuts down. Abbeville's Matthew Drive stays open for business until dawn, as those still in a festive mood fill the Blue Goose, the Knead-2-Feed Bakery, Las Abuelitas Cocina Mexicana, and the cafe at the general store kept open by Bridget, Ted, Daisy May, and Fred Barns.

Sunday, July 3, 10:00 a.m.: Over the loud speaker, the winners of yesterday's cakewalks are announced and the news blares out that Hector "gravedigger" Flores, the crematorium attendant at the Abbeville Cemetery, won the logrolling contest.

Howls and bellows from the turkey shoot mingle with carnival sounds, as Edgar and Fenway warm up for the fly fishing contest at Salmon Creek Winery Pond.

"See that green inner tube, Fenway. A couple of sweeps of the rod for rhythm and timing and I should be able to side cast my fly over the wild raspberry bushes and under the limbs of that pine tree and drop it perfectly."

Talking to Fenway calms Edgar's nerves. Lost in the wonder of fly-fishing, Edgar casts and floats his fly exactly through the space between the top of the bush and the overhanging pine limb, but the fly falls short and bounces off the front of the inner tube and drops into the creek.

"Ah rats, close enough for a practice try though, Fenway old girl, I'm almost there. I've got the touch today."

Edgar is up against nine expert fly casters. He has been there before and relishes the opportunity to test his skills against the best in the Sierra's. This time "Beetle" Hampton wins. "Stone Fly" Radford is second, and Edgar snags third place.

"Not a bad days work, Fenway. If my underhand cast under tree limb into the red tube had dropped, I would have had Beetle by the short hairs."

Fenway seems to agree. Edgar takes the shuttle to Yuba River Park and purchases pink cotton candy on a paper cone for a buck twenty-five and joins Conrad, Desiree, Mo, and Ellen, Curtis, Cannon, Florence, and Nick Simmons at the Oktoberfest table for a beer.

"Third place isn't bad Edgar," Cannon calls out, as Edgar nears the table.

"Third out of a field of a hundred twenty fly fishing nuts, not bad at all," Edgar boasts, "That means I will not have to pay the seventy-five dollar entrance fee again next year."

That brings a burst of hyena-pitched laugher from the group.

"So what does third place win?" Ellen asks.

"Ellen, third place earned me an M-series eight compartment fly box and an assortment of fine flies—the White River Fly Shop Parachute, an Adams Dry Fishing Fly, an Orvis Adams Trude Fly, and the brand new Barnsley-Adams Irresistible 16 Dry Fly."

Mo interjects, "So far, that's better than the green fish tie you won for first place last year, Edgar."

Edgar takes a bite of his cotton candy and offers some to Ellen, Desiree, and Florence, who pinch bits of cotton candy off with their fingers.

"The rest of you smart mouth guys don't get any!"

Bruce says, "That reminds me. I thought I saw Anne last night over by the candy cotton machine. It must have been my imagination playing tricks on me."

"Maybe not, "Edgar pops up, "I thought I saw the same thing from the Ferris wheel."

"What do you think the odds are that the two of you hallucinated about the same thing at the same time last night?" adds Conrad.

Florence jumps in, "I'd say the chances of that happening are better than even given the emotional stress you two are under. Lots of people resemble each other, especially at a distance. And, you saw what you thought was Anne in carnival lights at nighttime. Very suspect at best."

The loudspeakers interrupt with the announcement that anyone interested in breaking wild horses should meet at Salmon Creek Stables in fifteen minutes.

"Now there's one event I won't mind missing," Nick admits.

"How about going to the stables to watch others break their bones?" Mo asks.

Florence says, "I'll pass on that. I see enough broken bones, ruptured spleens, and kidney failure at the clinic."

The next announcement plugs the Chili Cook Off at Spring Creek Park.

"That's more to my liking," responds Bruce.

At that moment, Elders Jones, Richmond, and Lawrence pass by.

"Beautiful day," Elder Jacob Richmond greets the table, "A good day to go digging for gold."

"Elder Jacob," Conrad greets back, "You're looking fit as a fiddle. I understand the haunted mines above Sand Pond are beautiful this time of year."

Conrad receives a combination of cringing and disapproving looks from his friends.

"Why on earth would you want to pull their chains Conrad?" snaps Florence.

"Grab the ungodly fiends and spit in their eyes, I say."

"Next time, could you spit in their eyes when I'm not here?" replies Bruce, "I have to work with these guys."

"They make my skin crawl," Mo admits.

Sunday, July 3, 2:00 p.m.: Emma Jane Walters' Wog Hill Chili Pot recipe wins the chili contest, hands down. The chili contest wets the crowd's pallets for the California Style Barbeque served by Bronco and the boys at

Spring Creek Park. The barbeque lasts for three hours and feeds over four thousand people. Stuffed like Thanksgiving turkeys, half of the crowd goes home by nine o'clock in the evening and hit the sack early to be fresh and ready for the last day of the festival.

The evening's jazz is smooth and dreamy and perfect to slow dance to on the grass. It's Not The Pale Moon That Excites Me is the final song played at jazz on the grass festival, ending the second day on a high note and ensuring big crowds return for the last day of the bicentennial festival.

Chapter 2

❦

M onday, July 4, 4:00 p.m.: A good sized crowd shows for the festival's final day, which is focused on kiddies-games and carnival rides for the young ones. As the festival winds down, family picnics are the activity of choice for most of those attending the festival.

Announcements over the loud speakers report cakewalk winners for the final day of the festival. The top spots in the Fly-Fishing Contest go to "Stone Fly" for catching two fish weighing a total of 18 pounds. "Beetle" took second with a total of 16.35 pounds of fish with four fish. Edgar is skunked this time, allowing "Big Belly" Wilson to walk away with third place. Alex Temecula won the final day's Logrolling contest, making it a gravedigger's sweep of the two-day competition. With ten out of ten turkeys nailed, "Mole Baby" Sutton wins the Abbeville Bicentennial Turkey Shoot and walks away with a Columbia Men's Omni Heat Wader Widgeon Parka and a Horn Hunter Slingshot with twelve gold tip trophy hunter arrows. The announcements fade to silence, as Big Momma Thornton's *Hound Dog* plays throughout Abbeville.

Good news for Florence and Dr. Preston, no legs are broken riding wild horses or riding Brahma bulls on the last two days of the festival. The Big Sand Pond Weenie Roast hosted by the Bar-B Cattle Ranch was a huge success that almost turned into a disaster, when the weenies were mistakenly delivered to the Boy Scout Camp down Packer Lake Road. Although Edgar chooses to skip the fireworks at Upper Sardine Lake, the pyrotechnics are spectacular and are the perfect ending for Abbeville's Bicentennial Festival.

As immensely popular and financially successful as was the festival, more townsfolk can't wait to pull up stakes and move from Abbeville to other towns that are safer than Abbeville and offer more of a future than becoming the richest ghost town in the Sierras. On the way home from the evening's fireworks stories begin to spread through Abbeville. Townsfolk's report seeing shadows move by the abandoned mines above the Sardine lakes and Sand Pond. And later, reports of shootings in Abbeville reach the patrons of the Sardine Resort Bar and Restaurant and the Blue Goose. Rumors about shadows on the hillsides and shootings after the festival fireworks quickly spread from the bars and restaurants through the town.

Tuesday, July 5, 12:10 a.m. Dr. Preston and Florence are contacted by Lieutenant Milo Freeman about a shooting at Harvard Elgin's residence and arrive at the crime scene. They examine Elgin's gun and determine five shots to have been fired. The gun is bagged and marked as evidence #J410-E8-001 (Gun) and placed in the custody of Sergeant Dirk Jacobson.

Tuesday, July 5, 1:07 a.m. Dr. Jeffrey Martin Mayes of the Sierra County Sheriff Department Medical Examiner and his forensic team arrive and deploy in the forest and systematically search for evidence. All evidence is collected and marked as called for by the medical examiner protocol. The chain of evidence is duly recorded.

Two of the five bullets shot from Elgin's gun are found in the wall and ceiling of his house. Three more bullets are found lodged in trees in the forest, where blood and tissue spatter are found on one of the trees. Blood and tissue-splashed bark is remove from the tree and placed in evidence boxes. Bloody leaves found on the forest floor where Elgin and his family saw the shadow of a person fall are bagged and marked for analysis and evidence. All bullets are bagged and properly marked as evidence.

Dr. Preston, as an officer of the Court, takes samples of the blood soaked leaves and one bullet for her own analysis. Those are properly marked for evidence as #J410-E8-008 (Blood Leaf Sample) and #J410-E8-009 (Tree Lodged Bullet). A thorough forensic sweep is made of the house, grounds and forest with all evidence found appropriately marked.

In all, thirty-seven pieces of physical evidence from the crime scene are marked that morning, but no signs of bodies exist. No footprints are found.

Tuesday, July 5, 6:30 a.m. The forensic team, Sheriff deputies, Silvia and Florence leave the crime scene. For further study in the old Sierra Meat Company's meat locker at the Abbeville Town Morgue, Dr. Preston keeps several samples of blood and tissue, which she is allowed to do by past practice of the Medical Examiner's Office. Silvia is one of Dr. Mayes' secret weapons in his war against crime. They have formed a trusting relationship over the years.

Tuesday, July 5, 6:43 a.m.: Silvia loses no time calling in outside experts to help her with the analysis of the blood and tissue samples she has collected from the Elgin shooting. Dr. Michael Greenstone is the chief forensic pathologist and medical examiner for Alameda County and an adjunct lecturer at the University of California in Berkeley. He has followed the bizarre course of events in Abbeville and is eager to lend a helping hand. A call to Professor Gene McIntyre produces the same results and the three agree to meet on July 12 to study the collected samples.

Tuesday, July 5, 10:00 a.m.: What was first thought to be twisted rumors about someone being shot after the fireworks display at Upper Sardine Lake turns out to be true. Betzer Morrison, KWAB's moderator on the Good Morning Yuba Pass Show, continuously plays a frantic 911-call recorded at 11:55 p.m. on the evening of the Fourth of July.

Dispatcher: "This is 911 police dispatcher Karen. How may I help?"

Caller: "My name is Harvard Elgin and I live at 8 Central Spring Creek Lane in Abbeville Estates. I think we have been robbed and I see shadowy figures running across West Spring Creek Lane into the forest. No, something stopped at the edge of the forest."

Voice in Background, "Look! There, it's coming toward us. I'm scared Dad.

Dispatcher: "Who is that in the background, Mr. Elgin?"

Elgin: "My daughter Peggy."

Another Voice in the Background: "Oh My God! It's coming back to kill us! (Screaming is heard.)"

Dispatcher: "Mr. Elgin, sheriff deputies are on their way. Breathe, stay calm, you are doing well. You have a right to protect yourself, but be sure you are in actual danger. (Sounds of shots being fired) What is going on Mr. Elgin?"

Elgin: "This man came into our house again and I shot at him."

Dispatcher: "Mr. Elgin, did you hit him?"

Elgin: "I don't see how I missed. He was right on top of us. He's running into the forest. No he's fallen. I think I hit him. Oh no, please God let him be alive."

(Sounds of police arriving; conversations grabbled.)

Lieutenant Freeman: "Mr. Elgin can you identify who it was that entered your home?"

Elgin: "Not exactly, Lieutenant. Everything was a blur. My only thought was to protect my family from whatever it was."

Lieutenant Freeman: "How tall was the assailant?"

Elgin: "Taller than me. When he went out the door he appeared to be five ten or so."

Lieutenant Freeman: "What was he or she wearing?"

Elgin: "Now that I think of it, Lieutenant Milo, I couldn't tell you if they were wearing anything."

Lieutenant Freeman: "You're saying they were nude?"

Elgin: "I can't be sure, but I'd say yes. Maybe they were looking for something to wear. I don't know. It was dark."

Lieutenant Freeman: "You think there were two people, Mr. Elgin?"

Elgin: "Yes, I think so."

(End of transmission.)

Abbeville's gossip mill makes the news about the Elgin shooting so ghastly that more and more Abbevillians leave town. The first business to fold is the Tree Trimmer's Barbershop. Auggie can't take the constant pounding of endless rumors trafficking through his shop. He is also losing business to the Hair Falls Salon, which is now so popular that men want Ellen to cut their hair. The problem is not that the barbershop closing is so much of an economic hit to Abbeville, than the shop's closing further unsettles the confidence of the town's inhabitants—the rats are leaving the sinking ship.

Thursday, July 7, 2:15 p.m.: As promised Doctors Greenstone and McIntyre arrive at the town morgue on time. Silvia introduces the two and invites them to sit around the morgue, drinking coffee and getting to know each other better before analyzing the forensic evidence collected behind the Elgin household.

"Where do want to start, Dr. Preston," inquires Greenstone.

"I have the blood stain pattern analysis and chemical lab DNA, blood type and Rhesus antigens factor results and find them interesting to say the least. You have samples of blood from the blood soaked leaves I collected at the scene of the crime. I suggest you and Dr. McIntyre analyze your samples, so we can compare the results with the pattern analysis and lab report and go from there."

The blind blood sample analysis Silvia suggests is agreeable to McIntyre and Greenstone. They take the necessary time to conduct their separate and independent tests. Two hours later they are finished with phase-one.

"Now what?" McIntyre asks.

"I suggest we each examine the blood and tissue showered on the bark fragments we removed from the pine tree. I've done my analyses and have my opinion about where they came from, but I'll wait until you two have conducted your analyses and drawn conclusions about what they mean. Then, let's compare and discuss our findings."

Drs. Greenstone and McIntyre take another hour examining the evidence from the pine tree. Finished with their preliminary analysis, the doctors begin to share their findings and opinions.

Dr. McIntyre starts, "The blood sample isn't human, but it is very close to being human. Need a blood transfusion? Our bodies will not reject this blood."

Doctors Greenstone and Preston agree to the extent that whatever they found it was not exactly human blood, but close to it.

"Gentlemen, what do you have to say about the substance found on the bark fragments and leaves?" Dr. Preston continues.

Greenstone answers, "Although it is close, the blood and tissue definitely did not come from a human. Neither does the tissue and blood belong to any animal I know of. The sample reminds me of colonies of protists or microorganisms, which take the place of human tissue like minerals take the same structure as the wood of petrified trees."

McIntyre adds, "That's it! We have a replication of human tissue, using the microorganisms and protists already in our human bodies. Amazing! Fascinating, there are no signs of the tissue decomposing. The tissue, if anything, is maintaining itself!"

"The only information I'd add is, according to my thermal cycling of the blood samples, the assailant was a male," Dr. Preston contributes, "Otherwise, our findings match perfectly."

Greenstone speculates, "We may well have found a mutated human being, an improved model of the old human, maybe even a new species."

McIntyre cautions, "A new species of human! We have a long way to go before we can be certain we have discovered a new anything from few drops of blood and microscopic bits of tissue."

"Agreed. No one is suggesting for a moment that we go out an write a scientific paper on this baby," Dr. Preston emphasizes.

"But, it is an interesting notion we're entertaining. Think of the questions raised by the existence of a new species of human? Where did it come from? How was it formed? Then, the philosophical questions who or what formed it, how, and why?" Greenstone ponders.

"If we put information out in the public about a new species with tissues and blood that regenerates itself, we'll all be drawn and quartered, burned and have our ashes tossed in the Yuba River!" McIntyre exclaims.

"Now, there's a comforting thought. That will inspire our youngsters to want to become scientists." Jokes Greenstone.

"You think Darwin had it rough; I can hardly wait," Silvia muses.

"Very funny. Okay, let's get the nervous humor out of our systems and screw our heads on straight and decide what we are going to say and do," Dr. McIntyre advises.

Silvia comments, "Oh, I'm all for us keeping our heads. What precisely are we going to say? This little meeting of our hasn't exactly gone unnoticed by the fine citizens of Abbeville."

McIntyre suggests, "Whatever we do say must be the truth, must convey the facts, and we must be on the same page. Let's start with answering the question: Why are the three of us here?"

"Easy," Greenstone responds, "We're here to examine the evidence found at the Elgin shooting. Dr. Preston called us in to review the evidence and give our professional opinions. We found nothing that would say anything more than Mr. Elgin fired and hit the assailant and the evidence suggests the assailant was not mortally wounded. That's the end of our public statement."

Silvia says, "So far so good, but what do I tell the county medical examiner?"

"Don't you think the medical examiner's blood and tissue analyses will lead them to the same conclusions we've reached?" Dr. Greenstone makes a compelling point.

"Possibly, possibly not. Either way, the ball is in the county medical examiner's court. Let's see what Dr. Mayes and his forensic team come up with. I suggest we put the new species idea on the back shelf for a while. It's merely speculation and we are not legally or morally compelled to climb out on a limb without verifying our scientific speculations." Dr. McIntyre advises.

Greenstone agrees, "We would be rather premature, releasing our preliminary findings without substantial scientific verification. Announcing a new species would create quite a political whirlwind that kicks our Christian theology, as well as our biological theory, in the head."

"Not necessarily so, Dr. Greenstone," McIntyre muses, "According to Scripture, ever so often God wipes out individuals, groups, and most of the human race to start a new slate. Several times, God tried to give humans another chance to return to him. The flood Noah experienced wiped out the earth, as he knew it, except for his family and the animals he collected. That was a meteorological event used to hit the restart button. The destruction of Sodom and Gomorra purged the earth of evil. That was a cosmological event that hit the reset button. God has always used natural disasters, acts of God—fiery destruction from the skies, plagues, earthquakes, and floods. Why can't God give humans another shaking up by upgrading their DNA through biological evolution?"

"I'll believe that, when you scientifically verify your theory," declares Greenstone.

Dr. Preston is quiet. She is well aware that forest shadows may exist, a phenomenon she can't quite scientifically explain, but one that goes beyond the physical.

McIntyre observes, "Silence! Dr. Preston? I've never known you to miss an opportunity to give your professional opinion. Could it be that you think there's merit in what I say?"

"Too early to tell. I certainly don't believe in what I can't scientifically prove. Like Dr. Greenstone, I'll need a whole lot more before I sing your tune, Professor. But, I can't falsify your thinking, quite yet, either."

"You two can't categorically disprove the possibility that we've found a newly evolved form of human being, strictly on biological terms, either. I find the theological possibilities irrelevant, at this point. But, the science is promising. We certainly can trace the DNA of this new species of human being from the old." Dr. Greenstone argues.

"In any case, let's not start celebrating anything, until we have our scientific data lined up like ducks in a row." Dr. McIntyre states.

"That's a point we all can agree upon," Dr. Preston replies.

"One thing for certain, Dr. Greenstone and I do not have to say anything as consultants called into the case. All our recommendations are funneled to Dr. Preston," Dr. McIntyre states with a twinkle in his eye.

"That's exactly the way I like it, gentlemen. I'm in control of all the communication here, perfect." Dr. Preston summarizes the group's position.

Book Seven

❦

Utter Destruction

Chapter 1

❦

Friday, July 8 12:15 p.m.: Airing Harvard Elgin's 911-call on the radio grabs the attention of everyone in Abbeville. Sacramento Courier reporters won't let the story die, and the Abbeville gossip mill has a field day with Elgin shooting at shadows in Abbeville Estates. Eating her lunch on the park benches by the fountain statue of Samuel Beckett, Joyce Lawrence, head librarian, discusses the Elgin affair with Fredrika, Bunny, Edna, and Holly.

"I hate to say this, but Mr. Elgin shooting at forest shadows tells me something sinister is sweeping this town. Elder Jacob Richmond stirring the town up with his ravings about Reverend Henry murdering Alma and dumping her body in an abandoned gold mine isn't helping matters any."

Fredrika runs to Jacob's defense, "Elder Richmond is a good Christian gentleman, a little indignant about the infidelities of Alma and Reverend Henry to be sure, but a man of God justifiably outraged by the sins of this godless pastor and his temple whore? I hear it was Alma that was shot by Mr. Elgin as she ran from his house. Alma and Henry are not dead; they are living, hiding deep in the forest protected by Edgar, Dr. Preston, and their cronies. I feel it in my bones."

"I heard the same thing, only, according to my sources, Alma and Henry are protected in the forest by Chief Silver Squirrel. You heard those Indian go on and on at the bicentennial about their secret burial grounds and all. Indians know everything going on in the forest," Bunny reveals.

Joyce admits, "I too am a little annoyed about the shenanigans of Alma and Henry. They've brought nothing but shame to our town and church. Everybody is feeling sorry about Edgar. How pathetic!"

Fredrika is pleased with herself for turning Joyce around so easily. Since Joyce Lawrence replaced Bob Winston as head librarian, Fredrika acquires a strong ally to do her bidding.

Bunny asks, "Who's holding down the fort, while you're on lunch break, Joyce?"

Joyce exclaims, "Oh my God you're right! I've been out here too long and my new assistant, Abigail Sorenson-Valdez—she needs the work being a new mother with a three month old baby boy they named Hermano or Umberto or something like that . . . besides, who knows if a father is in the picture? Noon is a popular time for visiting the library. Sorry. Got-to-go, girls."

Again exercising her power Fredrika says, "Joyce. You trained her well, didn't you? Abigail will do fine."

"You are right, Fredrika. I can stay a little longer."

"Exactly," purrs Fredrika.

Holly erupts, "You know Tree Trimmers sold their business to a new church."

The news catches everyone flat-footed.

"No!"

"Yes! And, that little dinky space is the home of the Church of Self Reflection. I talked to the new pastor Sister Joyce McMichaels," reports Holly.

"What kind of church is that?" Edna shrieks.

"I don't know if you can call it a church with a woman running it? Sounds like an abomination in God's sight. I know it's an abomination in my sight," Fredrika retorts.

Holly Spears, gossiper par excellence and another of Fredrika's loyal followers, agrees with Fredrika.

"Fredrika's right," echoes Edna, "It's an abomination, an abomination, an abomination! Well, Holly, what did Sister Joyce have to say?"

"Like I said, I talked to that woman and she said they already have six church members. She even asked me to join. I said no, of course," Holly continues.

"Holly, what did she say they believed in?" Bunny demands.

"Some gibberish like we are made in the image and likeness of God and need to reflect on our inner selves. Can you image?" Holly broadcasts.

"We'll have to let the elders at church know," insists Edna.

"I did phone Elder Dean and told him the whole story and he said he was going to give Sister Joyce McMichaels a visit." Holly informs the group.

Head elder Bruce Dean and several elders had talked with Joyce McMichaels for a couple of hours. Sister Joyce was clear the Self Reflection Church is about discovering and acting upon spirituality God placed within us to help others. That she plans to open a kitchen to feed Abbeville's needy favorably impresses the elders, who want to support Sister Joyce.

Friday, July 8 7:15 p.m.: That night, during the council meeting, the good news spoken about the new church drives a wedge between church elders. As is the tradition of Damascus Church, disputes are decided by standing votes of the elders. Elder Richmond stands at the meeting and rails about Henry and Alma, he protests the new church and calls for Damascus church to be reformed.

"Who will stand with me and the Lord this day against Satan?" Elder Jacob declares.

Eight elders stand with Elder Jacob. Elder Richmond holds his open hand out to Bruce Dean, who hands him the gavel. With the exchange of gavel, Jacob immediately becomes the head elder of the council.

The first action taken by Jacob's council is appointing Elder Jacob Richmond to the temporary position of pastor of the Damascus Church. In turn, Pastor Jacob appoints Elder Elroy Jones to fill the newly created position of Assistant Pastor of Family and Community Outreach. Elder Martin Lawrence is appointed church treasurer. The last action of Jacob's council is to change the name of the church to the Damascus Reformed Church; and, on a vote of eight to four Damascus Church becomes the Damascus Reformed Church.

Elder Harvard Elgin asks, "Pastor Jacob, what duties do you have in mind for the FCO assistant pastor?"

Pastor Jacob hands out a half-sheet job description and says, "The main responsibility Assistant Pastor Jones has agreed to take is purifying the community, which means identifying members of the Sisterhood and praying for the salvation of their souls. It also means we will begin to take action to close Sister McMichael's Church of Self Reflection."

Elder Bronco Brown challenges Pastor Jacob's ideas, "Christ never tried to close other churches or other religions. Christ never took actions against women for testifying on his behalf. Instead, we are to embrace others with the love and compassion Jesus showed us."

"Jesus cast the demons into a herd of pigs and they destroyed themselves in the sea. These demons in our midst will be treated the same way Jesus treated the demons of his day."

The answer doesn't sit well with Elder Brown, who, like the Apostle Peter, continues to passionately speak out. With eight of the elder votes in his back pocket, Pastor Elder Jacob has the political power to do anything he wants.

"Reverend Henry briefed us on sermon topics he was thinking about presenting to the congregation and asked us for input. Will you continue to follow that policy Pastor Jacob?" asks Elder Sherman.

"Discussing my prospective sermons with the entire council takes away important meeting time that can be better spent praying and meditating on God's word. Reverend Henry's past practice will not be followed. I've created a small group of elders to advise me on important church matters, including sermon topics and content.

"Who is on the committee Pastor?" asks Elder Dean.

"Elders Jones, Lawrence, and Elder Robert Crane are in the circle."

"How does the circle work Pastor?" Bruce asks a follow up question for clarity.

"I follow Christ's ministry. The Bible shows Jesus was close to three apostles, Peter, James, and John. We work like Christ's Inner Circle in the management of our council and church congregation affairs."

"Christ didn't have an inner circle, Pastor. He dined and worked with the twelve apostles. Elroy, Martin, and Bob has a little different ring to it than Peter, James, and John, but I get the picture," quips Elder Brown.

Sunday, July 10, 9:00 a.m.: Pastor Elder Jacob Richmond portrays the Damascus Reformed Church being in a struggle not against flesh and blood humans but against authorities and powers of petty town councils, against the dark powers ruling from the forests and spiritual forces of wickedness in heavenly places. The congregation understands Jacob's message, a call to action against the sinister powers seizing Abbeville.

Attendance at church services, which had dropped by more than half, since Henry's resignation, drops by half again.

Sunday, July 17, 9:00 a.m.: In the following Sunday's sermon Pastor Jacob preaches on the rapture and end of the world. He predicts the rapture will take place on July 17 of the next year, followed one hundred fifty-nine days later by the end of the world. His sermon, which was hotly debated at the Friday elder's council meeting before the sermon, is delivered to a congregation numbering seventy-five people. What is Pastor Jacob's reaction to the drop in church attendance under his leadership?

"Many are called, but few are chosen. I am the instrument God is using to destroy dangerous forces within our church. Only you, the true believers, know this truth to be reality. I rely on the command of Jesus Christ, telling us to keep our eyes on the glorious future Christ promises. This is the work of the reformation of our church."

Pastor Elder Jacob's message and Abbeville's gossip mill are finally on the same page. Alma and Reverend Henry's death and disappearance, the shooting at forest shadows behind Elder Elgin's house, and the establishment of the Church of Self Reflection are evil signs, demanding the forces of righteousness take action. Pastor Jacob sees himself as one of the great generals of God's brigades, preparing to fight the last war, Armageddon on January 30, a little over a year and five months from now.

Sitting in the back of the church, Sydney Cameron furiously takes notes on the new Pastor's sermon. Monday morning headlines tell the tale: PASTOR JACOB'S DECLARES WAR ON EVIL IN ABBEVILLE. The next day's headlines air the other side of the Damascus Church split: ELDERS OPENLY DISAGREE WITH PASTOR JACOB'S LEADERSHIP. In an interview with Elder Bronco Brown, Cameron successfully draws out differences of Bible interpretations about the rapture and the end of the world held by elder council members.

Cameron: "You disagree with Pastor Jacob's apocalyptic message?

Elder Brown is quoted as saying, "I don't disagree with Pastor Jacob on the Biblical fact that there will be a rapture, when Christ comes back and glorifies the bodies of Christians. I don't disagree with the Pastor that the end of the world will follow that event. That's straightforward New Testament Scripture. But, according to Scripture, no one knows the time when the rapture and end of the world will take place."

Cameron: "So you disagree with Pastor Jacob because he predicts exactly when the rapture and the end of the world will happen?"

Elder Brown quote is, "Absolutely. We also disagree how our bodies will be glorified."

Cameron: "How does that work?"

Elder Brown's quote continues, "Pastor Jacob and his followers believe our bodies will be transformed and glorified, as we meet Christ in the air, like some kind of magic. A number of the elders and I believe our bodies begin the transformation and glorification process, when we accept Jesus as our personal Savior. Paul is quite specific that our perfection in Christ is a process. First, Christ justifies us. Second, Christ saves us. Third, Christ glorifies our bodies."

Cameron: "Elder Brown, your belief sounds like a magical process too?"

Elder Brown's reply is reported, "No magic is involved. We're dealing with scientific facts. The science of Intelligent Design tells us God, the intelligent designer, made us in his glory, his image and likeness. When we sin against God, our bodies deteriorate. When we accept Jesus as Lord of our lives, our restoration process begins and ends with our bodies being glorified as God first created us."

Cameron: "Scientific facts?"

Elder Brown is quoted as stating, "Eventually, science always proves Scripture to be accurate. I believe God's process for glorifying our bodies is changing the biology of our bodies for the better."

Cameron: "Biological in the sense our bodies will be biologically transformed to the glorified state you and Pastor Jacob talk about?"

Elder Brown quotes from the Bible to prove his point, "Exactly. Read Philippians 3.20 and 1 Thessalonians 4.15-17. There are many ways to interpret these Scriptures. Every Christian's body begins developing his glorified body while he is on earth. The process is completed when he meets Jesus in the sky. I'm not dogmatic about it like Jacob is. Pastor Jacob believes it's his way of believing or the highway. Most of our church is taking the highway."

Headlines about the theological banter among elders at the Damascus Reformed Church play in the newspaper day-in-and-day-out. It is not the kind of press wanted by the town's chamber of commerce or the town council. The good news is that all the hoopla distracts attention from Dr. Preston's meeting with Drs. Greenstone and McIntyre. The shooting on July fourth takes a backseat to elders of the DRC, shooting off their mouths.

Taking advantage of being out of the spotlight, Silvia accepts Dr. Mayes' invitation to meet with him at his office in Downieville. Meeting at the county medical examiner's office frees her from prying eyes and the possibility of being the subject of town gossip.

Monday, July 18, 2:45:00 p.m.: Dr. Preston arrives on time at Dr. Mayes' office, where she is greeted by quite a surprise. She is scheduled for not one but three meetings that afternoon. Dr. Preston calls Florence and cancels her late afternoon appointments and asks Florence to move their Sisterhood meeting time from after work until some time further into the evening. Florence agrees, suggesting they meet behind the mausoleum whenever Dr. Preston finishes her business at the medical examiners.

"Good afternoon Dr. Preston. You know everyone here. I thought it would be a good idea if we met earlier, before meeting with Dr. Collin Fitzsimons of the CDC and Major Souk Kwai from military intelligence."

"By all means," Dr. Preston agrees, "How did CDC and the military get into this?"

"Didn't you find the blood and tissue samples strange, Dr. Preston?"

"Yes," she responds.

"We did too and contacted CDC with our findings. They contacted the military because of suspicions of biological warfare possibilities or some such?"

"Understood," she acknowledges.

"We are stymied about what's going on. Dr. Artisia Brown, would you brief Dr. Preston on what Agent Fitzsimons told us?"

Artisia Brown, a registered nurse that went on to receive her Ph.D. in forensic psychology from John Jay College in New York, specializes in evaluating credibility of witnesses questioned during coroner's inquests and determining the risk of violent behavior of suspects and persons of interest held for questioning by the Sierra County Sheriff Department. Her serious, almost austere appearance coats a sensitive, highly venerable woman, who has experienced the harder knocks of life that have given her great insight in human behavior. She is Dr. Mayes' right hand and operates the day-to-day operations of the medical examiner's office.

"Dr. Fitzsimons is an FBI agent working with the Centers for Disease Control and Prevention. He's probably from the Department of Homeland Security. We expect him to tell us about a highly contagious disease, a virus of some kind, that he believes could be uses as weapon of biological warfare, an obvious threat to national security. At this point, we have no specific idea of what CDC research labs have found."

After her comments, she immediately leaves the conference room. Dr. Preston listens attentively, as Jeffrey Mayes introduces Hopper Jensen, head forensic team leader.

"In short, we're not sure what the military has to tell us. We'll have to wait and see what Major Kwai has to say when he gets here."

Zack Curry, one of the county forensic technicians, asks Dr. Preston whether her findings are any different than the possibilities outlined. She answers truthfully and does not go into detail about what she thinks.

"Diseased tissue is a possibility. I called in Drs. Greenstone and McIntyre to give their opinions and the three of us agree the tissue and blood samples we examined are consistent with some kind of microorganism or protist invasion of a human body. However, we are not sure which parasite, bacteria, virus, protist or combination of microorganisms is or are affecting the tissue and blood samples and are we are not sure how the biological agents work to produce the changes in tissue and blood samples."

"Exactly what we've found," Mimi Gastineau pops into the conversation.

It seems odd that a technician would jump into the conversation without being invited. But there is no pecking order in Dr. Mayes' operation. He has created a collegial team of intelligent and divergent thinkers to help solve the mysteries that routinely pass through the coroner's office. Mimi's comment is acceptable in Mayes' eyes.

Dr. Brown knocks, opens the conference room door and escorts Dr. Fitzsimons from CDC into the room. After introductions, Dr. Fitzsimons asks that only essential personnel remain and specifically identifies Dr. Mayes and Dr. Preston, as the essential personnel, thereby excusing the rest of Dr. Mayes' Forensic Team by inference. Dr. Mayes nods assent and his team leaves the room.

Dr. Collin Fitzsimons comes from a different culture, one where loose lips sinks ships. He strongly advises Drs. Mayes and Preston not to share with anyone what is discussed.

Dr. Fitzsimons begins, "What we say in this room stays in this room."

Irked by Fitzsimons imposing command, Mayes argues, "I am the one that the media will hound for statements about the Elgin investigation. I can hold them off with the 'No comment the crime is under active investigation' for only so long. Then, the public has the right to know the truth."

"Not when it comes to issues under the authority of the CDC," counters Fitzsimons, "We determine what is to be said to the public and when to say it. If we do not have your cooperation, this meeting is ended."

Mayes retreats, "We can work the details out later. What do your people say we have going on?"

"There will be no such thing as 'working the details out later,' Dr. Mayes. Everything discussed at this meeting will not be divulged to anyone else, including the sheriffs department and your superiors. Strict confidence is the rule."

Dr. Preston jumps into the conversation, "I understand your position clearly Dr. Fitzsimons. I agree; and, I will excuse myself from this meeting. I'm a doctor and have taken an oath to protect the health and safety of my patients. I cannot give you the guarantees you require. So, if you will please excuse me gentlemen. Dr. Mayes, I will stick around for our other meetings."

Silvia does not want to be subject to probing by Fitzsimons or anyone from military intelligence. Based on her work with Greenstone and McIntyre, she has a pretty good idea what Fitzsimons has to say. More importantly, she needs to keep her theory about the tissue and blood samples to herself and protect the Sisterhood from exposure by probing governmental agencies and from the prying eyes of the public.

Mayes is shocked by Dr. Preston's abrupt exit from the meeting. Fitzsimons waits placidly until the door closes behind Silvia and he hears the sound of her footsteps diminish before he continues.

"Are you on board, Dr. Mayes?"

"Yes, Dr. Fitzsimons, I'm fully on board."

"The tissue samples you sent, Dr. Mayes, show evidence of Creutzfeldt-Jacob's disease, which is usually transmitted to humans by consuming infected meat from cattle."

"But, we've seen no outbreaks of mad-cow disease in the Sierra's. There have been no reported cases of spongiform encephalitis in area hospitals," Mayes informs Dr. Fitzsimons.

"That's good to know. But, the mutation of the samples you sent, we believe results from a variant form of Creutzfeldt-Jacob's called M7 that is not fatal to humans. Matter of fact, instead of finding infected proteins destroying normal cell proteins, leading to brain death, we find the infectious proteins actually enhancing normal protein materials."

Dr. Mayes responds, "Improving human tissue cells? Amazing. How does that work?"

"M7 seems to repair cells and cellular structures damaged by genetic defects, pre-existing diseases, and the effects of aging." Dr. Fitzsimons reveals.

"Fascinating. An infection that restores human tissue, that's a switch. The cattle industry is going to be happy to hear good news for a change." Mayes quips.

"We haven't a clue, as to where M7 comes from or how it gets in our food supply?" continues Fitzsimons.

"We are in agreement about what we've observed in the tissue and blood samples; but you have no more of a clue than I do as to what is causing the changes in the samples. You've just made up a name and slapped it on the observation. Your Creutzfelt-Jacob's theory is thin on scientific facts, as far as I can see."

"You're right, doctor. As far as the CDC higher-ups are concerned, M7 is caused by the Creutzfeldt-Jacob's mutation and is the highest priority issue on CDC's plate. "

Mayes states, " Oh, I understand, Dr. Fitzsimons; but, just how do you explain that to the public?"

"We don't explain it to the public. At this point, what difference does it make to the public whether the blood and tissue structure of the alleged perpetrator Elgin shot is normal or abnormal? M7 poses no harm to humans. As you say, we don't have enough of a scientific understanding about M7 to make a definitive statement to the public," Fitzsimons responds.

"Eventually, Dr. Fitzsimons, other doctors examining their patients will come across the M7 phenomenon and questions will be raised, which will find their way into public discourse. The news media is sure to pick this up. Once that happens, all eyes will turn to me for answers. Then, what am I supposed to say?" Mayes asserts.

"You will have to do the best you can without going into detail. It's more politically complicated than you think. We don't know if what we are dealing with is human." Fitzsimons replies.

"We're talking about alien invasion? Flying saucers and goofy stuff like that? Awe, that's just great!"

"I'm not authorized to discuss the particulars with you, Dr. Mayes.

Hold your questions for Major Kwai. That's his jurisdiction. What concerns us at CDC and certainly will concern you is whatever is causing the change in the tissue and blood samples is found in our food supply."

"Are you saying M7 is contaminating our meat?"

Dr. Fitzsimons is quick to answer, "That's our guess. Alerting the public before we know the short and long term effects of M7 will cause panic in the streets. The political outcomes of prematurely announcing M7 are horrendous. We need to be sure our scientific facts and sure our recommendations to the public are sound. We don't want to go off half cocked."

Mayes "Let me get this straight. You think our meat supply is being contaminated by aliens that put microorganisms in our meat supply, which causes the changes we've observed in the tissues and blood samples we've found?"

Fitzsimons, "That's what we think at this time. However, as you know, we only have small amounts of the M7 blood and tissues to base our theory on. We need to find the whole body or bodies these samples are from. Next week, a team of scientists from the San Francisco Academy of Sciences will begin to research the effect of bark beetles in the Sierra National Forest. They will send teams to comb the forests below the Buttes, surveying the number of trees infested with bark beetles."

Mayes blurts out, "Bark beetles! What do bark beetles have to do with our problem?"

"Nothing, that's the beauty of it; bark beetles have been unstoppable in the forests of British Columbia and the United States. The only thing that stops them is running out of healthy trees to infest. To protect the forest industry and the environment, the Environmental Protection Agency is conducting the research. It is a perfect cover for our agents and the military to search for the bodies Elgin shot."

"The Academy field study of the western pine beetles is linked to the shadows shot at by Elgin?"

"For years CDC and the military have worked this way with the San Francisco Academy of Sciences on scientific expeditions all over the world."

"The Academy of Sciences is a covert operation?"

"No, the academy is not aware that some of their scientists and technicians also work for us. Their research expeditions around the world are legitimate scientific endeavors that we sometimes tag along with for our purposes. Their western pine beetle research project is a perfect example. The academy is studying how to stop the beetles in an area we need to access without raising public awareness. Scientists will go about their work, while we search for the missing bodies infected by M7. At the same time the Sierra County Sheriffs Department will be investigating the Elgin shootings and the missing bodies of Alma Whitman and Reverend Henry Johnston."

"Everything's tied up with one big bow," Mayes comments."

"Correct. The Academy scientists and the police know nothing about what we are talking about; and, you need to keep it that way. The blood and tissue evidence you sent us was sent to the FBI for analysis. They sent samples to the military. Here we are, one big happy family.

"The Academy of Sciences operation is an unknowing accomplices to CDC, FBI, EPA, and military investigations around the world?" Mayes observes.

"That's about it. But, and I'll say it again, the Academy and the Sierra Sheriff's Department are to be kept in the dark about our operations!" Fitzsimons is adamant on this point.

"Okay, okay, I'll keep it to myself. But groups of scientists accompanied by the military searching the national forests around Abbeville are sure to attract lots of attention. How do you intend to handle that public relations problems?" Mayes further inquires.

"Transparently, in the full view of the public. The academy has arranged with the Abbeville town council to make a full report to them at their next public meeting. The scientists from the academy will carry the ball in public. We stay out of it."

The Fitzsimons-Mayes meeting ends with both in full accord on the plan. The academy will go about searching out and destroying the western pine beetles to save the forests and lumber industry with CDC and FBI agents searching for M7 infected human bodies. The Sheriff's Department has murders to solve and the military is on an alien hunt.

Waiting for the next shoe to drop, Dr. Mayes wonders what he's gotten himself into. Maybe Dr. Preston took the best way out of this quagmire. Run, while you have a chance. A knock is heard at the door and Dr. Mayes welcomes Major Souk Kwai to the conference room. After presenting his credentials, Major Kwai begins his briefing.

"You realize this meeting between us never happened?"

"Yes, Dr. Fitzsimons informed me of the need to keep everything in the strictest confidence."

"What I'm saying goes beyond strictest confidence. This meeting literally never happened. Do you comprehend the difference, Dr. Mayes?"

"I understand, but my staff and Dr. Preston was informed of our meeting."

"That may be so, but the scheduled meeting never occurred."

"Right but," Mayes divulges, "our conference conversation is being video recorded as we speak."

"When you review your video recording, you will find quite a different conference and conversation." Major Kwai explains. "You will see Dr. Fitzsimons informing you about the academy's Operation Beetle in this area and inviting you to attend the Abbeville town council meeting, where Dr. Darius Porter, the Operation Beetle's team leader, will describe the project to the council and to the public."

"But, Dr. Preston . . ."

"That's been taken care of. She never attended the meeting."

"I see." Dr. Mayes replies, "Still, I'm uneasy with all the intrigue going on."

"Understandable. As was explained to you Operation Beetle is a legitimate scientific project. All you have to do is play it that way, convincingly in public. You know nothing more."

"Aliens?"

"Yes, aliens." Major Kwai affirms, "We think Harvard Elgin may have possibly shot an alien. You may recall some news a few decades ago about Hangar 18 and Area 51? The idea that extra terrestrials exist is part of our American folklore and a worldwide phenomenon."

"Those stories are true?" Mayes asks.

"You know the answer to that question, Dr. Mayes. I can neither affirm nor deny stories about the existence or nonexistence of extra terrestrials. We'll leave that to the imaginations of science fiction writers."

"I think you're on a wild-goose chase, Major Kwai. The thinking, rational public will laugh you off the face of the earth. Until you provide hard evidence that aliens do exist, no rational person will take you or the government seriously."

"Let's keep it that way, Dr. Mayes," responds the major.

Chapter 2

❦

onday, July 18, 5:35 p.m.: As soon as Major Kwai leaves the
medical examiner's office, Dr. Mayes looks for Dr. Preston. He
finds her in the third floor cafeteria.

"How did everything go, Jeff?

"I'm surprised to see you here Silvia. I didn't think you were a junk
food addict. Everything went into deep freeze. You know I can't talk about
anything that took place during the meetings I've had."

"Oh yes, I'm quite aware of that, thanks to my little visit with the
major. I'm not here to pry on your conversations with Dr. Fitzsimons and
Major Kwai. I'm here to get our wires uncrossed because both of us are up
to our necks in quick sand."

Mayes is relieved, "As chief medical examiner for this county, I have
two problems on my plate. I am sworn to silence about the Fitzsimons-
Kwai information. At the same time, I have the legal responsibility to
provide information to the sheriff to further their investigation of the
deaths of Alma and Henry. Plus, my duty to inform the public of health
issues is compromised. Both of us can't give statements to the newspapers.
Silvia, I have to be in control of all the information. It's too risky to play
it anyway else."

"Agreed. My lips are sealed unless I'm called on the stand to testify
under oath."

"Testifying under oath will be a problem," Jeff admits, "Here's a little

276

news flash. Lieutenant Freeman intends to press for a coroner's inquest on the deaths of Henry and Alma and you will probably be called as a witness."

"Right. I guess we'll cross that bridge when we come to it," Silvia says.

Avoiding information disclosed to him by the CDC and MI, Jeffrey invites Silvia to go for a walk with him to discuss the murder theories the Lieutenant discussed with him.

"The walls have ears, Silvia. Let's go for a walk outside to continue our discussion."

Across the street is a small park, where they find a bench.

"Quite frankly, Silvia, I don't see any connection between the blood and tissue samples and the sheriff departments murder theories Milo Freeman and Dirk Jacobson are pursuing."

"Without their bodies, Jeffrey, we can't compare samples. We may never know what went on at Upper Sardine Lake or who or what Elgin shot in the forest."

"Exactly," Jeffrey agrees. He adds, "From the evidence all we know is Elgin shot an unidentified person or thing behind his house. That's about it."

"Unless Lieutenant Freeman and Sergeant Jacobson come up with more evidence supporting their theories, I'm holding fast to my preliminary determination that Alma Whitman and Reverend Henry's deaths were accidental," Silvia continues.

"So, we are on the same page on that determination, which is good for us."

"That means, if an expert witness on forensics is called for, you could fill the bill as well as I. Why call for a coroner's inquest at all?"

"Lieutenant Freeman wants to call for an inquest into the alleged murders of Henry and Alma. That way Marcus can ask witnesses questions about what they know without being restrained by Constitutional protections afforded defendants in a criminal case."

"Clever. So everything's going to see the light of day at the inquest," Silvia says.

"It's going to be some wild mouse ride from here on out, Silvia. Fasten your seat belt."

As the heavenly shades of night descend, Silvia leaves Jeffrey in the park. She drives the short distance from Downieville to where she knows Florence will be waiting for her. Silvia turns from Highway 49 onto Old Gold Lake Road, stopping in a patch of mist below the mausoleum. Florence and Desiree are sitting with their feet dangling over the dark green marble terrace platform. They watch Silvia making her way up the hill from the dirt road below.

"Fancy meeting you two here," Silvia greets the pair.

"I hope you don't mind Desiree being here," Florence says.

"There was a time when the sight of Desiree would have driven me into a state of apoplexy, but we have straitened things out and I am glad you invited her. I have a lot to get off my chest with you two."

"So, what's bothering you Silvia?" Desiree pushes the conversation forward.

"Lots of loose ends rambling around in my head. Everything revolves around what happened to Alma and Henry. The Sierra County Medical Examiner is of the opinion they died of accidental drowning. That is, of course, the apparent cause of death. But I found no water in their lungs, which means they were dead before they hit the water. Then there's the matter of where are the missing bodies? My guess is they have been whisked off somewhere by someone for some reason."

Looking at Desiree, Florence flippantly says, "Oh, that really narrows the possibilities, doesn't it?"

"Thank you Florence," comments Silvia. "We don't have much to go on, but I want you two to give me your ideas about what I have in mind."

"That's novel," jests Florence.

Silvia becomes dead serious.

"Novel yes, but I need to see how what I think sounds from a layperson's perspective, ladies. You two already know what information about Alma and Reverend Henry is out in public. So let's try this on for size. Given what you know, what is safe for me to tell the public?" Silvia challenges Desiree and Florence.

Regarding what information is out there, Florence knows far more about the situation than does Desiree. Matter of fact, Florence knows far more about the situation than does Silvia, who is limited by her scientific way of examining things.

"What do you mean by 'what is safe to tell the public?'" Florence inquires.

"Safe in the sense that whatever I may have to say in public is accepted as reasonable, believable by the public."

"You're looking for a lie to feed the public to keep them from what, Silvia?"

"A lie, yes, a little white lie to keep the public from being concerned about anything I say."

"What are you trying to hide, Silvia?" Florence continues.

"I can't tell anyone, just yet. Trust me on this," Silvia pleads.

"Okay, I'll play your silly game, Silvia." Desiree begins, "From what I know and what I know is out in public, dead people don't bleed. So, whatever or whoever Elgin shot is or was alive. You've told me shadows are pure spirit. Spirits don't bleed either. That eliminates the rational public of being scared of the folktales around her about shadows and shades roaming the forests. "

"Go on," urges Silvia.

"I think and I believe the public can go three ways on this. Elgin shot Alma or Henry, Elgin shot another person or he shot an animal. That's my guess."

"An animal, maybe like a stray cow," Silvia muses out loud. "I hadn't thought about that. I'll have the medical examiner check that out in the morning. Go on, Desiree."

"After Alma and I toured this cemetery," Desiree continues, "she gave me a few pieces of a puzzle to put together. She asked me why I thought ten spaces are vacant in the Abbe Family Mausoleum? That's easy to figure out. Only the founding fathers, their wives, and direct descendants are buried in the mausoleum. This leaves the Whitman wing of the family, who are descended from Matthew Abbe's only daughter Carol Ann, out in the cold."

Silvia asks, "I still don't understand. Why are the descendents of Carol Ann Abbe-Whitman not buried in this mausoleum?"

"You've answered your own question, Silvia. Alma said her great grandfather, Samuel Whitman, built the Abbe Family Mausoleum. He thought someday he and his descendents would be buried in the crypt. But the last of the 'pure' Abbe's, those offspring with the last name of Abbe, ended with the death of Matthew Abbe Jr., in 1946."

"Oh, I see," says Silvia, who hadn't put that together. "A Whitman isn't an Abbe in the eyes of the old guard. What else?"

"When we were walking through the cemetery, I saw something in the forest. Alma implied it was my imagination, shadows made by the trees and tombstones that were playing tricks on us. If I had taken her comments figuratively, Alma was telling me that shadows, in the sense of spirits or ghosts were playing as they always play in the forests. If I'm right on this point that Alma was talking about real shadows playing in the forest, who are these tricksters? Where do they come from? What is their purpose, hanging around?"

Desiree muses on the questions she's posed.

The moonlight shining through the mist hanging in the trees behind the mausoleum accentuates the drama. Lengthy moments pass.

"Of course," Desiree continues, "the public doesn't literally take the stories about shadows in the forest for real or do they?"

Florence sits quietly, taking in all that Desiree is sharing. She carefully observes Silvia's body language in response to Desiree seriously considering the possibility that forest shadows exist. Of course, shadows are for real from Florence's perspective and from most of the women in the Sisterhood. Certainly, the gossip mill knows there's a factual base to the tales about spirits and witches and shadows in the forest, although they have the facts twisted somewhat. Silvia, however, does not respond in any telling way to Desiree's account of and musings.

"Go on," Silvia urges Desiree. "What else did Alma say to you and what do you think it means?"

"Alma said in time, injustices would be righted. I believe the injustices she's referring to are first, the fact that the Whitman line of Abbe's is not buried in the mausoleum. Second, the fact that the Abbe women were considered inferior compared to Abbeville's founding fathers. And

third the fact that to this day, the whole structure of Abbeville society—
from the name of the town to the names of the drives—reflects only the
contributions of the Abbe males."

Silvia is confused. She's not getting any information from Desiree
that sheds light on what happened to Alma and Reverend Henry. Neither
does Desiree reveal information that could be pertinent at a coroner's
inquest into the disappearance of Alma and Henry. Florence evaluates
Desiree's take on things and knows Desiree is right on target about Alma's
quest. Florence thinks that Alma was right. Desiree is a good fit for the
Sisterhood.

"What are you talking about Desiree? You're not making any sense."
Silvia reacts.

"Alma told me one other piece of the puzzle that her bones would never
see the grave," Desiree says as a light dawns on her.

Desiree looks at Florence. She senses Florence is as enlightened as was
Alma. Florence understands the meaning of Desiree's glimpse into part
of Alma's Journey. However, the truth of this moment escapes Silvia's
attention. Silvia is trying to understand Desiree's comments within the
confines of her first posed question: given what you know, what is safe for
me to tell the public?

"Now, I'm really lost Desiree. What has any of this to do with what I need
to say to the public about Alma and Reverend Henry's missing bodies?"

"Alma was saying the final chapter hasn't been written." Desiree
continues on her train of thought, "that in time, these injustices will be
righted. Wow, Alma's righting the wrongs done to the Whitman's and to
those cast in second class by Abbeville's founding fathers."

Silvia listens closely to Desiree. All Silvia wanted to know is who Elgin
shot and what happened to the bodies. It seems Desiree is making the
problem more complicated. But, Florence knows Desiree is solving the
mystery of the missing bodies at a different level. Silvia lives in a world of
hard evidence, facts and logical conclusions. Desiree knows she must speak
in those terms to clearly communicate with Silvia. Desiree also knows the
full answer about Alma and Reverend Henry's bodies missing lies beyond
natural explanations.

"Silvia," Desiree continues, "your guess is Alma and Henry were whisked off somewhere by someone for some reason. My guess is Alma and Henry were whisked off by shadows, into the forest, so Alma and Henry could set right the wrongs done by Abbeville's forefathers."

"Let me catch my breath, Desiree," Silvia says, mulling over Desiree's hypothesis.

Silvia hears the words, but doesn't exactly understand because Desiree's thinking is based in some kind of fantasy folklore, not scientific fact or scientific theory.

"Desiree, how does all of what you've said work in the real world? I need to know in concrete terms what is going on, starting with who Elgin shot and what happened to the people he shot?"

Florence knows what Desiree is saying better than Desiree herself knows and pushes Silvia to recall her experiences with forest shadows.

"Remember Silvia, when we first saw Alma and Henry at the bottom of the lake? There were shadows around them that flew up the mountainside when we turned our lights on them. Desiree thinks the forest shadows swept them away from the mortuary in the dead of night and brought them back to life."

"Brought them back to life! I was the physician that pronounced Alma and Henry dead. Alma was autopsied. There's no coming to life after that!"

"The forest shadows, Silvia. How do you explain the forest shadows you've seen on many occasions?" Florence pursues.

"I too am of the Sisterhood. Florence, I know the stories about shadows. But until shadows are scientifically verified and other scientific theories are falsified, I cannot accept explanations based on ghosts and goblins and folktales. I wish I could. It would make things a lot easier, but we live in a real world with real happenings."

"Silvia, how do you explain seeing shadows around Alma and Henry fly up the side of the mountain when we approached them?" Florence asks.

"Figments of our imaginations. Where are hard facts? The testable theories?"

Florence does not answer. She holds back from telling Silvia and Desiree what Alma, had said about relinquishing her flame, as it has been done in the Sisterhood for centuries. She knows Dr. Preston deals with facts not metaphysics. Suggesting Alma somehow willingly gave up her life to right two centuries of wrong and fulfill the promise of the Sisterhood, as it has been done thousands of centuries before the founding of Abbeville, would be unintelligible to Silvia. Desiree, on the other hand, is beginning to realize that maybe Alma chose to give up her life and pass the flame onto Florence. But Desiree doesn't get what purpose Henry's dying served."

"Florence, you've been quiet through all this. Given what you know— and I know you know a lot—what is safe for me to tell the public?"

"There is nothing you can tell the public about the passing of Alma and Reverend Henry that will be believed by the public."

"So both of your ideas about the why, how and where of the missing bodies of Alma and Henry are based in mysteries beyond the reach of science?" Silvia concludes. "That's a big help!"

"How can you rule out theories simply because you don't understand them, Silvia? The shadows are a phenomenon you kiss off as figments of imagination. Don't you have to play by your rules of scientific inquiry too?" Florence says challenging Silvia.

Turning to Florence and Desiree, Silvia says, "You think and believe, as many others of the women of the Sisterhood think and believe that shadows do exist. I'm not at the point where forest shadows are as real as the laws of physics."

"So you have to give public statements that reflect your science-first self, Dr. Preston. In public, don't talk about shadows in the forest, which you have seen but not yet understand."

Nodding in agreement Desiree says, "Okay, we laid our cards out. What are you going to do, Silvia?"

Silvia decides to share the theories she and Drs. McIntyre and Greenstone developed. She knows she's must walk a tight rope. She cannot divulge the silly ideas about Elgin shooting an M7-infected human or MI's ridiculous theory about alien interventions. She will hold her tongue for the moment, as it's too early to let Florence and Silvia in on the new species thinking of Drs. McIntyre and Greenstone that is also the front-runner in her mind. She begins to lay the facts out and waits to see what her sisters think.

"Analysis of the blood and tissue samples found behind the Elgin house indicate whatever was shot was not exactly human."

"Now who's dreaming stuff up?" jokes Florence.

"My, my," is all Desiree utters for the moment.

Silvia presses on, "My analysis of the evidence suggests Elgin shot something human, but not human like us. The question is what does this information do to your theories, my sisters?"

Desiree responds with Florence acquiescing in agreement. "Alma and Henry being now something not exactly human doesn't change the premise of our belief that the answers are beyond the natural explanations of things that have happened around here."

Florence restates Silvia's new disclosure in the form of a question, "The shadows fired on by Elgin bled red blood similar to human blood, had organ tissues similar to human tissues and are running alive in the forest. Is that what you intend to say in public, Silvia?"

"According to the way you two described the shadows at Upper Sardine Lake, I thought the shadows were pure spirits. If that were true, there would be no blood or tissue to be forensically analyzed! It makes common sense that Elgin shot a person, an animal or something humanlike." Desiree reasons.

Pushing Silvia's idea Florence asks, "Now you've tickled my scientific curiosity. Silvia, from your perspective as a scientist, I need you to better define what you mean by not exactly human?"

Making the connection for the first time, Desiree interrupts, "The shadows I've felt and seen in the forest were once live humans!"

Frustrated that shadows are back in the conversation, Dr. Preston protests, "Nonsense, Desiree. Let's stay on the reasonable side of the line. Someday we will discover natural causes explaining our imaginary friends, the shadows."

"Silvia, I thought you were the physician with an open mind about what she doesn't understand. Desiree is constructing her hypothesis. If you disagree, scientifically disprove what she is saying. Don't browbeat her about it! Where's your verifiable truth to the contrary?"

"Okay Florence, I'll let Desiree have her how-many-angels-dance-on-the-head-of-a-pin guess without being critical. Now, let's be empirical about this. I analyzed the tissue and blood samples and at this point I believe they are humanoid."

"Humanoid? What's that mean? Something half fly, half human or are we talking about Jo-Jo the dog-faced boy?"

Florence's humor breaks the tension.

"Silvia, are you're holding out on us?" Desiree inquires.

"Oh, I'm holding out lots of information that I am pledged not to disclose. What I can say is the gross microscopic anatomy of the cells and tissues I examined are clearly human, but the erythrocytes, for example, are enhanced. These blood cells carry ten times the amount of oxygen to the body cells, than our blood cells deliver in our bodies."

"Interesting," Desiree comments.

"My microscopic observations of the tissue samples show regenerative properties."

"Your tissue samples are growing?" Florence says.

"I know it sounds incredible, but the skin and liver tissue traces that first showed broken cells under the microscope have renewed themselves to a healthy, functioning state. The tissues don't die. If I didn't know any better, I'd say we have a new, improved species of humans."

"Have you confirmed your findings with anyone else, Silvia?"

"Yes, but I can't quite yet disclose who is working on this with me," Silvia earnestly confides, "And I'm asking you and Desiree to keep even this information in strict confidence until it becomes public."

Of course, both Desiree and Florence agree to support Silvia.

"When do you think your information will be made public?"

"Hard to say. People are looking at this problem from different directions. They have conflicting opinions. I don't know what will be disclosed in public. But, at least you know what scientific data I have and my opinion that whatever Elgin shot was an improved model of a human being. Please keep it to yourselves."

Florence and Desiree assure Silvia that her opinion will be held in strict confidence.

"Got it. We don't know what will surface in public, but, how is it going to be aired in public?" asks Florence.

"Yea," Desiree chimes in. "We need a heads-up here so we are not caught off guard."

"After listening to you guys, I'm not saying anything in public except I haven't come to any conclusions and I see no evidence of foul play. Next week, people from the San Francisco Academy of Sciences are making a special presentation to the Abbeville town council about eradicating the pesky western pine beetle from the Tahoe National Forest."

"News to me," Florence responds, "where did you hear that?"

"Can't say," Silvia replies, "but let's go to that meeting and keep our eyes and ears open."

For the moment Silvia's answer satisfies Desiree and Florence's scientific curiosity. Desiree is beginning to understand the shadows and the role Florence will play in the future. Silvia remains, as ever, the empiricist, the scientist, and the doubting Thomas. And based on Silvia's humanoid but not human blood and tissue analysis, Florence is beginning to consider the possibility that the spiritual and the physical may be more entwined than she previously thought.

Throughout the night, the women talk and draw closer. They respect each other's worth, feelings, and opinions. They understand things are never going to be the same in Abbeville and there is more to come than currently meets the eye. In spite of their differences, they seem to be destined to become the inner circle of the Sisterhood.

Chapter 3

❧

Tuesday, July 19, 12:00 Noon: The mercury in Abbeville hits one hundred ten degrees, when the Sacramento Courier carries the story about the San Francisco Academy of Sciences asking permission from the Abbeville town council to stage Operation Beetle in forests around their town. That evening, Abbeville's special town hall meeting on the western pine beetle goes better than expected. Interest is stirred in Abbeville about eradicating the pine beetles, which have destroyed over 40 million acres of forest timber in North America. Townsfolk are grateful the pine beetle problem will be aggressively addressed in their forests, which is a large piece of their economy.

At the meeting, Abbeville's town council Chairman Silva reports the governor of the State of California is authorizing the National Guard to assist Academy of Science researchers to find and destroy the pine beetles. The Guard's involvement comes as a complete surprise to Drs. Mayes and Preston, who almost miss Dr. Fitzsimons' introduction and acknowledgements, thanking them for their support of Operation Beetle. Sitting in the audience, Desiree and Florence wonder if this is the public announcement Silvia was referring to when they last met. What the connection is between Operation Beetle and the Dr. Preston's humanoid blood and tissue samples remains a mystery to them, however.

Abbeville's town council enthusiastically approves the Academy's request to stage the project in their town and reserves the southwestern corner of Spring Creek Park and Campgrounds below the Buttes for the Academy's use.

Sacramento Courier's editorial piece by Editor and Chief Louis Jones couldn't be more enthusiastic: "SCIENTISTS AND GUARD ENGINEERS FIGHT BEETLE INFESTATION." "In a day when government agencies fight among themselves to protect their territories, Abbeville's Operation Beetle is showing the good that comes when government by the people works for the people. Teams of San Francisco Academy of Sciences researchers supported by the California National Guard Core of Engineers are conducting wide-scale search and destroy operations to eradicate the western pine beetle that plagues forests in California and ranges from Oregon to British Columbia through Colorado, New Mexico, and western Texas."

Abbeville and the Sacramento Courier buy wholesale Dr. Collin Fitzsimons' pitch to the town council. The FBI and MI cover-up is executed perfectly. But Fredrika's gossip mill and Pastor Elder Jacob does not buy the academy's pitch to the town council. Their twist on the involvement of scientists and the government runs contrary to the town's elation. Familiar themes about "godless scientists," "government interference," and "sinister happenings in Abbeville" flood the community from the Damascus Reformed Church pulpit and gossip mill.

While most people view town rumors as coming from nuts in the community, there is a ring of credibility in what they say, because the information leaks coming from the medical examiner's office are from a reliable source. The little known fact is Mimi Gastineau's Godmother is Bunny Grimmer. Mimi, however, does not ever spill the beans accurately to Bunny. She always finds a way to spin the information to protect her job, which only adds to the absurdity of the rumors. Mimi feeds Bunny the news that the shadow Elgin shot was trying to steal food from the Elgin household and was a person dying of malnutrition. In turn, Bunny launches the rumor that Alma and Henry are alive and hiding in the forest. Bunny's gossip beats the morning edition of the Sacramento Courier to the streets of Abbeville. When people read Louis Jones' editorial piece about Operation Beetle, the seeds undermining the editorial have already been planted, the scientists and National Guardsmen are really looking for Alma and Henry. Ironically, the rumor is true, not by design, but by happenstance.

The rumor that Alma and Henry are starving in the forest, after being shot at by Harvard Elgin causes more businesses to close. By the end of July, the Belcher Brother's Mortuary is sold to Jackson Smythe of Samuelson and Connolly, a nation-wide chain of mortuaries designed to operate the cemetery and provide inexpensive funeral services. Smythe and his wife, Dixie, buy a home in Abbeville Estates. The Belcher's retire to Beaverton Oregon.

Wednesday, August 3, 7:00 a.m.: The continued sweltering heat in the Sierras make Abbeville a living hell. Death is claiming Abbeville's locals at an alarming rate. Bridget Silver, 25, dies in a car accident; Jack Thomson, 40, of a heart attack; Kelly Watson, 67, dies of emphysema; Freddie Sherman, 2, of pneumonia; Noreen Correra, 53, of cancer; Sally Blanca, 75, dies of natural causes, as does Samantha Cross, 72. Simone Fletcher, 76, dies of undisclosed causes; Terri Sanders, 30, dies in a hiking accident and Vicky Reyes, 19, commits suicide. Only three weeks after presiding over the town hall meeting, William Silva, 66, retired truck driver, bicentennial festival marshal and chairman of the town council passes away from an aggressive form of pancreatic cancer. Martin Lawrence, 57, banker and elder at the Damascus Reformed Church dies suddenly, leaving openings for new blood at the Abbeville Savings and Loan and the elder's council. Elder Lawrence is the first to be buried out of Samuelson and Connolly Mortuary. Adding to this recent total the names of Alma Whitman, Henry Johnston, Jeremy Paxton, Anne Dean, and Bob Winston brings the grand total of deaths to seventeen before the end of the seventh month of the year. For a town that sees an average of 4.7 deaths per year it is an astounding figure. People begin to feel the only business booming in town is the mortuary business. Abbeville is coming apart at the seams before their eyes.

The real shocker hits town, when Saturday morning Courier Headline reads: ASTOUNDING NUMBER OF DEATHS UNACCOUNTED FOR IN ABBEVILLE.

Sydney Cameron's article reveals that according to Sierra county records of the seventeen deaths reported, since January, only ten bodies were buried in the Abbeville Cemetery. Her article raises the question, what ever became of Alma Whitman, Reverend Henry Johnston, Kelly Watson, Noreen Correra, Sally Blanca, Samantha Cross, and Simone Fletcher? Citizens of Abbeville are shocked by the news that six of the seven missing corpses are women.

The gossip mill fuels the fires about the six women, who died and are missing without a trace. Rumor has it that God is striking down members of the witch's cult, starting with their leader, Alma and her warlock counterpart Reverend Henry. Few Abbevillians venture out in the streets after sunset. The reputation of the town sinks further to an all-time low.

Businesses continue to close.

Abbeville Savings and Loan is taken over by Sacramento Commercial Bank, which in turn is taken by Chase Manhattan Bank. Chase opens in a week with all new staff, beginning with the new bank manager, Jenny Chin. Townspeople feel strangers are overrunning their town.

Next to slip under is Sanders Attorney at Law. With the death of Terri, his only daughter, Peter Sanders sells his building to Royce Willet, who opens Willet's Pizza Joint. Peter moves out of town and opens a new practice in Lodi, California.

Within the space of two months, the barbershop, savings and loan, law offices, mortuary and church have been sold or have changed hands, unsettling the town even more.

Monday, September 5, 9:00 a.m.: The Labor Day weekend brings record crowds to Sardine Lakes and Sand Pond, as temperatures reach into the hundreds. Hundreds of families take their last hoorah before the kids go back to school, swimming and hiking in the Buttes. The population of Abbeville may have been cut in half, but the lakes, streams and campgrounds around Abbeville boom with the excitement of vacationers and family fun.

Fingers are crossed throughout Abbeville, in the hope that the last big vacation day of the summer will be enjoyed without a mishap. The hope is dashed as Jake Langdon, the San Francisco stockbroker with ties to Fredrika and Edgar, is found dead in Upper Sardine Lake.

Detective Lieutenant Milo Freeman of the Sierra County Sheriff Department brings Edgar Whitman in for questioning. Fenway sits outside the interrogation room. Against Conrad's advice, Edgar, feeling he has nothing to hide, waves his right to counsel. He also waives the offer to have coffee during the interrogation, as his stomach is upset.

Lieutenant Milo begins, "Edgar I'm sorry to have to ask you questions about your sister and Reverend Henry. I know this is a sensitive topic. What kind of relationship did Alma and you have with Henry?"

"The three of us were friends. I played chess with Henry every Sunday after church services. Alma would make lunch for us and served tea or lemonade to refresh us. For years that was the extent of our relationship."

Milo presses, "Your relationship changed within the last year?"

"Yes, Reverend Henry and Alma had a strained relationship over matters of belief until the big January snow storms when Anne and Jeremy died. Henry was unnerved by Anne's death and turned to us for advice."

"Us, meaning you and Alma?"

"Yes."

"What kind of advice?"

"Henry felt responsible for causing pain to Anne's family because of the rumors that he and Anne were having an affair, which wasn't true, but Henry felt in his role as Pastor of Damascus Church he needed to be above such accusations. Alma and I assured Henry he was being to hard on himself."

"Reverend Henry didn't know he couldn't stop what people were thinking and saying?"

"He knew, but being close to Anne and her husband, Henry felt if he could have done things differently the gossip about Anne and him would not have happened. It was ridiculous for him to feel that way, and Alma, Dean Curtis, and I tried to convince him otherwise, but he persisted in feeling guilty."

"I understand that through this ordeal Alma and Henry drew close to each other. They would go for walks. They became confidants."

"Yes."

"Alma was away from you for longer periods of time than usual?"

"Yes."

"How did that make you feel Edgar? Your only sister, who always cared for you, who was always there for you, suddenly spending more time with Reverend Henry?"

Edgar thinks for a while, mulling over the implications of Lieutenant Milo's questions.

Breaking the silence Milo says, "Do you want to have a lawyer with you before answering my questions?"

Edgar feels like saying yes. Realizing Lieutenant Freeman called him in as a suspect in the death of his sister and is spelling out the motive for why he murdered Alma, Edgar's heart is in his throat. His emotions are mixed. He feels Milo is putting together a ridiculous theory. On the other hand, being honest, Edgar did feel a little twinge of jealousy at the beginning. That disappeared, when he realized Alma was trying to help Henry overcome his anxiety.

"Lieutenant Freeman, no, I don't need an attorney. At first, yes, I did feel a little let's say separation anxiety. Since I was born I always have been the center of Alma's attention of her life. When I realized Alma was, as was I, trying to help our dear friend shake feelings of guilt, guilt for something he had no control over, my twinge of jealousy vanished."

"You knew Jake Langdon?"

"Yes, he was Alma and my financial adviser. He managed the stocks and bonds we had bought years ago."

"Is that all Edgar?"

"Yes."

"You didn't know Mr. Langdon's other clients were criminals?"

"I never asked Jake who his other clients were."

"You didn't check out Mr. Langdon, who was going to manage your entire financial assets?"

"No."

"How did you come to choose him as your financial advisor?"

"He contacted me by phone and explained annuities. Alma and I thought it was a good idea to put a little something aside and bought into the program."

"He changed financial institutions several times before becoming an independent financial advisor. Each time you authorized pulling your investments out of the financial institution Langdon left and reinvesting your holdings with Mr. Langdon wherever he went."

"He always made us money. Alma and I trusted him."

"Mr. Langdon always made you big money, even when the market tanked. Do you know what he invested your money in, Mr. Whitman?"

"Not exactly."

"You were never curious why you always made substantial profits, Mr. Whitman?"

"Alma and I thought he knew the investment business well and know how to make money in up and down markets. We had no reason to question him."

"Did you know Mr. Langdon was indicted for fraud by the Securities and Exchange Commission?"

"No."

"Did you know Mr. Langdon invested money for Albert Castillo?"

"I don't know any of Mr. Langdon's clients."

"You have never heard of Joaquin Guzman, Hector Ortiz, Jimmy Jones?"

"No."

"Do you know Juan Aquino and Alex Temecula?"

"Yes."

"You drink with them often at the Blue Goose Tavern?"

"Yes, I've had a drink with about everyone who drinks at the Blue Goose."

With his last answer Edgar feels defensive. Edgar's reaction lets Milo knows he's hit a nerve. He decides to conclude the interview, leaving Edgar in a state of discomfort. He can always call Edgar in for further questioning.

"Edgar, that's about all for today. I'll save the rest for another day. Thank you for your cooperation. It's greatly appreciated and you have been very helpful," Milo says, cutting the interview short.

Believing Milo will hound him until he gets what he wants, a dejected Edgar leaves the sheriff's office with Fenway. He answered Milo's questions as honestly as possible and hopes for the best.

Two days later headlines in the morning edition of the Sacramento Courier read: FREEMAN DEMANDS CORONER'S INQUEST IN WHITMAN, JOHNSTON AND LANGDON DROWNINGS.

Lieutenant Milo Freeman stated, "The fact that the bodies of Alma Whitman and Reverend Henry Johnston have been missing with out a trace for five months with out raises suspicion of foul play. I have requested the medical examiner reopen the case to place witnesses under oath to answer question respecting their deaths and disappearances." Asked why a coroner's inquest has been requested, Lieutenant Freeman was quoted as saying, "The circumstances of Mr. Langdon's death clearly indicate foul play."

Gossip has it that Juan Aquino, a gravedigger at the Abbeville Cemetery, confessed to the murder of Jake Langdon. Rumors spread that Edgar Whitman hired Langdon to arrange for his sister and Henry's murder and disappearances. Also, the townspeople are well aware Lieutenant Freeman had Fredrika escorted to Downieville for interrogation in the deaths of Alma, Henry, and Jake Langdon. Fredrika had business connections with Jake Langdon. He was her financial adviser too. The gossip girls fear the white-hot spotlight of the public inquest will shine directly on them. Edgar is probably the only one that doesn't fear the coroner's inquest. His strategy was tested during Freeman's interrogation. Henry tells the truth as he sees it and lets the devil take the hindmost.

At this moment, Lieutenant Freeman knows his office does not have sufficient evidence to arrest suspects, including Edgar, on charges of first or second-degree murder in the deaths of Alma and Henry. Maybe, if some of his suspects are squeezed hard enough at the inquest, the evidence needed to charge people with first or second-degree murder will come out. In addition, the death of Jake Langdon is sure to be a high profile case because of the horrendous way Langdon died. Although the links between

Langdon and Edgar, as well as the links between Langdon and Fredrika are weak, Lieutenant Freeman thinks calling a coroner's inquest in the death of Jake Langdon will put tremendous pressure on Edgar, Fredrika, Juan, and anyone else who is connected to Langdon's murder. His experience in murder cases tells him the chances are exceptionally good that someone is going to slip under the intense scrutiny Marcus Chao will place on witnesses at the inquest.

At another level, Drs. Preston and Mayes know Lieutenant Freeman won't go away; and, if there is an inquest, they will be in the middle of it because they examined Whitman, Johnston, and Langdon's bodies. Dr. Mayes will be the first one to go under oath at the inquest because he is the county medical examiner. He has a lot of secrets and needs to be careful not to commit perjury under oath. If the inquest verdict leads to civil or criminal trial proceedings, a perjury conviction could lead him into real trouble with Dr. Preston thrown in besides.

Due to the involvement of Native Americans, complicated legal issues will be raised by the inquest. Generally speaking, the Mandoo Nation, which includes the Kitwa, Miwok, Maidu, Wintun, and Yokuts tribes, is a sovereign nation, enjoying limited diplomatic immunity from United States and California judicial proceedings, concerning internal tribal affairs and religious tribal matters. News of the upcoming inquest motivates the Native Americans to seek legal advice. Langdon's murder took place on the lands hunted by the Kitwa Native Americans. The Kitwa tribes and the Mandoo Nation occupied northern California long before the white man entered the scene. They have witnessed the forest shadows, which they place on par with their sacred grounds at Forest Patch, where live those whose hearts have gone away. They have observed the activities of the Sisterhood from the beginning. In the death of Jake Langdon, if summoned by the court, how will the Kitwa braves respond to being subpoenaed to testify at the inquest? Chief Silver Squirrel convenes the tribal council to hear the words of Black Feather, the tribe's counsel.

Black Feather carefully explains the legal meanings of the phrases "limited diplomatic immunity" from judicial proceedings, "internal tribal affairs," and "religious tribal matters."

"Black Feather," Grey Fox speaks, "We cannot lie to the white ghosts. We cannot speak with forked tongues. If I am asked my knowledge about the taking of life I must answer as straight as an arrow flies."

Black Feather replies, "Yes, you can not lie about what you have seen, regarding the killing of Jake Langdon. But you are not compelled to reveal the mysteries of volcano cave and secrets of Forest Patch: Hipinningkodo, Yongkodo, or Kukinimkodo."

"No," Grey Fox says emphatically, "I would never reveal that which belong to hearts gone away. Nor would I reveal secrets of our lives."

"Good. Then there is no problem with white-man laws or tribal laws. But if we know about or have material evidence relevant to a capital crime—murder in the first degree, murder with aggravating circumstances, or kidnapping, we must, if subpoenaed, testify."

Wise Snake stands, "We witnessed no murders or kidnapping on our land."

"And, the killing of Jake Langdon?" Black Feather inquires.

"None of our tribe saw Langdon's death take place."

"If that is true, Wise Snake, our tribe, our sacred beliefs, and our ancestors are protected by white ghost law."

Further in the Buttes, the Sisterhood is being convened by Florence. The sisters pick a familiar clearing below Lookout Tower to meet. They face two major problems coming from two very different directions.

Florence addresses the community, "First, if sisters are called to testify at the coroner's inquest, how will they respond to questions about the Sisterhood? This problem is dispatched quickly. The Sisterhood is an idea, not a reality. All women are connected by the fact of their biology. If summoned to testify, what is there to hide? Is there anything to hide about women gathering in homes, coffee shops, and churches to talk about whatever women talk about? What is wrong about women gathering on sidewalks or along forest paths to talk about things that matter to them? Is there a problem with women having a conference around a campfire or a picnic in the forest?"

The Sisterhood's silence following Florence's questions signals agreement that the answer to each question is in the negative.

Florence continues, "If you are called to testify at the inquest, you will honestly answer as to what you personally know about Langdon's killing and questions you can answer from direct experience about Alma and Reverend Henry. Questions about the Sisterhood are irrelevant to matters probed at the inquest."

The second is a series of questions and concerns, which raise more thorny issues that directly bear on the very fabric of the Sisterhood. Florence has invited men to join them later at this gathering of sisters. At dusk, Florence stands next to the fire at the center of the clearing, surrounded by one hundred sixty-four sisters to respond to their questions and concerns.

"My dear sisters, Alma and Reverend Henry's hearts have gone into the forest. The shadows, wolves, and raptors protect them. They are renewed and will soon show us the path of all histories. Alma's message is clear. We too must include men in our gatherings. This is our destiny, dear sisters."

Carefully weighing every word Florence says, two-thirds of the Sisterhood takes exception to Florence's attempt to bring men into the Sisterhood. Changing the ways of the Sisterhood that have stood for hundreds of thousands of years is unacceptable. Emma Jane Walters addresses the Sisterhood.

"Florence, you know my personal story, as does every one around our flame. Men's hearts are evil. Their souls are possessed. They treat us in terrible, despicable ways. I for one am against opening our sanctuary to them."

"Emma Jane, do you feel Reverend Henry is evil? Do you believe his soul is possessed? Has he treated you in terrible, despicable ways? How would you judge the hearts and souls of Edgar Whitman, Bruce Dean, Conrad Corbett, Mo Jackson, Washington Reyes, Larry Sherman, and Bronco Brown?"

Emma Jane nods. Her body relaxes, as she returns to the gathering seated in the clearing around the open-air fire. Helen Simmons stands by the fire.

"For hundreds of years our gathering of sisters has been held in secrecy from the men in Abbeville. There are good reasons behind keeping our assemblies closed to the outside world."

The humble bookkeeper quietly returns to her place.

"Helen is absolutely correct," Florence, acknowledges. "We still need to keep our meetings closed to the outside world. Before Abbeville existed, the Mango Nation lived in our area, as they do to this day. They have watched us develop from the beginning, before we knew we were being watched. The Kitwa's keep our secrets as they keep their secrets about their burial grounds. The men invited into the heart of the Sisterhood are of sterling quality and will keep our secrets too."

Stella May Fields speaks next.

"Florence, I have a lot of confidence in you and your judgment, but how were these men picked?"

"Good question Stella May. You sisters have spoken highly of these men. The wives of these men have talked in the highest terms about their husbands. Alma and I have seen the truth in what you've said over the years. The Sisterhood picked these men to stand with us."

Stella May continues, "Each of the women invited into the Sisterhood were unanimously selected by all members of the Sisterhood. Tonight, you place before our gathering the names of men, who are acceptable to those you mention. But the whole of the Sisterhood has not had their say in this matter."

"You are correct, my dear sister. Is there anyone who has an objection to voice about accepting the men I've mentioned into the Sisterhood?"

Florence's comments remove all but Silvia's objections.

"Florence knows where I'm coming from. She makes a compelling case for bringing selected men into our midst. I agree. Yes, the Sisterhood needs to embrace men of good character, men, who love peace and exercise self-control. Men, like Reverend Henry, who have an open heart, have an open mind, and honestly question their own beliefs need to be part of the Sisterhood. Continuing an all-girls club today is as bad as continuing the all-boys club from the past. But all this mumbo-jumbo about hearts that have gone away into the forest, shadows that and wolves and raptors protecting Alma and Henry . . . What's that all about?"

Silvia's two feet are firmly planted on the ground of empirical science.

She needs to be convinced by facts and theories that stand up to objective, independent testing. Florence looks up through the trees.

Florence responds, "Welcome my sisters."

In response to her greeting, the pines circling the clearing suddenly bustle with the sounds of wind, as the trees twist and sway backwards and forward. It is no secret to some of the Sisterhood that such sounds in the trees testify to the presence of shadows among them. Silvia looks into the treetops and sees what appear to be shadows dancing. Looking from the clearing she sees the rest of the forest's trees stand straight and still in the night.

"Impressive," Silvia reports, "but the winds along the Buttes are unpredictable. Pure coincidence, Florence."

Shadows fly among the sisters and into the open fire, dancing among the flames. A sweet scent wafts through the clearing.

Florence whispers in Silvia's ear, "Now how do you scientifically account for what you see happening?"

"I can't come up with a scientific explanation at the moment, Florence, but in time you know I will."

"Well, put on your thinking cap and hold on to your seat, Silvia because you're going to witness something your eyes and your science have never seen."

"I've been waiting for years to have the chance to demystify your forest secrets, Florence. Be my guest."

Florence signals for the men to join them. Several minutes pass before the blindfolded men enter the circle and kneel around the fire. Florence and Silvia still stand at the center of the gathering. Florence explains to the women that the men have accepted being one with the Sisterhood and have been oriented about the ways of the Sisterhood by Shanice Jackson, Ellen Jackson, and Concha Santiago.

"Ladies and gentlemen," Florence commences, "we are about to conduct a scientific experiment, which should shed more light on the mystery many of us know to be fact. Watch and listen with open hearts and minds."

Many of the women look around, not knowing what to make of things, as the forest pines continue to bustle, as the winds blows through them.

Among sounds of creaking and breaking tree limbs the whisper of names can be heard as one-by-one shadows swoop through the fire and take glowing hot embers into the sultry sky, crowning the treetops with a ring of fire that does not burn. The men can't deny the presence of swooping things, the heat and smell of fiery embers, and rush of vocalizations filling the air. The Sisterhood is in awe of the spectacle, as embers fly like flaming arrows from and to the trees and the darting sounds of Franc, the whoosh of Tasha, and the cries of Francis are plainly heard. Whispers of Anne Jeane, Mary and Josie sail past the onlookers. Dr. Preston stands amazed. She has heard the names Carol Ann, Carol Ann Abbe, and Susan on the wind. Except for the unmistakable sound of Anne, the men hear names they have never before heard, but names that are very familiar to the Sisterhood.

Over the years, Silvia will have much to process about this night. The phenomena she witnessed needs to be explained on her terms, scientific terms. She stands quietly. The men invited to the gathering stand and take off their blindfolds. There is no need for comment. Their experience in the forest speaks for itself. Unruffled, Florence calmly returns to the practical issues that soon will face the sisters and brothers of the Sisterhood.

"Next week, an open public inquest will be held to find out what the circumstances are surrounding the death of Jake Langdon. Desiree, Silvia, and I know Lieutenant Freeman intends to probe these forests to discover what happened to the bodies of Alma and Reverend Henry. The subject of the Sisterhood will undoubtedly be inadvertently examined too. We know we have nothing to fear, the mysteries of our Sisterhood will continue to be hidden in the forest, if we do our jobs well."

Abigail Sorenson stands and asks, "What does doing our jobs well mean?"

"Answering questions truthfully in ways that do not betray the Sisterhood," replies Florence.

"How does that work Florence?" asks Edgar.

"We live in multiple worlds, my brothers and sisters. Our answers will fall true on the ears of those at the inquest and satisfy their questions without betraying the Sisterhood. The shadows will make it so," answers Florence.

The forest shadows manifest approval, as a rush of wind that gently bends the tall pines back and forth.

Conrad stands and asks the gathering of sisters, "What do you expect from us?"

"Be yourselves, as nature intended you to be. Do what's right."

Rising to his feet, Bruce Dean testifies, "I heard my wife's name in the wilderness."

His testimony is validated by every man present saying, "So did I."

Florence responds, "We all heard Anne's name on the wings of the wind"

"For now, Anne is a shadow dancing in a flame, embers glowing in a fire, and a fleeting sensation. But, soon, my dear brothers and sisters, you will see her as well as you now see me," Florence says.

Edgar asks, "And Alma and Reverend Henry. I did not hear their names in the wind."

"The forest has not finished its work. In time, you will be reunited." Florence replies,

As with the ending of each meeting of the Sisterhood, not a word is spoken; everyone goes back to their way of life. But never can they, nor ever would they, even if they could, return to what they were. Forest experiences constantly alter their kaleidoscopic understandings of reality. They hear a wolf howl into the night, as if giving tribute to a greater power.

Book Eight

❦

Judgment Day

Chapter 1

❦

*M*onday, September 12, 10:00 a.m.: Before a full house packed into Abbeville's town hall, the Honorable Judge Caroline Abbington gavels Coroner's Inquest Case #2039712 to order in the death of Jake Langdon. After swearing in and instructing the jury of four women and three men, Judge Abbington directs Downieville's Chief County Counsel, Marcus Chao, to make his opening statement. A skilled and experienced trial attorney, who has proved his mettle working some of the most sensational, publicized trials in California history, Mr. Chao unassumingly approaches the jury.

"Your Honor. Good morning ladies and gentlemen of the jury. You have been chosen to use only the facts presented and your judgment to identify the deceased and to determine when, where, why, and by what means he died. I ask you to clear your mind of whatever you may have heard about this case and make your determinations solely on the credible physical evidence and sworn testimony of witnesses presented at this inquest."

The personable and understated attorney pauses, allowing the gravity of the jury's responsibility to settle deeply in their minds. Judge Abbington apologizes for the humid conditions in the courtroom, explaining that the courthouse is old and the air conditioning has failed during the heat wave. She directs Kruko to open the courtroom windows.

"Your honor, I call Detective Lieutenant Milo Freeman to the stand."

Deputy Sheriff Bailiff Steve Kruko swears in the lieutenant.

"Detective Lieutenant Freeman, please state, for the jury, your full name and qualifications."

"My name is Milo Octavio Freeman. I am the chief homicide detective for the Sierra County Sheriffs Department. I have worked seven years in this capacity. I was a police detective sergeant for the city and county of San Francisco for fifteen years, before coming to Sierra County. My undergraduate degree is entomology. I hold a Masters degree in forensic science."

"Please tell the jury, Lieutenant Freeman, how you came about finding and identifying the deceased."

"At 7:23 a.m., on the morning of September 5th, I was called by Ranger Patrick O'Reilly who informed me that Yinka Nigel, the father of Kanan and Ortha Nigel, and his wife Mamba Nigel had discovered a body in the shallows of Upper Sardine Lake, near the parking, at approximately 5:45 a.m."

"What were the Nigel's doing at Upper Sardine Lake that early in the morning?"

"Bird watching. The family walks the trail around the lake each morning, sighting and identifying wildlife, mostly birds."

"They found the diseased at that time?"

"Yes."

"Have you identified the body found in Upper Sardine Lake?"

"Yes. The body has been identified as Jake Langdon, 33 year-old single Caucasian male, muscular build, and six feet and three inches tall. Personal effects of Mr. Langdon—his wallet, brief case, registration, insurance papers, and phone book—were found in his truck, his iPhone and papers found in his cabin at the Sardine Lake Resort. His effects indicate he is the managing director of Cain, Cross, Leon, and Saxes Wealth Management Firm, located at 3205 Eureka Street in San Francisco, California. He resided at 45326 Lincoln Drive, Belmont California."

Marcus throws another softball question, "Lieutenant Freeman, what is your professional opinion regarding the circumstances surrounding Jake Langdon's demise?"

"He was murdered. People don't drown in the shallows of Upper Sardine Lake. Drowning takes place in the deeper parts of the lake. The shallows run from zero to two feet at the depth Langdon was found. He was only eleven and one half feet from the shoreline. The man's face was covered with welts and deep bruises. His skull was fractured in several places, his jaw was broken, he sustained a broken clavicle and he was bleeding from his ears. It appears Mr. Langdon tried to protect himself by extending his arms in an attempt to stop the blows he sustained. His right and left ulna bones were broken in several places. It appears from the deep bruises on his chest and from several broken ribs when Langdon tried to cover his face and head he was struck in the chest and back with a blunt instrument."

"Is there any possibility that Mr. Langdon fell while mountain climbing?"

"None. He was wearing tan slacks, a blue sports shirt and had on street shoes. As far as I could tell, none of his valuables were missing. He was found wearing his watch and jewelry. His wallet was full of money and credit cards. His truck keys were in the ignition of his truck."

"Could he have fallen while walking the trails?"

"No. From the scuffmarks on his shoe tops it appears he was dragged from the parking lot to the shoreline, then dropped in the lake unconscious or dead. There were sets of shoe prints along each side of Langdon's drag marks, as if two people were carrying him under his arms. There was another set of fresh shoe prints further away, as if someone was trailing whomever was dragging Mr. Langdon from the parking lot into the lake."

"As to location of his body and the cause or causes of Mr. Langdon's death, what is your professional opinion?"

"Jake Langdon was murdered and after being beaten to death in the parking lot next to Upper Sardine Lake, his body was dragged and dumped into the lake shallows"

"Your Honor, I would like to recall Lieutenant Freeman later this afternoon."

Judge Caroline Abbington excuses Milo from the witness stand requesting him to wait in the witness room, so as not to hear the testimony of other witnesses.

"Call your next witness, Mr. Chao."

I would like to call Dr. Jeffrey Mayes to the stand.

Deputy Kruko swears in Dr. Mayes.

"Good morning Dr. Mayes. Please state, for the jury, your full name and qualifications."

"Good morning," replies Jeffrey, "My name is Jeffrey Martin Mayes. I am the chief medical examiner for Sierra County.

"Based on your examination of Mr. Langdon, Dr. Mayes, when would you place his time of death?"

"Judging from the amount of blood lost and the freshness of the body, I would place Mr. Langdon's time of death between three and five o'clock in the morning of Monday, September 5th, Labor Day."

"Dr. Mayes, did you perform an autopsy on Mr. Langdon?"

"Yes."

"According to your medical examination, what would you say was the cause of death?"

After a lengthy graphic, detailed report of his findings, complete with photos supporting each observation he makes respecting Langdon's autopsy, Dr. Mayes concludes his statement.

"The immediate cause of Mr. Langdon's death was traumatic brain injury caused by repeated blows to the head with a heavy blunt instrument."

"Do you know what kind of heavy blunt instrument was used to kill Mr. Langdon?"

"Yes, a five pound crow bar was found in the brush on the hillside near the lake parking lot. Blood found on the crow bar was identified as Jake Langdon's blood, which also match blood splatter patterns found on the back window and cab of Mr. Langdon's truck."

"Thank you Dr. Mayes. Are you available for further questioning later this afternoon?"

"Yes."

Judge Abbington excuses Dr. Mayes from the witness stand, directing him to wait in the witness room and not discuss testimony with Lieutenant Freeman.

Abbington directs Bailiff Kruko to order lunch for the two witnesses and remain with them until the inquest reconvenes at two o'clock. The jurors are released to go to lunch and are reminded not to discuss matters relating to the inquest with anyone.

Except for the reporter for the Sierra Morning Star, journalists rush to phones to file their stories before the evening edition deadline. Sacramento Courier field correspondent, Sydney Cameron, encapsulates her view: STOCK BROKER'S BRAINS BASHED OUT IN ABBEVILLE. Sacramento Bee's Lindsay Patton headlines her story: LANGDON MURDERED, DUMPED IN LAKE.

The Sierra Morning Star is a new paper with a new policy. Focus on Abbeville's local news in a positive way. Marti Morgan, writer for the Sierra Morning Star, drafts a front-page story entitled: VACATION PARADISE. She reports on the crowds at the lakes this Labor Day and the fun-filled family activities happening. She doesn't ignore the inquest, as she centers on what people think and feel when they exit the inquest. The news, which is a more personal, more in-depth interview of townspeople, carries more weight in the town than what outsiders have to say. Her front-page underneath story reads TOWNSPEOPLE VOICE THEIR VIEWS OF INQUEST. Pictures of townspeople, giving their opinions, are imbedded in their comments.

The Sacramento Courier and Sacramento Bee front-page banner headlines hit the streets of Abbeville before the day's inquest is over. Their articles highlight the gruesome details described by Detective Lieutenant Freeman and county medical examiner Mayes. As people like the good news about their town and like reading the bad news told by people they know, copies of the Morning Star fly off the newspaper racks and off counters in Abbeville, until the paper is sold out.

After lunch the jury files into court. Judge Abbington immediately reminds them that they are still under oath. She individually polls the jury.

Looking at each juror, Abbington asks, "Have you discussed the details of these proceedings with anyone, juror number one?"

"No." answers Manheim Dawson.

"No Your Honor," responds Carol Lewis.

"No Judge Abbington," replies Larson Rogers.

"No." answers Linda Murphy.

"No." says Olivia Nicholson.

"No." replies Paige Robinson.

"No Ma'am," answers Xavier Powell, juror number 7, the final juror on the panel.

"Mr. Chao," the judge says, turning toward Marcus, "You may proceed."

Chao recalls Milo and Jeffrey to the stand and draws more information from them about whom they have contacted and questioned about the death of Jake Langdon. Lieutenant Freeman reveals he has interrogated Edgar Whitman, Bunny Grimmer, Edna Pinkney, Fredrika Handley, Holly Spears, Joyce Lawrence, and Jenny Hobbs. Dr. Mayes reports discussing the case with his forensic team—Dr. Artisia Brown, Hopper Jensen, Zack Curry, and Mimi Gastineau—and consulting with Dr. Silvia Preston on the Langdon case.

Chao requests a *subpoena duces tectum* of all interviews made by Lieutenant Milo and all recordings of the autopsy of Jake Langdon and all discussions pertaining to the Langdon case among members of the county forensic team. Judge Abbington orders a summons for the production of all evidence, pertaining to the interrogations conducted by Milo and of all discussions held among members of the forensic team. Next, Mr. Chao requests subpoenas to appear as witness at the inquest are issued for all the individuals named by Lieutenant Milo and examiner Mayes. After questioning Dr. Mayes with regard to his consultation with Dr. Preston, Chao does not compel Silvia to testify. In a surprise move, Marcus requests Pastor Jacob Richmond also be commanded by the court to bear witness at the inquest.

Judge Abbington asks Mr. Chao to approach the bench. She asks Chao to justify his request, demanding a member of the clergy to testify at the inquest. Mr. Chao hands Abbington two pieces of paper. Abbington calls a thirty-minute recess and directs Marcus to follow her into the town hall conference room. With the door closed both sit at a corner of the large conference table.

"This new information puts a whole new light on our coroner's inquest, Marcus. With Alex Temecula confessing he murdered Jake Langdon, Juan Aquino confessing to be an accessory to murder and Christopher Jenkins plea bargaining to lesser criminal charge, we seems to have a wrapped up our inquest."

"Only part way."

"Go on, counselor."

"I intend to prove to the jury there was a conspiracy to murder Alma Whitman and Reverend Henry, a conspiracy which I believe includes Jake Langdon, Jacob Richmond, Juan Aquino, Alex Temecula, and others I have yet to identify."

"You're linking Langdon's murder to a conspiracy to commit the murder's of Alma and Henry?"

"Yes."

"The court cannot act on what you believe and think, Mr. Chao. Who are the others you refer to and what is your hard evidence, connecting the members of the supposed conspiracy?"

"As for others involved in the conspiracy, Judge Abbington, I don't exactly know. That will be sorted out when I question the subpoenaed witnesses. Then, I will have the hard evidence, you require."

"If you stay clear of violating Pastor Jacob's Constitutional rights under the first and Second amendments, Marcus, I will allow your little fishing expedition, but only for a while. You did not subpoena Dr. Preston, why is that?"

"Dr. Preston in her consulting capacity to the county medical examiner is technically an officer of the court, plus she is not a hostile witness. I've talked with her and she is willing to be available and testify at the inquest if needed."

"Anything else, Marcus?"

"I will need time to thoroughly comb through the subpoenaed documents and videos related to Detective Milo's interrogations, the autopsy of Jake Langdon, and the discussions of Dr. Mayes and his forensic team."

"I'll give you two days, Marcus."

"Thank you. I think, after reviewing the police records, I would like meet with you before the inquest convenes. By that time, I will give you a better idea, where my fishing expedition is heading."

Judge Abbington agrees and they return to the inquest.

In light of the number of people and records subpoenaed, Judge Abbington adjourns the coroner's inquest until Thursday morning, September 15, at ten o'clock.

By six o'clock that evening, Bailiff Kruko has personally served Lieutenant Milo with the court summons to surrender all documents and media recordings of his interrogations. By eight o'clock Edgar Whitman, Bunny Grimmer, Edna Pinkney, Fredrika Handley, Holly Spears, Joyce Lawrence, and Jenny Hobbs receive writs to testify in the matter of the death of Jake Langdon.

Chapter 2

ᏫᏯᏫ

Tuesday, September 13, 7:00 a.m.: Today will be a busy one for Drs. Preston and Mayes, as they have the full day scheduled to work with the San Francisco Academy of Sciences research teams, surveying the extend of damages cause by the western pine beetles.

As Silvia and Jeffrey walk into the Academy's field biology staging area in Springs Creek Park, teams of scientists accompanied by National Guard personnel, tractors, and guard dogs organize to investigate the mountain terrain.

Dr. Darius Porter, the Academy of Sciences Operation Beetle team leader and his field assistant Joel Lambert, Ph.D. in entomology at Cal Berkeley, walk from the field laboratory tent across the clearing.

"You must be Drs. Preston and Mayes. Glad to meet you and show you around our humble accommodations," Darius calls out, as he approaches the two.

"Pleasure to meet you, too," Joel warmly greet Silvia and Jeffrey.

"Let's go over to the lab tent and I'll show you how Operation Beetle works," Darius says, leading the way.

Drs. Mayes and Preston are impressed with the quality of the equipment and the lighting in the makeshift laboratory tent.

Darius continues, "Joel supervises the science teams in the fields. They photograph western beetle habitats, collect specimens, and direct the National Guard engineers to mark beetle-infested trees to be cut. Once the trees are cut we section them and bring tree samples back to the lab for study."

Joel contributes, "Each beetle brought here is identified, labeled, and preserved for storage at the Academy. Some tree sections are examined and everything living is preserved for storage. Now, here's the interesting part. Other tree sections are kept alive for observation and testing purposes."

"Testing for what?" Mayes inquires.

"Testing to see which strain of forest ant has a taste for western beetle eggs and larvae," responds Joel.

"The idea is to release ants on beetles, as lady bugs are released on aphid infested plants and trees."

"Right," replies Darius, "We have several promising species of ants that might work."

"Doesn't cutting trees destroy the forest habitat?" asks Dr. Preston.

Joel almost jumps out of his skin, "Absolutely and that is why I'm here to ensure only a small sample of trees are taken for our purposes. Most of the trees we take are infested to the extent they would die. The forests around Abbeville are mature and are the prime habitat for the Pileated Woodpecker and other endangered forest creatures."

"Won't introducing a genetically mutated ant specializing on sap beetles pose problems too?" injects Dr. Mayes.

"We are aware of some of the consequences of our interventions. We will have to proceed cautiously. But first things first, we have to find the natural forest predators that loves sap beetles at every stage of their lives," Darius comments.

"I can't help but notice each of the science teams going into the forest have two or three dogs assigned. All those dogs are needed to find beetle infested trees?" Silvia inquires.

"I thought so too. Guard engineers pointed out there are a lot of trees in the forests and the dogs also serve to protect their equipment. Over there, those gentleman talking by the edge of the clearing . . . You have to ask them if you have more questions about the dogs."

Obviously Darius knows nothing about the purpose of the dogs or is playing dumb. Dr. Mayes recognize the gentlemen at the clearing's edge to be a CDC agent and Major Souk Kwai, but he doesn't see Dr. Fitzsimons. Drs. Preston and Mayes keep silent on the matter.

"Maybe later on this afternoon," Mayes says. "What else do you have to show us, Darius?"

"Do you want to go out with one of the field teams?"

Jeffrey and Silvia are eager to join one of the research teams as Darius suggests. Both are enticed by the science and curious about how the CDC and military are going to go about searching for western pine beetles, while they ostensibly search for Alma, Henry, the aliens, and mad cows. As for the guard dogs, they know cadaver dogs, when they see them. The canines and their handlers can't hide the fact they are specialized in the detection of human remains. The search for the unknown person or persons Elgin shot is in full swing.

"Dr. Mayes, Dr. Preston, let me show is in store for you this afternoon."

Joel points to the large map, showing how the Academy search and study teams are assigned regions throughout the Tahoe National Forest.

"You'll be heading up to the Saxonia Lake area. It's a fairly desolate area that not too many people know about. The crowds that swarm to popular destinations like Sardine and Packer Lakes certainly don't frequent it. It's an almost forgotten body of water."

"That's pretty rugged country; Silvia, are you sure you're up for it?"

"Worry about yourself, Jeffrey. I hike these mountains several times a week. If you poop out on the trail, just tell me. I'll understand."

"Appears you two are ready to go," Joel continues, "The Saxonia Region 77 truck is about to leave. Good luck."

Jeffrey and Silvia run and jump into the bed of the truck, as it winds to its destination. Without a jeep trail access to the shoreline, the team hikes three miles to Region 77, which is located above the lake.

"What a view. I think that's Mount Shasta in the distance?" Jeffrey says, as if standing on the top of the world.

"Spectacular," sighs Silvia. "Unbelievable."

Team leader Jenna Franks breaks into the conversation, "We're going to set up our field staging area here. You two are welcome to join us. Our job isn't glamorous. Just start stripping the bark off the selected trees, like you see the other members of our team doing over there and look for beetles or beetle larvae."

"It's going to be hard to take our eyes off the view, but count us in," Silvia responds.

Four hours of striping fallen logs and trees in search of beetle yields no findings, which is good news, telling the scientists the spread of the western beetle hasn't penetrated the sparse forest around Lake Saxonia. Returning to the Spring Creek Academy base camp, Mayes sees Dr. Fitzsimons.

"Silvia, I'm going to talk to Collin. So, I'll meet you a little later in the field laboratory."

"Sure," Silvia replies, "I'll tag along with Jenna and listen to the report she's going to give Darius."

As the two women head to the tent, Mayes waves to catch Collin's eye.

"How's your search coming along Dr. Fitzsimons?" Mayes says, throwing Collin an open-ended question.

"What do you mean?" responds Dr. Fitzsimons.

"It's just you and me Collin. Have the cadaver dogs detected anything."

"Not a sign," Collin grudgingly responds.

"Nothing? The dogs found nothing?"

Dr. Fitzsimons is uncomfortable sharing anything with Mayes.

Mayes presses, "Relax Collin, we're in this together. What about the other CDC and MI agents?"

"Not a trace of human remains was found by any of the teams."

"That surprises me," Mayes continues, "You'd think with Academy teams searching hundreds of square miles today that something would turn up."

Collin doesn't respond.

Mayes continues, "I'm shocked. You'd think the dogs would have come across the remains of the Native Americans we know are scattered in burial grounds throughout the Sierra's?"

"Mayes, all you need to know is we found nothing; and, keep it to yourself."

Tuesday, September 13, 10:00 p.m.: Since they were delivered to him by Deputy Kruko, early this morning, Marcus has been pouring over the fifteen hundred pages of interrogation transcripts and discussion tapes from the medical office. Blessed with a near photographic memory, he sorts and cross references the topics discussions made by each person until past midnight.

Wednesday, September 14, 7:00 a.m.: Marcus studies the two digital film discs of the interrogations and the videos of the Langdon autopsy and video records of the discussions that took place with Dr. Mayes and his forensic team. He studies the mannerisms of each person interrogated by Milo and each person participating in the medical examiner's office. He notes Edgar's honesty, Holly's skittish nature, the coolness of Fredrika, and how Bunny looks for assurances when answering questions. He knows what Pastor Jacob and Christopher Jenkins will say. Marcus is sure they will make predictable witnesses. Based on his experience and judgment, he determines the final line up of witnesses he'll submit to Judge Abbington on Thursday at their eight-thirty morning meeting at the Knead-2-Feed Bakery.

Chapter 3

❦

Thursday, September 14, 5:48 a.m.: Marcus wakes and stretches his toes in one direction, his head and outstretched arms in the other, squeezing all of his muscles tightly. He lets out a big groan, a sigh, and thinks, "Today is that day I said yesterday was an other day." He sits on the edge of his bed.

"What's the matter, Tweety?" asks Ling asks, calling him by her favorite name for him.

"All I have to do is pull one thread a little and their stories will unravel in front of the judge and jury."

"That's sweet dear," responds his wife Ling, as she rolls to the other side of the bed and falls to sleep.

Looking into the mirror Marcus wonders, "Who in the hell is that?"

Thursday, September 14, 6:50 a.m.: Marcus' kids run and hit both of his legs like he's a tackling dummy.

"Daddy, Daddy is you taking us to school today? Mommy said you would," says his youngest daughter Sophia, age three, who is now perched on his foot.

Lan Ying is that blue glittering pajama clad child on his other foot, wanting him to give her a ride around the house. She's seven. He knows it is useless to debate his wife over who drives the kids to school; he always loses.

As for his daughters, Marcus shaves and gets ready for work with the both of them clinging to his legs. Only the call of breakfast and their mother's demand to get ready for school release their grip on Tweety's leg.

Each morning is a miracle. By eight o'clock, before heading to the bakery for coffee and donuts with Judge Abbington, Marcus watches his daughters walk all the way into their classrooms.

Arriving at the bakery by eight thirty, Marcus greets the judge and hands the list of witnesses to her, before he gives her a heads-up on what he plans to do. She reads the order of the to herself.

Bunny Grimmer

Fredrika Handley

Pastor Jacob Richmond

Christopher Jenkins

"You're not calling Edgar Whitman, Edna Pinkney, Holly Spears, Jenny Hobbs, or Joyce Lawrence to the stand? You added Christopher Jenkins to the list. What gives?"

"After hearing the testimonies of the witnesses I've given you, I want the other subpoenaed witnesses to stew in their juices. These witnesses have deadly weakness in the stories, which I intend to hit hard at the inquest. They do appear to me to have something they are hiding about the murder of Jake Langdon and the deaths of Alma and Reverend Henry. I'll call other witnesses, if I need to, but I don't think that will be necessary with the batting order I've lined up."

Judge Abbington approves the starting order of witnesses for the morning's session.

"What next?"

Marcus pushes another paper in front of the judge requesting the placement of deputy sheriffs inside of town hall as well as outside. She looks at him.

"Security reasons," he whispers across the top of his coffee, "Plus I may need for you to place certain witnesses into immediate custody."

Abbington agrees.

"Is that it, counselor?"

The number of witnesses Marcus intends to call is short. But the list of possible witnesses is long. The space inside the town hall witness room is limited. Marcus requests that all witnesses be sequestered at the library, under the watchful eyes of sheriff deputies, until they are called to the inquest.

"Agreed," Judge Abbington replies, "Any more tricks up your sleeve, counselor?"

"None, Your Honor. But, I object to you saying I have tricks up my sleeve."

"Overruled," the judge says standing and commenting, "If that's about all Marcus, I have work to do myself before today's inquest begins. See you promptly at ten."

Marcus acknowledges the judge and watches her leave the bakery.

He thinks, "That's a woman of few words."

Nine o'clock in the morning, Marcus stands on the town hall steps and watches the townspeople and curious outsiders fill the auditorium. Several people come over and greet him on their way inside the town hall. Marcus sees the two surprise, voluntary witnesses he didn't tell Judge Abbington about, as he doesn't want them to be sequestered. However, he wants them clearly visible, during the inquest. Jackson Smythe and Allen Belcher enter town hall and avoid looking in Marcus' direction. With everything set, he moves to the attorney's table. Judge Abbington, the court reporter, and the jury enter the hall from the town council's conference room.

Judge Abbington instructs the jury about their responsibilities under the California Code of Criminal Procedure Section 1514, namely, to set forth who the killed person is, and when, where and by what means he came to his death, and, if he was killed or his death occasioned by the act of another by criminal means, who is guilty. Finally, she instructs the jury to place their verdict in writing, containing the information she quoted from the Code of Criminal Procedure.

You may call your first witness, Mr. Chao," permits Judge Abbington.

"Your Honor, I call Mrs. Bunyon Grimmer to the stand."

Bunny trots to the front of the town hall, smiling, before she sits in the witness chair and is sworn in to testify.

"Would you state your full name for the jury?"

"My name is Bunyon Linda Grimmer, but you can call me Bunny. I've been a resident in Abbeville for thirty-three years."

Mrs. Grimmer, did you know the deceased Jake Langdon?"

Bunny looks in the audience for Fredrika, but Freddie is sequestered under guard at the library.

She answers hesitatingly, "Ah, Jake, I know Jake Langdon. He was my financial adviser, I told that to Detective Lieutenant Freeman."

"Did you know that Fredrika Handley knew Jake Langdon?"

"Why yes, I believe she did," responds Bunny more confidently.

"Did you know Alma and Edgar Whitman knew Jake Langdon?"

"I don't recall."

"According to the transcript of your interrogation at the Sheriff's Department, you stated in answer to Lieutenant Freeman's question about knowing Mr. Langdon: 'Jake is my friend and financial advisor who many years ago put together a stock partnership for Fredrika, Alma, Edna and me.' Is that a true statement you made to Lieutenant Freeman?"

"Remember you are under oath to tell the truth," Judge Abbington reminds the witness.

"Of course, I told the truth. Now, I remember, we were all in a kind of a financial partnership."

"Mrs. Grimmer, if one of the partners died, how was the principle and the earnings of the deceased partner to be divided?"

"Well, let me think for a moment?"

"Take your time, Mrs. Grimmer."

"I don't remember. All those legal words and contracts confuse me."

Marcus takes three certified copies of the financial partnership agreement from his briefcase. He gives one to Judge Abbington, hands one to Bunny, and begins to read the appropriate contract provision from the other copy.

"According to the financial partnership contract you signed with Fredrika, Alma, and Edna, each of you hold one forth of the financial partnership and if one dies: 'The surviving partner's share of the financial partnership would increase to one third with the deceased partner's personal estate compensated for the full market value of the deceased partner's share by the life insurance policy each partner has on his or her life.' That means that Alma's share of the financial partnership would compensate Alma's estate a total of $96,000.78. In turn, you, Fredrika, and Edgar's share of the financial partnership would be increased to one third share with a value of $128,001.78."

"You're not saying I killed Alma so I could increase my share to one third. That's preposterous! And, anyway, what's this got to do with the death of Jake Langdon?"

"It establishes the fact that you, Edna, Alma, Fredrika, and Jake Langdon knew each other very well and that Edna, Fredrika, and you financially gain some $32,000.00 each by Alma's death, which your friend, Jake Langdon, manages."

Bunny is visibly frustrated, her face and ears are bright red.

Bunny indignantly fires back at Marcus, "Jake Langdon is Edgar Whitman's financial advisor too. Why aren't you dragging him here? Everyone knows what happened between his sister and Reverend Henry!"

Judge Abbington warns the witness, "Mrs. Grimmer, please confine your statements to answering the questions Mr. Chao asks."

Bunny still ruffled assents to Abbington's direction.

Marcus continues, "Do you know Mimi Gastineau?"

"Yes."

"Do you know what she does for a living?"

"Yes."

"Do you talk to Ms. Gastineau, often?"

"Of course, I do she's my Goddaughter. We talk a lot."

"Does she tell you about the work she does?"

"Yes, she tells me a lot about her work . . . how she gets to solve mysteries and all the terrible things that happen to people."

"Like what, Bunny?"

"Oh, like the time they found poor Alma and Henry at the bottom of that lake, simply horrible, terrible, how sad."

"Yes, sad indeed," Marcus says empathetically.

"Yes, and how they may have died of some contagious disease."

"I didn't know that?" Marcus says as if in friendly conversation.

Bunny adds, "Yes, when Mr. Elgin shot at those shadows, they found blood on the ground that turned out to be diseased."

"'They,' being the county medical examiner and his forensic team?"

"Oh no! Dr. Preston and Florence de la Rosa were there before any of those people.

"Honestly," Marcus flips through his notes of the medical examiner's report and says "The records indicate Mimi was not with the forensic team that night."

Bunny quickly adds the missing information, "Mimi, poor darling, had a bad cold that week; she found out about what happened at the Elgin place days later, when she was briefed by Dr. Mayes at one of their meetings."

"I understand. You've been quite helpful, Mrs. Grimmer. Thank you for your testimony," Marcus says politely.

Judge Abbington informs Bunny, "You may step from the witness stand, Mrs. Grimmer. You may be seated in the front row reserved for witnesses."

"Thank you Judge. You too, Mr. Chao."

Bunny steps from the stand and is escorted by a sheriff deputy to the front, where they sit together, the deputy on the aisle.

"May we have Fredrika Handley called to the stand?" Marcus requests.

Fredrika is escorted from the library, confidently walks to the front of the town hall, and sits expressionless, while sworn to testify. Marcus waits before questioning Fredrika. When he is sure Fredrika has spotted Bunny sitting in the front row, he begins his line of questioning.

"Would you please state your full name for the jury?"

"My name is Fredrika Cameron Handley. I've lived in Abbeville for forty-seven years."

"Thank you Mrs. Handley. Did you know the deceased Jake Langdon?"

Fredrika looks at Bunny.

"Jake Langdon was my financial adviser and when Alma Whitman,

Edna Pinkney, Mrs. Grimmer, and I wanted to pool our money to buy securities, he put a financial partnership together for us."

"Are you aware of what happens, when one of your financial partners die?"

"Yes. Using money from the deceased partner's insurance policy, the surviving partners buy the decease's one-fourth interest so it will not be transferred to the personal estate of the deceased."

"Did you know Jake Langdon was connected with criminal elements in San Francisco?"

"No."

"Did you know Jake Langdon had served six years in the Ohio State Penitentiary for the negligent homicide of a client, for whom he too put together a financial partnership?"

Fredrika glances at Bunny who looks very frightened sitting with the deputy in the front row of the auditorium. She takes a deep breath, as if exasperated by the whole proceeding.

"No."

"You looked at Mrs. Grimmer before answering. Does Mrs. Grimmer know of Mr. Langdon's prison record?"

"I don't know."

"Mrs. Handley, do you know Christopher Jenkins."

"Slightly."

"Do you know whether Christopher Jenkins knows anything about Mr. Langdon's prison record?"

Fredrika looks away and sees Jenkins sitting between two sheriff deputies next to the far wall in the town hall.

"I have no idea." She answers with disinterest.

"I have no further questions for Mrs. Handley, Your Honor."

Judge Abbington excuses Fredrika and directs her to sit in the front row. She sits next to Bunny. Both ladies avoid eye contact. Another sheriff deputy walks over and sits right of Fredrika.

"Judge Abbington, given the evidence placed before the jury this afternoon, I request a warrant be issued for the arrest of Mimi Constance Gastineau."

"On what charges, counselor?"

"Based on the testimony of Mrs. Grimmer that she received information on a regular basis from her Goddaughter, Mimi Gastineau, who is a forensic technician at the Sierra County Medical Examiner's Office. One misdemeanor count of giving government information to unauthorized sources and one felony count of destruction of physical evidence in an ongoing homicide investigation, You Honor," submits Marcus.

"So ordered."

Judge Abbington orders Mimi Gastineau be placed under arrest, knowing Marcus has only the thinnest of grounds to base his request. Marcus knows his is not a solid case against Mimi, but knows ordering a bench warrant for the arrest Mimi will send Bunny into a state of panic.

"I would also request, after booking Ms. Mimi Gastineau on the two counts, that she be brought to this inquest for questioning," Marcus continues.

The judge directs two sheriff deputies to make the arrest and bring Mimi Gastineau to the inquest. Judge Abbington calls a fifteen-minute recess, directing the witnesses, Fredrika and Bunny, to remain the front row, during the recess. Marcus signals the two deputies guarding Christopher Jenkins to assist him to the front row during the recess. Marcus watches the reactions of Fredrika and Bunny, as the shackled, hand cuffed Jenkins shuffles by and is seated next to Fredrika and her sheriff deputy.

"The noose seems to be tightening," Marcus observes to himself.

After the recess, Judge Abbington calls on Marcus to continue with the inquest and call his next witness.

"I request Pastor Jacob Richmond take the witness stand, Your Honor.

Pastor Jacob Richmond is sworn in to testify. Fredrika, who has been cool as the underside of a pillow throughout the proceedings swallows hard and begins to squirm. Marcus knows Pastor Jacob will answer each question posed to him without equivocation. Bailiff Kruko asks the pastor to give his full name and occupation for the court record.

"My name is Jacob Isaiah Richmond; I am the pastor of the Damascus Reformed Church and live in the cottage in back of the church," replies the pastor.

"Pastor Richmond, do you hate Reverend Henry and Alma Whitman?"

"Yes, as God hates sin," Jacob answers.

"Did you plan to kill Alma Whitman and Reverend Henry Johnston?"

"Yes, as God is my witness in His Holy Cause. I planned to kill the wicked Alma and Henry, as God told Moses to kill and replace the wicked people living in the Promised Land."

"Were you alone in your plans?"

"No, as Joshua had his army that utterly destroyed Jericho and every man, woman, child and every ox, sheep and donkey with the Edge of God's Sword, I have my army too."

"And, Pastor Richmond, who is in your army?"

"My commander, Elroy Jones, who has fled Abbeville with the true believers to the Promised Land in the Emerald Triangle. Fredrika Handley, my high priestess, and Bunny Grimmer, her hand servant."

Bunny and Fredrika come straight to their feet and cry, "Liar, you damnable liar, this man is crazy . . ."

Abbington gavels the court to order over the uproar. She advises Fredrika and Bunny to remain quiet throughout the proceedings or have their mouths duck-taped. Even though they believe Judge Abbington would not do such a thing, the judge's comment stuns the courtroom into silence.

Mimi, who is being escorted by two sheriff deputies down a side aisle in the town hall, hears her Godmother and Fredrika screaming at Pastor Jacob and hears the judge's comments. Mimi is seated in the front row next to the deputy guarding Christopher Jenkins.

"Were there other soldiers in your army, Pastor Jacob?"

"Captain Christopher Jenkins, Lieutenant Jake Langdon, and their two loyal soldiers, Alex Temecula and Juan Aquino, plus their hand maiden Edna Pinkney."

Marcus summarizes, "Is it true to say that you and Commander Elroy Jones; your high priestess Fredrika Handley; hand servant Bunny Grimmer; Captain Christopher Jenkins; Lieutenant Jake Langdon; solider Alex Temecula; solider Juan Aquino; and hand maiden Edna Pinkney planned to murder Alma Whitman and Reverend Henry?"

"Yes. And that harlot in Downieville, the spy who gave us inside information to throw the police investigations off track."

"Who would that be?"

"Mimi Gastineau?"

"Did Mimi Gastineau plan with you to murder Alma and Henry?"

"No, she gave us valuable information that we used to drive Reverend Henry from the pulpit."

"Your Honor, I have no other questions to ask Pastor Jacob."

Pastor Jacob is dismissed with the thanks of the court and takes his seat in the front row accompanied by his assigned deputy sheriff.

Marcus calls his last witness, Christopher Jenkins. Cutting a deal with the Sierra County Council's Office to avoid facing a possible death penalty for the first-degree murder of Jake Langdon, Jenkins agrees to tell all he knows. Christopher sings like a bird, but can't fly because of his shackles, handcuffs, and two deputy sheriffs guarding him.

"Mr. Jenkins, please tell the jury your full name, occupation and residence."

"My name is Christopher Franklin Jenkins, I am the head gardener and landscaper at the Abbeville Cemetery and reside at 12 East Spring Creek Lane in Abbeville."

"Did you with Pastor Jacobs, Elroy Jones, Fredrika Handley, Bunny Grimmer, Edna Pinkney, Jake Langdon, Juan Aquino, Alex Temecula meet and plan to commit the murders of Alma Whitman and Reverend Henry Johnston?"

"Yes, I and the individuals you named meet on six separate occasions to plan the murders of Alma Whitman and Reverend Henry."

"Did you take steps to put the plan to murder Henry and Alma in action?"

"Yes."

"And Mr. Jenkins, was there agreement on who in your group of conspirators was to murder Alma and Henry?"

"Yes. At our last meeting on the evening of Monday, May 23, 7:30 in the evening at the home of Edna Pinkney at 145 Salmon Creek Drive in Abbeville, we agreed Jake Langdon would execute Alma and Reverend Henry."

"How were the executions to be carried out?"

"I was to meet with Pastor Henry, Alma, and Jake Langdon at the Abbe Family Mausoleum to discuss plans for financing a perpetual memorial in commemoration of the Abbeville founders. Langdon was going to shoot Alma and Henry dead and Alex and Juan would cremate the bodies in our crematorium."

"Were you, Jacob, Elroy, Fredrika, Bunny, Jake, Alex, Juan, and Edna present at the home of Edna Pinkney for the entire meeting on the evening of Monday, May 23?"

"Yes, everyone you mentioned was present for the whole meeting."

"Were you, Jacob, Elroy, Fredrika, Bunny, Jake, Alex, Juan, and Edna in full agreement on the manner you describe to murder Alma and Henry."

"Yes, we were in full agreement."

"Was any part of the plan put into operation?"

"Jake Langdon was given a check in the amount of $25,000.00 to kill Alma and Henry. Here is the canceled check in that amount from the Damascus Reformed Church treasury, signed by Elders Martin Lawrence, treasure and Pastor Jacob Richmond."

"Mr. Jenkins, getting back to Alma and Henry. After their cremation, where did you plan to dispose of their ashes and bone fragments?"

Sheepishly looking at Allen and Jackson sitting in the courtroom, Christopher answers.

"Me and the gravediggers did a little grave robbing on the side to help make ends meet."

"Yes, go on Mr. Jenkins," urges Marcus.

"Hector Flores, Alex Temecula, Juan Aquino, Richard Aguilar, and I robbed graves for about a year, but so many graves were empty, it wasn't worth it. We were afraid of getting caught and for what?"

"You see Mr. Belcher and Mr. Smythe sitting in the audience.

"Yes."

"Did you report the empty coffins and graves to them?"

Before answering, Christopher gives another quick glance at Allen Belcher and Jackson Smythe.

"No we didn't. We would have lost our jobs."

"How many graves did you and your fellow grave robbers open Mr. Jenkins?"

"Hundreds I suppose. We didn't find much in the mausoleum either."

Marcus turns to the jury and explains that Christopher Jenkins has agreed to tell why, how, and by whom Jake Langdon was bludgeoned to death and who dumped Mr. Langdon in Upper Sardine Lake. Mr. Jenkins is under oath and is confessing his part in the death of Jake Langdon in exchange for pleading guilty to the lesser crime of the unlawful act of manslaughter.

"Mr. Jenkins, tell us what happened to Jake Langdon and why he was beaten to death?"

"Beating Jake to death was an accident. He was only supposed to be roughed up a bit. After he received the money for putting the final hit on Alma and the Reverend Henry, he wanted more money or he would tell the newspapers about our plans to murder the two. I met with the rest of the group . . ."

Marcus interjects, "The 'group' being you, Fredrika Handley, Bunny Grimmer, Elroy Jones, Jacob Richmond, Edna Pinkney, Alex Temecula, and Juan Aquino without co-conspirator Jake Langdon, who was not invited to the meeting I imagine?"

"Yes, that's the group. They decided that me and my guys beat Langdon around a little to see things our way."

"The guys?"

"Yea, Alex and Juan. When Langdon hit Alex and pulled a gun on Juan, things got out of hand. I jumped Jake and we wrestled him to the ground. The next thing I know, Alex is in a rage, beating Jake's head into the ground with a crowbar. We couldn't stop him. Jake was a bloody mess. I had the boys drag Jake from the parking lot and drop him in the lake."

"Upper Sardine Lake?"

"Yes, it all took place at Upper Sardine Lake."

"On the morning of September 5, Labor Day?"

"Yes, around four thirty in the morning."

"Thank you Mr. Jenkins. I have no further questions of this witness, Your Honor, and I have no further witnesses to call to the stand. Your Honor, I would like the jury to have the certified signed copies of the confessions made by Alex Temecula and Juan Aquino, which supports Mr. Jenkins' testimony."

Judge Abbington directs Christopher Jenkins to remain in the witness chair until the end of the inquest and permits Marcus to hand copies of the murder confessions to the members of the jury.

"Mr. Chao, do you have a closing statement to present to the jury."

"No, Your Honor. I believe the jury is ready to hear your instructions, as to their duties under the law."

"Very well," Judge Abbington responds, "Ladies and gentlemen of the jury the California Code of Criminal Procedure, Section 1514, asks you to place in writing, based on your understanding of the evidence presented at this inquest: who the killed person is, and when, where and by what means he came to his death, and, if he was killed or his death occasioned by the act of another by criminal means, who is guilty. Do you have any questions before you begin your deliberations?"

"Hearing no questions, the jury is dismissed to deliberate until a verdict is reached or until the jury declares it is impossible to reach a verdict. The time is four o'clock. The jury is sequestered for the night and dinner will be served at seven thirty."

With that, Bailiff Kruko takes charge of the jury, as they file into the town hall conference room and begins deliberations. The judge adjourns the inquest until such time as the jury has reached its conclusions. She directs the sheriff deputies to sequester the witnesses in the library until the verdict is reached. Bailiff Kruko is responsible for the care and feeding of the jury until they reach a finding.

During jury deliberations, Judge Abbington and Marcus drive over to get a bite to eat at Las Abuelita's Cocina Mexicana Restaurant. Tucked away in a back booth they attract little attention and are able to enjoy a quiet meal and pleasant conversation mixed with a little business.

"Are you satisfied with your case, Marcus?"

"Everything fell in place perfectly, Caroline; and, the best is yet to come: *Pinkerton v. United States (1946).*"

"You're going to use the Pinkerton Rule to link the conspiracy to murder Alma and Henry with the murder of Jake Langdon at their criminal trials. Just how do you intend to do that, Marcus?"

"Under Pinkerton a death that comes from a felony is murder, even if the death was caused accidentally. In this case, Jake Langdon's death resulted from the felony conspiracy to murder Alma Whitman and Reverend Henry Johnston. If I can prove that, then each member of the conspiracy is guilty of the murder of Jake Langdon."

"Clever boy," Caroline comments, "Under the Pinkerton rule guilt extends to all members of the conspiracy, even if the conspirators did not cause, intend, or foresee the death of Jake Langdon."

"Of course, our discussion bars you from being the judge in any of the upcoming criminal trials."

"Of course."

Judge Abbington's cell phone vibrator goes off at nine o'clock. Baliff Kruko informs the judge that the jury has made its determinations. She instructs Kruko to have all the witnesses present and under guard at the hearing. Judge Abbington asks Deputy Kruko to inform the newspapers.

Marcus and Judge Abbington arrive at town hall fifteen minutes later. Ninety to a hundred people have waited to be among the first to hear the jury's finding. The press is seated. Sheriff deputies usher the witnesses to the first two rows of seats in the hall. Shortly, the jury files out of the conference room and take their seats in the jury box.

"Has the jury agreed on their findings in the death of Jake Langdon?"

The jury spokesperson, Paige Robinson, stands.

"Yes we have, Your Honor."

"Please read your findings."

Paige Robinson reads, "After inspecting the body of the deceased and hearing the testimony, we the jury render the following finding: On Labor Day, Monday, September 5th on or about four thirty in the morning Jake Langdon was beaten in and around his head, arms and upper body in the parking lot at Upper Sardine Lake until he was dead. The evidence and testimony presented at this inquest and the assailant's signed confession clearly indicates Alex Temecula in a fit or rage repeatedly and violently beat Jake Langdon to death. In addition, the jury finds Mr. Langdon's murder was occasioned by the act of others linked by criminal means. In this regard, we the jury find Christopher Jenkins, Pastor Jacobs, Elroy Jones, Fredrika Handley, Bunny Grimmer, Edna Pinkney, Jake Langdon, Juan Aquino, and Alex Temecula guilty of conspiracy to murder Alma Whitman and Reverend Henry Johnston."

Judge Abbington asks the jury, "Is the jury in full accord with the finding read by jury forewoman, Paige Robinson?"

The jury indicates they are in full accord with the statement as read. Bailiff Kruko takes the jury's written finding and hands it to Judge Abbington, who certifies the document and approvingly signs her name to it, as presiding judge.

"On behalf of all the judges of the superior court in Sierra County and the people of the State of California, I thank you, the members of the jury. You are dismissed."

After the last juror has left from the jury box's two-level raised platform and exited into the public seating area, Marcus Chao stands and addresses the court.

"Your Honor, as Christopher Jenkins, Alex Temecula, Juan Aquino, and Mimi Gastineau are in custody, I ask the court to order the arrests of Pastor Jacob Richmond, Elroy Jones, Fredrika Handley, Bunny Grimmer, and Edna Pinkney on charges of conspiracy to commit murders of Alma Whitman and Reverend Henry Johnston. I ask that they be held over for arraignment in the Superior Court of Sierra County."

"So ordered."

Sheriff deputies immediately take the alleged conspirators present at the inquest into custody.

"Your Honor, I ask that Christopher Jenkins, Alex Temecula, Juan Aquino, and Hector Flores be arrested and charged with trespassing and grand theft grave robbery."

"So ordered."

"I also request permission of the court to exhume the bodies of Anne

Dean and exhume the bodies from graves robbed by Christopher Jenkins, Alex Temecula, Juan Aquino, and Hector Flores."

"So ordered. Mr. Chao, do you have anything more to bring to the court's attention?"

"No, Your Honor."

With that, Judge Abbington gavels the Sierra County Coroner's Inquest to a close. Although justice has been served, the bodies of Alma, Reverend Henry, Anne Dean, and the hundreds of persons exhumed from the Abbeville's Cemetery were never found.

Book Nine

❧

Apocalypse

Chapter 1

❦

F*riday, September 15, 7:00 a.m.:* NINE CHARGED WITH CONSPIRACY TO COMMIT MURDER runs across the morning edition of the Sacramento Courier. Again, the Sierra Morning Star takes the less sensational road and runs large banner lines across its early bird edition: POPULAR SCHOOL TEACHER KICKS OFF THE NEW SCHOOL YEAR. Strange as it may seem, the lives of the townspeople begin to normalize. The news that Abbeville's children are back in the good hands of Desiree Parker begins to quell the turmoil that threatens to destroyed the town.

With justice served, Abbeville's gossip mill dismantled, and Pastor Jacob gone, people's fears begin to disappear. Even the fact that so many bodies remain missing and so many questions go unanswered does not distract from the new hope people begin to feel. People trust the ministry of Reverend Doctor Ezekiel Gates. Elder Dean returns to lead the elder council; and, the name of their church is restored to Damascus Church. Within a month, the paltry thirty-eight-member church bounces to over four hundred members.

Pastor Gates partners with Sister Joyce McMichaels of the Church of Self-Reflection and creates and operates the Helping Hands Food Bank to serve the poor and hungry in the Sierra's. In honor of his sister and Reverend Henry, the Abbeville General Store joins with the Damascus Church and the Church of Self Reflection partnership and donates virtually all the food the food bank needs.

Thomas Cochran, editor of the Sierra Morning Star writes a front page editorial on the town's struggle to stay alive: WILL ABBEVILLE BOUNCE BACK? He answers his question by featuring the good that has come about since the bicentennial festival: increases in church membership; absence of small town gossip; and Abbeville's treasury filled to the brim. Cochran writes, "Although the town's population has precipitously dropped over the past six months from over seven hundred to four hundred fifty people, Abbevillians have not lost their spirit or love for life in the Sierras. Abbeville is still a great place to live."

Saturday, October 15, 7:45 a.m.: Dr. Darius Porter and Joel Lambert call a news conference to announce the results of Operation Beetle—the San Francisco Academy of Sciences' month-long search and study effort to eradicate the western pine beetle from the Tahoe National Forest. Because the western pine beetle is a problem on a national scale all the major media networks cover the news conference. Darius gives the big picture.

"We are happy to announce the Academy has successfully found a solution to the problems cause by the western pine beetle. To keep our forests healthy for centuries to come, a genetically altered *Camponotus laevigatus*, a common harvester ant, that already nests in dead and living trees in the Sierra's will be introduced into the forests surrounding Abbeville. We believe this new strain of ant will keep the western pine beetles in check."

CNN reporter Shelly Manning asks, "Can you explain exactly what is being genetically altered in the ant and what danger such genetic tampering will have in the future?"

Joel takes this question; "Danger from our genetic engineering is virtually non-existent; however our Academy scientists will be closely observing the behavior and genetic outcomes over generations. We have altered the harvest ant's genetics in two ways. First, we have added to the list of foods harvest ants already eat in the forests: living and dead insects, aphid, scale insect honeydew, the juices of ripe fruit, seeds and now western pine beetle eggs and larvae. Second, we have made the harvest ant react to the adult pine beetle as if it were a threat to their ant colonies. When alarmed by the pine beetle, harvest ants secrete formalin, which causes the colony of ants to swarm and destroy the adult western pine beetles. Also harvest ants close to the colonies sensing danger drum against the walls of the ant colony to call the colony to arms to swarm and destroy the enemy."

FOX reporter Andrea Michael Forbes follows up, "Once you let the ants out of the jar how are you going to get them back in the jar if something goes wrong?"

Darius responds, "These ants are already out of the jar and in our forests and can be found in almost any habitat on the face of the earth. They are herbivores like we are. Nothing is going to go wrong any more than adding a different food to our diet that we've never tried before. You've never tried calamari, try it you may like it. These harvest ants like to eat beetle eggs and larvae."

Jacqueline Lang from ABC News, "Will this super ant you've created kill the entire population of pine beetles?"

Joel responds, "Killing all the western pine beetles would be a mistake. First, we do not know what the effects of annihilating the complete western beetle population would be. Life on this planet is complexly interrelated. Second, the pine beetle usually infests weak and dying trees, so it is a positive animal in some respects. We look to cut the western pine beetle population in half over the next ten years. We will be observing and studying our progress as we go."

The positive news about the genetically changed ants curbing the destructive western pine beetles is broadcast worldwide. Thanks to the worldwide coverage of Darius and Joe's announcement to the press, Newtown is placed on the world's map in a big way. ACADEMY OF SCIENCES WORK SUCCEEDS reads the headline of the Sierra Morning Star. The positive recognition the town receives builds new confidence in the town.

With the passing of time, Abbeville's economy thrives and normalizes. Business prospers. Abbeville's gossip mill becomes a dimly recollected nightmare few remember. Jacob Richmond's apocalyptic predictions fail to materialize. The ways of the Sisterhood become the new town's fabric.

Wednesday, November 30, 7:15 p.m.: The night of Abbeville's final town hall meeting witnesses a partial lunar eclipse that for many townspeople symbolizes the town emerging from its dark ages. That night, by unanimous vote of the town council with the virtual support of every townsperson, Abbeville is renamed Newtown. The council's plan to rename the streets in honor of the founding men and women wins unanimously approval.

The old town's preoccupation with what happened to Alma and Henry fades. The criminal trials of the nine-conspirators and Langdon's murderers result in life sentences without parole. Mimi and Hector Flores are convicted of their crimes, serve their time and move away. Lingering questions about empty cemetery coffins die away.

With the town forgiven the sins of its fathers, Abbeville is allowed to die away peacefully.

Chapter 2

❧

Twenty years later, Tuesday, November 18, 11:36 a.m.: Tom Mooreland, historian, author of *The Sutton Hoo Mysteries*, and Shelby Howard, his research assistant, travel over Yuba Pass on Highway 49 to Newtown. They are contracted by the State of California Historical Society to chronicle the history of Sierran towns established before the rush for gold. Although Shelby's research has turned up secondary sources that refer to the existence of Abbeville, the exact location of the town is not found on current or archived maps of California. Tom and Shelby are on their way to pay a visit to the Newtown Library in search of whatever maps and documents they may have to help them find Abbeville and understand some of the history of the town.

Passing a sign marking Newtown—elevation 5,560 feet, population 1,239—they slow down to turn up Edgar Whitman Drive.

"What a beautiful setting," Shelby comments, as she looks through the open moon roof at the Northern Buttes towering above them.

"Absolutely," Tom responds keeping his eyes on the road.

They motor past a stable, chicken farm, and winery then through town to the library, where they are scheduled to meet with the Assistant Librarian, Mrs. Abigail Sorenson-Valdez.

After a four and a half hour drive from San Francisco, they arrive at the library parking lot and get out of the car to stretch, getting the kinks out from their bodies. Looking around, they see children playing in the

Newtown Elementary School playground and people walking up and down the streets. The valley town is ideal, peaceful. The warmth of the Indian summer sun feels good on their faces and backs, energizing their bodies.

They climb the stairs and walk through the lobby to the library desk.

"Good morning, you must be Abigail Valdez?" Shelby opens.

"Yes, and you must be Drs. Mooreland and Howard, pleased to meet you. I am free to help you with whatever questions you have, as Carol Ann will cover the desk for me. What is it you're looking for?"

"We've received a grant from the State of California to film a documentary about the history of Abbeville. Where would you suggest we begin our research?" Shelby explains.

Mooreland is the consummate observer. He watches and studies human behavior and environmental surroundings, as Shelby takes the lead.

"Our newspaper archives would be a good place to start," Abigail replies, "Follow me. Our newspaper files are back here."

They walk to the back of the library where the historical archives are located. Abigail turns on the old fashion microfiche and invites Tom to sit before the large screen.

"Do you remember how to operate one of these, Dr. Mooreland?"

"I think I remember from my elementary school days, when I was the class projector monitor."

After a quick look at the old newspaper headlines, Tom is surprised to find no mention of the murders, deaths, ghosts, inquests, and mystery he was expecting to find. And, there is little mention about the town of Abbeville that gives him much of a clue as to its location or history.

"I only see articles in the Sierra Morning Star articles about Newtown There's nothing written about this area older than twenty years ago. The Sacramento Bee started in 1857. I'm sure there must have been something written about this area that showed up in the Bee or the Sacramento Courier."

Abigail recalls, "Oh, those old stories were lost when the Sacramento Courier building burnt to the ground. They went out of business ten years ago. Unfortunately, the Sacramento Bee relied on the Courier's archives for storage of all of their historical files. When the Courier archives were lost, the Sacramento Bee's corporate memory about Abbeville was wiped clean."

"Sounds like something fishy's going on here. It's like Abbeville never existed. Did someone wipe the books clean? A cover-up of some kind?"

"I've been here for over thirty years. I'm not aware of anyone deliberately trying to wipe all traces of Abbeville off the map. The newspaper records were burnt in that fiery accident. The only paper we have is the Sierra Morning Star."

"Abigail, we've heard rumors about murders and missing bodies in Abbeville. What's the story about that?" Asks Shelby.

"I do recall one murder happening in Abbeville around that time. Maybe the records at the public defender's office in Downieville could help you. As far as missing bodies, everyone I know is accounted for here in Newtown.

"Are any of the people living at the time of the coroner's inquest still living in Newtown?" Tom asks.

"The records of coroner inquests are also located in Downieville at the county medical examiners office. People living around here at that time . . . Yes, start with the Kitwa Tribal Council members, elders from the Damascus Church, retired members of the Newtown Town Council, and townspeople going in and out of Whitman General Store . . . the Bakery and Blue Goose Tavern are good spots to find people who know a lot about the history of this area. I would also pay a visit to Preston Medical Clinic to talk with Florence, the nurse practitioner and Dr. Preston, if she's in. When he gets back from kayaking the Snake River, I will have the head librarian, Mr. Winston, call to set up an appointment for an interview. He's been around for a long time."

"Those sound like excellent sources of information," Tom replies, "We'll finish up taking notes and walk around town and look for some of these people.

"Oh, one last question," asks Shelby, "You've been here what . . . thirty years or so? May I ask you what happened to that exhumed body ordered by the judge at the coroner's inquest?"

"Anne Dean's grave was opened, the casket was raised, and the body was gone, missing like other bodies have disappeared around here. But that was a longtime ago."

"What other bodies have turned up missing?" probes Shelby.

"Lots of bodies turned up missing around here twenty years ago. A third of the graves and some of the crypts in the Abbe Family Mausoleum were opened and robbed by transient workers, gravediggers, and the garden and landscape contractor who worked at the old cemetery. As far as I know, they're still doing time in Mule Creek State Prison."

"None of the bodies were found?" asks Tom.

"No."

"Hum. Well, thank you. You've given us some great leads. We'll finish up here like we planned and take that walk through town," concludes Shelby.

Tom and Shelby complete their work around three o'clock as the Newtown Elementary School bell rings. Kids run past them up to the library and into the parking lot to get a ride home. They go into the school and introduce themselves to the teacher, Desiree Parker.

"Ms. Parker," Shelby begins, "When you first came to Abbeville you saw a small town with a small town culture. Newtown is still a small town with a small town culture. What would you say are the differences between those towns?"

Quick and insightful as always Desiree reverses the question, "Small towns are small towns; I've not seen anything quite like it. How did your visit go with Abigail?"

"Who told you about our visiting the library?"

"Forest eyes see and ears hear. The news carries on the wind."

"Word gets around in small towns," responds Shelby.

This brings a smile to Desiree's face and triggers a startled look from Tom.

"Small town gossip, I suppose," Tom replies.

"Once upon a time in Abbeville, yes, but, not in Newtown."

"You're saying Newtown is a utopia?"

"Not a utopia, Mr. Mooreland, a new start."

"A new start? How can the whole of Newtown be a new start? And, a new start of what?" Shelby follows up.

"The children, Miss Howard, You're a woman. Within you and every woman there is the possibility of a new start for society."

"You're saying nature gives women the power to change the course of humankind with the birth of each new child?"

"Absolutely. Nature or the force behind nature empowers women to change the course fo society for the better—no offense to you, Mr. Moorland. You and every man have an important part to play, too"

While Shelby and Tom mull Desiree's comment, she excuses herself from the conversation.

As Desiree walks away, Tom can't help but think, *"I believe I've just been told to stay out of the biological kitchen!"*

Walking further down Whitman Drive they pass Damascus Church and read the large revolving electronic billboard at the corner of Jane Franc Street and Edgar Whitman Drive. The billboard advertises the Sunday sermon message, "Love the Way You Lie." They are surprised and amused by the fact Eminen and Rihanna's music is coming from the billboard.

"Sounds interesting," Shelby comments, "Let's see if anyone around knows what that's all about.

The door to the church is open and a very pleasant voice greets them as they approach the church office desk.

Shelby sends a greeting back, "We were passing by and couldn't help but notice Sunday's sermon is a song title."

The church secretary, an affable woman in her mid thirties or so, smiles.

"The pastor always picks popular songs to attract the attention of young people and their parents. The sermon messages relating to popular song titles are quite effectively. I don't know what pastor is going to say this Sunday, but last Sunday's message was on the rock and roll classic, "Walk This Way."

"But that song has lots of sexual connotations," voices Tom.

"The sermon is about avoiding walking that way and following in Christ's footsteps."

"Oh, I get it," Tom comments a bit embarrassed.

"Yes, Reverend Henry loves to catch people off guard with his sermons; they're wonderful messages I might add. Hope you can stay till Sunday and hear him."

Tom and Shelby say they would love to but business calls them back to San Francisco before Sunday. They will be back to Newtown in a month or so and promise to definitely hear one of the pastor's sermons.

Crossing the drive, they enter Preston Medical Clinic.

"Good afternoon," Florence says with her usually bouncy personality, "How can I help you?"

Tom speaks up, "Shelby and I, my name is Tom Moorland, are doing a documentary on the town before 1849 and wondered if we could catch Dr. Preston for an interview."

"I'm sorry. The doctor is teaching classes at Holman College this afternoon, but I do know a fair amount about that period of time. I'm an avid student of women's history. My expertise is in the period from 1750, when only Mandoo nation tribes lived here, to 1839, when Abbeville was founded."

"I've studied that period of time," admits Shelby. "The Kitwa Tribe is part of the Mandoo Native American Nation that still lives in this area."

"Chief Silver Squirrel's Kitwa Tribe is located in forests below the Northern Sierra Buttes to the west of town. He is the tribe's shaman. He must be at least eighty-eight years old and I bet can help you with the history of this area."

"Good idea. We'll try to meet with him tomorrow. Shelby and I are getting the lay of the land today and will comb through the town more thoroughly later. What do you know about the time before Newtown, Florence?"

"The history of this town goes back to when the Abbe brothers, Matthew, Mark, and John established the town of Abbeville. Their wives had a hand in influencing the way the town developed, but were never given credit."

"I've never read that Florence, how do you know that's true?" asks Shelby.

"Good question. Not much is written about the women of Abbeville. In those days men ruled the roost, at least from outward appearances.

Studying the inscriptions on gravestones and on crypts in the Abbe Family Mausoleum gives a lot of information about the women, mostly indirectly. You have to read between the lines."

"Is there anyone who can personally testify as to what happened to Abbeville and why the name of the town was changed from Abbeville to Newtown?"

"Chief Silver Squirrel and Edgar Whitman are your best bets. They know the story of why the town council changed the name of the town and more. Chief Silver Squirrel's ancestors were here thousands of years before Abbeville became a town. Kitwa tribal songs tell about the women of the forest."

"Women in the forest? What's that?" Tom asks.

"Yes, women walked through the forest gathering seeds and herbs for cooking, very much like women do today in the forests surrounding Newtown."

Fascinating," Shelby picks up on Tom's questions, "But is there anything acknowledging the work accomplished by these women?"

Florence responds, "The bronze plaque on the wall in the Newtown Town Hall is a tribute to the women who made Newtown the ideal place it is to live. They were all of the Sisterhood."

"Is that why all the streets in Newtown are named after women?" Tom inquires.

"When the town was renamed, the street names were changed to recognize the contributions of the women who, along with their husbands, sons and a daughter, founded and lived in Abbeville," Florence responds.

"What happened to the men's names?" Tom says with a smile.

"Nothing. The men and women of Newtown are equally recognized. The men's names, the founding fathers are also found naming the drives, avenues, streets and one of the roads in Newtown."

"Makes sense to me," says Shelby, "Crediting the men and women who made this town what it is today, rounds out the history of Newtown.

"You summed the process of how history should be told very well, Shelby," Florence remarks.

"Is there anything else you can tell us, Florence, that will help us better understand why Abbeville is virtually wiped off the the face of the earth?" Tom asks.

"A walk in the forest?"

"How will a walk in the forest reveal anything else about Abbeville's history?" Tom presses.

"Walk through the forests and your questions will be answered." Florence suggests.

Thanking Florence for the time and information, Tom and Shelby leave the clinic. Checking her watch, Shelby notes that it's getting late. They'd better find a room soon. Thomas flips a coin to see who's going to go back to the library and get the car. He loses as usual and agrees to meet Shelby at the Whitman General Store.

"Tom, one more thing before you go," Shelby calls as Tom heads up the street.

"What's that?"

"Give a call to the county court house and set up a meeting so we can go over the corner's hearing and the murder trial transcripts."

"Good idea, Shelby. I'll do just that."

"Oh, and Tom."

Tom stops, looking Shelby's way to hear the next pearl of wisdom coming from his research assistant.

"Find out what happened to Judge Caroline Abbington and that prosecuting attorney, Marcus Chao."

"Okay, will do."

Shelby crosses Mary Sand Street and enters the Knead-2-Feed Bakery. She orders a raspberry scone with lemon icing and a cup of coffee to tide her over till dinnertime. She engages Stella May Fields to pick up the latest gossip around town.

"Delicious, I can't believe how well the sweet-tangy lemon ice goes so well with raspberry. You make these fresh?"

"Every day rain or shine everything is baked fresh at the Knead-2-Feed Bakery," Stella May sings out.

"I bet you've heard about everything that goes on in this town," Shelby says, pausing for Stella May to fill in the gap.

"If it's gossip you want here it goes, Honey! This morning Helen Radcliff was telling Mary Kenyon about the new strain of wild flowers she's growing in her back yard. And, the school teacher chimed in about the height of the tomato plants the schoolchildren are studying in science."

"That's the caliber of gossip around here?" Shelby is shocked.

"That's about as stinging as our gossip mill gets these days. However, it was not too long ago when the girls used to sit at the same table you're sitting at and shot the gossip around like gunslingers, but those days are long gone. Thank goodness. That was the way Abbeville was."

"Where did the gossip girls go?"

"Prison. They're serving life sentences for murder," Stella May says in a matter of fact way.

"Murder!" Shelby exclaims causing some raspberry scone crumbs to fall from her mouth into her coffee.

"The bunch was convicted of conspiracy to murder the church pastor and Alma Whitman and got sent to the slammer for good."

"Reverend Henry Johnston who's the pastor at the Damascus Church up the street?" Shelby exclaims.

"Yep."

"Didn't I read where his body wasn't found?" Shelby says trying to entice Stella May to reveal a dark secret of the town.

"Honey, don't believe everything you read in a newspaper, didn't your mommy every teach you that?"

"Yeah, but that's kind of strange isn't it?"

"Strange, a lot of things were strange in Abbeville."

A little bewildered, but amused at the same time, Shelby leaves the bakery. A half a block down Whitman Drive and across Susan Smith Street, she sticks her head into the Blue Goose and looks around. The only person in the bar is Nick, who is wiping clean the beer glasses before stacking them up in a pyramid.

"Hello, my name is Shelby."

"What's your pleasure, little lady?"

"A little information, old man," Shelby snaps back, not knowing exactly why she bristled at Nick's comment.

"Yes ma'am. You want a little information. Shoot."

"Thank you," Shelby says politely after her bristles have settled, "How long have you been here . . ."

"Nick, Nick Simmons, I've owned and bar tendered this place for over forty years."

"You don't look a day over sixty, Nick."

"I'm fifty nine, ma'am."

"Shelby. Remember, you can call me Shelby?"

"I'm fifty nine, Shelby."

"You've seen a lot of this town go through your tavern doors, haven't you, Nick. What sticks out in your mind as the most memorable event happening in your tavern?"

"The time Pastor Henry came through those doors for the first time. It was like the Blue Goose receiving a blessing from God. You know like a priest going to the harbor and blessing the fishing fleet or something like that."

"That's a great memory. What other great memories do you have of things happening at the Blue Goose and Abbeville?" Shelby asks.

"When the president of the town council, Bill Silva, may his soul rest in peace, he sat here for a month or so, putting together the finishing touches of the town's bicentennial celebration, parade, carnival, and all. That was the best of times."

"Beautiful memory and an important event in the life of this town."

"Yes, yes it was, little lady."

Accepting Nick's address more gracefully, Shelby continues, "Anything else come to mind Nick?"

"Eh, that's about it, except watching the drunks fall off the barstools flat on their backsides. That's always memorable."

"Yes, that is memorable. I see you have a starving author's special on the wall."

"Turkey sandwich on dark rye with your choice of beer. It's a big draw here on the last Friday of the month."

"How does it work?"

"I take it you're writing a book?"

"The script for a documentary film about the Sierra's."

"That works too. Well, we have a lot of writers up here. There's nothing to do for some folks except eat, write, and fart. So the writer that comes in here with the smallest royalty check gets the Author's Special."

"When this script is finished to our documentary, I'll certainly keep that in mind, Nick."

"That's okay with me little lady, I mean Shelby."

"No harm, no foul, Nick. I've enjoyed our conversation."

"Shelby, if it's information you're looking for, you may want to talk to that fellow sitting in the corner."

"Thanks Nick."

The corner of the Tavern is dark in the shadows. Shelby can't exactly make out what or who is sitting in the corner. She stops in front of the table, peering into shadows to see whom she's addressing.

"Excuse me sir. Nick said you might be able to help me. My name is Shelby Howard and I'm researching the history of this town to before Abbeville was settled?"

Not a word comes from the shade. Shelby stands uneasily in the silence before the dark corner.

"Chief Silver Squirrel is his name, Shelby, he may be asleep."

"Thanks Nick." Shelby replies.

Again, Nick calls across the barroom, "Don't be scared Shelby, The Chief has a flare for the dramatic. Sit, he won't bite.

Chief Silver Squirrel retorts, "After all these years round-eye doesn't understand our native ways."

Still not quite certain of what is going on, Shelby slides into a worn wooden chair, across the table from Chief Silver Squirrel."

"My partner and I read in the Sierra Morning Star that no one has ever found the bodies of Alma and Henry in the mountains and forests around here. More surprising to me was the article said there were no signs of Native American burial sites either, which defies logic. We know the Mandoo's bury their dead in the forests and mountains close to where they live."

"Where hearts have gone is mystery."

"You're saying the burial grounds are hidden?"

"In plain view of the Great Spirit the hearts that have gone live again where human eyes cannot see."

"You have presided over ceremonies for the dead of your tribe somewhere around here, haven't you?"

"I have placed those whose hearts are gone in bear skins and danced."

"And where is that Chief Silver Squirrel?"

Nick yells, "He won't tell you Shelby. He's never said a word in all the time I've known him."

"Hearts gone cannot be disturbed."

"I won't disturb the dead, Chief Silver Squirrel, all I want to know is why there is no trace of their remains."

"It has been this way from creation to this day. Those whose hearts have gone live well in another place."

"Chief Silver Squirrel, I do not expect you to betray your ancestors."

"I know," Chief Silver Squirrel replies.

Shelby can charm the birds out of the trees, but fails to pull a credible piece of information from Chief Silver Squirrel. Feeling she has squeezed about all the information she can out of the Blue Goose, Shelby thanks the Chief.

On her way out, she waves to Nick, "Thanks for all your help, Nick. I've enjoyed meeting you."

"Good-bye little lady and come back soon?"

"You can count on it Nick! Good-bye."

Shelby walks out the side door of the tavern to Tasha Gorbi Street and walks to the corner and stops. The view from the town up to the top of the Buttes is breath-taking. Walking along Matthew Drive, she saunters a block past a large vacant lot and crosses Carol Ann Street. Entering Whitman General Store, she bumps into a very young looking woman, who apologizes profusely.

"No problem. I wasn't watching where I was going, sorry," Shelby responds.

"No, the fault was all mine. Say, you're new in town. Welcome."

"Thank you," Shelby replies."

"Any time you want your hair done, come in to the Hair Falls and see me."

"I will. Thanks for the invitation."

Shelby watches the woman walk across the parking lot for a moment and turns back into the store. Fenway, as frisky as ever, crashes at her feet and rolls over for some loving. After scratching and petting the dog, Shelby stands and looks into the piercing blue eyes of a man, appearing to be in his mid-eighties.

"Hello young lady, my name is Edgar Whitman. You have a kind heart. Fenway likes you."

"Fenway looks like she loves everyone, Mr. Whitman."

"Call me Edgar. Yes she does, but she likes you best of all."

"Only because I'm the only one in the store, Edgar."

"True, but I still think she especially likes you. I should know. Fenway and I have been paling around for years."

"That's a pretty energetic dog you've been paling around with for that many years. How old is Fenway?"

"I can't rightly remember. But it's been a long time."

"I've heard about you Edgar. Your the last of the line of the founding fathers of this town."

"Guilty as charged."

Thomas finally catches up with Shelby and walks into the store. Fenway immediately assaults him.

"What is this? I can't believe a dog can be this starved for affection. Hello old girl, how yawl doing."

"Edgar, that's my boss, Tom Moorland. He's doing a documentary about this town before the time California became a state, before your family established Abbeville. Everyone we've met tells us you're the man that knows the most about Abbeville."

"That I am, young lady."

"Please, Edgar, call me Shelby."

"Shelby, I know a lot about the fishing in these parts. I know what the Witka tribe knows or, at least, what they share with me, which isn't really much. My sister Alma knows the most about these parts though."

As Fenway is rolling around making weird sounds like she's talking between barks, Shelby only hears parts of what Edgar says. Standing up after paying homage to Fenway, Tom surveys the store.

"Excuse me Edgar. I have a bone to pick with Tom!" Shelby exclaims, "Then, I'll introduce you two."

"Sure, pick away."

As Shelby passes Tom on her way out of Whitman's store, Tom looks at Edgar.

"This may take some time. Once she's finished with me, I have a little something to tell her too.

Showing complete understanding of the situation, Edgar smiles and nods his head, as Tom follows Shelby out to the wooden sidewalk in front of the store.

"It's about time you waltzed in Tom!" Where have you been for the last two hours?"

"Looking for you all over town, Shelby. The question is more where have you been for the last two hours. You don't have to answer because I already know. Every place I've been people said you had only left a few minutes before I arrived."

Sorry. Next time I'll leave a trail of breadcrumbs for you.

"Okay, I guess I had that coming. Did you strike it rich with your interviews?"

"Only fool's gold. No one has anything to say about the past. This Mr. Edgar Samuel Whitman is our last and best chance to get at the real story about Abbeville," Shelby says, allowing the full emotional impact and substance of her comment to sink into Tom's mind."

"Yeah, I guess so," Tom responds, meeting Shelby's pep talk rather nonchalantly.

"Yeah, I guess so?" Shelby says exasperated with Tom's inability to grasp the importance of the moment, "He's the Edgar Whitman whose family settled Abbeville! If we can't crack this guy open like a watermelon, it's going to be a long ride back to San Francisco!"

Tom takes time to digest everything Shelby's telling him.

"You're right Shelby. You may be more right than you realize. I checked with the county court house to set up the meeting to look over the transcripts from the coroner's inquest and the murder trials . . . and they are gone, missing."

"What do you mean, gone? Missing?"

"I talked to the district attorney and he told me that when Judge Caroline Abbington retired all of the transcripts from the inquest and the trials were mysteriously deleted."

"Nothing's left at the court house!"

"Only the final verdicts of the inquest and the trials are on record," Tom responds.

"Great! Just great! We only have a few newspaper clippings to go on. Where's Judge Abbington now?"

"No one knows where she is," Tom answers.

"And, Marcus Chao?" she continues.

"He's a federal court judge in San Francisco."

"Did you call him?"

"Oh yes, I called him alright, and all he could tell me was what we already know from the newspapers."

"The whole town is conspiring to lock down Abbeville's past. Edgar is our last time at bat," Shelby concludes.

"Okay, we're on the same page now. Let's go back inside so you can formally introduce me to Edgar and get the show on the road."

When Shelby and Tom reenter the store, Edgar is standing about where they left him. Fenway is sitting by Edgar's feet, wagging her tail like a windshield wiper in a hailstorm. Her eyes are fixed on Tom and Shelby for signs of encouragement or doggie treats.

"That didn't take long," Edgar warmly says, greeting his guests, as would the good host that he is.

"Thank you for being so patient with us, Edgar, much appreciated," Shelby responds.

"No problem at all," Edgar replies.

"Edgar, like I was saying a while ago, this is my boss, Tom Moorland, who's doing a documentary about this area before Abbeville was established as a town."

"Good to meet you, Tom," Edgar says with his usual smile and engaging personality.

"Indeed, it's my pleasure to meet you, Mr. Whitman. I'd like to set up a time for us to meet and talk about the history of your town."

"Please Tom, call me Edgar. What about right now? Bridget can take care of the store while we sit over here in the booth by the window and talk."

"Its beautiful this time of day, when the sun is setting behind the Buttes," says Shelby in almost a sigh.

"The greatest place on earth to be," agrees Edgar.

Edgar, Shelby, and Tom converse about every imaginable topic there is to talk about concerning the Sierra's. From Edgar's earliest recollections to blow-by-blow descriptions of the old Abbeville gossip mill to event-by-event descriptions of the Abbeville Bicentennial Summer Festival.

Edgar gives his honest opinion about everything, but only in generalities. Noting specific is mentioned about the murder conspiracy, the empty graves or forest women. The more Edgar talks, the less Shelby and Tom seem to know. Tom has pages and pages of notes. As he flips through them, he realizes only a vague outline, beginning to take shape. As the evening rolls on, Edgar continues to give Tom more fluff than stuff.

As the nine o'clock hour creeps up on them, Bridget has locked the store up and bids Edgar and his guests a good night.

"Oh, I almost forgot, Edgar. We need two rooms in your lodge to stay over night," Tom says quickly before Bridget leaves from work.

Edgar waves to Bridget, signaling to her it is all right for her to go home, and says good night.

"You guys have been at this for a good long time. You must be tired and hungry," Edgar says empathetically, "Tell you what. My sister is the greatest cook in the world, and I know she would love to have both of you over for dinner tonight. You can stay the night with us and I won't take no for an answer."

Shelby and Tom look at each other with incredulous expressions. What is Edgar talking about? His sister has been gone for over twenty years?

Observing the looks on their faces, Edgar repeats himself more emphatically, "No! I won't take no for an answer from you two. Stay right there while I go in the back and turn off the lights."

Still in disbelief, Tom and Shelby watch, as Edgar and Fenway disappear in the dark.

"I'll be with you in a minute. Come on Fenway!"

"Good girl, Fenway, good girl."

Acknowledgements and Credits

Writing this novel, I have drawn on the experience and knowledge of people from many different educational backgrounds, beliefs, and walks of life. I am especially indebted to the work of Desirée Latour, Effie Kontonickas, George "Rich" Richmond, Hayley and Drew Lyon, Jack McKay, Jerry and Judith Guerino, and Kay Schwindt for helping knock the rough edges off the first drafts.

My thanks to the folks at the Bassetts Station General Store—Ed Amende, Mike and Carol Williams—for spending time with me and answering my questions about the history of the area. Your information was very helpful. You and your general store are reflected in the outgoing natures of Alma and Edgar Whitman and how their general store provides everyone in the area with needed supplies and a warm, friendly place to eat and socialize.

A special thanks goes to Shirley Welcome Kerns—an excellent storyteller, who read *Alma's Journey* aloud with full dramatic expression—a fascinating experience for this author, who became the audience and heard *Alma's Journey* voiced and theatrically transformed.

To my Literary Consultant, Isabel Christina Sanchez, who when I took to flights of fancy or chased rabbits down trails, challenged me to justify how such escapades were true to my story line. Steadfast in her task, Isabel never compromised her voice of reason. Thank you.

The *Ladies H.E.L.D. Literary Society* was the second wave of eyes that scanned the semi-rough manuscript: Audrey Gross, Dennell Richardson, Gayle Banks, Kathy Jensen, Leslie Michalak, and Sandy Kratville. Your discussions and comments were highly instructive and indispensable in the refining stages of the final manuscript.

A third wave of eyes proved extremely helpful, thanks to Bob Golling and his Placer County Writer's Group. The perspectives of writers about other writer's work are powerful tools along the path of writing and rewriting.

Janice Friesen and Leslie Johnston patiently and expertly combed each page of the final manuscript with Dr. Linda Lambert reviewed the final manuscript. Their close-up readings of the manuscript are not only appreciated, but the manuscript would not moved forward to the publisher without their observations and insights taken into account.

It only remains to be said that the ideas expressed in the novel are mine. The names of the characters are fictitious. Similarities between events depicted in this novel and events actually happening in the Sierra's are coincidental. If you spot weirdness and error in this work of fiction, there is no need to inform me by snail-mail or email, telephone or microphone, as weirdness and error are friends that follow wherever I go. However, I will respond to comments about *Alma's Journey* sent to me on my Amazon. com Author Page by clicking on the blue author name by most of my books. Or, follow along and make comment on my blog at cypherbuzz. blogspot.com.

CREDITS

The front cover photo of Lower Sardine Lake with Upper Sardine Lake at the next level and the California Butte's in the background was taken by Taylor Lyen.

A map of Abbeville allegedly drawn by Elder Jacob.

Marie Lyen (1935-2009) dedication photo by Connie Castellanos.

Judy Gurerino (1944-2011) and Marie Lyen dedication Photo by Jerry Guerino.

Book photos taken by author unless otherwise noted. Book One: Alma and the Sisterhood is a photo is one of the Sisterhood (Shutterstock); Book Two: Winter's Deadly Touch is a photo of the late Anne Dean, the beloved Damascus Church secretary (Shutterstock); Book Three: Spring Break is a photo of mountain wildflowers in Springtime (Thinkstock); Book Four: Fall From Grace is a photo of Lookout Tower (Thinkstock); Book Five: Earthly Miracles is a photo of Upper Sardine Lake from which Alma and Henry mysteriously disappeared take by author; Book Six: Bicentennial Festival is a of a typical town carnival take by author; Book Seven: Utter Destruction is a photo of vultures circling above Abbeville taken by author; Book Eight: Judgment Day is a depiction of a Native American, representing justice restored (Thinkstock); Book Nine: Resurrection is a photo of one of the Sisterhood inviting humankind to take a different path (Thinkstock).

Fenway, affectionately known as "Fen," is Drew Lyon's golden retriever that he named after Boston's Fenway Park.

The *"About The Author"* photo by Hayley Lyon

A map of Newtown by Shelby Howard based on Jacob's map of Abbeville.

The back cover photo, taken by Taylor Lyen, is one of the trails traveled by Alma and the Sisterhood that leads to hidden meeting places in the forest.

Back cover author photo by Isabel Sanchez

Citation Credit: Debbie Friedman, *T'filat haderech, Mishlan T'filah,* A Reform Siddur; Central Conference of American Rabbis, p. 649 (2007), which is found embedded in Reverend Henry's benediction in Book 2, Chapter 2.

Questions for the Reader

Recall preface to this book, where this challenge was made: However, the diligent sleuthhound, when all is said and done, when all the information has been fairly weighed, one and only one reasonable solution will be found that accurately describes the events that took place in Abbeville and the events that are now taking place in Newtown.

I am interested in what those who have read *Alma's Journey* think are the answers to the following questions. I would love to understand how you have put the story together in your minds.

What happened in Abbeville and what is happening in Newtown?

How did it happen and how is it happening?

Why did it happen and why is it happening?

And, of course, what was Alma's Journey?

One month after the book is published, I will post your and my responses to these questions on my blog at cypherbuzz.blogspot.com. Also, I am also open to discussing the book on my Author Page at Amazon.com. Just click on the blue author name by most of my books.

About the Author

Taylor Samuel Lyen was born in Oakland, California in 1939. He grew up in a mortuary with his mother and father, where his father was as an embalmer. From an early age, he was taught anatomy, embalming science, and, under the supervision of his father, embalmed his first body, when he was eight years old. His father was a Third-degree Mason of the Blue Lodge and educated him in freemasonry. An open-minded man, his father allowed him, however, to become a Catholic and attend Saint Francis de Sales Elementary School, where under the close eye of the Sisters of the Holy Names, he received an excellent education. Unfortunately, he did not benefit from the fine instruction of the sisters, but he was considered bright enough not to be held back. He attended Saint Elizabeth High School, but did not apply himself and was academically disqualified in his freshman year. When invited by his best friend to attend Oakland Neighborhood Church, an evangelical fundamentalist Christian church, he did so and a year later they voted him president of Omega, the church's

300-plus-member high school group. During these years, he learned how Protestants viewed the world.

He attended San Francisco State University and received his BA in Education with a distributed minor in music, art, dance, science, and an emphasis in philosophy in 1961. He worked as a teacher and reading specialist. As president of the Castro Valley Teachers' Association, he was awarded the California Teacher's Association Arthur F. Cory Award for Editorial Writing. Later, he was appointed as a principal, director of special education and employer-employee relations, deputy superintendent of schools, and the chief negotiator for the board of education.

August 23, 1963, Marie Helen Castellanos married Taylor Lyen. They had two wonderful children, Kim and Michael, who grew up in the loving care of their parents and the love and care of the large extended Castellanos family. Marie met Taylor in the Castro Valley Unified School District, where they taught at the elementary school level. Marie was an excellent teacher and recognized several times as Teacher of the Year. She taught and was loved by her students at the elementary, middle school and high school levels. When illness forced her to retire in June of 1999, Marie was the Chairwoman of the Foreign Language Department at Castro Valley High School. On January 31, 2009, Marie passed away. *Alama's Journey* is dedicated to Marie, whose heart has gone away and exists in some curved dimension yet undiscovered.

Today, Taylor volunteers as a grant writer for the Jenny Lin Foundation and Sacramento Child Advocates. He plays golf, writes, and maintains two residences—one in San Francisco to be with his son and the other in Gold River to be with his grandchildren, daughter, and son-in-law.

Other Books

⁊⁊

All Points of the Compass
(First Chapter posted November 2011 on cypherbuz.blogspot.com)

Oxbowl Incident
A Case For Jesus Christ Through Scientific Inquiry (2010)

Life Ain't All Kitties and Bunnies (2007)

Thanks for the Share ... Thanks for the Chair (2007)

Mischievous Rascal: Breaking the Seventh Seal (2005)

Student Science Research Associates (1995)
Principal Investigator, Lawrence Livermore National Laboratory

Establishment Clause Doctrine and Public Schools (1986)

Seashore Zoology (1963)

BOOKS IN PROGRESS

Pembroke (2012)

The Adventures of Dr. Greenstone and Jerrythespider Series:

Top Hat Forest (2012)
Spanish Steps (2014)
Beijing (2016)

Newtown Map*

❧

ALMA AND EDGAR'S CABIN
SPRING CREEK ESTATES
JEFF JR. MEMORIAL PARK
SIERRA COUNTY LIBRARY
NEWTOWN HALL
JOHN JR. MEMORIAL PARK
NEWTOWN LIBRARY PARK
NEWTOWN SQUARE PARK
NEWTOWN CEMETERY
NEWTOWN ELEMENTARY SCHOOL
CHASE MANHATTEN BANK
SAMUELSON AND CONNOLLY MORTUARY
DAMASCUS CHURCH
WHITMAN CHAPEL
SPRING CREEK PARK AND CAMPGROUNDS
NEWTOWN TOWN MORGUE
PRESTON MEDICAL CLINIC
FABRICS PLUS
CREMATORIUM
KNEAD 2 FEED BAKERY
WILLET'S PIZZA

---

* *This is the only map of Newtown known to exist and was re-drawn by Shelby Thomas from the copy of the old map of Abbeville supposedly drawn by Jacob Richmond.*

WHITMAN CHAPEL
BLUE GOOSE TAVERN
NEWTOWN FARMER'S MARKET
CHURCH OF SELF-REFLECTION
HAIR FALLS SALON
LAS ABUELITA'S COCINA MEXICAN RESTAURANT
SALMON CREEK WINERY
WHITMAN GENERAL STORE
MEADOWS AUTO SERVICE
EMMA JANE'S WOG FARM
SPRING CREEK STABLES
CALIFORNIA STATE PARK AT YUBA RIVER

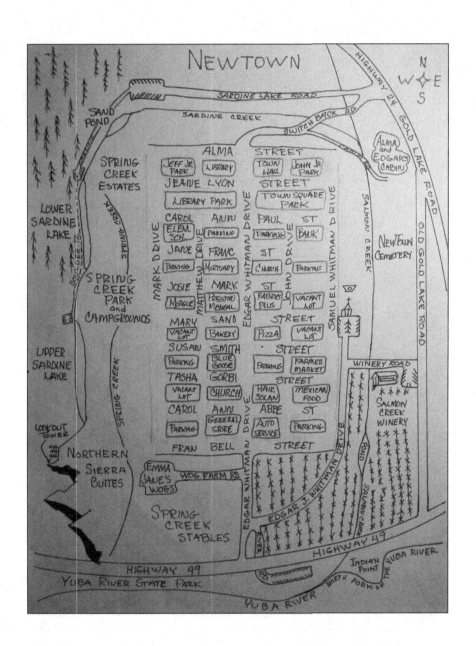